BACK BLAST

BACK BLAST

MARK GREANEY

 BERKLEY BOOKS, NEW YORK

BERKLEY

An imprint of Penguin Random House LLC
375 Hudson Street, New York, New York 10014

This book is an original publication of Penguin Random House LLC.

Berkley export edition ISBN: 978-1-101-98917-3

Library of Congress Cataloging-in-Publication Data

Greaney, Mark.
Back blast / Mark Greaney.—First edition.
pages ; cm
ISBN 978-0-425-28279-3
I. Title.
PS3607.R4285B33 2016
813'.6—dc23
2015022109

FIRST EDITION: February 2016

PRINTED IN THE UNITED STATES OF AMERICA

10 9 8 7 6 5 4 3 2 1

Cover photograph of Washington, D.C. © Tim Martin / Getty Images.
Cover design by Richard Hasselberger.
Title page art © ZWD / Shutterstock.
Text design by Laura K. Corless.

Penguin
Random
House

For Devon

ACKNOWLEDGMENTS

I'd like to thank Mike Cowan, Chris Clarke, Natalie Hopkinson, Scott Swanson, Maria Burnham, James Yeager and Tactical Response, Lt Col Rip Rawlings (USMC), Keith Thomson, Jeff Belanger, Dorothy Greaney, Devin Greaney, Nick Ciubotariu, EJ Owens, Ben Coes, Brad Taylor, Dalton Fury, Nichole Geen Roberto, and Patrick O'Daniel.

Special thanks to my agents, Scott Miller at Trident Media and Jon Cassir at CAA, my editor, Tom Colgan, and his assistant, Amanda Ng, at Berkley, and Mystery Mike Bursaw.

Why seeketh thou vengeance, O man! With what purpose is it that thou pursuest it? Thinkest thou to pain thine adversary by it? Know that thou thyself feelest its greatest torments.

—AKHENATON, EGYPTIAN PHARAOH

Three can keep a secret, if two of them are dead.

—BENJAMIN FRANKLIN

CHARACTERS

COURTLAND "COURT" GENTRY: The Gray Man, call sign Sierra Six, code name Violator—ex–Special Activities Division (Ground Branch) paramilitary operations officer, CIA; ex–CIA Autonomous Asset Program operative

CATHERINE KING: Senior investigative reporter for the *Washington Post*

ANDY SHOAL: Metro (cops) reporter for the *Washington Post*

DENNY CARMICHAEL: Director of National Clandestine Service, CIA

JORDAN MAYES: Assistant Director of National Clandestine Service, CIA

MATTHEW HANLEY: Director of Special Activities Division, CIA

SUZANNE BREWER: Senior Officer, Programs and Plans, CIA

ZACK HIGHTOWER: Call sign Sierra One, former CIA Special Activities Division (Ground Branch) paramilitary operations officer—Court Gentry's former team leader

CHRIS TRAVERS: Special Activities Division (Ground Branch) paramilitary operations officer, CIA

JENNER: Special Activities Division (Ground Branch) paramilitary operations officer, CIA

MAX OHLHAUSER: Former Chief Council, CIA

LELAND BABBITT: Director of Townsend Government Services

MENACHEM AURBACH: Director of Mossad—Israeli Intelligence

YANIS ALVEY: Senior officer in Mossad—Israeli Intelligence

MURQUIN AL-KAZAZ ("KAZ"): Washington, D.C., Station Chief—Saudi Arabia General Intelligence Presidency (Saudi Intelligence)

"DAKOTA": Joint Special Operations Command—Special Mission Unit team leader

PROLOGUE

The host of the garden party accidentally left his phone in the kitchen, so when it all went to hell he was the last to know.

Seconds before the debacle he stood on the patio with his wife, chatting with guests over the music from a four-piece jazz ensemble set up by the pool. It was late evening and too cold for an outdoor event like this, but the host and his wife had erected a dozen flaming gas heaters, and enough red wine had been consumed to warm the blood of everyone in attendance.

Denny Carmichael was in his sixties but lean and tan, with a deeply lined but razor-sharp face and a formidable bearing. One of his wife's friends had once confided in her by saying he looked like Abraham Lincoln's evil twin. Denny and his wife traded gossip with a couple who lived in D.C. but weekended in nearby Easton, Maryland. Denny was wholly uninterested in the petty chitchat but his wife lived for this shit, so he stood there and faked it, swigging pinot noir that did little to ameliorate his boredom.

While his guests droned on about the cost of their neighbor's new swimming pool, Denny looked around his property, regarded the Italianate patio, the opulent saltwater pool, and the meticulously maintained lawn sprinkled with their well-heeled friends. Eleanor liked to flee D.C. and drive out here to their estate in rural Maryland every week or two. It was expensive as hell, but his wife came from money, and this was what she wanted.

Denny thought of this place as his wife's house.

And these friends were hers, as well.

Carmichael didn't "do" friendships. He barely did marriage, for that matter. He lived for his work, and while everyone around him partied, he would much rather have been back at the office.

The jazz band finished a sedate rendition of "Sentimental Journey" to polite applause, but before the four-piece could fire up their next song, heads began turning towards several sets of headlights racing up the driveway.

Denny watched the lights approach, his already dark mood quickly blackening full-on to anger.

Three black Yukon XL SUVs parked on the grass alongside the driveway, fifty feet from the patio. All in attendance knew government motor pool vehicles when they saw them, because this patch of Maryland was only twenty-five miles from D.C., and most everyone here worked in the District.

Carmichael felt around in his jacket and realized he'd left his phone inside. He'd missed an important call, he had no doubt. He placed his wineglass on a café table next to him, made a quick apology to the couple standing nearby, kissed a perturbed Eleanor, and then started towards the driveway.

A dozen men in suits climbed out of the vehicles, and the gray veins in Carmichael's forehead throbbed. The guests were *not* supposed to see these security officers, because they didn't know what Denny really did for a living.

None of his wife's friends knew he was the director of the National Clandestine Service, which made him the top spy at CIA.

The rage he felt over his protection detail alarming the guests was blunted by the fact that he knew these men wouldn't be spun up like this without one hell of a good reason. Every security officer on Carmichael's detail knew their boss would tear their head off for overreacting to a threat, so Denny took this show of force to mean something serious was going down.

"Talk," he demanded when he was still strides away from the armed men.

The team leader was a forty-one-year-old former army major named DeRenzi, who was just like his protectee: all business, all the time. "Sorry, sir. You didn't answer your phone. Orders are to cordon you off from the guests and hand you my mobile so you can take a call from the office."

Five men moved between Carmichael and the stunned party guests, and squat P90 bullpup submachine guns came out of their coats, held at the low ready by men with intense, searching eyes.

Every one of the guests, the band, the caterers—even Denny's own wife—stared, mouths agape, at this spectacle. Most in attendance knew Carmichael had served as an officer in the Marine Corps, but all thought he now worked in something banal at the Department of Homeland Security, as that was his official story.

Denny ignored the attention and asked no more questions of DeRenzi—he only mumbled an explanation that he'd left his phone in the kitchen.

DeRenzi responded with, "The office is sending air."

To this Carmichael cocked his head. "*Air?* Jesus Christ." He thought over the outrageous spectacle of a helicopter landing in the yard and whisking him away. "Are we at war?"

"Dunno, boss." DeRenzi was muscle. He had no answers. Instead he handed his phone to his protectee and led him briskly towards the house.

Carmichael snatched it and held it to his ear while he walked. "Who is this?"

"It's Mayes." Jordan Mayes was Carmichael's number two at NCS. He was a dozen years younger than his boss, but Carmichael could barely recall a time when Mayes was not by his side.

"Talk."

"He's here."

"*Who's* here?"

A brief delay from Mayes. Then one word. "Gentry."

Carmichael stopped in his tracks. After a few seconds he spoke again, but his voice cracked. "He— Here? Here *where?*"

"Worst-case scenario? He's got eyes on you right now."

Carmichael looked around the lawn. In an instant his emotions cycled from fury through confusion, and then straight on to terror, and his voice went hoarse. "He's in the goddamned States?"

"Best intel puts him in *your* state, Denny."

Carmichael spoke quickly now; there would be no more pregnant pauses. "Get me the *fuck* out of here." He began walking briskly, still cordoned off from the rest by DeRenzi and his men.

"Helo inbound. ETA five mikes."

As he hurried along, Denny scanned his property. The tree line of pines in the distance, half-covered by thick mist, suddenly appeared foreboding.

Carmichael barked into the phone, "Five mikes, my ass. Expedite it!"

1

The band started back up tentatively, but the revelers' attention was firmly fixed on the dozen serious men in the driveway surrounding the host.

Carmichael's eyes searched from left to right, locking on human forms, because everyone at the party was a threat now. A congressman from Nevada, a prosecutor from Virginia, a horse breeder from Kentucky, the co-owner of a fashion magazine on Fifth Avenue. Caterers, musicians, and an event organizer standing by the pool with his hands on his hips, gaping at the armed Neanderthals destroying the mood of this glorious spring garden social. Carmichael double-checked everyone's faces as he neared the back door, and the men and women he did not recognize—there were just a few—he triple-checked. He knew Gentry's appearance—he'd been thinking about it for years—but he also knew the man could disguise himself better than anyone he'd ever known.

When he was inside and completely surrounded by his detail, he stood there a moment breathing heavily. He remembered he was still holding the phone to his ear. He said, "We're sure?"

Mayes replied in a clipped, efficient tone. "Israelis tracked him to a freighter that embarked from Lisbon eight days ago. It's now anchored in the Chesapeake Bay, just west of Easton. He might be heading west into D.C., but if he goes east, that's less than fifteen minutes from you by car. We've sent a Marine FAST team to hit the boat, but—"

"Gentry won't be on it."

"Not a chance. He would have slipped off the second he got near the shore. Have to clear it anyway. Might find some clues on board as to what his play is here in the States."

"Where did the Israelis come across this intel?"

"Unknown. I have a conference call set up with Menachem Aurbach at Mossad. We'll initiate it as soon as you get to Langley."

Just then, Carmichael saw heads turn to the south. Seconds later he heard the thumping. He knew the sound. It was one of the Agency's sleek new Eurocopters.

Jordan Mayes added, "Denny, sorry about the party. I know it was important to Eleanor."

"*Fuck* this party. I want the Violator Working Group assembled in sixty mikes. Everyone."

"Roger that."

The landing of the helo and the exfiltration of the host of the garden party went down in a fashion just as obnoxious as Carmichael feared it might. He'd spend the rest of his life explaining this moment away to his wife's friends, but the fallout wasn't even on his radar now. As he boarded the aircraft, along with DeRenzi and three other bodyguards, his mind reverted into combat mode.

Carmichael had fought as a lieutenant in Vietnam, as a lieutenant colonel in Lebanon and Grenada, and as a CIA officer against the Russians in Afghanistan. He'd HALO jumped into Panama, jetted into the Balkans, dune buggied into Iraq, and helicoptered back into Afghanistan twenty years after his first visit. Denny knew combat, and he knew how to push everything extraneous out of his mind, leaving it solely committed to the utter simplicity of kill or be killed.

This was his mind-set now.

The helo took off towards the south, leaving the party behind as it rose over misty, rolling farmland. The pilot pushed the cyclic forward and then twisted the throttle to pick up speed in the cold air.

Carmichael ordered Mayes to hold the line, then he moved to a seat just behind the flight crew and put on a set of headphones. Pulling the microphone down over his lips, he tapped the pilot on his shoulder.

The man turned back to him. "Yes, sir?"

"You have countermeasures on board?"

The pilot seemed surprised by the question. He glanced to his copilot, then back to the windscreen in front of him. "Yes, sir. Chaff and flares."

Denny said, "Be prepared to employ them. I want your head on a swivel."

The copilot spoke up. Unsure. "We were rushed into this . . . uh . . . Anything you can tell us about what we're up against would be helpful."

Denny shrugged. He said, "The threat is an ex-asset, code name Violator. A former Agency paramilitary officer with one hell of a grudge."

The pilot spun his head back around sixty degrees and stared through his visor at the much older man. "One guy? All this is about *one* guy?"

Denny's leathery face turned even harder as he looked back into the pilot's visor. "Son, do I look like I scare easily?"

"Not at all."

"Well, this son of a bitch scares me to death. Turn around and fly this thing to Langley, and be ready for inbound missiles."

"Sir," he said with a slight nod, and then he focused fully on the flight.

Twenty seconds later Carmichael was back on the phone with his number two. "Get my family out of town. Have them taken to the ranch in Provo. If Violator is here for me I want them out of the way so I can do what I need to do."

The helo began swaying to the left and right, not quite in jerking movements, but certainly nausea-inducing to those in back.

DeRenzi moved forward and sat down next to Carmichael. He had his own intercom-ready headset on. He tapped the pilot on his back, but the man did not turn around.

The security officer asked, "Why the hell are we flying like this?"

Carmichael answered for the pilot, who was fully occupied with his work. "We have to operate under the assumption that Gentry has a SAM, or at least an RPG. We'll stay low to counter the SAM threat, but we need to fly like this over population centers to counter an RPG."

DeRenzi then asked, "Why do you think Gentry has a SAM or an RPG?"

Carmichael looked out the window, focusing on the twinkling lights of the D.C. suburbs below him. "Because he's the fucking Gray Man."

2

A dimly lit street in the center of Washington Highlands was a hell of a place for a nighttime stroll.

The Highlands were in the southeastern corner of the District, over the Anacostia River in Ward Eight. Full of high-rise government housing, low-income apartment complexes, and derelict single-family homes on tiny lots strewn with garbage, Ward Eight had been the second most dangerous ward in the District behind Ward Seven, but it had recently retaken the lead thanks to a triple murder in the last week of the reporting period.

But despite the late hour and the area's infamous reputation, a lone pedestrian ambled calmly through the misty evening, heading north on Atlantic Street SE as if he didn't have a care in the world. He walked along a broken sidewalk, catching the glow of most all of the streetlamps that had not been shot out or burned out and left black by a city that didn't give a damn about its poorest residents. He wore blue jeans and a wrinkled blue blazer, his dark brown hair was tousled and damp, and a clean-shaven face revealed him as white, which, around here, at this time of night, meant he was probably up to no good.

It was ten p.m., and the neighborhood appeared devoid of any life other than the solo pedestrian. But while the street itself was barren, several sets of eyes tracked the man's movements. Astonished senior citizens looked out from behind their barred apartment windows. A single mother up with a sick kid watched through the bolted Plexiglas door of her duplex unit with a wince of regret, knowing good and well the damn fool in the street was going to get rolled at best and murdered at worst. And a teen with a cell phone on a darkened stoop of an apartment building watched the man carefully, reporting what he saw to an acquaintance at the other end of the connection with hopes of collecting a finder's fee if his friend showed up with a crew and beat every last item of value off of the hapless outsider.

But the teen and his friend were out of luck, because another group of predators were closer, and they also had their eyes on this target of opportunity.

Three dark silhouettes watched the white man from where they stood in a driveway, in front of a fifty-five-gallon drum filled with burning trash.

Marvin was the oldest of the three, and at thirty-one he had eleven priors, most for B&E or armed robbery. Only two arrests had really stuck, the first one earning him eleven months, twenty-nine days in a city lockup. And then, on the inside, Marvin had bought himself a full dime at Hagerstown for manslaughter.

He did six years before being released on good behavior—a relative term in prison—and now he was back on the streets.

And he wasn't looking for work. He was looking for a score.

In this pursuit he had taken on the two young men with him. Darius and James were both sixteen, and they looked up to the older Marvin since he'd done time and he'd killed a man, and because of this they would follow him anywhere. For Marvin's part, he liked running a crew of kids because they could take chances; any convictions they earned would likely be expunged on their eighteenth birthdays.

Marvin carried a handgun in his waistband under his baggy boxers. It was a rusty Lorcin Arms L380, a piece of junk, even compared to the other pot-metal pistols ubiquitous on the low end of crime here in the "gun-free zone" of D.C. He'd never shot the weapon, it was for show, really, which meant he kept the grip of the gun on display, sticking out from below his faux leather jacket, but only when the cops weren't around. If he saw a patrol car a couple of shakes would drop the little automatic down the inside of his warm-up pants and out onto the ground. He could then kick it away or under something, or else he could just fucking run.

Marvin had been running from trouble since long before the two boys standing with him were born.

The two kids had thin switchblades they'd shoplifted from a head shop in Hyattsville. The knives were comically cheap novelty items, but the boys didn't know any better and they thought themselves impossibly badass for carrying them inside their jackets.

Darius and James fingered their knives under their clothes as they watched the white man disappear in the mist, just past an overgrown hedge strewn with blown trash. As one they turned to each other, smiling in surprise at this evening's outrageous fortune. The pedestrian seemed oblivious to the fact he'd just walked past the three men standing by the fire, which made them think the fool was drunk, high, or perhaps a combination of both. Even though they rarely saw whites walking around this section of Washington Highlands at night, men and women of all races certainly drove into this neighborhood to buy drugs all the time, *especially* at night, and the two boys couldn't imagine any reason for this fool's presence other than a buy.

That meant he either had cash or drugs, and it didn't matter which, because around here, drugs *were* cash.

Darius and James looked back over the flames coming out of the oil drum, towards their leader.

Marvin nodded back to his crew, giving them the prompting they needed. All three left the warmth of the drum and headed down the driveway to the sidewalk, following the white man with their hands hovering inches from the weapons they kept tucked inside their clothes.

At the same instant three hunters were stalking their prey on 8th Street SE, a twenty-four-million-dollar Eurocopter streaked high over D.C., flying from Maryland in the northeast and heading towards Virginia in the southwest. The men on board discussed the chances someone below them was lining up the advanced optical sights of a man-portable surface-to-air missile on the tail rotor behind them, or perhaps tracking the nose of the helo with the iron sights of a rocket-propelled grenade launcher. Onboard countermeasures were ready, the pilot made defensive maneuvers, and all eyes were focused outside the helo and down at street level, scanning for the bright flare of a missile launch.

But there was no flare and there was no launch, because although the man they feared was, in fact, somewhere below them, he had no SAM, nor did he have an RPG.

He didn't even have a pistol or, for that matter, any cash.

Court Gentry walked alone through D.C.'s most dangerous district, as aware of the footsteps closing on him as he was of the throbbing in his right forearm and the maddening itch under the plaster cast that went from his elbow to his wrist.

He knew three men were following him—a definite leader and two subordinates, much younger and completely subservient to their boss. Gentry determined all this from a quarter-second half glance as he passed them on the driveway, as well as from the sounds of their footfalls. The man in the middle was more sure, the men on either side uneasy, slowing from time to time, then rushing to catch back up to the one in charge.

Court knew something about the psychology of crime. These street thugs weren't looking for a fight; they were looking for a victim. The strength of the attackers' resolve would be reflected in how quickly they acted. If they messed around and followed him for blocks, then they would probably never go through with it. On the other hand, if they challenged him right now, that meant their confidence was high and they wouldn't be expecting any resistance, and this would indicate to Gentry they were probably armed and they'd done this sort of thing before.

Just then, still half a block from the next intersection, the man in the middle of the three called out.

"Yo! You know what this is. You don't gotta get hurt."

Court was pleased this guy was getting right to it. After all, he didn't have all night. He stopped, but he did not turn around. He just stood there, facing away. The three men behind came closer.

"Turn around, motherfucker. Do it slow."

Court took a few calming breaths, but he did not turn.

"Yo, bitch! I'm talkin' to you!"

Now Court slowly pivoted to face the threat.

The three attackers stood only six feet away on the sidewalk. Court scanned their eyes. It was always the same in a threat situation. Determine the will, and determine the skill. He pegged the leader as cocky, amped up from excitement, but not from concern. The other two tried to show confidence, but their furtive eyes sold them out.

All three clutched weapons. The leader had a small gunmetal blue pistol and the two men with him— actually now to Court they appeared to be teenagers—each held up a knife.

Court spoke calmly. "Evenin', gents."

The leader cocked his head in surprise. After a second, the thin black man said, "I want that wallet. And that phone." He looked around on the street, then asked, "Where your car at?"

Court ignored the man's voice and focused on the pistol in his hand. "What do you have there?"

"It's a gun, motherfucker!"

"Right. What kind of gun?"

"The kinda gun that's gonna pop a cap in your ass if you don't pull out that wallet and drop it off, real nice and slow."

The man raised the pistol to eye level, in Court's face now. Even though the light was bad, Court was able to identify the weapon quickly here, just three feet from the tip of his nose.

He sighed. Disappointed. "An L380? What the hell am I supposed to do with that piece of shit?"

The armed man stiffened his gun arm, then smiled. "Oh, I got it. You tryin' to die tonight."

Court looked around at the two others. "Any chance you kids are strapped?" The boys glanced at their boss, confused. After a second they held their knives up higher. "I didn't think so." Court looked up into the wet sky with a half smile. "Just my luck."

3

M arvin had been pointing guns at people since before his thirteenth birthday, and in all this time he'd never seen anyone so utterly unimpressed. Normally eyes widened to saucers and fixed on the muzzle of his weapon, and no matter what he did for the rest of the encounter, the person at gunpoint never *ever* glanced away from the instrument in his hand. They rarely even blinked.

But this guy turned to the other men, looked around at the street, into the sky, and at the windows of the duplexes all around. He didn't seem at all concerned that there was a *motherfucking* gat in his *motherfucking* face.

The white man didn't look high, and he didn't smell drunk. His languid eyes were clear, his relaxed body did not sway. For some reason he just didn't give a damn.

And this infuriated Marvin. He had no plan B for intimidating a victim.

The two boys stepped to either side of their prey. Now Marvin had a pistol pointed to the man's forehead, and his crew had stilettos in range on the left and right.

But the white man wasn't worried about the knives, either. He just sighed more deeply now, his shoulders slumped all the way down. "Any chance I can persuade you guys to step off? I don't have any cash, no phone, no car. I don't have a thing to offer you but trouble, and I promise you, I'm a lot more trouble than I'm worth. What do you say we call it a night and—"

Marvin was tired of this asshole. He stepped forward a half step, raising the gun higher to drive his point home. As he did so the white man's left hand shot up and forward and he spun on his left foot in a blur, pirouetting his body out of the line of fire. Marvin was stunned by the movement. As the man turned, his strong hand locked onto the slide of the pistol, just aft of the muzzle, and he shoved the weapon to the side and down. Marvin instinctively pulled the trigger. The Lorcin cracked loud in the empty street, but the white man had both rotated his body away to Marvin's right and pushed the gun down low to Marvin's left just as it fired.

Marvin realized instantly he had missed.

James leapt into the air, the stiletto dropped to the ground as he grabbed at his lower leg with both hands. He fell into the grass by the sidewalk and wailed.

The kid had taken the .380 hollow-point round through the top of his foot.

Marvin knew he had fucked up, but he still had the gun in his hand, and for some inexplicable reason, his intended victim released his hold of the weapon. The man turned away from Marvin now, his attention on Darius and his blade, leaving his back exposed, just a couple of feet from Marvin's gun.

Marvin couldn't believe this fool could be so stupid as to let go of a loaded gun and then turn his back on it. Marvin raised the weapon and pointed it at the back of the fool's head, ready to kill the man before he did anything to Darius. He pulled the trigger.

Click.

Court ignored the asshole with the gun behind him because he knew the man was out of the fight for the next few seconds. By grabbing the slide of the weapon, Court had kept it from cycling after it fired. Now there was a spent shell inside the chamber of the Lorcin, and the dude behind him could pull that trigger all damn day and it wouldn't go bang, not until he racked the slide to eject the spent casing and load a fresh round from the magazine.

And Court didn't think for an instant he would figure this out for at least a couple of seconds. The attacker was in a fight for his life; his adrenaline would make him spastic and unable to process the flood of information coming his way.

Court had learned long ago that in any gunfight, one does not rise to the occasion. Instead, one defaults to the level of ability he has mastered.

And the asshole with the shitty pistol couldn't have mastered much of anything involving firearms, otherwise he wouldn't be carrying such a shitty pistol.

Now Court had time to deal with the stiletto in front of him. The kid jabbed straight out with it, lunging his body with the strike, and Court raised his right arm. The blade stuck into the plaster cast on his forearm, and Court used his left hand to catch the boy's knife hand in a wristlock, twisting until the knife dropped away. Court continued the backwards twist of the hand, then pushed against the sinews connecting the boy's upper arm and lower arm together. He wrenched it back at a forty-five-degree angle, cranking the arm awkwardly away from the bend of the elbow joint, spraining the tendons before the boy figured out his only defense to the move was to fall back onto the pavement on his back. He did this, then he rolled around on the cold concrete clutching an elbow that jolted with pain.

Court figured the man behind him would be in the middle of trouble-shooting his situation, so he turned back to him. The thin man had his hand on the top of the pistol, and he had just begun racking the slide. The spent casing ejected into the air, but before the slide sprang forward, Court's left hand shot out again and wrapped around the exposed barrel and the frame, restricting the slide's progress forward. Court's thumb pressed on the mag release button now, dropping the magazine full of bullets to the sidewalk.

Court let go of the gun.

Marvin retained his grip on the weapon, with his finger on the trigger. Before he understood what was happening he squeezed the trigger, and the striker fired on the empty chamber.

The gun went click again.

Marvin looked up at the white man, his own eyes as wide as saucers now. His "victim" looked back at him, still calm. Almost bored.

Marvin gaped at his empty pistol, and at the magazine on the ground. He did not understand what had just happened, but he was pretty sure his weapon was useless. He had a folding knife in his back pocket, but he wasn't thinking about it now. In fact, he wouldn't remember it until much later. For now his mind panicked. He turned and ran—Marvin had been running for his whole life, after all—and he left his teenaged crew behind.

Court watched the thin man race off into the mist, then he knelt down over the two injured boys. The teen holding his battered arm was sitting up on the sidewalk, but the kid with the hole in his foot still writhed in pain on the grass.

Their weapons were somewhere in the dark, out of reach.

Court scanned the buildings in all directions, the windows and doorways and driveways he could see through the mist, and while he did so he spoke softly. "Hell of a guy, your fearless leader."

Neither boy replied; they just both stared in horror at the calm man kneeling over them.

Court waited for some response, but when nothing came, he shrugged. "How much cash you carrying?"

They looked to each other briefly, then back up.

Court sniffed. "How 'bout that? *I'm* mugging *you*. The irony, right?"

Court reached out, felt through the clothing worn by the kid with the hole in his foot, and pulled a ten-dollar bill out of his front pocket. The boy with the wounded arm extended a shaking hand holding a wad of crumpled one-dollar bills, and Court stuffed them into the pocket of his jeans.

He then grabbed the first boy's injured foot and looked at the bloody hole in the top of his white tennis shoe. In a soft voice he said, "That looks worse than it is, so maybe you shouldn't look at it." He turned to the kid with the twisted arm and helped him back up to his feet. "You're okay. That will hurt a few days, tops. Less if you ice it. It's your job to help him. Take him to a hospital. When you get there tell the cops some dickhead was playing with his gun and it went off. They'll hassle you, but if you stick with your story, eventually they'll buy it and move on."

Both boys nodded slowly.

Then both Court's face and his voice darkened. "But if you tell them about me, give them a description, *any* information at all . . . I'll come back here, I'll find out whatever it is in this world that you love . . . and I will kill it. Are we clear?"

The boys nodded again, much faster this time.

"Good night."

The standing boy hefted the wounded boy, and together they hobbled off into the evening. Gentry noticed they went in a different direction from their boss, and he took that as a positive sign.

But he also noted no one had come out of any of the homes nearby to investigate the gunshot, and this depressed him a little.

Court had been away from the United States for five years. It occurred to him now that this America didn't feel much different than some of the more dangerous third-world countries he'd operated in. He'd always thought of the U.S. as home, as a sanctuary, as his safe place.

But that was fantasy. He knew the truth was just the opposite. This was Indian country. He was a wanted man here. There existed danger and menace at every turn.

After a moment, Court Gentry walked on, bundling his jacket around him to ward off the cold fog.

4

CIA headquarters in Langley, an unincorporated neighborhood in the city of McLean, Virginia, was open twenty-four hours a day, but the executive offices on the seventh floor of the Old Headquarters Building were normally deathly quiet at ten p.m. on a Saturday night. This evening, however, lights began flashing back on just before ten, and by ten thirty an entire office suite was occupied by nearly two dozen executives, assistants, communications specialists, and other support staff.

The Eurocopter from Maryland landed in the parking lot minutes later, and Jordan Mayes was there waiting for it in front of the large amphitheater known as the bubble, shielding his white hair from a light rainfall with a plastic file folder. Denny Carmichael climbed out of the aircraft surrounded by his four security men, but DeRenzi and company soon took up positions just behind their charge so Mayes could shoulder up to his boss while they all walked for the safety of the Old Headquarters Building.

As soon as they were inside and Mayes could be heard over the helicopter, he updated his superior. "Here's where we stand. FAST team reports no joy on board the cargo ship, but they found a bedroll and some personal items in a recess aft of the engine room. They definitely had a stowaway on board."

"How did he get off?"

"A supply launch left the boat two minutes before the marines boarded. Figure Gentry was on it."

Denny knew they wouldn't catch Gentry sound asleep in his cot. "He's in the wind. Who do you have assembled here?"

"The JSOC liaison, the NSA liaison, the NGA liaison, the DS&T guy read in on Violator, and the communications officer on the task force. We'll have eight in the meeting in total."

Denny kept walking, but said, "There are only seven in the Violator Working Group."

"I've asked Suzanne Brewer of Programs and Plans to join us."

The two CIA execs and DeRenzi all had their IDs scanned, and then they entered the elevator, leaving three of the bodyguards behind. Carmichael's clipped voice showed his displeasure. "What does Brewer have to do with this?"

"Among her other duties, she has been red-celling a lone-wolf attack on domestic CIA infrastructure for over a year. She's got the background of a good targeting officer, and she knows how to prevent an attack by a determined enemy. If Gentry is here, and if he's got CIA in his sights, Suzanne might prove useful."

"She doesn't know a damn thing about the problem at hand. Gentry isn't some raghead with an AK taking potshots at cars at the south gate, for God's sake."

"Brewer is as sharp a counterterror mind as we have. She's spent a decade on risk mitigation involving Agency facilities and personnel overseas, and she's developed protocols for dealing with sophisticated homegrown terror hazards as well as high-level foreign actors who might target Agency assets."

"I don't like bringing outsiders into the fold."

"Think about it, Denny. We're going to have to beef up your security protocols, and we'll be putting assets on Gentry's known associates in the city. There is no way that can happen without Brewer learning about it. She's an outsider now, but we bring her in and give her password access to the Working Group, and she'll become an ally instead of an impediment."

"And when she learns we don't want Gentry alive?"

Mayes didn't hesitate. "Operational expediencies won't trouble her. If you tell her this target needs to die, she'll make it happen."

The elevator arrived on the seventh floor. Mayes reached out and took Denny by the arm before he left the car. He spoke softly to him. "I was also thinking . . . if Gentry *is* here to target the Agency, and this manages to make some noise outside of the Agency, God forbid, we might want to frame this to the media as some kind of an external threat. If Suzanne is involved, beefing up the guns and gates of our facilities, it will only help us sell it as some lone-wolf terror attack on the Agency."

Denny looked at his second-in-command. In a louder voice he said, "One, this *is* a terror attack on the Agency. Gentry didn't come all this way to pick up an old paycheck. And two, keeping this shit in house is paramount. No one breathes a word. We'll take care of it." Carmichael took off, heading up a brightly lit hallway towards his office.

Mayes knew when to fight with his boss, and he knew when to let his boss wrestle with his own arguments. As he caught up with Carmichael he said, "So . . . Suzanne. Yea or nay?"

After a moment the director of National Clandestine Service gave in, to a point. "Maybe. But before I bring her into the program, I want to know more about her."

"She's reliable. I've worked with her myself. She'll play ball."

Denny slowed and turned back towards Mayes, but before he could say anything Mayes preempted him by handing over the plastic file folder. "Here's her two-page write-up. You want more, I can send it to your office."

Carmichael took the file, but said, "I want it all. Nobody gets read in on Violator unless I know them inside and out."

Ten minutes later five men and one woman converged in a glass-walled conference room that could easily accommodate sixteen, took their seats quickly, and then all eyes turned to a pair of side-by-side monitors on the wall. A satellite linkup had been established with Tel Aviv and fed to one of the monitors, but until the commo people on the Israeli side of the connection gave the word that their attendee was on camera and ready, the screen just glowed blue. Next to this, a larger screen displayed an interactive map of the greater Washington, D.C., area.

The responsibilities of those in the room represented some of the most secret departments and divisions within the CIA. Communications was there, as were the CIA employees charged with working with the National Security Agency, the National Geospatial-Intelligence Agency, and the Joint Special Operations Command, the military's most elite paramilitary fighting force. A CIA analyst sat across from a senior officer in the Department of Science and Technology. Jordan Mayes, assistant director of the National Clandestine Service, entered and sat to the left of the empty chair at the head of the table.

Most of these officers had been on the Violator Working Group for years. It had taken them, both physically and virtually, to locations all over the world. But this was most assuredly the first time any of them found need to refer to a map of the local area in relation to the Gentry hunt.

The one new face in the room was also the lone female. Suzanne Brewer was a thirty-nine-year-old Programs and Plans officer for the National Clandestine Service. She spent her days at CIA identifying and fortifying soft spots in Agency security protocols. She knew the name of every potential agent provocateur; she knew the details of threats against CIA personnel, every known operation targeting the Agency, every website that posted warnings to life and limb of intelligence officers all over the District. She wasn't a spy herself, but she saw it as her mission to keep the spies of NCS safe from harm.

Denny Carmichael marched in at eleven forty-five p.m., his brow pinched with purpose. DeRenzi was with him, and as Denny moved to his chair, his close protection officer took a position against the wall, present for the meeting in an observer capacity only. It was his job to keep his protectee safe from harm, after all.

Denny dropped into his seat at the head of the conference table, facing the large monitors on the opposite wall. He turned first to Brewer. "Suzanne, you're the odd man out here, if you will excuse the phrase. This is going to be a little out of your wheelhouse, but AD Mayes invited you in. Before I decide whether you are going to have code word access to the Working Group, I need to make a determination about your relevance to all this. What have you been told?"

"Only that there is a potential threat to local CIA personnel, and I would be briefed in the meeting and asked for my preliminary assessment."

"I've read your file," Carmichael said. "You've been solid in delicate situations. You've worked as a targeting officer as well as a counterterror officer, and you've excelled in both positions."

"Thank you, sir."

"But you haven't run up against a situation as difficult or as delicate as this."

Brewer said, "I only ask for an opportunity to show you what I can do."

Carmichael turned to Mayes, and with a nod gave him the go-ahead to brief her.

Mayes said, "Here's the sitrep. A former Ground Branch paramilitary operations officer, code named Violator, has appeared suddenly in the United States. We think it's likely he's in the immediate area."

Brewer was confused. "And this former employee. He poses some sort of a threat?"

Mayes just said, "His name is Courtland Gentry."

It was obvious to all that the name meant something to Suzanne Brewer. She blinked hard. "The Gray Man? You're talking about the Gray Man? *Here?*"

The reply was delivered in a biting tone. "We call him Violator, Suzanne. You aren't at the watercooler with the junior administrators."

Chastened, she said, "Of course. I'm sorry. But why is he a threat? My understanding was that *we* were after *him*."

Mayes said, "We are, and he knows it. Five years now. That's why him showing up like this is so problematic. It's possible his arrival in the area was coincidence, a waypoint towards his final destination, but we have to allow for the possibility that he is here on some sort of an offensive operation." Mayes added, "It's what he does, after all."

Brewer spoke with a tone of astonishment. "That . . . that would be suicide on his part."

On the monitor next to the map a new image appeared. A passport photo of Courtland Gentry, wearing a blue blazer and wire-rimmed glasses. The image was at least five years old.

Brewer said, "He looks so . . . average."

Carmichael broke into the conversation. "Do you know what this ex-asset is capable of?"

"I admit I only know the rumors. Cafeteria chatter and such. That file has been SCI code word classified," she said, and then quickly added, "which of course you know, because you classified it."

"I did," replied Carmichael.

She added, "If I am to help you, I'll need to know what we're dealing with. The more information you can give me, the better."

Jordan Mayes said, "Here's what you need to know. The threat is one man, but the threat is real. Gentry was, hands down, the best hard asset in the entire Agency while he was in."

"And how long was he in?"

"He was with us for nearly twelve years."

"Ex-military?"

"Negative. His potential was identified at a young age, then he was brought in to a pilot program designed to train exceptional young men for autonomous field work."

She lifted her pen and put the tip on the legal pad in front of her. She still seemed stunned by the thought of going up against the Gray Man, but she was quickly composing herself and getting down to work. "The name of this program?"

When no one spoke, Brewer glanced up from her pad. The room was perfectly silent and all eyes stared at the pen on the paper.

After a few seconds, she slowly put the pen back down. "I see."

Mayes broke the silence. "After 9/11 Violator was folded into a rendition and direct action task force in Ground Branch."

Brewer said, "I'm cleared for SAD ops. Will you tell me the task force's name?"

Carmichael answered with a wave of his hand, as if it didn't matter. "Golf Sierra. Run by Matthew Hanley."

Brewer just muttered, "The Goon Squad."

"So you've heard of them, too."

"Well, like it is with Gentry, I only know the legend. They were supposedly the best we had." Brewer glanced quickly around the room. It was evident to all she was wondering why on earth Gentry's former superior was not present. Matthew Hanley was now the head of the Special Activities Division; *surely* he was cleared for anything said in this room.

As she was about to bring up this concern, something else occurred to her. "I guess the most important thing you can tell me is why we are after Gentry in the first place."

She looked to Mayes, but Mayes only turned his head to Carmichael. Apparently Carmichael would determine if she was to be allowed to know this part of the story.

Before Carmichael could speak, a disembodied voice filled the room. "We have Director Aurbach ready on the satellite."

Mayes told the commo technician to send the feed to the monitor.

The large blue screen on the wall came to life. Menachem Aurbach sat at a desk wearing an open-collared white button-down. The man was seventy-two years old, and he had a thick neck and a thicker gut, but he also was in possession of a ruddy complexion and a coiffed black mane that was only peppered with strands of silver. His visage was tired and sullen, but Carmichael expected nothing else, because as long as he'd known the Mossad man, Aurbach had always looked as if he'd just been awakened from a deep sleep and told that his dog had died.

Carmichael and Aurbach had first met in a bomb shelter in Beirut in 1985, both intelligence officers representing their countries during Lebanon's insane seventeen-faction civil war. Denny was new at CIA at the time, but he'd already spent over a decade in military intelligence, so he and the rugged Mossad officer worked well together in those instances when CIA and Mossad found themselves in close operational relationships.

Carmichael and Aurbach had kept the relationship up in the nineties, and then after 9/11 they worked even more closely together. Carmichael became station chief in Hong Kong, then was promoted to head the CIA's Special Activities Division, a hard-charging unit of paramilitary officers that was called on constantly during the War on Terror. After several years running SAD, he was promoted again, this time to run the entire National Clandestine Service.

As high up on the American intelligence food chain as Carmichael was, Menachem Aurbach had reached even loftier realms in the Mossad, becoming the head of Israeli Intelligence several years earlier.

Denny hadn't spoken to Aurbach in months, and that meant this would normally be the time for pleasantries about health and family, but Carmichael wasn't in a pleasant mood. "What do you know, Manny?"

Aurbach spoke in a voice graveled by six decades of smoking. "I know that we owe you an apology. We had access to your man Gentry, but we let him slip between our fingers, and it appears he has escaped into your area of operations."

Carmichael responded, "The imprecision in your words is a concern. First off, Gentry isn't my man. He's my target. And D.C. isn't my AO. It's my damn home. CIA doesn't run ops here."

Aurbach raised an eyebrow, an act that looked like it took a significant amount of his low energy. "I imagine that will change immediately, in light of what I am about to tell you."

"Talk."

"As you know, Mr. Gentry recently saved the life of our prime minister. An inconsequential thing to me, really, as I don't have a high regard for politicians. But one of my top people was appreciative, and he single-handedly arranged for Mr. Gentry's escape from Europe. We only found out about this today. It goes without saying that I have detained my officer for further questioning."

"How did Gentry get out of Europe?"

"Via container ship leaving out of the Portuguese city of Aveiro. We tracked the boat, but by the time we began looking for it, it was already in your Chesapeake Bay. Of course we reached out to your office instantly, but we suspect Mr. Gentry would have had time to make his way off the ship and onto shore."

Carmichael took his time controlling his fury, then he said, "I take it your man was unaware of Gentry's importance?"

"He'd been told Mr. Gentry was wanted by the CIA. He'd been warned the man was both formidable and an enemy to both of our nations."

"And that's it?"

At the conference table, several people looked at one another in confusion. Jordan Mayes, on the other hand, seemed unfazed by the back and forth between the two veteran spies.

Aurbach said, "He did not know specifics of Gentry's crimes."

Carmichael rubbed his eyes under his glasses and leaned back in his chair. "Well, Manny, you've handed me one hell of a shit sandwich, haven't you? I'm not exactly sure how you can help me from over there, other than to shake down that traitor of yours to glean any scrap of intel you can get."

If Aurbach did not like the characterization of his subordinate, he gave no hint of it on his face, but he replied, "My officer is no traitor to his country. He rewarded the man who prevented the decapitation of our government. Having said that, I will question him personally to find out everything he knows, after giving him some days in solitary detention to soften him up."

"I hope you are thorough."

Aurbach's tired face tightened a bit. "Mossad doesn't need any tips on interrogation from CIA. I'll let you know what I find out." Aurbach leaned a little closer to the camera. "In the meantime . . . I suggest you lock your doors tonight. I've read the after-action reports regarding the swath of destruction this former asset of yours burned through Europe last month. He is quite the talented killing machine. I would not want him mad at me." Aurbach leaned back with a smile and reached for a button on the desk console in front of him. "My love to Eleanor." He punched the button and the feed went dead.

Carmichael paid no attention to the others in the conference room. Instead he exhaled, looking off into space. "Fucking Manny."

One of the analysts at the table interrupted his thought. "Director Carmichael, apologies for pointing this out if it's sensitive, but it seems clear Aurbach knows more about why we are hunting this target than I do. What does Violator have to do with Israel?"

Carmichael answered in an offhanded manner. "Gentry was involved in an op while working in SAD. Israel came out on the short end of things. Manny knows about it. You do not." He shrugged. "Not relevant to your operation."

The analyst said, "It might help us understand why he went to such lengths to protect the Israeli prime minister. That doesn't fit with what we know about the man."

"George . . . no." There was an annoyed finality in Carmichael's voice. George just held a hand up in surrender.

Brewer took this all in. She was fascinated to see other Working Group members asking questions about Violator. They were tasked with catching him, but their need-to-know apparently didn't include details of his former operations.

Carmichael turned to Brewer now, surprising her with the speed of the movement. "Okay, Suzanne. Time to earn yourself a seat at the table. You've heard what we're up against. What do you suggest we do?"

Brewer looked around, and her voice became unsure. "I don't see any outside entities represented here."

"Outside entities?"

"Protocol for something like this . . . a local threat, I mean . . . is to bring in the FBI."

Carmichael sighed. Disappointed in her comment. "No Bureau. This isn't going to be a DOJ dog and pony show. We have one man in the area, we can handle this. What steps do you say we take first?"

She said, "Honestly, if this were Paris, Buenos Aires, even Toronto, we would have more options from an operational standpoint. But D.C. isn't our turf. I can't just send a security team in a helicopter over the Capitol and a surveillance team in a van down Pennsylvania Avenue."

Carmichael shook his head. "There *are* counterintelligence protocols for resources at our disposal. On an ad hoc basis I can bring in various assets, I can order up contracted security with TS clearance. I can call in JSOC operators."

Brewer was astonished. "JSOC operators? You are talking about Delta Force?"

Mayes corrected her. "They haven't been called that for years, but yeah, special mission units. Those guys."

"To run a direct-action mission in the United States?"

"Yes," Carmichael replied flatly.

Brewer was realizing Carmichael had been right when he said she'd never worked on an operation of this magnitude. "You would need approval from the director, who himself would need approval from the president."

"I *have* approval from the director, who has an existing understanding with POTUS involving Violator." He smiled. "Welcome to the big leagues, Brewer. You want *in* this program, you're going to have to get *with* the program."

Suzanne Brewer composed herself for a moment, well aware that all eyes were on her. Then she reached out and touched the intercom button. Mayes and Carmichael exchanged a look, surprised that the subordinate was taking such liberties. She was the most junior officer in the room, but clearly she was no shrinking violet.

A communications specialist answered on the intercom.

"Commo."

"Where are we in accessing local police, D.C. Metro, and civilian camera networks?"

"We'll be up on all systems by tomorrow at seven a.m."

"And facial recog?"

"Ready to go. Once we have the feeds, we'll get to work. It will be a slow process. A lot of cameras for the computers to look at."

"I understand. Are we monitoring first responder bands?"

"Uh . . ."

"Do it. Police, ambulance, fire. We need to be on the lookout for anything anomalous in the District involving a single subject fitting his description. If he's a lone wolf, he might steal a car, break into a building, rob a pawnshop in the burbs. Hell, if he's been on a cargo ship for that long he might hire a hooker or get himself busted in a massage parlor."

"We'll get on it immediately."

The room was quiet. Then Carmichael looked to Mayes. "All right. I'm sold. Suzanne is in the Working Group, in charge of the tactical operations center. She runs defense, and she is subordinate to you on offense. She sees primary intel on Violator, beginning with everything we know about his actions in the past two years."

Brewer cocked her head. "You said he's been on the run for *five* years."

Carmichael stared her down. "You get two years. That is plenty of background for you to build a profile of his modus operandi."

Suzanne Brewer let it go. "Thank you, sir."

Carmichael addressed the entire table now. "Listen up. Violator has been running from us for a long time. Suddenly he's right back here in our midst. This gives rise to the possibility he has transitioned from defender to aggressor. That should be extremely disconcerting to you all."

He pointed a finger at the map. "The quicker we can find him out there, the better. The longer he's free on the streets, the more time he has to set up an operation to go on the attack." He shook his head. "We are not going to give him that time."

5

ourt Gentry stood in the darkness, a light rain falling on his head and
shoulders, the back of his jacket soaked from leaning against the steps
of a rusted playground slide. He shifted his feet back and forth for
warmth and blew into his hands.

As he stood and shivered in the tiny park he watched a young white
man in a red parka standing on the porch of a dilapidated single-story
home across the street. The man lit a cigarette and looked around in all
directions, his eyes searching for anyone watching him. Court was just one
hundred feet away but he might as well have been invisible. The man looked
through him and continued his scan, then he left the porch and headed
down the street.

Court kept his eyes on the man until he disappeared around the corner
a block to the south.

When he was out of view, Court turned his attention back to the house.
Sandwiched between a pair of low-rent and low-rise apartment buildings,
it had whitewashed wood clapboard walls and a small front porch, accented
by a black metal door that looked like it could withstand a direct hit from
an antitank missile. There were two security cameras visible on the property, one watching over the driveway to the right of the porch, the other
pointing straight down to the front door to record anyone who approached.

A tall wooden fence rimmed with barbed wire enclosed the small backyard, and an angry dog back there barked and snarled at any sound on the
street.

Court blew into his hands again while he took in the scene. The inner-
city location, the beat-up house with the fortified access point, the rough-
looking skinny white boys coming and going.

There was no mystery as to what he was looking at.

This was a stash house for a drug ring.

Thirty minutes after his run-in with the would-be muggers on 8th Street SE, Court had seen a man selling packets of either heroin or meth behind a gas station on Savannah Avenue. Court melted into the dark edge of the parking lot to watch, and soon he determined the man probably wasn't dealing H, because he looked like a meth head, which meant he was both a user and a dealer, and it stood to reason he used what he dealt. The bony man made a phone call after the sale. Court wasn't in a position to hear any of it, but from the fact the man started walking as soon as he hung up, Court thought he might be heading to a stash house to drop off money and pick up more supply.

And Court had been right. He followed the gaunt young man seven blocks, finding this surprisingly difficult to do because the man was amped up and paranoid, always looking back over his shoulder, ducking down behind things and even moving in and out through traffic racing by on Wheeler Road. But Court kept the tail, because he knew the low-level dealer was going someplace Court wanted to be.

The man finally arrived at this single-story clapboard house on Brandy-wine Street, where he knocked four times on the iron door, and then transferred something—almost certainly cash—through a slot at chest level, before receiving something—almost certainly drugs—in a paper bag. He headed off up the street and Court watched the man go, and soon another equally strung-out-looking white kid appeared and repeated the sequence, giving Court all the evidence he needed that he'd come to the right place.

Court had considered making his way into a neighbor's backyard to get a better look at the property behind the stash house, but the angry pit bull snarling there encouraged him to change his mind. The dog went positively ape shit every time one of the men stepped onto the property to knock on the front door, so Court decided he couldn't get any closer to the house without raising the alarm. Instead he moved to the derelict asphalt-covered park, stood on the playground, and cased the location from the front, planning his next move.

While he felt certain he knew what was inside the house, he had no idea *who* was inside the house. They could be MS-13, the Salvadoran gang, or they could be white supremacists. From the three motorcycles lined up and locked together on the drive he knew they could be some biker gang, as well, but the old, beat-up bikes weren't nearly as impressive as Court's mental image of what a biker gang would be riding, so he was betting against Hells Angels or Outlaws MC.

He was pretty sure who *wasn't* inside. There was a pickup truck in the drive, a late-model candy-apple red Dodge Ram, and the presence of a rebel flag decal on the back window gave Court the impression that the operation in the house probably wasn't being conducted by the D.C. Blacks, the Crips, or the Bloods.

But Court didn't really care about the occupants themselves; all that really concerned him was the security of the property, because he planned on making entry on the house. He wanted to know about any booby traps, false access points, mantraps, or other fortified areas. At this point he wasn't really thinking about the presence of guns because he *knew* there would be guns—no self-respecting drug dealer would operate in the United States without an arsenal within arm's reach—but to Court, this was not a problem.

In fact, he was counting on it.

He checked his watch. Twenty minutes till midnight. For a second he considered hanging out there until three a.m., when the average person's body clock was at its lowest. But almost immediately he decided against waiting. Meth heads kept weird hours, after all, and Court knew they might well be more wired and ready at four a.m. than at four p.m., so he made the decision to act now.

He left the darkness of the playground and stepped out onto the sidewalk.

He didn't go directly to the stash house. Instead he backtracked half a block, returning to an unlocked garage he had noticed as he was tailing the street dealer through the neighborhood. He entered the garage, felt his way around, and came across a pull cord for a lamp on a worktable. Before he pulled the cord, he took off his jacket and threw it over the lamp, so he could control the amount of light the bulb gave off.

He pulled the chain and then moved his jacket so that only a faint glow reached the rest of the little one-car garage. He saw a few items on the table, and a few more on a wooden shelf, and he took what he needed, turned off the lamp, and felt his way back to the exit.

Minutes later he crossed the street in front of the drug house, his hands empty and nonthreatening. As he approached he heard the sound of industrial heavy metal music coming from inside. He walked up the little driveway, passed the bikes and the Dodge pickup, and climbed up onto the porch. By now the frantic noise was blasting, which was impressive to Court, considering the windows were boarded and the door could not have been more secure.

Looking the door over, he tried to determine the security measures at this entrance. There would be dead bolts and multiple chain locks, and there would be a drop bar or a "dead man," a large metal shank that secured the door to the wall.

Court knew he would not be entering through that door unless someone on the inside wanted him to, and he didn't see much of a chance in that.

He banged four times, and the dog in the backyard barked like a maniac.

Seconds later, a four-inch-high and twelve-inch-wide slit opened in the center of the door at chest height, firing a bolt of light across the porch. From the inside, Court heard the loud metal music, and above that a voice high and harsh like a coffee grinder. "What the fuck *you* want?"

Court leaned down to look into the slot. A bald-headed, shirtless man in his thirties stood back a few feet from the door. His chest and neck were tattooed and glistening with sweat. He held a lit cigarette in his left hand.

Pure white trash.

Court looked over the ink on the man's chest quickly. The numbers 1 and 2 rode high above his left pec. Court knew the significance. The numbers represented the first and second letters of the alphabet. AB.

This asshole was Aryan Brotherhood.

Court also noticed the man was hiding something in his right hand behind his thigh.

"I said, what do you want, fuckhead?"

"I need a hit." Court was winging it; he didn't know the street lingo for meth these days; he'd been out of the States for several years and had never bought meth in his life. He saw the paranoia in the white supremacist's eyes now as the man realized this wasn't one of his regular street dealers.

He said, "Get lost."

"Your guy told me to come here. He said he ran out of stuff."

"What guy?"

"Skinny dude over at the Exxon on Savannah."

A younger man stepped up behind the bald man at the door. He had stringy hair and was wearing a wifebeater, and his arms were sleeved with shamrocks and the number 12. He also had 88 on his neck, and Court knew these numbers were representations of the eighth letter of the alphabet. HH.

Heil Hitler.

Charming.

The younger man said, "He's talkin' 'bout Junior."

"Junior, that's right," Court confirmed helpfully.

The bald-headed man reached back and punched the kid in the wifebeater in the chest, then shoved him out of Court's line of sight. He turned back to Court, his eyes wide with both suspicion and anger. "Fuck you. Get off my porch." He moved his right hand from behind his hip and exposed a black AK-47 assault rifle with a folded stock.

Court raised his hands. "It's all good, brother. Hook me up and I'll go." He pulled the wad of bills out of his pocket, the ten wrapped around the six ones. He held it up but kept it moving in front of his face, hoping it looked like significantly more than sixteen dollars. "See, I've got cash."

"This ain't McDonald's drive-through, you stupid fuck! Get out of here!" The man rushed to the door and slid the tiny panel shut. Court heard another male voice, different than that of the two men he'd already heard speak, and then a screaming female. Everyone was shouting over the music, but Court couldn't understand a word of what was being said.

He hadn't really expected to be invited in for tea, or for any transaction to take place. This was a stash house, hardly an inviting retail establishment. He just wanted to use the opportunity to get a look at the inside, to judge the defenses, to evaluate the opposition.

Four people in the front room, three males. He had seen just the one rifle, but he imagined each and every one of those drug-addled paranoid freaks inside would be carrying some sort of a weapon.

He had told himself earlier that if he knew there were more than three people inside, he would move on, find another target of opportunity.

But it was getting late, he was getting cold, and four was close enough to three.

He'd continue on with his mission here.

Just to get everyone inside a little more jumpy and overwrought, he knocked again.

"I'm going to kill you!" the bald-headed man shouted. And then, for added emphasis, he added a "Fuck off!"

Court heaved a big sigh. He gave a light "Have a good night," and he turned and left the porch.

But he did not return to the sidewalk or the street. Instead he walked over to the driveway and looked up at the camera peering down at him. It was on the side of the house, just under the awning, a foot and a half out of Court's reach. Its lens was centered on the Dodge Ram and the motorcycles.

Court moved to the side of the Ram, and as he did so he reached into his blazer and pulled a hammer from his waistband, an oily shop rag and a lighter from his pocket. He used the claw of the hammer to prize open the fuel door of the vehicle, then he removed the fuel cap and stuffed the oily rag most of the way in the fueling tube.

He lit it quickly.

Court stepped directly under the camera now and tossed the hammer up gently. It hit the camera and knocked the lens so that it pointed up to the rainy sky.

Court caught the hammer as it fell, then he moved up the driveway towards the back gate, but while doing so he turned around and heaved the hammer overhand into the windshield of the Ram. The glass cracked and the vehicle's shrill alarm began to wail.

6

Two men armed with 12-gauge shotguns raced out the back door of the single-story clapboard house, leapt off the side of the porch, and then charged to the locked gate that led to the driveway. One of the men slowed to release a ninety-pound pit bull from his chain, freeing him to run with the humans towards the noise in the front of the property and the man who had caused it. At the gate, one man unhooked a large, loose padlock from the staple hasp on the wooden fence, then kicked the gate open, his shotgun at the high ready in case someone stood waiting for him there. The dog took off up the driveway, and when the man saw no one in front of him, he ran towards the Dodge pickup to douse the flames licking up the side panel of the truckbed.

The second man followed close behind the first, himself waving his 12-gauge in all directions as he did so. He saw the flaming rag in the gas tank of the Dodge Ram and he hesitated a moment, not knowing if it would explode at any second. But his colleague was either braver or more foolish, and he charged at the flames, desperate to save the vehicle.

Court Gentry knelt in the bushes next to the gate and watched the pit bull bolt from the darkened backyard. The massive black form of muscle and gnashing teeth raced past Court's position on his way to freedom. Behind the pit, two men, both rail-thin and pasty white, sprinted through the gate, down the driveway, and towards the Dodge Ram, wooden-stocked shotguns out in front of them. One man slowed for a moment, hesitating, but soon enough he headed on, catching up with his friend at the burning shop rag.

Court slipped into the backyard and closed the gate behind him, locking it by dropping the padlock's shackle through the hasp.

There was no direct lighting back there at all, but the tiny bit of residual glow from the raining sky above gave him a dim view of his surroundings. The entire yard was surrounded by the ten-foot-high privacy fence. It was overgrown and filled with trash, and a broken-down and weed-covered Chevy Monte Carlo was on blocks alongside the fence near the back porch. The windows of the house back there were boarded, just as they were out front, and the back door was a metal and Plexiglas storm door.

As Court moved past the car he pulled an old, shredded tire out of the weeds. It was only a small-sized spare, but it must have weighed twenty pounds. His injured right forearm hurt when he held that much weight in his right hand, so he hefted it in his left and continued on towards the porch.

As he started up the stairs he stopped suddenly. Something about the scene triggered a sense of danger. He figured it out quickly—it was odd there were no bright lights back here; it would have made sense considering the other security measures on the property—unless, of course, the back entrance was booby-trapped.

Court still had the lighter, so he fired it up and held it out, and immediately he saw the glint of metal suspended two feet in front of his face. A dozen or more large metal fishhooks hung on fishing line five and a half feet off the ground, at eye level of the average man. The thin filament was attached to the columns on either side of the steps up to the back porch, and the hooks hung ready to dig into the face and rip out the eyes of anyone unaware of this security measure. Obviously those who lived or worked in the stash house also knew to avoid the stairs of the back porch and instead to come and go by stepping up onto the two-foot-high porch on either side of the stairs.

Court saw a milk crate positioned to his right to help with that, so he sidestepped the booby trap and climbed up the rest of the way to the door.

He heard shouting and barking in the driveway now, and the gate rattled off to his left. Court assumed the Aryan Brotherhood men and their Nazi dog had just figured out they'd been tricked.

As he made to reach for the handle of the heavy back door, light engulfed the porch and the door flew open. A man appeared in the doorway, backlit from a bulb in the room behind him, a Kalashnikov rifle held high. Court rushed forward, batted the weapon to the side with his right hand, and banged the twenty-pound rubber tire into the man's face with his left, striking him in the jaw, snapping the man's head back, and knocking him to the floor.

Court entered the house by stepping over the dazed man, and he closed and locked the metal door behind him. He found himself in a poorly lit dark-paneled hallway floored with cheap linoleum. The thick smell of cigarette smoke, pot, and rotting garbage assaulted his nostrils and clawed at his eyes, and the incessant music, played at a volume that made Court think of a concert in hell, further disrupted his senses.

He started to kneel to pick up the AK, but before he could get his hand on the weapon another man raced in through a dim doorway ahead and to his left, on his way towards the back door. This man also wielded a Kalashnikov, but he had not expected to see a threat inside the house, so his weapon was not up and ready to fire.

Court identified this man as the young Aryan Brotherhood member with the 88 on his neck. As the man raised his gun towards the stranger, Court swung the car tire at him underhanded, and it slammed into his face with a thud audible over the hammering drumbeat of the heavy metal.

The young man's head flew back, banged against the door casing. He slid down, unconscious and flat on his back on the hallway floor.

The Aryan Brotherhood man by the back door who had taken the tire to the jaw rolled slowly to his knees and reached for his weapon, but Court kicked him in his already bloody face and spun him into the air, dropping him against the locked back door.

Court lifted one of the AKs off the ground now, but as he did so a shrill scream caused him to look back over his shoulder. Down the full length of the paneled hallway, some twenty-five feet away, a woman held something over her head.

Court recognized the item immediately, although he could not help but recoil in surprise. It was a *katana*. A traditional Japanese sword.

Not good.

And it got worse. Court realized the sword was being brandished by a meth head. The woman might have been in her twenties or thirties, but her skin was dry and leathery and stretched across the bones of her pockmarked face, and every exposed inch of her arms and neck was covered in scabs and tats. Her white blond hair was oily and thin, and the black T-shirt and jeans she wore were torn and threadbare.

He was as afraid of the woman as he was of the deadly weapon in her grasp.

The meth head with the sword charged. She was no expert with this weapon of hers; Court determined this instantly. In the narrow hall she should have been advancing forward with the point of the katana, but instead she swung it from side to side, slamming the blade into both walls as she closed wildly.

Court did not see her any differently because she was a woman; any sense of chivalry or gender bias in a force-on-force encounter had been trained out of him years and years ago. He saw her only as a threat. A target. He brought the AK up to his shoulder, used his thumb to make sure the fire selector was set to semiautomatic, centered the blade sight on her chest, and moved his finger to the trigger.

But before he could press the trigger and drop the woman, fully automatic gunfire erupted somewhere in the house. Suddenly jagged perforations pocked the paneling of the hallway, waist-high, halfway between Court and the charging woman with the sword. Though the holes appeared in both sides of the hall, Court could tell the shooting was coming from his right, so he dropped down onto his left shoulder, landing on the cold linoleum, and he returned fire with his AK, sending rounds of lead back in the direction of the gunfire, shooting through the wall next to him.

The woman with the sword made it less than halfway to Court before she was cut down. One of the bullets fired by the unseen attacker ripped through the paneling and then sliced through both of her thighs, causing her to stumble and fall awkwardly to her knees. The sword flew from her hands and clanged along the floor, then it slid, hilt-first, all the way to Court.

Court ignored the sword and kept firing the Kalashnikov at the wall just inches in front of him. The crushing volume of the rifle's reports in the long, narrow space made his ears squeal, but he continued raking the barrel of his weapon back and forth, shooting all the while, desperate to suppress the incoming gunfire. Red-hot ejected shell casings bounced around the floor all around him and ricocheted back into his face, while splinters of paneling pricked his eyes and covered his hair and clothing.

It was clear to him by the incredible amount of gunfire that he was up against more than one weapon, perhaps as many as three. He emptied his AK and crawled for the other lying nearby, scooping it up. He continued firing, pushing himself along the floor with his feet and flattening himself even lower to the filthy linoleum as an incoming round punched a massive hole in the wall less than a foot above his head. Court jammed his Kalashnikov through the opening to return fire, again sweeping his muzzle back and forth. He had no idea who or what he was shooting at—his training and his years of experience commanded his actions now. He was in a fight for his life, and he did not pause to consider the consequences of each thumbnail-sized round he sent tearing through the wall at 2,350 feet per second.

Finally this second weapon clicked on an empty chamber and he took a moment to just lie there and listen. His ears were battered enough from all the shooting, and the heavy music coming from another part of the house droned on, but he was reasonably sure the incoming fire had stopped. The woman moaned on the floor ten feet away, but he ignored her as he climbed to one knee.

Court dropped the rifle on the floor there next to him and he heaved the sword. He stood back up and headed down the hall, hoping to make it to any more threats in the house before they had a chance to regroup and attack.

When he reached the woman he decided he needed to check her for any weapons. She had nothing on her other than a crack pipe, a thick roll of twenties, and a lighter. He saw her bloody thighs, and determined from the location of the wounds that the arteries in her legs remained intact, and she would probably survive.

He thought she was out of the fight completely, but before he could stand back up she looked up to him, bared her teeth, and tried to scratch at his eyes with her fingernails.

Court punched her in her left temple with the hilt of the sword, dazing her instantly. He then grabbed her by the waistband of her jeans in the small of her back, and he lifted her off the floor. He walked on, carrying her like a rag doll, holding the sword in his right hand as he dragged her along with his left.

He found the stereo in the main living room and turned it off, and as soon as he did so he heard the two men outside, frantically beating on the boarded windows next to the front door, trying to get back in.

He popped the disk out of the property's security camera system, and he snapped it in his hands and slipped it into his pocket, then he turned and moved down a hall, out of the main living area.

In a large back bedroom his eyes settled on a scene of carnage. An older man, covered in Aryan Brotherhood ink like the others, lay on his back in the middle of the floor. His arms and legs were splayed; his head was split open from a gunshot wound to the eye. Court determined one of the 7.62 rounds he'd fired into the wall had passed all the way through the man's skull. The dead man's gore had been splattered across a faux leather recliner behind him that had itself taken half a dozen rounds of hate from Court's borrowed rifles. Next to the body lay an AK, and next to this Court saw the bald-headed man he'd spoken to through the front door just minutes earlier. The Aryan Brotherhood meth dealer sat on the floor, leaning against the foot of an unmade bed, his eyes glazed but pointing in Court's direction.

The black polymer Kalashnikov lay in his lap, but his hands were resting on the floor. Court counted three gunshot wounds on the man. One in the right wrist, one in the left elbow, and another in his right hip.

The bald-headed man's chest heaved up and down rapidly, and he was covered in blood.

Court used the tip of the katana to flick the AK-47 out of the man's lap and beyond his reach. He then dragged the unconscious woman into the room and dropped her face-first on the bed behind the injured man. The bald-headed man lay there motionless as Court did this, blood pumping from his hip and arms. Court looked the wounds over and didn't give the man much chance for survival unless the bleeding was controlled and paramedics made the scene in the next fifteen minutes.

Court looked around the room. All the walls, all the furniture—all the people, for that matter—were riddled with bullet holes.

Court pulled a blanket off the bed. It was soiled and stained and covered in cigarette burns. He tossed it to the drug dealer on the floor.

The man pressed it against his hip to stanch the bleeding, groaning with pain as he put pressure on the wound. He held it in place with his injured left arm. "What do you want?"

"What do you think?"

"Drugs?"

"Guess again."

"Cash?"

"You're brighter than you look."

The white supremacist's voice slurred a little. "You . . . ain't . . . gettin' shit."

Court checked his watch. A stray round here and there might not garner too much interest in Ward Eight, but he knew the roar of a thirty-second full-auto firefight would draw out the police, and he sure as hell did not want to be hanging out in this meth den when the cops showed up. "I don't have time to dick around. I see from all that ink that you are no stranger to superficial wounds from sharp objects, so I'll have to go deep, won't I?" Court raised the katana chest-high, holding the hilt with both hands.

"What the fuck are you going to—"

The man stopped speaking suddenly and his focus shifted to a point somewhere over Court's left shoulder. Court knew the man was looking at the doorway behind him. Without hesitation Court flipped the sword around in his left hand and brought it underhanded back behind him, and he fired it back like a piston, launching it through the air blade-first without looking. Immediately he heard the steel strike flesh, and he turned around, saw a bearded man in the doorway ten feet away, armed with a massive Desert Eagle pistol. The katana had caught him in the solar plexus, driven through his lungs, and the tip now rested against the backside of the man's rib cage.

The big handgun fell from the man's hand and he reached up for the sword for a short time, his wide eyes on it, his face a mask of confusion. After a moment, however, he folded down onto the floor, ending up with his back propped on the doorframe, wheezing and grunting with the movement of his chest. His eyes went unfixed and glassy as he drifted away.

Court knew the look of the dying. It didn't sadden him; he felt little other than operational concerns. He knelt over the dying man, rummaged through his pockets, pushed the man's weakening hands away when they reached out to stop him.

Court found nothing of interest on the man, so he left him alone to die, and he turned back to the wounded drug dealer at the foot of the bed. "I'm going to make this really quick and simple. Show me where the money is, and you get help before you bleed out."

The man looked at his two dead partners, back behind him to the unconscious woman on the bed, then back to Court. "Go fuck yourself."

Court nodded, and he pulled the blanket out of the man's grasp. He looked down at the blood pumping from the man's hip. "Three minutes and you'll lose consciousness. Five minutes, you're dead."

"I don't give a shit."

"Well, that makes two of us. I'll find the money anyway. Or the cops will. Not that it will matter much to you, because you'll be in a fridge at the morgue."

Court saw the wheels spinning in the man's head. When he realized he would gain nothing from his obstinacy he said, "Windowsill. Pop the ledge up."

Court tossed the bloody blanket back to the wounded drug dealer, then he went to the boarded-up window. He yanked up on the wooden sill. With some effort, it pulled away from the wall. Inside was a channel in the frame of the house. He could see two bags there, and he fished them out quickly with a metal coat hanger he found lying loose on the floor.

The first paper bag contained a meth ball, a plastic bag holding small plastic baggies, each one containing a sixteenth of an ounce of crystal meth. Court wasn't sure what the street value of it all was, but there had to have been a hundred or more bags.

He turned and tossed the meth bag into the lap of the nearly decapitated corpse, just feet away. "Careful, this shit'll kill you," Court said, and then he looked in the second bag. This one was stuffed with cash. Tens and twenties, mostly, but there were a few fives and even some ones. He held it up to the wounded man on the floor. "How much?"

Even though he'd stanched the bulk of the blood flow, the man was weakening noticeably. Through gasps he said, "I don't know. 'Bout thirteen grand. Little more, maybe."

The soft wail of distant sirens caused Court to pick up his pace now. He shoved the money in his coat pocket and began looking for guns. He counted seven firearms in the house, but they were all wrong for his needs. The chrome-plated Desert Eagle pistol was as long as a shoebox and inefficiently heavy. He could get out of the area with the pistol if he hid it under his shirt, but he wouldn't be able to operate in the District with such a huge and flashy weapon. There were four AK-47–style semiautomatic rifles, none of which he could hide in his blazer to exfiltrate the scene with, even while folded.

He loved AKs—he knew he couldn't go wrong with the venerable Russian assault rifle. But it was hardly a low-profile weapon.

He also found two pistol grip shotguns. The shotguns were like the Desert Eagle, almost small enough to get away with, but way too big to use efficiently in the manner Court had planned.

He went back to the severely wounded man sitting up in front of the bed. He felt around his waistband, then frisked him down to his ankles, avoiding the blood on the man's clothing.

Court breathed a sigh of relief when his fingers brushed against a Velcro ankle holster low on the man's right leg. He yanked out a tiny Ruger LCP .380. It carried eight rounds of hollow-point ammo and fit nicely in the palm of Court's hand.

The drug dealer hadn't resisted at all. Court wondered if the man had even remembered the weapon strapped to his leg.

Court slipped the gun into the back pocket of his jeans, then walked over to a nightstand by the bed. It was covered with ashtrays, cigarette packs, crumpled beer cans, and candy wrappers, so Court used a forearm to knock every last item onto the floor.

He was back there in the corner for several seconds, long enough to arouse the curiosity of the wounded drug dealer, who was now lying on his side on the floor in front of the bed. "You got what you came for. There's nothing else."

When Court did not reply the man spoke in a slurred voice. "What the fuck are you doing?"

Court replied cryptically: "Sending a message."

"What?"

Soon Court headed for the door, passing the wounded man on the floor without a glance as he did so.

As he started up the hall, the wounded man called out from behind.

"Who *are* you?"

Court did not reply. He wouldn't give the man or his buddies, alive or dead, another moment's thought. His plans ahead were infinitely more important than these inconsequential street criminals. They were just a means to an end, nothing more.

Less than a minute before the first police car stopped in front of the house, Court stepped back out into the backyard, holding a loaded AK-47 high in front of him. He realized quickly the two Aryan Brotherhood men who had been out there were gone from the scene—even their damn dog had hit the road with the sound of approaching sirens—so Court tossed the AK into the grass, climbed up onto the Monte Carlo by the fence, carefully pushed the barbed wire out of the way, and dropped into an adjoining backyard.

He was out of the neighborhood two minutes after that.

Tonight had been more trouble than he'd envisioned, but it had all been a necessary opening move in his operation. He needed a portable and concealable weapon, and he needed capital to put his plan into action.

He wanted more gun than what was now sitting in the back pocket of his jeans. To be sure, he wasn't going to fight much of a battle here in the U.S. with the little Ruger, but it was a decent tool, and with it he had improved his defenses markedly.

But infinitely more important than the gun was the cash.

This was America, after all, and cash was king.

And with thirteen grand, Court Gentry could wage a motherfucking war.

7

By the time the meeting on the seventh floor of CIA's Old Headquarters Building hit the forty-five-minute mark, Suzanne Brewer was reasonably certain everyone else had forgotten she was still here.

Denny had admitted her into the Violator Working Group, true, but since then she had sat to the side, seemingly excluded from the conversation. The cross talk now was between Jordan Mayes and Denny Carmichael as they discussed moving Joint Special Operations Command operatives into the city. Apparently a quasi-legal precedent had been established for doing so, which came as a surprise to Brewer. It seemed clear that even though Carmichael wasn't concerned about doing things by the book himself, he knew "Jay-Sock" wouldn't operate without all the forms filled out to the letter, so he was making sure the CIA's JSOC liaison had all the details he needed to contact Fort Bragg and get the highly trained paramilitaries on the way to D.C.

Brewer found herself impressed with Denny. She'd never worked closely with him before, and knew him mostly as the old hard piece of shoe leather in a suit that she saw in the halls every now and then. She did know that Carmichael commanded a take-no-prisoners reputation in the Agency, and his colleagues knew to fall into step behind the man or to get the hell out of his way, because although he and the director weren't close, Denny got things done and clearly the president liked having a stone-cold killing machine like Carmichael in his bag of tricks.

Now Carmichael, Mayes, and the communications officer at the table began discussing the logistics of initiating a full-time Violator Working Group tactical operations center, or TOC, on the fourth floor. Carmichael had already said he wanted more boots on the ground, so Mayes ordered thirty contracted assets with security clearance from a private security company. These assets, and the JSOC operators, would need a central ops center to coordinate their movements and responsibilities, and the TOC would serve that function.

Suzanne Brewer was surprised they wouldn't use Special Activities Division assets for this, but Denny was adamant he didn't want SAD men operating on the streets of D.C. It seemed like an odd quibble for a man who just ordered up U.S. military forces and private contractors to do the same thing, but Brewer figured there was a piece of the puzzle she didn't understand, so she didn't bring it up.

When there was a brief lull in the chatter, Brewer fought her way back into the conversation.

"I'd like to know something about Violator's specific capabilities."

With Carmichael's approval, Mayes said, "Gentry has every tactic, every piece of tradecraft, every relevant training evolution you can think of. He can fly planes, scuba, rappel, fast rope, and free climb. He's a master in the Israeli martial art of Krav Maga, and he's the best close-quarters battle tactician to ever serve in SAD. He's been to jump school, sniper school, advanced surveillance school, explosive breaching school, SERE school."

Suzanne didn't know that one. "SERE school?"

"Survival, Evasion, Resistance, and Escape."

"Okay."

Mayes continued. "Ground Branch contains the finest one hundred fifty hard assets on planet earth. Gentry was as good as any one of them if not better, and that was before he went solo five years ago and *really* began to hone his craft."

Brewer asked, "When you say hard asset, I assume Gentry was involved in lethal operations for the Agency."

No one answered for a moment.

Brewer cleared her throat. "Look. You invited me in. If I can't be told the full scope of the danger, then I won't be much help to you."

Carmichael nodded, almost imperceptibly, and Jordan Mayes said, "Gentry began his career as a singleton operator, he graduated to singleton assassin, and then in the Golf Sierra task force he was the point man for an assassination and rendition team." Mayes cleared his throat. "Golf Sierra was absolute tip-of-the-spear stuff."

Brewer took it all in. The gravity of what was being asked of her was growing by the second. "I spoke of the rumors I had heard. As a private hit man he supposedly has executed over thirty lethal operations."

Mayes answered back. "Our confirmed number is much lower. Twelve."

"A large discrepancy," Brewer added. "But the fact remains he has managed to survive for a long time in that industry. My suggestion is we don't play into this threat. If he draws us out into a campaign on the streets of the USA, we will be vulnerable to counterattack, as well as exposure."

Carmichael shook his head adamantly. "Suzanne, we *are* going after him. We know he's in the area. We have no intentions of battening down the hatches and sheltering in place while he is here. I've been after this man for five years. This is an opportunity too good to pass up. I'm not going to just lock my doors and wait for him to move on."

Brewer had expected this reaction. "Very well. In that case, we need to bring in a brain trust to help us determine Gentry's potential actions. Who in the Agency knows him best? Who knows all of his TTPs?" She knew the tactics, techniques, and procedures of her target were an essential element in establishing his operational pattern, which itself was critical in figuring out what he would do next.

The NSA liaison spoke up. "Matthew Hanley at SAD knows him well. He ran Gentry and the Golf Sierra Task Force."

More to himself than to the others, Denny Carmichael said, "I don't trust Hanley. He's after my job."

Brewer smiled. Taking a chance with a joke she said, "*I'm* after your job, Denny."

There were a few chuckles at the table, but not from Carmichael. He sniffed. "You can fucking have it, today."

Mayes joined Brewer in making a case for bringing Hanley into the Working Group. "Court Gentry shot Matt Hanley in Mexico City a couple of years ago. He barely survived. Matt might not be your closest confidant in the halls here at Langley, but I feel sure he wants Gentry's head on a pike as bad as you do. Isn't that all that matters at the moment?"

Brewer knew Matt Hanley vaguely; she'd met him in Port-au-Prince when he was chief of the CIA station there, but had heard nothing about him being shot. Protecting CIA facilities and personnel was Brewer's job, so she couldn't believe she'd been kept out of the loop on something so big.

"Wait. The head of SAD was shot by the Gray Man?" She caught herself. "Violator, I mean."

Carmichael said, "Hanley wasn't running SAD at the time, he was COS in Haiti. It was kept quiet."

"From *me*?"

"From everyone." Carmichael drummed his fingers on the table a moment. "I don't want Hanley brought in. He stays on the outside of this, for now anyway."

Brewer said, "If you don't want him involved in this hunt, that's one thing. But if Violator has a beef with the Agency, that beef is likely to include his former case officer, especially if he's targeted him in the past. We surely need to give Hanley a heads-up that his rogue operative is on the loose in the area."

Carmichael seemed to acquiesce a little. "We'll put security on Hanley, watching his house, just to keep him safe. But let's keep it low-key. Don't tell Hanley."

Brewer dropped the subject and went back to her request for information from others who knew Gentry. "Who else worked with him? What about other members of his task force?"

The CIA liaison to JSOC said, "All dead. Gentry killed them."

Mayes and Carmichael exchanged another look. The liaison caught it, and he cocked his head. "What?"

Carmichael said, "Not exactly true. One man survived."

Mayes picked it up from there. "The team leader of Task Force Golf Sierra, Zachary Hightower, is not dead." With a shrug he said, "He might as well be. Denny shit-canned him after he botched an attempt to snatch Gentry in Africa."

Brewer said, "It stands to reason his team leader would know a great deal about his operational abilities. Do we know where he is?"

Mayes said, "No idea, but I'm sure he can be located."

Carmichael held up a finger. "I want to see him first, face-to-face, to evaluate what I'm working with. He was injured severely in Africa, then he was drummed out of the Agency. If he's like a lot of operators he'll be bitter, and a shell of the man he was when he worked for us."

Brewer nodded and made notes on her pad.

She started to switch the conversation to Carmichael's immediate physical security, but one of the communications technicians outside the room knocked on the glass wall and stepped to the door. Mayes pressed a button, and the door unlocked with a click.

Mayes asked, "What is it?"

"We picked something up on the scanner. PD reports a homicide in Washington Highlands. Home invasion, multiple fatalities."

Carmichael picked up his coffee mug and took a sip. "Sounds like any other Saturday night over there."

"A surviving victim reports a lone Caucasian assailant. Apparently he took down a house full of heavily armed Aryan Brotherhood drug dealers. Two dead, four wounded."

"When?"

"Less than thirty minutes ago."

"One guy did it?" Carmichael asked.

"Yes, sir."

Carmichael and Mayes nodded at each other, and Brewer picked up what her superiors were thinking.

She asked, "Why would Violator attack a house full of meth dealers?"

Carmichael said immediately, "Maybe he needs something."

"He needs *meth*?"

Mayes answered with confidence. "Resources. Arms and financing. No better place to get both if you don't mind a fight."

Carmichael said, "And Violator *loves* a fight." Slowly his lean face widened into a smile. "It's classic Gentry, isn't it?"

Brewer was confused. "Classic in what way?"

"He needs weapons and money, right?" Carmichael said. "What's the easiest way to acquire them? Knock over a pawnshop? Hit a liquor store with a security guard? Why doesn't he steal a shotgun out of a patrol car and rob a check cashing business? Why does he do it the hard way? Hit right up the fucking middle of a house full of armed meth head Aryan assholes?"

"Tell me why," Brewer said.

Mayes understood what Carmichael was getting at, and he answered Brewer's question. "Because Violator sees himself as the good guy. He only targets bad guys."

"But you just said you think he is a threat to us."

"Make no mistake. He truly thinks he's some sort of hero and *we're* the villains." Jordan Mayes stood now. "I'll check out the crime scene personally."

Suzanne Brewer stood as well. "Denny, I'd like to go along, too. I'm behind the curve on understanding this target of ours. If this was him, I want to get the feel of the scene, to see what he's capable of."

"Okay." Carmichael turned his attention to AD Mayes. "Mayes, it's possible you are in Gentry's crosshairs, same as me. I want you rolling in armor, with a full detail."

Mayes whistled softly. "Damn, Denny. I didn't even have a full security detail in Baghdad."

"Gentry was on our side back then, wasn't he?"

8

After dark, Andy Shoal lived on cans of Red Bull and cups of convenience store coffee. He wasn't a night owl by design but, over time, he had created a chemically structured superhuman version of himself that got him through the nighttime hours, allowing him to excel at his job as a crime reporter for the *Washington Post*.

As "on" as he was when most people were tucked away in their beds, there was a price to be paid—the physical crash came each day with dawn. He was usually back in his apartment in Arlington by eight and asleep by nine, but by four thirty p.m. he was on his way back to his tiny cubicle in the *Post*'s office on 15th Street NW, just a few blocks from the White House.

He told himself he wouldn't have to do this forever. Andy was ambitious, and he was four years into his five-year plan to get out of Metro and into something higher profile, a position on the national desk or on an investigative team that wouldn't necessitate him being a zombie every damn day, so he worked hard, he got along with his editor, and he didn't bitch.

All that taken into account, Andy still figured he must be doing something seriously wrong, because why else was he the one driving out to the shittiest ward in the District in the middle of this cold misty night to report on a double homicide?

Tonight's assignment didn't sound terribly interesting—the Watergate break-in this wasn't. From the info he picked up over the police scanner in his car it seemed to be a shooting at a crack house or something. Not anything new and exciting, as Andy had filed countless stories like this already, but there were bodies and there were injured and this was his job, so as soon as he finished a piece he was working on at his desk, he climbed into his Ford Festiva and headed out into the dreary night.

With luck, he told himself, he could get six column inches out of this shooting.

Now he followed the last instructions of his GPS and turned off 4th Street SE and onto Brandywine Street.

Even though he knew the depressing crime statistics for Ward Eight, Andy never really felt unsafe around here. He was from Philly and had been raised lower middle class, so he was no stranger to rough streets. He'd been mugged once in D.C., but that was just three and a half blocks from the Capitol building, so he didn't ascribe much more threat to the so-called bad parts of town.

As Andy pulled into the neighborhood he heard over his police scanner the crime scene was a possible meth stash house run by the Aryan Brotherhood, and as he parked and looked around he thought that possibility to be highly likely. He couldn't imagine this property in front of him being anything *other* than a drug house. It was basically a boarded-up ramshackle single-story with a pickup truck adorned with a rebel flag decal in the driveway out front. The front door was a big black iron monstrosity and the fence around the back of the property was high and ringed with barbed wire.

The entire property was surrounded by police tape, and a few locals stood around in the rainy night. In the street a dozen squad cars idled, all with their headlights facing the home, and many with their lights flashing. A pair of fire trucks were parked end to end out front, and a single ambulance sat in the driveway, the EMTs leaning against their vehicle.

Just another night.

Other than Animal Control wrangling a big pit bull in the parking lot of an apartment building three doors down, there was no sense of urgency to the scene, which told Andy this ambulance was here to pick up dead bodies, not injured victims.

As he parked he noticed a gray four-door Nissan that he knew belonged to a homicide detective he'd become friendly with during his time as a cops reporter. He grabbed his backpack, stuffed with a camera, notebooks, an iPad, and a digital recorder, and he climbed out of his car, locking it before heading across the street.

He'd gotten less than halfway to the police tape when a patrolman standing at the perimeter shone a flashlight in his face. The light clicked off quickly, and Andy recognized the burly black officer.

"How's it going, Mike?"

The cop held his hand up and said, "Not yet, Andy."

Andy stopped in the street. "What's that?"

"Can't let you in just yet."

"Really?" They always let Andy in, or at least up to the porch to take a quick peek. "Why not?"

"Dunno."

"Who's the detective in charge? Is it Rauch? Tell him I'm here, he always lets me poke a head in. Won't take but a minute."

"Rauch isn't in there."

"Why are you breakin' my balls tonight, Mike? I saw his Altima back there."

"Rauch is around, but not in the house. Hasn't been inside yet. I think he's on a canvass. Go talk to him."

"What's he doing on a canvass if he hasn't even looked at the scene yet?"

The cop did not answer. He looked a bit uncomfortable, but he also looked resolute. Andy knew he could whine about it a little more, but he also knew he *wasn't* getting in that house right now.

He noticed a flashlight's beam shining through a small opening in a boarded-up front window. There was definitely someone inside. "What's going on?" he asked.

Mike turned away. "Man, go talk to Rauch."

Andy found Detective Rauch five minutes later, a half block away, stepping down from the stoop of a duplex. From the look of him he hadn't gotten any good information from anyone inside.

"Hey, Bobby. How's your night going?"

Bobby Rauch was a wiry, thin, and balding fifty-year-old who always looked like he needed a sandwich more than he needed the cigarettes he constantly smoked. He kept walking as he said, "It's goin', Shoal."

"How come you're not over there at the murder? Seen ten thousand, seen 'em all?"

Rauch took the young reporter by the arm and turned him away from the duplex, and together they started walking up the sidewalk towards the house next door. He said, "Do me a favor and go back over the river. Come back in the morning."

Andy looked at his watch. In a tone that was much more good-natured than smart-ass, he said, "Twelve fifty-eight a.m. It's morning. Here I am."

Rauch sighed. "Sorry, but I can't let you get any closer to that scene."

"What's the deal? You got a dead celeb in there or something?" Andy half chuckled as he said it, but he turned quickly serious when he saw Detective Rauch just give him an uncomfortable look.

"Oh man." Andy got excited quickly. The prospect of this being a *real* story made him salivate. "Like a congressman's kid? Who is it?"

Rauch shook his head. "Nah, nothing like that. Just some white trash dealers, from what they tell me."

"Then what the hell is going on?"

Rauch stopped walking in the dark, and he leaned in closer, causing Andy to recoil at first. Quickly the *Post* reporter realized the detective wanted to whisper something. As weird as this was, Andy leaned in himself.

Rauch said, "Spooks."

"Come again?"

"There's a bunch of spooks in there. They won't let us in till they are finished looking around."

"What do you mean 'spooks'? Like, CIA?"

Rauch shrugged. "They didn't say that. But I was army, and they aren't military intel. I ran into a few CIA when I was working Vice. A couple of guys in trench coats show up, not spit-shined like Bureau types, more scotch breath and chewed fingernails. They flash some general-looking Homeland Security credos and push past the PD like they own the fucking place. Same deal tonight, except one of the guys is a serious-looking woman in a trench coat." Rauch shrugged his narrow shoulders inside his raincoat. "They're *definitely* spooks."

Rauch turned and looked back at the house, and Andy did the same, taking in the dilapidated property from a distance.

"This isn't exactly Embassy Row," Andy said. "What are they doing *here*?"

Rauch lit a cigarette, shielding the flame from the misty breeze. "In true spook fashion, they didn't volunteer much information about their motives."

"What else do you know?"

"Just what the responding officers and the EMTs said. Two DOA. One with his head blown half off from a rifle, the other skewered with some kinda ninja sword."

"Damn. And the injured?"

"They transported four to Medstar Trauma. All Aryan Brotherhood. One dude took three AK rounds, another's got a busted face, a third has a concussion and possible neck trauma, and some skank took two to the legs. I'll go interview them as soon as I am allowed in to see my crime scene." The annoyance was evident in Rauch's voice.

"On the scanner they said it was one guy who did all this."

"That's what the injured woman told the responding officers."

Andy thought for a second. This story was starting to get interesting. "How 'bout I wait at the tape so I can talk to the CIA guys when they come out?"

Rauch looked at Andy for an instant, then he shut down, like he just realized jawing with the reporter was the wrong call. "Look . . . *I* didn't say CIA. *You* did. I said they were Homeland Security. Do me a favor and get out of here till they leave. Come back in the morning."

Rauch tossed his cigarette in the gutter and headed up to knock on the next door.

Andy walked back to his car, then he stood there for a few minutes looking at the scene, awash in flashing red and blue lights. Finally one of the beat cops stepped up and asked him if he wouldn't mind backing off a block or two. Normally Andy would have told the man to kiss his ass, but not this time. He climbed in his Ford, then drove around the corner, parked, and got back out with his camera. He walked between a pair of apartment buildings, squinted out the reflections of flashing lights, and made his way one block north of the crime scene.

On the street in front of him were two black Chevy Suburbans that clearly didn't belong. Drivers sat behind the wheels, and each vehicle had a passenger in the front. Andy stopped in his tracks before the men saw him, then he retraced his steps back to the apartment buildings. Under a stairwell he found a place in the dark where he could keep his eyes on the vehicles, and there he waited.

Ten minutes later several figures in overcoats approached the Suburbans.

One was a white-haired man in his early fifties, flanked by a pair of men Andy took immediately for bodyguards. Next to him was a woman in her thirties wearing eyeglasses, with her brown hair in a professional-looking bun. He snapped several pictures of both of them before they drove off, careful not to use his flash.

Back in his Fiesta he looked at the images on the digital display of his camera. He hadn't expected to recognize either of them, even on closer inspection, and he did not.

But he knew someone who might. Sitting there in the shittiest part of the city, Andy looked up a number on his contact list and made a call.

A few miles west in Georgetown, a fifty-four-year-old woman slowly reached for the vibrating mobile phone on her nightstand. While doing so, she blinked the sleep from her eyes and checked the time on the phone's screen.

It was a quarter after one.

She made no effort to perk up her sleepy voice. "This is Catherine King."

"Ms. King? Andy Shoal here. I apologize for calling so late."

"Who?"

"Andy Shoal. Metro desk."

The woman sat up slowly, rubbing her eyes. "Metro? Sure," she said, but she'd never heard of this guy. "What can I do for you, Andy?"

"Again, sorry about the hour, but I'm doing a story on a double homicide in Washington Highlands and I could use your professional opinion."

Catherine lay back down on her right side. "The butler did it. Can I go back to sleep?"

Andy chuckled. "I can pretty much guarantee this dump didn't have a butler. No, actually I'm calling because I was told the CIA was here, looking over the crime scene. I haven't run into that before, so I thought I'd reach out to you."

Catherine King sat back up. "Hold on. Are you saying Agency personnel are investigating a homicide in the District?"

"That's the word I got. The dick who made the scene first—"

"I beg your pardon?"

"Sorry, the *detective* said he was told the men inside were Homeland Security. He didn't outright say CIA, but that was his inference."

"What's the connection to Langley?"

"I don't have a clue, and it doesn't seem like the cops do, either. The crime scene is a suspected Aryan Brotherhood property, but I don't know if that's relevant or not. I do know you are the paper's veteran National Security correspondent, so I thought maybe you could help, since nobody knows more about the intelligence community in this town than you do."

King picked up on the platitude, and it told her something about this Andy Shoal. Cops reporters were usually either grizzled old vets or else they were young and ambitious. Shoal, it was clear, was the latter, and he was sucking up to her a little. She absolutely hated to be called a veteran reporter; she found this almost as bad as when she was referred to as an institution, which also happened on occasion. But she was too intrigued by Andy's information to be either flattered or annoyed. "I can't think of a soul on that side of the Anacostia who would be of interest to CIA. I suppose if they are counterintel officers and they caught one of their people visiting a drug house then that would rouse Langley in the middle of the night, but that's just a guess."

"It was one male, with bodyguards, and one female. I got pretty good pictures of both of them."

"You did, did you? You need to be careful doing that with Agency personnel. They are camera shy as a species. Did they see you take their picture?"

"Absolutely not."

"You want to send them to my phone?"

"On the way."

Catherine reached for her eyeglasses, then turned on the light on her nightstand. While she waited she looked around her bedroom. She lived alone, and had no children, so the only disorder in the home was her own. An empty cereal bowl and a spoon on the nightstand, a pile of yoga tights and sweats on a settee in a far corner, a raincoat lying over a chair by the door to her closet.

She'd returned from a trip to Cairo three days earlier, where she'd been meeting with a source in Egyptian intelligence, and she'd yet to unpack fully, so a large rolling North Face duffel sat on a table in the far corner of the room, open with dirty clothes spilling out onto the floor.

Two images appeared on her mobile, and Catherine looked at them one at a time. She zoomed in on the first, a woman with light brown hair in a tight bun. She did not recognize her. She swiped down to the next image; this one was of a white-haired man in his early fifties. He seemed to have a two-man security detail shadowing him.

Interesting. If he was CIA this would be beyond odd. Other than the director and some division heads, CIA execs didn't ordinarily move with bodyguards in the USA.

She blinked away more sleep, and quickly rubbed her eyes. She looked at the photo of the white-haired man again. After several seconds she said, "That makes no sense at all."

Though she was talking to herself, Shoal asked, "Do you recognize them?"

"The gentleman with the white hair is Jordan Mayes. I haven't seen him since Iraq. Six years ago. Back then he was a senior officer, but now he's assistant director of the CIA's National Clandestine Service."

"Does that mean he's a big deal?"

"Big enough to where I can't think of a single reason he would be wandering through a crime scene in the middle of the night in the worst part of the city. Why would *anyone* do that?" With a little hesitation she said, "Hope that doesn't offend you, Andy."

"Not in the least. We can't all get the good gigs like the national security beat."

The comment barely registered with Catherine. She was still looking at the picture of Jordan Mayes. She said, "Mayes's purview is one hundred percent outside of the U.S. Denny Carmichael holds Mayes's leash."

"Who?"

"Carmichael runs the show at CIA."

"Director?"

"Directors don't run the show, Andy. Directors are political hires. Sent in to watch over, but to keep their hands clean. No, Denny Carmichael is head of the National Clandestine Service. He's the top spook in spook land. He does all the dirty things around the world."

"He's bad?"

"Depends on your perspective. He's done a lot of good I'm sure, but I've watched while Denny has grown his fiefdom to the point where he makes his own rules over at Langley. I'm not crazy about that."

"Are you going to ask Carmichael what his assistant was doing in Washington Highlands?"

Catherine thought this over. "No. That's not the right play here. I'd rather probe into Mayes a little. Figure out who this woman is with him at the crime scene. If I go to Carmichael as clueless as I am now, he'll know he can sell me anything. Once I have some facts, just enough to scare him into thinking I know more than I really do, I'll confront him."

Andy didn't respond to this. Finally Catherine said, "Did I lose you?"

There was obvious amazement in his voice. "That's genius."

"I talk to men and women who lie for a living. You develop techniques to mitigate some of the BS along the way. Will you keep me posted on anything you learn about the Highlands incident?"

"Of course I will. What would you say to the two of us sharing a byline?"

Catherine smiled at the phone. "Let's not get ahead of ourselves, Andy. I don't know there is a story there just yet. I get five 'can't miss' earth-shattering leads a week that turn into nothing. For now, let's just pull this thread from both ends and see what turns up. That sound good to you?"

"Sounds great. I'll let you know what I find."

Catherine King hung up the phone, pulled off her glasses, and lay back down on the bed. But after thirty seconds she rolled back up, climbed to her feet, and headed downstairs to her home office.

Whatever was going on that involved spooks from the CIA, the Aryan Brotherhood, and a double homicide was much more important to her than a few hours' sleep. She'd sit at her computer and dig around on Mayes, Carmichael, and the mystery woman, and see what she could find.

9

Arthur Mayberry was nearly seventy, and he looked it. Weatherworn black skin, a silver mane of hair, and Coke-bottle glasses. He had been 11-bravo, army infantry, back in Vietnam, and then he came home and drove a bus for Washington Metro Transit for forty-one years while his wife worked her way up to food services manager at a hospital in Falls Church. Arthur sired four kids along the way, which made him a man rich in many blessings, but not in much else. Now he and his wife were grandparents and empty nesters, retired and living frugally in a large but rickety two-story home in Columbia Heights.

Prices in the District had skyrocketed in the past few years as the federal government became one of the few growth industries in America, and for this reason Mayberry's property taxes had shot through the roof. Even though his street was one of the edgiest in Columbia Heights, which was one of the lower-end neighborhoods in the heart of the District, Arthur and his sixty-eight-year-old wife Bernice could barely afford their mortgage, so they'd taken to renting out a tiny and not exactly up-to-code basement bedroom for two hundred fifty a month. They'd recently lost their last tenant when he was arrested on a possession charge, so when the knock came at their front door first thing after church on Sunday morning, Arthur found himself hoping it was someone who'd seen the For Rent sign stuck in the tiny front yard.

This street was seventy percent African American, and twenty-two percent Hispanic. There were as many Asians as there were whites, and the vast majority of the whites who lived around here were elderly, so Arthur's hopes that he'd get a new tenant today were effectively dashed when he looked through the peephole and saw a clean-shaven white man in a blazer standing alone on his stoop.

Bernice came up beside him in the entryway. She was still wearing her hat from church. "Who is it?"

"Some man."

"He's here about the room," she said confidently.

"I doubt it."

"Why do you say—"

Arthur opened the wooden door, but left the storm door and its iron grating alone.

"Oh," his wife said, seeing the youngish Caucasian face on the other side of the storm door.

"Yeah?"

The white man spoke through the bolted door. "Good morning."

"Yeah?" Arthur repeated, the suspicion obvious in his voice.

"I saw your For Rent sign. Can I take a look at the room?"

What the hell? Arthur had no intention of renting to a white man. It wasn't that he was racist, but he was a realist, and no young white man in this area with a job would want to live in a tiny basement on this street.

"Sir?" the man said after waiting ten seconds for a response.

"You from around here?"

"No, sir. Just in from Michigan. My uncle had a place in Petworth, but he passed away. I'm in town for a couple of months getting the house ready to sell."

Arthur softened just a little. "Sure sorry to hear about that."

"Thanks. What are you asking for the room?"

A pause. "Three hundred."

"Really? I saw the notice you put on the board at the Giant up the street. It says two fifty."

Arthur stiffened right back up now. "Then why'd you ask?"

A little smile from the white man. "I guess just to see if you'd rip me off."

Everyone stood awkwardly for a moment in the doorway till Mayberry said, "Well, now you know. Price went up. Take it or leave it."

"Can I *see* it?"

Arthur could feel an icy stare from his wife, standing just next to him. Bernice was generally more suspicious of people than was Arthur, and considering Arthur didn't really believe this man's story, he assumed his wife was ready to kick the door shut in the man's face.

But Arthur was thinking about the three hundred bucks now, as well as the fact this guy could go and get a lawyer and make trouble if some black landlord refused to rent to him.

Mayberry snatched his keys off the wall and headed out onto the porch. Bernice followed close behind silently, but Arthur felt her misgivings. He knew if he rented the room to the man she'd tell him he was a fool, because the man was probably out of work and on drugs.

With a fatalistic sigh he led his wife and the white man down to the driveway.

Court almost didn't give a damn what the inside of the room looked like, because the outside was as close to perfect as he could hope to find from an operational security perspective. The entrance to the basement room was off the driveway, just six steps down to a tiny patio with a storm door that looked substantial, and on the other side of that was a wooden door that looked sturdy enough. There was just a small slit window at eye level, but it afforded a full view of the driveway and, since this was a corner lot, he could use the window to see a good distance to the south, east, and north.

Court and the Mayberrys stepped into the basement room, and with three people there was little space to move around. It occurred to Court that there would be a bit more room to move if the heavyset lady took off her huge hat, but he made no mention of it. Instead he checked the space over quickly. It was just ten feet by ten feet with a tiny bathroom off the back, a kitchen counter that ran across the rear wall, and a knee-high refrigerator taking up floor space.

It was obvious this setup had been built by hand. The cheap linoleum flooring buckled from water damage and the paneling on the walls looked like a weekend project by the homeowner, and a water pipe ran across the middle of the room so that anyone over five-six would have to dip his head to move from the bed to the bathroom. But even with these limitations, it was as nice a place as any other Court had lived in the past few years, and better than most.

The bed was just a twin, but it was all that would fit. There were a table and a chair by the one little window and even a small TV that looked like it was plugged into a cable box.

Cable?

Court wondered if he'd died and gone to heaven.

On the southern wall right behind where the front door opened was an accordion door covering a small closet. The storage space was just two feet deep but six feet wide. Court peered in and noticed the back panel of the closet was rippling, as if from moisture or excessive heat on the boards.

"What's all that?" he asked.

"Oh, that ain't nothin'," the landlord said. "I built this room in a corner of my basement. The water heater and the furnace are on the other side of that wall. Maybe I shoulda put a little more insulation in the wall or something, but it don't bother nobody who stays here."

Mayberry leaned into the closet and knocked on the wood. "See? It's solid."

It sounded hollow as a drum to Court, but he considered that a feature, not a glitch. The basement would have access to the main house, which meant Court would just have to make a small "adjustment" in that wall and he'd have an escape route in case someone he didn't like came to the front door.

Court looked around the room again. "I like it," he said.

"Didn't get your name."

Court was always quick with a name and a story, though like his trip from Michigan and his dead uncle in Petworth, it was *never* the truth. "Jeff. Jeff Duncan."

"Got to ask, Jeff. How come you ain't stayin' up at your uncle's place?"

"I won't be able to afford the property taxes on the house, so I'll have to sell it. Before I put it on the market, I'll be doing some renovations. Have to shut off the water and heat while I work on the plumbing and HVAC."

Court saw the older black man soften to him even more. It was basic social engineering. Court would say things to create an instant bond between himself and his potential landlord.

When the man replied with, "I know that's right. Taxes are through the damn roof. It's gotten real bad around here," Court knew he was in with the man, but Court noticed the wife was still gaping at him like he was a fucking unicorn.

"It's three hundred a month for the room?" Court asked.

"That's firm," the man replied.

Court pretended to think it over. Then he said, "I can give you first and last month's rent. Will that do?"

The old man was on the spot. He clearly didn't expect an offer. He stammered for a moment, then said, "No room in the driveway for your car. Hard to find parking around here."

"No problem. I'll keep my car parked at my uncle's."

The man bit his lip. He glanced to his wife, then said, "Not much of a kitchen. Toilet runs a little bit. TV is just basic cable."

"That's all I need."

"Okay, then," Arthur said. Then, "Of course I'm gonna need to see your driver's license. Run a background check."

Court smiled a little. "What do you say we make it four hundred a month?"

Despite the fact that he was being offered one hundred fifty dollars more per month than he'd originally been asking, Mayberry frowned. "Son, I can't allow no criminals in here."

"Not a criminal, Mr. Mayberry. Just a guy who's hoping to avoid some red tape."

"Well, that's a problem, because I'm by the book. I guess this place isn't for you."

Court turned his head back and forth, scanning the small room. "You're right. By the book is best."

"That's what I say."

"Cool. Can I take a quick look at the back door?"

"The what?"

"The back door?"

"Uh . . . just the one door."

"Huh," Court said. "I could have sworn building codes say private apartments have to have two exits in case of fire. I could be wrong, though. How 'bout while you are running that background check on me, I check with the city to make sure you've complied with all the building and zoning laws. That way we *both* know what we're getting into here."

The African American man glared at the white man for a long moment.

Court smiled. "Like you said. By the book."

Bernice reached out and took her husband by the arm, giving it an anxious squeeze. Slowly the corners of Arthur Mayberry's mouth rose, and he smiled a wide, toothy grin. "All right, then. You gonna have it your way, and I'm gonna have me five hundred dollars a month, plus two fifty security deposit."

Court calculated he'd have to burn this tiny room to cinders to do two hundred and fifty dollars' worth of damage. But with a little smile he reached for his wallet. "A hard bargain, sir, but I like your style."

Bernice spoke up for the first time, and apparently none of the new mutual respect between the two men had rubbed off on her. "I'll tell you right now, young man, we're not gonna stand for no parties."

Court had never thrown a party in his life, but still he wondered how much of a party one might actually throw in a ten-by-ten basement with a metal water pipe running across at forehead height. "I'll be gone a lot. I guarantee I'll be the quietest tenant you've ever had."

"And no drugs," the woman added.

"Absolutely not."

Jeff Duncan" handed Arthur Mayberry $1,250 and took a key, and when Arthur asked the younger man when he would actually move in, Jeff replied he'd been up all night so he'd go right to bed, and then bring some things over from his hotel that evening.

Arthur and Bernice left him in his new apartment and headed back to the front of the house. As soon as the storm door shut Bernice said one word. "Drugs."

"You're probably right," replied Arthur. Plaintively he added, "But what was I gonna do? First and last month's rent ain't nothing to turn your nose up to. And all that bonus money."

Bernice made a clicking sound with her tongue and said it again. "Drugs."

Arthur sighed. He knew he'd be hearing this a lot over the next two months.

Court wedged one of the metal chairs under the door and then he took a shower, his first in days. He took the .380 pistol into the stall with him, leaving it in the soap niche. There was no soap or shampoo, so all he really did was rinse off, and there were no towels so he did little more than drip-dry, although he patted himself down with the thin comforter from the bed. He put his clothes back on, even his shoes, and then he pulled a pillow and a wool blanket off the bed and threw them in the long narrow closet behind the door to the outside. He rolled the damp comforter around the remaining two pillows and he put them under the bed sheet in the center of the bed, making an approximate man-sized shape under the sheets.

He turned off the lights in the room, walked over to the blanket and the pillow in the closet, and lay down, drawing his pistol from his pocket and putting it on the linoleum floor to the right of his body.

He thought about the locks on the doors and the wedged chair. This wasn't exactly a high-security facility, but he was dead tired and he could barely think. Anyone who kicked open the door would see the bed, and Court hoped they would assume someone was sleeping there. They would open fire on this target first, giving Court a little warning. They wouldn't see Court here in the closet until they stepped a few feet into the room and looked to their left, at which point Court would shoot them dead.

That was the plan, anyway. Court wondered if he'd even wake up at the sound of a shattering storm door. And of course, most attackers came in pairs, or in long lines of jocked-up operators, and his little .380 peashooter wouldn't do much more than kill the point man and maybe one of his buddies.

No, this wasn't much defense at all, but Court realized he needed to try to get his energy back before doing anything else to fortify the room, so he lay there with his eyes closed and tried to will himself to sleep.

He'd been on the go for over a month. Moving from place to place in Russia, in Sweden, in Germany and Belgium. Then to Spain and into Portugal, where he met up with the cargo ship that brought him to the U.S.

Eight days on the water, the daylight hours in his hiding place in the bowels of the ship like a bilge rat, the late nights walking or running the holds for exercise.

He'd had help in his escape. A Mossad officer who felt like he owed Court a debt, though in truth Court knew the man owed the debt to someone else. Still, the guy worked as Court's genie in a bottle, granting him his wish and getting him into the United States.

Court had decided he'd have no more dealings with the Mossad officer. Court knew personal relationships were points of vulnerability, so his plan all along had been to use the man as a conduit into the U.S. and then to break contact, to go his own way.

He'd done exactly that by leaving everything behind on the cargo ship save for the clothes on his back. He hadn't planned it exactly that way, but he heard the helicopters approaching, and he knew they were coming for him.

On shore he hotwired a car and drove it to the Greenbelt metro station on the outskirts of D.C. He used some coins he found in the car's ashtray to buy a Metro card that got him as far as the Congress Heights Station.

He needed cash and a weapon, and he knew this area would afford him the most target-rich environment in which to obtain both.

He got what he'd been after and now he had a suitable base of operations, at least for the time being. He knew it was possible he'd have to relocate multiple times during the next few days, but he'd do what he could to keep his new safe house free of compromise.

Court's mission here in Washington, as he saw it anyway, was very simple. His former employer, the Central Intelligence Agency, had spent the last five years trying to kill him, and he did not know why. He'd been running all that time, living abroad, off grid, staying away from relationships and ties. Looking over his shoulder all day, every day.

They'd almost caught him a few times, and during his flight from the Agency, other entities out there had come even closer to killing him.

He had grown tired of running, so he decided it was time to end this, once and for all.

In his years of small unit tactics training he had learned a great many truths, but one stood out from the rest. When the opposition attacked, it expected you to play your role; to run, to cover. But turning the tables, attacking *into* a threat, was often the most useful way of defending oneself.

Court's principal trainer at CIA, a man he knew only as Maurice, used to say a mantra over and over, so often Court now heard it in Maurice's gravelly voice. "You can run, but if you can't run anymore, then you can hide. You can hide, but if you can't hide anymore, then you can fight. There is *nothing* after the fight, so you fight until there is nothing."

Court couldn't run anymore, and he couldn't hide anymore, so he came back to fight. To attack into the threat, to get answers and to get closure.

He knew he would not be leaving D.C. without a resolution to this nightmare. Either he would uncover the CIA's motives behind the shoot-on-sight sanction against him and somehow end the sanction, or else he would die trying.

He had come up with a working theory as to what this was all about.

At the beginning of Court's career with the CIA he had been part of a small initiative called the Autonomous Asset Program. He and several other young men like him had been given individual instruction by a cadre of the CIA's best operations officers, and then they had been sent into the world, allowed to run solo ops, tasked with difficult, deniable missions, and left, in large part, to their own devices.

The program was disbanded, Court was folded into another unit, and other than the fact that he had been given better solo training than the other CIA Special Activities Division men, the Autonomous Asset Program was behind him.

But Court had just found out the previous month that he was the last man alive from this entire program. Seventeen other young men had all been killed in the intervening years and, by necessity, Court himself had killed the only other remaining singleton asset out there.

Court saw it clearly now. For some reason the CIA was erasing anyone who had been in AAP. All the others were gone.

And now it was down to Court Gentry. The last man standing.

What he did not know was why.

He could reveal what he knew about the program and the termination order for the assets, but first he needed proof. Without proof—if he just called up the *New York Times* and told them what he suspected—he'd be considered a crackpot and there would be no story.

The CIA would deny his allegations, and the CIA would win, because the CIA had significantly better media outreach than Court Gentry had.

He needed proof. If he found proof, he would find justice, and that was what he was after.

Not revenge, he told himself. Justice.

There were men here, in the area, who Court felt sure would have the answers he sought. He had no illusions that they would give up their answers willingly, but Court was prepared. He'd seek these men out, find out what they knew, and rectify the mess his life had become. He told himself it was doable, that he wasn't naive, but part of him wondered if he'd just grown too tired of running, if he was racing headlong into his own death just to end it all.

He pushed the negativity out of his mind as best he could, and he drifted off just before ten a.m., and, for the first time in months, he slept the sleep of the dead.

10

Denny Carmichael lay on the leather couch in his dark office, but his eyes remained open, fixed on the ceiling. He'd stayed up working until past seven a.m., then he slept for a couple of hours, but only fitfully. Now he lay awake, brooding and plotting. Worrying and calculating.

The door opened slowly, letting a little light into the room. This startled the director of National Clandestine Service. No one walked into his office unannounced. He had a vision of the Gray Man, his face darkened with coal, a hooked knife with a flat black finish in his hand, his eyes cold and dark and dead like those of a snake.

Carmichael rolled quickly up to a sitting position and reached out in the dark, finding and then pulling the chain on the banker's lamp on the desk.

Jordan Mayes stood over him with two cups of coffee. "Sorry. I thought you'd be sleeping."

Carmichael rubbed his eyes and took a cup, and he motioned for Mayes to take a seat on the other side of the coffee table.

"What time is it?"

"About ten a.m.," Mayes said. "I'd have given you another hour, but I just got word from the homicide detective in charge in Washington Highlands."

"Talk."

Mayes rubbed his own eyes, the all-nighter evident on his face. "Brandywine Street was Violator, no question."

"We know this how?"

"Fingerprints left at the scene."

Carmichael shook his head. "Bullshit. PD doesn't have Gentry's prints on file. None of the Ground Branch boys are in any domestic database. Only we have his prints."

"I know that. The prints haven't been analyzed yet."

"Then how did the D.C. police—"

"Because Gentry *wanted* us to know it was him. He pressed his thumbprint onto a nightstand in the room where he left the bodies. Multiple times. Leaving clear prints in the shape of a six."

Carmichael sat up straighter. "Sierra Six. Gentry's call sign with the Goon Squad."

"It was a message. 'I'm back and I'm pissed. I want the Agency to know I'm here.'"

Carmichael sat back on the sofa and blew out a full chest of air. A chill ran down the back of his neck and into his shoulders. "Fucking brazen. He's not going to skulk around then. I guess that means he won't be running, either. What did he take from the Aryan Brotherhood?"

"According to survivors, he got a bag full of cash. No agreement on how much. The narcotics detective I spoke with guessed about ten grand, but that was just based on the size of the operation being run out of the house. PD recovered a lot of meth, apparently."

"That's it? Violator just took money?"

"None of the survivors copped to any more weapons than the half dozen or so found on the property, but that doesn't mean anything. He could have walked out of there with a bazooka and they wouldn't tell the cops, because that would mean they'd been keeping a bazooka in the house. The detective did find an empty ankle holster on one of the victims. It was sized for a subcompact pistol."

Carmichael ran his fingers through his short hair. "Okay. Gentry's in the wind with a mouse gun and enough money to finance a small op."

Mayes asked, "What's he after?"

Carmichael just looked into his coffee. "Revenge, I guess. I assume his next step is to make contact with known associates here in the area."

"Well, we're covered on that front. We've identified four possible contacts, people he used to work with in one capacity or another. We've put assets on them."

"Just four?"

"Most everyone he worked with is dead. We've got everyone covered, all except you and me, because we're here. Oh, and Zack Hightower, because he hasn't been located yet."

"What about Matt Hanley?"

"Right now I have four contract security officers watching Hanley's house. When JSOC gets here I'll put hard assets on him."

"Good. Gentry *will* go to Hanley."

Mayes hesitated a moment and said, "We need to get SAD involved in this. We can put twenty-five Ground Branch shooters in the mix with one call."

Carmichael shook his head. "We can't involve Ground Branch without involving Hanley. I don't want anyone breathing a word to Hanley about this. We have enough armed assets without going to SAD."

"You really think Hanley is a threat to the operation?"

"No, but he's next in line to run NCS."

"So?" asked Mayes. "When you take the directorship, he'll move up here. But you'll be the damn director, so why do you care?"

"I don't like the guy, and he doesn't like me. No Hanley. You have guys watching him. That's it. Gentry will go to him, and that's where we'll get him."

"So . . . we're using Hanley as bait."

"It's the best way that prick can serve the Agency." Something occurred to Carmichael. "We need to watch Gentry's family, too."

"His only close living relative is his dad. He's sixty-four, lives in a little town in Florida. But they've been estranged since Gentry was a teenager."

"I don't care. I want him covered."

"Agency watchers are already in place. Hard assets would, of course, need to fly down there if Violator shows, but we can move them out of Fort Bragg, and that's no more than ninety minutes' flying time."

Carmichael's secretary spoke over the intercom, telling him Suzanne Brewer was on the line. He asked her to put the call through, and seconds later the voice of the thirty-nine-year-old targeting officer emanated from the speaker.

Carmichael was customarily succinct. "Any word on the location of Zack Hightower?"

"Yes, sir. We'll have him in hand in a couple of hours. Do you want us to put him in a safe house?"

"No. I want him brought up here. Put the intimidation of the seventh floor in him. Let's see if he will play ball."

"Yes, sir."

After Carmichael hung up, Mayes said, "You want to stay here till he is brought in?"

"No."

"Okay. I can schedule the movement to a safe house right now. You can get a little sleep before Hightower is brought in."

Carmichael looked uneasy a moment, an expression Mayes wasn't used to seeing. "What is it?"

Carmichael said, "I have to leave the building for a few hours. A meeting with an asset off-site. I need to go alone."

Mayes stared at his boss for several seconds. Then he got up and closed the door. Standing back at the desk he said, "You're joking, right?"

"I understand your concern, but it has to be like this. No one is to know but you and DeRenzi. I'm only telling you because you'll have to cover for me, and DeRenzi because he won't be able to shadow."

Mayes remained incredulous. "Gentry's out there somewhere. You *do* know that, don't you?"

"You don't think I can do low pro anymore?"

"You aren't safe on the streets. Whoever you need to meet, we can set it up here with secure comms."

"Has to be in person."

Mayes said, "Then send me."

Carmichael just shook his head.

"Look, Denny, if you've got a mistress or some shit like that, you need to put a cork in it until this all blows over."

Carmichael sighed. "If I had a mistress and you didn't know about it, you'd be a sorry excuse for an assistant director. I'll be out of pocket three hours, four tops. I won't have a phone, so you'll have to come up with something convincing."

Mayes held the look of disbelief on his face. "Tell me you understand what's in the balance here."

Carmichael rolled his eyes. "Is this where you tell me Gentry is a dangerous man?"

"This is about more than Gentry, and you know it. You want the directorship. You've *earned* it. The one thing that can fuck that up is the Gentry story getting out. You won't just lose the directorship. You'll lose everything."

"It's not going to get out, because we are going to handle this."

Mayes pressed one more time. "You keeping me out of the loop is not a good idea."

"Some burdens are my own, Mayes. And that's just how it's going to stay."

The U.S. Army UC-35A jet touched down at Joint Base Andrews and taxied into a hangar on the far end of runway 36 Right. Once the hangar doors were closed and the aircraft's wheels were chocked, the hatch opened and a set of rolling stairs was positioned by the ground crew. Twelve men, all in their thirties and forties, stepped down the stairs of the U.S. Army's version of the Cessna Citation V. Each man carried a massive black duffel bag over his shoulder and, as soon as they vacated the stairs, they dropped their heavy bags onto the hangar floor.

Although this was a military base and the UC-35A a military aircraft, the dozen men wore various styles of civilian clothing. Few soldiers would get away with such a transgression while on base and on duty, but this small force was no regular army unit. They were a cell of operators from Joint Special Operations Command; specifically an elite offshoot of JSOC with a mandate to assist the United States on Homeland Security issues.

There were two main direct action ground asset components of JSOC—the navy men of DEVGRU, otherwise known as SEAL Team 6, and the army men of the unit that for decades was commonly known as Delta Force. The unit members even used that name in open sources from time to time, but their classified designation had been changed.

It was thought by the brass at JSOC that their operations and abilities had been compromised in the past few years due to an unprecedented spate of books, movies, articles, and interviews about and by Joint Special Operations personnel, so when they were given their new name, the name itself was codeword-classified.

The army boys of JSOC were happy to leave center stage to the Hollywood-loving navy SEALs.

JSOC had been on the Gentry hunt for years, but not this crew, because Gentry had been outside of the United States. These twelve operators worked inside the USA by special arrangement with the Department of Homeland Security.

The twelve men in the hangar at Joint Base Andrews were tip of the spear of the military on domestic operations, so it only stood to reason they would get the call-up for this mission. Their brass had been contacted late the evening before by the CIA and told of the in extremis mission to eliminate a rogue CIA man gone mad in D.C., and a short time later these men rushed to their headquarters inside the wire at Fort Bragg, geared up, and boarded the waiting army transport jet.

Ninety minutes after that they were on the ground at Andrews, and now they unpacked and assembled equipment, loaded it into three nondescript Chevy Suburban SUVs, and headed to a safe house in the Capitol Hill section of D.C.

The dozen men in street clothes didn't know much about the reasons behind the hunt, other than the facts that Violator was ex-Agency, he'd gone off reservation, and he had killed a bunch of his colleagues. The guys figured that was more than awkward and ugly enough to put you on a presidential kill list, so they didn't see the need to know more than that.

The leader of this unit was a forty-three-year-old lieutenant colonel with the code name Dakota. Soon after he and his men arrived at their safe house, Jordan Mayes, Suzanne Brewer, and the security detail traveling with Mayes arrived at the front door. Mayes, Brewer, and Dakota met for a briefing in the living room while the rest of the JSOC team prepped and tested their hi-tech communications equipment in the dining room.

Dakota took notes on a pad and asked relevant questions of the CIA officials, and together they went down a list of surveillance assets at their disposal. They then discussed Violator's known associates and the other CIA brass who would need to have their homes watched in case their target tried to make contact with them.

When Brewer indicated the briefing was complete, Dakota looked across the table to the two Agency execs. He said, "We've done lethal ops in the U.S. before. Rare, but it's happened. Know this. If we go in, collateral damage will be limited or nonexistent. Any other means you might use—local PD, federal SWAT, even CIA shooters, whatever assets you have available to you—they aren't going to be as precise as my men and myself. We have experience in doing this sort of thing quickly, cleanly, and quietly."

Mayes said, "Believe me, you are our first choice. Gentry has already committed two murders in the city. We are concerned that local police might run up on him before we do, but we will move you and your men to any sightings or possible sightings as soon as possible."

Dakota stood, shook hands politely with the two CIA execs, and then said, "Very good. You get us to him, and we'll put him down. For now we'll kit up and hit the streets. Let's stay in touch."

11

Denny Carmichael climbed aboard a Bell JetRanger that was already spinning up in the parking lot at the CIA's McLean campus.

DeRenzi was with him, for this leg of the movement, anyway. He threw an understandable fit when Carmichael told him he would run a surveillance detection route and then continue on to a meeting alone, but it wasn't DeRenzi's job to tell Director Carmichael what he could and couldn't do, so the close protection officer just made sure the director of National Clandestine Service was wearing his .45 caliber HK semiautomatic pistol in his shoulder holster like he normally did. CIA officers virtually never carried firearms, but Denny had always been a different sort of animal from every other CIA officer around, and he often strapped a sidearm during movements, even in the States.

The JetRanger landed at Washington Executive Airport in Prince Georges County just fifteen minutes after it took off, and there Denny left DeRenzi in the helo and climbed into a beige Toyota Highlander that another CIA employee had positioned in the parking lot with the keys under the mat. He drove out of the airport grounds and into late-morning traffic, heading north on the 210 back towards D.C. He kept his eyes in his rearview and he turned east on I-95, and only after he was sure there was no one on his tail did he get off the freeway and head back west. He took the Woodrow Wilson Bridge over the Potomac into Alexandria, Virginia, and there he spent twenty minutes driving through the narrow streets of the Old Town section on a surveillance detection route.

After fifty minutes in the vehicle he parked on King Street and continued his SDR on foot. He meandered through the neighborhood for thirty minutes, wandering into gift shops and antique stores, heading down side streets and then back up again on the other side. At twelve fifteen he stepped into a sandwich shop and ordered a pastrami on rye. Eating his lunch at a counter by the window, he kept his eyes out on the street, all the while searching for anyone who might be following him.

His trained eyes saw nothing out of the ordinary, so at twelve thirty he threw the remainder of his sandwich away, headed north on King Street, and then ducked into the courtyard in front of the Kimpton Lorien Hotel.

Once in the lobby he walked straight to the counter and asked for a suite for one night with an early check-in. He used a credit card from a cover identity he kept ready and the woman behind the counter gave him the card key to his fourth-floor suite. He stepped around to the bank of elevators behind the check-in desk, and while he did so a distinguished-looking man stepped out of the men's room and walked over to the elevator bank to wait alongside him.

The two men stood in silence as the car delivered them to the fourth floor. There Denny walked down the hall to his suite, and the other man followed. No words were exchanged.

They entered the suite together and Denny shut the door.

The man who shadowed him in was in his early fifties, lean and handsome in his gray pinstripe suit. Olive-skinned and delicately featured, he had a kind, gentle bearing about him, in sharp contrast to the stern manner of Denny Carmichael.

Only when the door was shut behind the two men did the olive-complected man offer a handshake to the American.

He spoke perfect English with only a slight accent. "Nice to see you, Denny."

"Hello, Kaz."

Carmichael turned away, took a cell phone–sized device out of his pocket, and turned it on. He headed to the center of the room and placed it on a coffee table. It was a radio frequency signal jammer, designed to block the transmissions given off by eavesdropping devices.

While he did this Kaz took off his suit coat and hung it over a chair, and then he moved to the sofa. There he sat calmly and watched Denny adjust the instrument.

Kaz was not his name, but Denny had called him this for fifteen years, because Kaz was easier to say than Murquin al-Kazaz. He was now chief of station here in the United States for Riasat Al-Istikhbarat Al-Amah, the intelligence agency of Saudi Arabia, but the two had known each other since back when Kaz was a lowly operative in Saudi intel.

The Saudi smiled while watching Denny. "Clandestine meetings in hotel rooms. This feels like the good old days, my friend."

Carmichael replied brusquely, "Don't romanticize the past. It wasn't any better than the present." While talking Denny pulled out his mobile phone and slipped an earpiece in his ear.

"We were younger, at least. I romanticize my youth, regardless of how I might have misspent it."

Denny tried to send music from his phone to his earpiece, but he couldn't get a signal to go through. Satisfied that his jammer was operational, he pulled the earpiece out of his ear and slipped it, with his phone, back into his coat.

Kaz said, "You must have gone to some trouble to come and see me like this on a Sunday afternoon. Tell me, what is it that could not have been handled through a secure phone call?"

Denny ignored him for the moment, took his time to turn on the TV in the adjoining bedroom, then returned to the living area and turned on the flat screen there. The televisions were set to different stations. An action movie in the bedroom and a news interview program in the living area blanketed the entire suite with conflicting sounds.

Denny sat down on the sofa, close to Kaz, and he spoke softly. "A wayward asset has returned to the United States. To Washington, in fact."

"One of yours, or one of mine?"

"Used to be one of mine."

"Code name Violator, perhaps?"

Carmichael looked carefully at Kaz's face, struggling to see any hint the Saudi knew this information already. "That is correct."

Kaz looked neither surprised nor unsurprised. His face was a cipher, betraying nothing but pleasant calm. He said, "A bold move on his part. I am sure this is troublesome for you, but I hope you see this as an opportunity. He has been out in the four winds of this earth for some time, and now he is here, on your turf."

"D.C. is not my turf."

Kaz raised his eyebrows. "By saying that, you mean to say . . . it's *my* turf."

"That's right. It's yours."

Al-Kazaz smiled a little. "A fact you remind me of from time to time. I don't know why you invited me here, but if it's a confession you want, I assure you I had no knowledge of Gentry's movements. Perhaps you should talk to your dear friends the Israelis. Doesn't the great Mossad know all things at all times?"

Kaz was an enemy of the Israelis—and whenever he spoke with Carmichael he never passed up an opportunity to get in digs about the United States' good relationship with them.

In the intelligence sphere, Israel, the United States, and Saudi Arabia formed an incredibly awkward love triangle.

Carmichael said, "I'm not after a confession. I know you were not aware that Violator was here. What I need from you is action."

"Sounds exciting," Kaz said with a smile that appeared more than a little sarcastic.

Carmichael didn't hide the fact he was losing patience with the flip attitude of the other man. "I don't have time to play. We both know exactly what's at stake here."

"As far as I can tell the only thing at stake with the arrival of Violator"—Kaz paused; his mouth morphed into a smile—"is *you*, Denny. Surely you realize that he is here for you."

"Whatever his intentions, I plan on terminating him. In the city. I will have other tools at my disposal for this, but I need you and your people involved, as well."

Kaz shook his head. "Out of the question. The leadership of my nation has me quite busy at the moment. Nothing that would interest you, I can assure you of that, but I'm not in a position to retask my assets to your needs at this time."

Denny loomed a little closer. "You and I have had a good working relationship. You give me some space for my people in the Middle East. I give you space for your people here in D.C. I want that relationship to continue."

"As you said, it *is* a good relationship. Why on earth would it not continue?"

"If the Gentry situation isn't handled quickly and quietly, I'll be the one taking the fall, and I will fall hard. You think the next man in my position is going to allow the same arrangement with Saudi Arabia that I've allowed?" Denny leaned closer. "No . . . *fucking* . . . way. You'll be expelled; your cell here doesn't have dip immunity, so they will be rounded up and tossed into prison, if not tossed into an unmarked grave."

Kaz said, "Threats of death and destruction? Really, Denny? Those who complain about you . . . and excuse me for saying so, but there are many . . . all say the same thing. That you don't possess the nuance for intelligence work. I defend you, you know. But opening the conversation with an overt threat to our long-standing agreement is exactly the boorishness that others accuse you of."

Denny said nothing, waiting the other man out.

Kaz calmed. "Look, dear friend. You are correct. Our mutual relationship is good for everyone. When our countries are friends, things are good. When you and I are friends, things are great."

"Then help me."

"What is it you want?"

"I want you looking for him. You and your team."

Kaz blew out a sigh. "Who else do you have hunting him?"

"Agency and military assets. But I need more. I need your best men."

"Sounds like a crowded playing field. That makes it dangerous for my men."

"I can keep you aware of other entities involved in the hunt. You can vector your assets away from American assets when necessary." Carmichael then asked, "How many men do you have working in D.C.?"

"Apologies, but that is something I would rather not say."

"Ten," Carmichael said. "You have ten. I want them all on this. If you want to bring others in, I can facilitate that."

Kaz seemed reluctant, but after a few moments he acquiesced. "Professional trust and good manners are two things I don't seek in this line of work. But you and I, Denny, we have shared interests. I will help you in this, provided you return the favor to me somehow."

Carmichael had been expecting this. "You help us find Violator and you have my word you will have more latitude in the District. You won't be off the leash, but I will let a little slack out of the leash so you can sniff around the yard a little more."

Kaz nodded.

Carmichael then said, "I am sure you realize Gentry can't be taken alive."

Kaz reached out and patted Carmichael on the arm. "If we get to him first, he won't be." Kaz stood, extended a hand. "Let us work together to finally put an end to this difficult affair."

"Excellent. You and I will deal directly. I'll let you know what I know, as soon as I know it."

Kaz stood and reached for his suit coat. Slipping it on, he said, "I do have some advice in the short term."

"What advice?"

"Get off the streets. If Gentry is within ten miles of you right now, you are in peril driving yourself around."

"My relationship with you is unsanctioned, Kaz. I can't just roll with a detail into the Saudi Embassy."

"Then let's pretend it's the old days. In Lebanon. Or in Sana'a. Or in Tunisia. You and I can play the role of young field operatives. Dead drops and coded messages."

Carmichael wiped his eyes under his glasses. He was already fighting sleep deprivation, and he expected no real rest until Gentry was located and terminated. "Don't be dramatic, Kaz. I'll use the secure mobile, it's on my person at all times. Keep yours with you."

The Saudi shrugged. Feigning disappointment. "Very well."

The men left separately, Carmichael first. He'd have one of his people drop by the hotel in the evening and spend the night, then check out in the morning using the hotel services screen on the television so he did not have to go to the reception desk and do it in person.

The automated world of travel made some things easier for spies.

12

Carmichael returned to the Highlander parked on King Street, then he began a new SDR that would lead him, eventually, to the helicopter and DeRenzi at the airport. He'd be back at Langley by three p.m., and only then would he and Mayes both breathe a long sigh of relief.

As he drove he thought of the unprecedented challenge before him: find one man in a metropolitan area of six million. Killing the Gray Man had been a top priority for the past five years, and still he had failed to accomplish it. In those same years he had directed human intelligence assets all over the globe, assassinated high-value targets in remote locations, successfully executed major intelligence operations against world powers, thwarted terrorist attacks on the homeland, and even had a hand in winning a regional war in Africa.

But Courtland *fucking* Gentry somehow managed to remain alive. He'd been a hard target for a long time, but now Carmichael was certain Gentry had miscalculated. Whatever it was he thought he would accomplish here, there would be no escape from the United States.

Not with Kaz and his men involved.

Carmichael had allowed Kaz to run a small team of operatives in D.C. for three years now. Carmichael had even helped Kaz steer clear of FBI counterintelligence schemes designed to identify and arrest foreign operatives in the U.S., alerting his Saudi colleague to sting operations. And no one knew. Not the FBI, not the director of the CIA, not even Jordan Mayes. Mayes was aware his boss had a good working relationship with the director of Saudi intelligence in the U.S., but he had no idea of the quid pro quo that existed between the two men.

It was entirely against the law, an unsanctioned relationship, but Carmichael wasn't interested in rules; he was interested in results.

In return for this, Kaz fed Carmichael intelligence of the quantity and quality no American intelligence chief had ever been given by an Arab nation. Kaz had personally passed Denny al Qaeda bank account numbers in Dubai, names and addresses of high-value targets, recorded intercepts of suspected ISIS officers working in Iraq, and many other items the CIA would have no access to otherwise, but an intrepid Saudi could obtain through his connections in the Islamist world.

Kaz's intelligence had not decimated the jihadists, not by any stretch of the imagination. AQ always seemed to find new avenues for funding, and ISIS found new men to put into leadership positions. But Denny was more than satisfied with the product he was getting from Kaz. That he had to keep the close affiliation under wraps was unfortunate, but Denny knew he would never in a million years receive authorization to allow foreign operatives to work freely in the USA. The closed minds of the FBI and the political minds of the White House would be horrified if they knew.

Denny understood the intel business; you had to pay to play. And he also understood what Kaz wanted. Kaz wasn't here in the U.S. running ops against the U.S. No, he was working against his country's enemies. Economic intelligence against other oil-producing states. Political intelligence against those of Saudi Arabia's Middle Eastern neighbors who swam in the waters of the United Nations, the American media, and D.C.-based think tanks.

Denny had known Kaz a long time, and although he couldn't say he trusted the man—Saudi Arabia was always looking out for the interests of Saudi Arabia, after all—Denny felt like he understood the man's motivations. Kaz wasn't running around America with a team of assassins knocking off congressmen. Allowing the Saudi intel chief some latitude to pursue his nation's objectives in the United States was, as far as Denny Carmichael was concerned, a fair price to pay for what he was getting in return.

As he drove back over the Woodrow Wilson Bridge on his way to Prince Georges County airport, Denny allowed himself a moment of pride and satisfaction. He saw himself as the chess master, controlling the pieces on the board.

The moment faded as he thought about Gentry. Not because Gentry was the problem at hand. No, he thought about Gentry now, because in the fifteen years Denny Carmichael had worked closely with Murquin al-Kazaz, there had only been one major misstep in the relationship. One time where intel from Kaz had led, for one reason or another, to an unmitigated intelligence disaster.

That time was years earlier, and the end result of that intelligence failure was now running free on the streets of America, wholly unaware of what he did to bring the full force of the U.S. intelligence community down on him like so many missiles from the sky.

Murquin al-Kazaz sat quietly in the suite at the Kimpton Lorien for twenty minutes, using the time to send text messages and to clear other matters out of his inbox. Then he, too, left the suite, wiping the door latch with a handkerchief on his way out.

He was picked up on Duke Street, two blocks from the hotel. He folded into the back of a Jaguar sedan, and then he was off to his office in the center of a small motorcade of unmarked Land Rovers and Escalades.

Kaz stared out the window silently as they returned to the Royal Embassy of Saudi Arabia, just across New Hampshire from the Watergate complex. His offices were there at the embassy, taking up a large portion of one wing of the building.

Saudi Arabia had a robust intelligence apparatus here in D.C., for three main reasons. For starters, many young Saudis came to the U.S. to study, and here they learned English and the ways of America. Kaz therefore had a large selection of good intelligence officers to choose from to staff his stable in D.C.

Secondly, Saudi Arabia had an incredible amount of money. Liquid funds. Easily accessible U.S. dollars. Good intelligence work did not rely on money alone, of course, but money was an effective lubricant to all manner of espionage. Kaz had a budget of millions with which to buy equipment, rent real estate, and bribe men and women in all social strata in the U.S.

And the third reason Saudi Arabia's intelligence service was so damn effective in the U.S. was because of the special relationship between CIA's Clandestine Service Director Denny Carmichael and U.S. Station Chief for the Saudi General Intelligence Presidency Murquin al-Kazaz.

The secret pact between the two men stipulated that Kaz could only use his operation here in the States to target other nations, not the U.S. itself. And

Kaz was not allowed to work against any of the U.S.'s main allies. Both men understood this to mean Israel, because Denny could not very well have Kaz getting caught in the District, for example, conducting surveillance on the home of the Israeli ambassador.

Denny's understanding of their agreement was that Kaz and his men were free to do other types of collection. They might use long-distance listening devices against the Russian consulate to learn about oil pipeline deals, they could run collection operations on other Middle Eastern embassies to obtain information on diplomatic and military affairs important to the Saudi kingdom, and they might surveil foreign nationals dangerous to Saudi interests who were here in the District to visit think tanks or speak to aid groups or conduct protest rallies.

Denny knew there was plenty for Kaz to do without conducting operations against Americans.

Until now, that was.

But despite Denny Carmichael's understanding of the agreement, Murquin al-Kazaz had his own ideas about just what his men would do here in the U.S. He took advantage of the protective wing of America's top spy, and he used Denny's secret sanction to run lethal direct-action missions here in the United States. His men had killed an Israeli blogger, a prominent author who wrote books critical of U.S.-Saudi relations, and a German businessman in the defense sector who stood in the way of the Kingdom obtaining a lucrative contract for aircraft engines.

All the murders had been passed off as muggings, car jackings, automobile accidents—and Denny had not suspected a thing. He never understood that his friend and partner Murquin al-Kazaz was actually more like a fox in a henhouse.

And now Kaz was being asked by the most important man in American intelligence to devote all his energies to finding and killing a single American operative, inside the United States of America. At first blush it had nothing to do with Kaz's overarching mission here in the States, but Kaz would do as Denny requested, because Denny Carmichael's survival was in the interests of the kingdom of Saudi Arabia.

13

The three fraternity brothers were stone-cold sober, but that wasn't the worst part. The worst part was that they were also wet, hungry, and pissed, and they hadn't even killed anything yet.

They'd begun this weekend with such high hopes, and Friday had been a blast. It was Jay's twenty-second birthday and his father had arranged a memorable time for him and his two best friends. They left the Sig Ep house at Cleveland's Case Western Reserve Friday afternoon and headed to the airport to climb aboard a Cessna Citation Mustang that was owned by Jay's dad's law firm. The three boys sipped rum and Cokes served to them by the jet's leggy flight attendant while they flew to Greenbrier Valley Airport in Lewisburg, West Virginia. From the airport they were driven to the hunting lodge, and as soon as they checked in to their rooms they hit the bar and drank shots with a group of old-timers till late in the evening.

Saturday morning they rolled out of their bunks, groggy and hungover, but riding on adrenaline. Dressed in their new camo, they shouldered their rented rifles and heavy packs and sauntered down to breakfast.

The plan called for their guide to meet them in the lobby, and then they would discuss the strategy of their full-weekend wild boar hunting excursion over pancakes and bacon. The boys figured after that they would all climb onto four-wheelers, drive up into the mountains, and kill shit—maybe do a shot of Fireball or Jägermeister every time a hog went down.

But when they met the guide in the lobby by the entrance to the breakfast room, he turned them away from the food and walked them directly out into the rainy morning. When Jay asked the gruff-looking, middle-aged, bearded man what the rush to get out of the lodge was all about, he just said they would be doing less four-wheeling and more "humping" to get to their hide site.

The three boys got the impression humping meant something different to their guide than it did to them.

The man then went through each of the frat boys' gear and began pulling things out and throwing them in a pile on the gravel drive without a word. Out came the 12-pack of Natural Light, the bottles of Fireball, Jägermeister, and Pappy Van Winkle, then the M&M's, fried pies, and even two bags of Cheetos.

Jay's dad was a high-profile attorney, Meat's mom hosted a satellite radio show about Chicago politics, and Stuart's dad had been deputy mayor of Cleveland, but all three boys were too intimidated by the rough-looking guide to protest. They'd been warned at the lodge by the old-timers that the man was surly and taciturn, but along with these cons, they'd been promised he was also the best hunting guide in the state, so they just rolled with his gruffness.

The bearded man all but pushed them into his huge pickup, although he did promise them food and coffee on the road. As soon as they left the lodge, however, it became clear their breakfast would consist of bagged military meals ready to eat and Folgers instant that they heated in a plastic bag with a chemical heater and then drank out of dirty tin cups.

They drove for two hours with the guide barely speaking, then they slung their packs and rifles and began walking into the mountains.

The guide led them off the trail after another hour and into impossibly dense forest.

They walked, climbed, and stumbled through the woods all day, and they failed to drop a single wild boar. Stuart had fired twice and missed twice, Jay blasted an anthill that sort of looked like a boar from distance, and, although he expended a lot of ammunition, the only thing Meat had killed was three pouches of marbled pound cake and two helpings of beef stew out of the MRE stash in his pack.

The guide was clearly disgusted with them all, but he had not even brought a rifle of his own, so as far as they were concerned he couldn't prove he could have done any better.

They made camp before last light and ate more MREs, and by then the Sig Ep frat brothers had begun complaining loudly. When they did, the guide gave them the evil eye and a gruff retort about how they looked like they needed the exercise more than they needed pork chops, and then he promised them better results on Sunday.

But it was Sunday now, past two p.m., thirty hours after setting out, and the frat boys still hadn't killed a damn thing. They sat in a hide on the side of a hill that looked down over broken ground divided by a winding creek. On the other side of the valley, some 250 yards away, sat another rocky hillside, thick with pines and brush that was lush and green in the wet spring.

All three boys had sat silently on the cold ground for the past hour, waiting for something to happen, but Jay ended the silence when he turned to the guide and cleared his throat. "Hey, man. This is bullshit. You promised us we'd shoot some hogs."

The bearded man covered in camo didn't even turn Jay's way. He kept looking out over the valley, then he spit chewing tobacco on the grass between his knees. "We're hunting, not chasing. Best when your prey comes to you."

Stuart looked at his watch. "Any idea when that might be?"

"You just have to open your eyes, ladies. They are out there if you look."

The boys all picked up their binoculars and searched the valley floor with their lenses. They'd missed most all their shots under two hundred yards, so they didn't bother to scan any farther out than that.

Finally Meat said, "There's nothing down there but squirrels."

The guide said, "I thought you said you kids came from Case Western. Sure you don't go to the School for the Blind?"

Jay took his eyes out of his binos and looked to the guide. "I don't want to be a dick or anything, but you know I could make one call to my dad and get you fired. He's friends with the old dude who owns the lodge, you know."

The guide spit again in the grass in front of him.

Stuart finished scanning the valley floor, then he moved the glass up and searched the opposite hillside. He stopped the movement of his binoculars suddenly.

"Wait. You aren't talking about those hogs up *there*, are you?"

It took a minute, but Stuart got his two fraternity brothers to see what he was looking at. Far on the other side and almost as high as the hunters' hide site, eight wild boar rooted in the wet grass and pine needles.

Jay said, "You're kidding, right? Those hogs have to be four hundred yards away."

The guide looked across the valley with his naked eyes. "Not an inch more than three seventy. Actually, I'd say . . . three sixty-three."

Jay pulled his brand-new laser range finder out of his brand-new backpack. After nearly a minute's work with the device, he retracted his eye out of the eyecup and turned to the guide, a look of astonishment on his face. "That's incredible. The closest hog is three sixty-one."

The guide spit again. "That one in front is a little underdeveloped. I was talking about that big black fella about two meters behind him."

Meat just muttered, "Holy shit."

Stuart said, "But we aren't shooting from here." A pause. "Are we?"

"Why not?"

Jay got over his awe at the guide's natural distance-calculating ability. "Look. It's your job to get us within range, not just to within sight."

The guide replied with annoyance, "I could hit him."

Jay laughed now. "Well, you're the fucking guide, so you're supposed to be better than us. But since you didn't even bother to bring a rifle, you can't prove it, can you?"

Meat held his bolt action Winchester out. "You want to take a shot? I'd like to see you try it."

The guide said, "Why not?" but he didn't reach for the rifle. Instead he spit once more to the side, rolled forward from a seated position into a prone position, unzipped his camouflage jacket, and reached into the folds of his clothing. To the utter confusion of the three fraternity brothers in the grass next to him, he slowly drew a perfectly ordinary-looking black handgun.

Jay said, "You're crazy."

The guide did not speak. He just leveled the semiautomatic pistol out in front of him, holding it in his right hand and resting his right forearm on top of his left forearm, which he positioned perpendicular to his body on the ground.

Stuart said, "That's an impossible shot with a handgun."

The guide spoke now, but it sounded as if he was talking to himself. "Humidity's got to be seventy percent. Four-point-five-inch barrel, forty-cal hollow point, it's gonna be pretty draggy, but I've got a full-value five-mile wind to work with. I'd say I need about a twenty-four-foot holdover."

Meat said, "Even if you *could* hit one of those hogs from here, you couldn't possibly kill it. That bullet will go an inch into its hide and get stuck in the fat or the muscle."

The guide nodded slowly, not taking his eyes off his pistol's iron sights.

"You're right. Let's do a twenty-five-and-a-half-foot holdover, go for the brain pan."

The three boys sat there agog, staring at the big bearded man lying in the grass next to them. They saw the barrel of the black pistol rise just slightly.

"You are fucking nuts," muttered Jay, but then he quickly brought his binoculars up to his eyes. The other two did the same, and they focused on the target.

A single gunshot pounded the air next to them. Jay jerked his binos away from his eyes with a flinch, but he got them recentered on the dark brown hog on the far hill. The animal just stood there, his snout rooting idly in the pine needles.

"You missed," Jay said.

And then the hog shuddered, its head twitched, and it dropped snout-first into the shallow hole it had been digging. It fell on its side, its legs kicked out, and then it stilled.

Only then did all the other wild boar on the hillside begin running off in different directions. And seconds after that, the echo of the pistol's report made its way from the far hillside to the four men.

Jay, Meat, and Stuart all moved as one. Eyes slowly lifted out of their binoculars and turned to the man next to them.

Mouths opened slightly, but no one spoke.

Zack Hightower rolled back up to a sitting position, reholstered his Glock 22 on his hip under his coat, and spit in the grass. He looked over to the three sissy college boys next to him. In a tone not quite as snide as he intended he said, "I'll kill him for you, but I sure as shit am not going to go get him for you."

Meat was the first of the three boys to speak. "One of the old dudes in the lodge said you were in the SEALs. We thought he was full of shit."

Hightower sighed. "You aren't 'in the SEALs.' You are in the navy. You *are* a SEAL."

Jay said, "So . . . you were a SEAL?"

Hightower did not answer. Instead he cocked his head to the left and looked up to the sky.

"What is it?" Meat asked.

Zack kept looking around, trying to find the source of the engine noise he was hearing. After several seconds, he said, "Helo."

A black helicopter appeared over the ridge on the other side of the valley, flew past the downed wild boar, and approached the four men.

"EC-130," Zack added.

Jay asked, "What's it doing here?"

Zack smiled a little now—he couldn't help it—then he stood, grabbed his pack, and slung it over a shoulder. He brushed some of the mud and wet leaves off his clothing. "I do believe he's here for me."

The aircraft hovered above a rolling pasture, the flattest area on the hillside, just one hundred feet away from the hunters. It lowered down onto its skids and Zack started towards it.

Jay shouted after him. "Hey! Where the hell are you going?"

Zack turned back around and snapped his fingers, like he'd forgotten about the three boys sitting in the grass. He reached into his pocket, removed the keys to his pickup, and threw them overhand to Jay.

He said, "The truck is seven point five klicks east-southeast."

Meat asked, "Which way is that? And what's a klick?"

Jay stood now. "Wait! You can't just leave us!"

Hightower turned around and headed for the helo. Over the sound of the Eurocopter's engine he shouted back to them. "Call your dad. I hear he knows the old dude who owns the lodge."

Zack Hightower climbed aboard the helicopter with a nod to the crew, nonchalant, like he'd been expecting it all day, and the helo lifted back off into the gray sky while the boys watched from below.

14

atherine King didn't always come in to the office on Sundays, but she was here today, preparing an investigative piece on a recent drone attack in Syria with a deadline of noon on Monday.

She had a corner cubicle area that wasn't quite an office, but it was more than what most of the reporters at the *Post* got. A ten-by-ten space filled with books, magazines, newspapers, file folders, rolling duffels and backpacks, yoga mats and other fitness-related items, along with a few pictures pinned into the fabric of the wall of her cube.

Catherine had never married, never had children. She'd felt sure it would happen in her thirties, and when it hadn't come to pass by her forties she felt sure she'd become too old and set in her ways to settle down. Now in her fifties, she threw herself into her only real loves: her work and her yoga practice.

This morning she'd come directly from her Sunday class at Georgetown Yoga, and she sat at her desk now in full loose-fitting exercise attire. She wasn't concerned with her appearance, because the few people who worked in the office on Sunday afternoon had known her for years, and there was no one around she was out to impress.

Catherine focused on her article till a reflection in her computer monitor caused her to spin around in surprise. When she did she found a young man with thinning blond hair and a wispy mustache-goatee combo, a smile on his face and a backpack over his shoulder.

"Let me guess," Catherine said as she stood and extended a hand. "You must be Andy Shoal."

"A real pleasure to finally meet you." He shook her hand eagerly. "I've followed your work since J-school. Before, even."

"How nice." Catherine forced a little smile at the comment, then she scooped a stack of manila shipping pouches off of one of the two extra chairs in her cubicle area and offered the seat to Andy. He plopped down and dropped his backpack on the floor, and she sat back down in front of her monitor, holding the pouches in her lap because she didn't want to foul up her filing system by placing them on any other surface in the messy cubicle.

"Hope you don't mind me dropping in unannounced," Andy said, looking around at the mess while he spoke.

"Not at all. Apparently you not only work nights, but you also work weekends. Is that it?"

By way of explanation, Andy said, "I'm a cops reporter."

Catherine understood. "I guess criminals don't work bankers' hours."

Andy smiled. "Only bank robbers."

Catherine returned a polite smile at the joke. "Did you find out anything new about the Brandywine Street murders?"

"The victims are all still in the hospital—one is in ICU—but I doubt they will be talking to me or the cops."

"Why do you say that?"

"They are all getting charged with possession with the intent to distribute. They will lawyer up, and their lawyers will tell them to button their lips."

"Any more from the police?"

"No description of the killer other than male, white, thirties. There was one thing that was really weird, though."

"What's that?"

"The killer left a bunch of fingerprints."

Catherine scrunched up her mouth. That didn't seem weird to her at all.

"In a symbol," Andy added.

"A *symbol*?"

"Well, a number. He used his right thumbprint to make a big number six on a nightstand in the room with the dead guys."

"It sounds like a calling card of some sort. Have you seen that at any other crime? A gang sign or something?"

"I haven't, and I checked a nationwide database on gang signs. A six by itself doesn't seem to mean anything."

"Could be a message."

Andy said, "You mean, to the CIA?"

Catherine gazed out the window and down onto 15th Street. "I don't know."

Andy asked, "Did you find anything out about the spooks who toured the scene?"

"Jordan Mayes I told you about. The woman's name is Suzanne Brewer. She's CIA as well, in their Programs and Plans office. Her job is to identify threats against the Agency, terrorists and such, and then task assets to eliminate the threats."

"What does she have to do with Mayes?"

"No idea," said Catherine. "According to my contacts she served in Baghdad protecting facilities, and then she served in Kabul and Sana'a, Yemen. She came back to HQ three years ago with a lot of accolades and commendations for her work and a promotion to go with it. She has an excellent reputation in the Agency."

Catherine sat quietly a moment, just thinking. Andy did not get in the way of the process. She said, "It makes me wonder if Mayes and Brewer had information about the perpetrator last night. That he was somehow related to a threat against CIA. It would have to be something substantial to bring out the AD of NCS and a senior program officer."

"What do you want to do now?" Andy asked.

"I'd like to know more about the man they are after. I'll stay away from Carmichael for now."

Andy said, "If you want I can reach out to Mayes. Just play dumb and ask him what he was doing there."

King shook her head. "He won't talk. At this point the best we can hope for is an official CIA press officer comment, which would be worthless."

Andy sighed. It was clear to Catherine that he wanted a story, and he wanted it now. He said, "In your world, you can't get people to talk. When I go to a crime scene to get an interview, I usually can't get people to shut up."

Catherine laughed. "Do what I do long enough and you learn to read between the lines. Often I get more information by what the CIA *doesn't* say." She spun back around to her computer, indicating to Andy she was ready to get back to work. "Keep your nose to the ground, Andy. My interest is piqued about Mayes and Brewer."

Zack Hightower had been handed a garment bag in the Eurocopter, and in it he found a suit and tie. The control officer on board asked him to change out of his hunting gear, not because CIA demanded formality, but rather so he did not draw attention to himself in the building dressed in camo and muddy boots. He stripped down to his boxers as they flew high over Northern Virginia, and as he did so he could immediately tell his new outfit had been borrowed off another man; it didn't fit very well around his muscular arms, and there was a hint of both antiperspirant and BO.

Zack smelled like a goat, however, so he just shrugged and put on the suit. The control officer kicked off his own wing tips and Zack slipped them on, finding them just one size too small.

The helo descended over the rolling hills of Virginia and landed on CIA property at seven p.m., setting down in the nearly empty parking lot on the bubble side of the Old HQ building. Even before the rotors spooled down, Zack was led out and then through the side door. He followed his control officer through the security checks, then to the elevators, where he stepped inside.

The Langley headquarters was familiar to him, but only from visits for an occasional briefing, seminar, or retirement party for a senior coworker. He'd never had a desk here, and as far as Zack was concerned, that was okay with him.

He raised an eyebrow when he realized they were heading up to the seventh floor. Zack worked for the Central Intelligence Agency for eleven years before being dismissed, but this was his first trip all the way to the top. Seven wasn't exactly a hangout for paramilitary operations officers, after all.

Zack had spent the majority of his stateside time with CIA in training, mostly in Virginia and North Carolina but also in the mountains of Montana and Colorado, firing ranges in Mississippi and Arizona, the deserts of Nevada and the streets of D.C., where he and other SAD men honed their surveillance skills.

Zack's unit of Ground Branch officers did have its own headquarters, an unmarked building in Norfolk, Virginia, but Zack had spent several years leading his six-man outfit of shooters to all points in the War on Terror, and in those years he and his team spent very little time stateside.

As he rode the elevator up with the other man, Zack did his best to act like this sort of shit happened to him every day, but in truth his mind was racing. Why were they pulling him in? Some old op needed a full accounting? Some new op needed the eyes of a veteran to straighten it out?

Was he being offered a way back in CIA?

Hightower didn't dare hope for this.

A minute later Zack took a seat at a mahogany table in a dark-paneled conference room, and within moments of his sitting down, a side door opened and in walked Jordan Mayes, the second-in-command at NCS.

Zack was surprised to see such a highflier, but more surprised that Jordan Mayes looked like hell, as if he'd been up for forty-eight hours.

Hightower knew Mayes from both of their days in SAD, although Mayes had always been enough rungs higher on the management ladder to where he didn't need to slum with labor much. From time to time Hightower would find himself face-to-face with Mayes, but he could count those occurrences on one hand.

Zack knew Mayes had always worked directly for Denny Carmichael. He hoped that was no longer the case. Carmichael had fired Zack a couple of years earlier, unceremoniously and cruelly. Hightower had been in intensive care at the time with a gunshot wound to his chest and a dangerous infection in his lungs, and Carmichael sent word down through a low-level flunky that his services would no longer be required. Zack had been devastated by this, but he was a good soldier. He filed no protest; he made no complaint. He just lay alone in the hospital till the doctors released him, then he went home from the hospital to his apartment in Virginia Beach, and did nothing but lay there and watch TV.

For a year.

He had no family other than an ex-wife who lived somewhere in Colorado with a daughter Zack had never met, so he basically sat at home and recuperated, watched the news and wished he was still part of it.

He'd only picked up the hunting guide gig in West Virginia when he ran out of money. He hated shepherding rich assholes through the woods just so they could shoot a fucking pig that wasn't bothering anybody, but the money was good, and all the hiking, climbing, and shooting had molded Zack into reasonably good shape within a short period of time.

He'd fantasized about getting back on, if not with CIA, at least with some private military company, but Carmichael had stripped Zack's Top Secret clearance, so Zack knew no real PMC would touch him. He had no interest in doing stateside static security work, so he just kept hauling rich civvies out on wild boar hunts, hoping something interesting would happen in his life.

And now he was face-to-face with the number two spy at the Agency, on the seventh floor of the Old HQB.

This was, at the very least, interesting.

Zack Hightower stood smartly, not quite at attention, but certainly displaying a show of respect.

Mayes nodded and sat down after a quick handshake. Under his arm he carried a thick file, and Zack suspected that his operational life, and perhaps his post-operational life, would be in that file.

"Thanks for coming in," Mayes said.

"Happy to help in any way I can."

"Denny wants a word."

Zack swallowed. "Can I ask what this is about?"

"Better if Denny gives it to you cold."

Carmichael pushed open the side door and all but stormed up to the table. If he had pulled an all-nighter with Mayes the evening before, then he was clearly a vampire, because Zack thought he looked good to go now at seven p.m.

Zack stood. This time it was at full military attention.

Carmichael's greeting was, to say the least, several degrees cooler than that of Jordan Mayes. "I don't do apologies, Hightower, so if you are waiting for one, prepare to be disappointed."

Zack followed Carmichael by sitting back down, and pulling himself up to the table. "Not expecting one, sir."

"You aren't pissed about what happened to you two years ago?"

Zack shook his head. "I failed on a mission. That was unacceptable to you, but it was also unacceptable to me. I would have been disappointed if you'd not released me after that."

Carmichael took in the comment. Then asked, "Fitness-wise, where are you?"

"One hundred percent." Zack realized his tone had sounded hopeful, and he told himself to keep it flat till he knew what the hell was going on.

Carmichael looked to Mayes now. Mayes shrugged.

Hightower clarified. "Took a handgun round center-mass two years ago, but I've recovered. Been shooting every day. Long-range I'm better than ever. Running some, too. I'm not twenty anymore, but that's an asset, not a liability. I'll get any job done you need me to do."

Carmichael looked doubtful.

"I can run a PT course right now."

"I'm questioning your mental state."

"My head is right, sir. I could put my hand in a candle and show you, if that's what you are looking for."

"That's *not* what I want, either. I need to see that there are no hard feelings about what happened two years ago."

"None at all, sir."

Carmichael drummed his fingers on the table for a moment, then he seemed to let it go, and he went immediately to the subject at hand. "Courtland Gentry appeared in the D.C. area last night."

Hightower had planned on keeping a cool stoic face, no matter what craziness Carmichael threw his way, but now he could not hide his surprise. "Oh, *shit!*"

"Killed two drug dealers in the slums, apparently to obtain money to finance his activities here."

"Only two?" Zack quipped. The execs stared back at him, so he went on the defensive. "Look, if you think I knew about this, then you—"

Carmichael interrupted. "Any idea why he might have come here?"

"Permission to speak freely, sir?"

"This isn't the fucking navy, Hightower."

Zack shrugged, as if the answer was obvious. "He's come here to kill you."

It was silent in the dark conference room for a moment, and Hightower worried he might have overstepped his bounds. Then Mayes said, "That's our assessment, as well."

Hightower nodded slowly and a smile grew. Suddenly it felt like all his problems had just melted away. The past two years of his life, the depression born out of being ostracized by the Agency after failing a mission, disappeared. He had a job, a purpose. The old Zack was back.

With a wide grin he said, "I get it. I get why I'm here. You need me to stop him."

Carmichael sniffed. "Don't get ahead of yourself. You didn't stop him last time out, did you?"

The cocky smile remained. "Sir, that op you sent me on in Sudan was as wrong as dick cancer, and you *know* it."

Denny Carmichael did not reply to this. After a moment he said, "We brought you in to see if you could help us determine where Gentry might be, what he might do. Tactics and the like."

"Damn straight. Nobody knows him like I do."

After a gentle rapping on the side door a woman in a conservative blue outfit entered. Zack's first impression was that she was hot. Not stripper hot, he told himself, but hot in sort of a sexy librarian kind of way.

She walked up to Hightower, who fought the urge to look her up and down. Instead he stood up, and she extended her hand.

Jordan Mayes made the introductions. "Hightower, this is Suzanne Brewer. She is the officer in charge of the Violator tactical operations center. As long as Gentry is in this area of operations, she is tasked with finding him. We'd like you to spend some time telling her everything you know about the man—his tactics, techniques, and procedures. Together you can fine-tune the hunt so the shooters know where to go."

Zack was disappointed. A minute earlier he would have been happy plunging the toilets here at CIA, but now he wanted in on the hunt itself. "Who are your shooters? Ground Branch?" he asked.

"Negative. We are using JSOC," Carmichael said. "They are already out on the streets. Until we have a positive sighting of him, we won't have anything more than what you and Suzanne can develop."

"Why not Ground Branch?"

"We are keeping Matt Hanley out of this for now."

Hightower nodded slowly. There was some sort of intra-office feud going on between Hanley and Carmichael; this Hightower could see on Carmichael's face.

Hightower put aside his desire to run and gun, and he nodded to the hottie in the business suit. "I look forward to working with you, Ms. Brewer."

He'd do more than that if he got the chance.

"Suzanne is fine," she said, and from her tone he instantly realized he would *not* get the chance. Despite the first-name, this one was all business. "The operations center is on the fourth floor. I have an office there where we can talk further. Violator has been in country about twenty hours, so we don't have a moment to lose."

"Then let's get started."

Mayes said, "That's it, Hightower? You haven't asked for anything. No money. No request for us to clarify your status. Why not?"

Hightower did not hesitate in his reply. "I understand what's happening. This isn't just about bringing me in to discuss Gentry's habits. No, you need a guy like me on the street, in the hunt. You want me to remain off book. Better that way for you. If this breaks bad with a running shoot-out down the National Mall, you don't want to be tied to it. You are bringing me on to help with TTPs, but if he's located on U.S. soil, you'd rather some nobody like me went out and did the killing. Not a special mission unit tied to the military, or an operative tied to the intelligence community.

"You want some loser you can leave swinging in the wind in case you need to deny responsibility."

No one said a word for an awkward moment. Then Zack added, "And I'm good with that."

Carmichael and Mayes exchanged a look. Finally Carmichael reached a hand across the table. "Good to see you again, Hightower."

The two men shook hands, and Zack looked to Brewer. "How 'bout you and me go and find that son of a bitch?"

15

Court Gentry accomplished more in his first day back in the United States than most could accomplish in a month. After sleeping five hours he rolled out of bed and looked through his small driveway-level window, checking for any new cars or strange people wandering the neighborhood. Atmospherics and patterns of life. The more he knew about his area of operations, the easier it would be for him to notice something that did not belong. But he saw nothing that triggered his threat radar, so he folded a massive wad of twenty-dollar bills into his pocket, left his rented room, and walked to a discount department store a mile away.

Here he filled a shopping cart with clothing in just minutes, because he knew what he was doing.

There were few people on planet Earth more skilled at changing their look on the fly, and Court knew the colors, styles, and sizes he needed to make himself invisible in a crowd. The temperatures in D.C. this time of year fluctuated between the low forties and the mid-sixties, with periods of rain nearly every day, so Court knew he could fit in with others on the street by wearing several layers.

With two long-sleeve shirts, a dark green baseball cap, a beige knit cap, and a brown hoodie under a reversible black raincoat, Court could, in under a second, switch between seven different and distinct looks as he walked down the street.

He bought six complete sets of clothing and two nondescript black backpacks, two different pairs of cheap sunglasses, brown work boots and rubber overshoes, a small fanny pack, a ten-dollar digital watch, and a quality kitchen knife with a plastic sheath.

Near the Columbia Heights Metro station he found an electronics chain store, and here Court bought a tablet computer and a battery charger, two contract-free smartphones, and a few other gadgets.

He'd done this sort of thing many times before, of course. In Ireland, in Brazil, in Laos, in Russia. But it felt different prepping for action here in the USA.

He made a stop at his room to drop off his shopping bags and change into some of his new clothes, then he walked to a hardware store and bought a high-end glass cutter, a multi-tool, a tool kit, a tool belt, binoculars, a small hacksaw, a rain parka, and more work clothes in colors and fashions that would help him fit into the fabric of the city as a construction worker or some nonspecific manual laborer.

At all three stores he was pleased to see he could make his purchases without having to speak to a single human being. No one in the stores asked to help him, and instead of going to cash registers, he could instead scan his own items, bag them, and pay a machine.

Court liked his chances of keeping a low profile if he could conduct as much of his business as possible with automation.

At a convenience store he purchased food and water, a prepaid Visa card loaded with $500, and two more contract-free phones.

He returned to the safe house below the Mayberrys' home and he dumped his new gear and clothing on the bed. He then knelt down in the narrow closet and felt around the paneling that had been damaged from the moisture and heat from the water heater on the other side. He rapped gently next to it until he found a two-foot-square section that sounded completely hollow. Using his hacksaw, he punched through the paneling on a seam, then he began cutting.

In minutes he had created a small and nearly undetectable escape hatch into the Mayberrys' basement proper.

He grabbed his flashlight and crawled through to the pitch-black basement, expecting to be able to stand up immediately. But shining the light around, he saw he was in a three-foot-high channel that passed below some water pipes next to the home's old water heater. Court followed the crawl space for six feet before he was able to stand up next to the furnace.

Looking around the main section of the basement, he got the distinct impression the Mayberrys didn't spend a great deal of time down here. A thick coating of dust covered most parts of the room, except for the area near the wooden staircase up to the ground floor. Here a shelving unit was filled with canned goods, paper towels, toilet paper, and cases of soft drinks.

In the flashlight's beam Court found Arthur Mayberry's workbench, along with a good selection of tools, most lying around haphazardly. Court could tell Mayberry was something of a handyman, which was no surprise considering this was an older home and probably required a lot of upkeep.

There was a propane tank for a gas grill, and a few lawn care items that Mayberry inexplicably stored down here instead of in the little shed at the end of the driveway that Court had noticed that morning.

Taking stock of all the equipment in the room, Court had an idea about how he could improve his defensive position in the little basement studio apartment. He shook the propane tank to make sure it was full, and then a slight smile drew across his face as he formulated his plan.

Using his tool kit to disassemble some items that did not look like they would be missed by the Mayberrys in the short term, he made two trips on his hands and knees, bringing all the equipment back to his rented room through the tiny crawl space. He then left his room again, running out to a nearby sporting goods store to buy everything he needed to finish his project.

While at the sporting goods store he picked up a Walker's Game Ear—a behind-the-ear device not unlike a hearing aid, used by hunters to hear the faint sound of game in the woods. Court had used similar devices with CIA, and although he expected this over-the-counter bit of technology to be a little inferior to the top secret kit he'd used in the field, he knew it would help him pick up distant conversation or alert him to anyone trying to sneak up behind him whenever he had it in place.

He returned and spent the next hour building a booby trap, rigging it to slow down or even stop anyone trying to make their way in through the one door to the room. He designed the entire contraption so he could break it down and hide it in minutes when he left the house, in case the Mayberrys themselves decided to drop in.

Satisfied his device was functional, Court checked his watch. It was already seven p.m. He logged on to the Internet via his 4G mobile phone and surfed to a computer hacking website. Here he downloaded an open source copy of Aircrack-ng, a Wi-Fi password-cracking tool that used brute force to guess log-ins to Wi-Fi networks.

When the software was ready on his phone he searched for all nearby Wi-Fi signals and found four that were strong enough for him to use here in his basement room. He chose one, then initiated Aircrack-ng. The software began running its algorithm to determine the password, trying hundreds of thousands of combinations against the targeted network.

After several minutes without success he gave up on the first network, determining that whoever selected the password had done an excellent job. Most people spent little time creating passwords, and it was a rare occurrence when Aircrack-ng failed to discover it. He moved on to the second network. This time Aircrack-ng divined the code in less than three and a half minutes, so Court then logged on to the neighbor's network with both his phone and his tablet.

Once online, he turned his attention to Craigslist, the classified advertising website. He spent less than fifteen minutes on the site before making a series of phone calls, then heading back out into the night. He took a cab to an address in nearby Petworth, and here he bought a 1998 gray Ford Escort for $1,100 from a private seller. Although the car was old, it had a reasonable 145,000 miles on it, and there were no major dents or scratches that could make the vehicle easy to ID by trained surveillance.

The seller said he was selling the car cheap because he'd lost his copy of the title, but he assured Court it wasn't stolen. It would be a tremendous understatement to say Court was skeptical in nature, but in this case he actually believed the man, because he saw from the listing the car had been for sale for over a month, and he knew police trolled Craigslist looking for stolen vehicles.

He drove the little four-door back to Reagan Washington National Airport, and here he parked in a long-term lot. He wandered around for a moment, then dropped down behind a vehicle parked rear-in against a back wall. He removed the car's Maryland license plate, attached it to his Escort, and then left the airport.

It took him another hour to purchase a motorcycle. He found a black-on-silver Yamaha 650XS on Craigslist. It was almost as old as Court himself and had some issues, but it was fast, perfectly nondescript, and, after a bit of haggling, only 750 bucks. The seller tossed in a helmet and a plate he had lying on a workbench off another old project bike of his.

Court rented a twelve-by-twelve storage unit within walking distance of his room and parked both vehicles inside, along with one of his two backpacks, this one filled with clothes.

By ten p.m. Court was back in his basement apartment and back on his tablet computer, calling up a website called USCrypto.org.

Even surfing through the pages of the site made the former American intelligence operative feel dirty.

USCrypto was the brainchild of a group of self-proclaimed anarchists and fervent anti-Americans, and it billed itself as an online library and repository for stolen and hacked classified documents, information about secret intelligence sites and personnel, and articles, photos, and videos that it claimed proved illegal U.S. intelligence eavesdropping.

One subsite on USCrypto.org was called Spycatcher, and Court clicked the link to take him there. On the pages contained in the subsite, USCrypto employees revealed the addresses of secret government facilities, and the names and home addresses of employees of American intelligence.

The site even provided Google Maps Street View images of the homes of clandestine personnel.

All this information was divined from open sources by USCrypto staff, so it was completely legal, but the very existence of Spycatcher made Court sick to his stomach.

The site could easily serve, and had probably already been used, as a tool by terrorists and other agents provocateur to allow them to physically target installations and personnel. But now USCrypto.org was an asset to Gentry, because he found himself in an adversarial relationship with his former employer.

It occurred to him that, if he were still working for CIA, he would love to be assigned to target the founder and author of this website, because the head of USCrypto.org was certainly a danger to every man and woman who worked in the U.S. intelligence community. Court would think nothing of killing the founder, although Court had never killed for his country on U.S. soil.

Court searched for the names of several people, and he found only one, because although USCrypto.org was good, Court's old associates at CIA were among the blackest of the black. He jotted down the address, pulled out his phone, and recorded it all on a mapping application. He also looked up addresses for several clandestine government contractors. There he had more luck, and he noted these on a pad and in his phone.

Quickly he ate a microwave enchilada and drank a bottle of water. As soon as he was done he took off his shirt, grabbed the hacksaw off of the little kitchen counter, and sat on the edge of his bed.

Court slowly and carefully began sawing the cast off his right arm. Less than a month earlier he'd taken a handgun round straight into his forearm, snapping the ulna in two. His doctor's orders were to leave the cast on for six weeks, and it had been less than four, but Court decided the time was right to free himself of this annoying burden. He'd have to be careful with it, of course; the broken bone and soft tissue had healed, more or less, but there was still some more growing together that needed to happen, and certain high-stress actions to his arm could quite easily reinjure it.

But Court knew his body. It came from a lifetime of hurting it and watching it heal. He knew he could go without the cast as long as he was careful with the arm, and he also knew he was out of time.

Each and every day he remained in the U.S. with the CIA's shoot-on-sight sanction in effect he compounded the risk. He had to begin his operation now. He didn't have time to nurse his wounds.

As soon as Court had the cast off his arm, he put on several layers of his darkest clothing, loaded his pockets with gear, and headed back out into the night.

He'd already had a busy day, but his real mission was only now about to begin.

16

Chris Travers ordered his fourth shot of Jameson at last call, then he polished off the last few gulps of his draft beer. He'd been drinking since before ten p.m., it was nearly one a.m. now, and he wanted one more for the road, or more precisely, one more for the six-block walk back to his apartment.

This was Travers's favorite pub and he was a regular here, but he drank alone now. A couple of mates had sat with him for the first round, but they had to push off because the next day was Monday and, after all, who really hung out sipping whiskey till closing time on a Sunday night?

Chris Travers did, because he didn't work a nine-to-five job. For large swaths of the year he was on the clock 24/7, and for other sizable chunks of the year he was in training and away from home. But for a few precious weeks here and there he was free from training, off from deployment, and on his own to do whatever the hell he wanted to do with his time.

And this evening he was determined to take advantage of one of the all-too-rare respites.

He held the whiskey up to the little light hanging over the bar of the Irish pub to appreciate the amber color, and while he did this he looked out the window into the night. By force of habit, he always kept an eye open. Even here, in the States.

He was surprised to see trash blowing down 19th Street. There had been only the lightest breeze when Travers headed out to the pub hours earlier, so he'd not bothered to dress for warmth—he'd just thrown on a flannel shirt and khaki pants, and boat shoes with no socks. Suddenly he found himself regretting his rare moment of poor preparation.

He'd not thought twice about making the six-block walk down here from his apartment to the Irish Whiskey, because Chris Travers had braved elements a hell of a lot more severe than a D.C. spring. His mind took him back to a mountain in Pakistan where he'd once spent three days in temperatures below zero; he'd handled that without a second thought. Granted, at the time he'd been under fire from Taliban snipers, so he had bigger fish to fry than catching a chill, but still, he told himself, tonight's ten-minute hump back to his apartment would be no big deal.

Travers had joined the army out of high school, served two years in straight-legged infantry and, with that, three tours of Iraq. He then earned his way into the Green Berets, spending three more years in 7th Special Forces Group. From there he left the military and went straight into the CIA, found his way to SAD Ground Branch, and, with his paramilitary unit, he had deployed all over the world for the past ten years.

This had been a life well spent, but he had a long-term plan for his life ahead, too. He'd earned his private and commercial pilot's licenses along the way and, he told himself, once he got too old or too beat-up for the shooting and scooting life, he'd stay with the Agency, flying spooks and techs all over the world as a pilot for Air Branch.

But that was somewhere in the future. For now he was between deployments, spending his evening alone in a bar and thinking about all his mates who didn't make it back home from Iraq, and from a dozen other shit holes of the world. He'd lost a lot of good friends, and he always dedicated his last drink of the night to them. Then he gave a silent wave to the bartender, a little wink to the waitress, whose attractiveness, like the wind outside, had increased dramatically in the time he'd been sitting on a bar stool drinking, and he headed out into the blustery night.

His apartment was on Florida, several blocks north, and it was directly into the wind, so he jammed his hands into his pockets, and leaned into it as he climbed the hill. There were next to no pedestrians out on a Sunday night, but he was careful to keep watch for movement on the sidewalk or on the street, ready to give a scrutinizing eye to anyone or anything that looked out of place.

He wasn't aware of any specific threats, but men like Travers had personal security and counter-surveillance techniques trained into their muscle memory.

He saw nothing out of the ordinary.

Court Gentry was completely enshrouded in his hoodie and neck gaiter; only his eyes, forehead, and the bridge of his nose remained visible. His hands were stuffed in his pockets, and he kept his head low into the wind. He stood on the sidewalk, three doors down from Chris Travers's apartment, and he waited for his target to appear, walking back from the pub.

Once he saw the man in the distance make the turn onto Florida, he tucked himself into a little alley that ran south off the street, found the deepest and darkest place, well out of the wind, and waited with his hand on the pistol in his jacket pocket.

He imagined Travers was probably a little drunk, but Court also knew the majority of the effects of the alcohol would disappear almost instantly when the adrenaline kicked in, so he knew he had to presume Travers would remain formidable.

Court was also aware Travers would be hardwired with every counter-surveillance protocol and tactic known to man, and he would treat everyone he saw as a potential adversary. That said, Travers could not evaluate what he could not see, so Court waited here, just out of the sight line of his quarry.

Court knew where Chris Travers lived because Court knew Chris Travers.

Travers had been an SAD Ground Branch operations officer at the same time as Gentry. While they weren't on the same task force, they had trained together from time to time and, to the extent Gentry got along with anyone, he had gotten along well with Travers.

The first time they met was in Court's early days with the Goon Squad. Travers and some of his team were assigned to play the opposition force against Court's Golf Sierra task force at a shoot house in Moyock, North Carolina. For two days Zack Hightower and his boys, all jocked up in combat gear, kicked in the doors of the shoot house and cleared rooms, opening fire on the other team, who were all dressed in robes or other Middle Eastern attire.

They fired Simunitions at one another. Plastic bullets loaded with paint that left a splotch on the clothing and blistering welts on the skin.

After the training the guys on both teams would go out to a local watering hole. For the most part the teams stayed to themselves, but Travers saddled up next to the bar alongside Court and complimented him on his skills. He asked questions of a tactical nature, bought Court a couple of drinks, and rolled his eyes when Court's team leader, Zack Hightower, told Court to stop fraternizing with the enemy and sit with his Golf Sierra unit.

The last time Gentry and Travers had run into each other had been at a funeral in D.C. Court barely knew the Ground Branch officer who'd been killed, but Zack Hightower had mandated all his team to go to the funeral because they were in town that week and few other SAD shooters were around to pay their respects.

Travers had been there; he'd been best friends with the man who had died, and after the funeral he invited all the Ground Branch men in attendance to his place, just a few blocks away. It was a two-bedroom second-floor walk-up in a part of town where 700-square-foot apartments sold for north of a million dollars. When Hightower asked Travers if he'd taken to spying for the Chinese to pay his mortgage, Travers replied that his mom owned the building and he lived here for free, and due to the deal he was getting and the convenience of the location he wouldn't think about moving as long as he was CIA.

Court remembered the location, and although he didn't know for sure if Travers was in town, as soon as he took up surveillance on the building tonight he saw the second-floor lights flip off and his old colleague step off the stoop and head south on foot.

Court had remained a hundred yards back, keeping out of the streetlights, while he tracked the distant figure to an Irish pub on 19th Street. Confident he'd return home after a few drinks, Court retraced his steps and found an alley nearby with a place to sit and wait.

He told himself it was Sunday night, and he doubted Travers would hang out at the bar till last call.

He'd been wrong. Court was bored and freezing now, but not for much longer, so he shook his arms and stamped his feet to prepare himself for action.

Travers had been a decent guy, Court remembered, but that was years ago, and in those intervening years Travers had no doubt been told that Gentry was both a rampaging murderer and an enemy of America. Court was here to talk to his old acquaintance, but he knew he had to take the other man down quick and hard. It didn't have to get bloody, but Travers would make the ultimate determination of how rough things were going to go tonight.

Now Travers passed along the sidewalk, moving abreast with the alleyway. Instinctively the man's head turned to scan for threats in the dark, but it was already too late.

Court stood there, face obscured, with his small pistol in his hands. In a tone that was measured perfectly to command attention without being loud enough to alert nearby apartment dwellers, Court said, "Hands on your head, Chris, or you die."

Travers stopped in his tracks, and his hands rose slowly. "What the fuck is this?"

"I'm going to search you for weapons, then we are going up to your place."

"Who are you?"

Court knew the man wouldn't remember his voice, and there was no way Travers would recognize him from just his eyes in a darkened alley.

"I'm only a threat if you make me a threat. I just want to have a little talk."

"You can't talk without a gun?"

"Of course I can. The gun is so *you* talk. Turn around and back up to me."

Travers complied, clearly now aware that this man not only knew his name, but he also knew Travers had some training.

Court pushed him up against the brick wall of the alleyway. While keeping his gun leveled at the man's back, Court felt over the man's waistband with his left hand. Finding nothing there, he checked Travers's pockets. He had a mobile phone, which Court slipped into his own pocket, a billfold, which Court left alone, and a set of keys, which Court took from the pocket and placed in Travers's left hand.

Court then knelt quickly and grabbed at the man's ankles. There was no ankle holster.

"I'm not carrying," Travers said.

But Court wasn't finished. He reached around to the front of the SAD operator's body, grabbed the man's belt buckle, feeling for a knife there, then he pulled Travers's shirt out of his pants and swept his hand up the man's chest.

Hanging from a chain around Travers's neck Court found a small blade in a sheath. He yanked the chain, breaking it free, and he threw it into the alley behind him.

Travers grumbled, "That cost me three hundred bucks."

Court finished the frisk and stepped back. "Bullshit. You can get them for sixty on the Internet."

"Who *are* you?"

"Move."

17

ravers led the way to his building and up his stoop, used a key on his chain to unlock the door, then climbed the stairs and entered his own apartment with a second key.

The space wasn't large, less than a thousand square feet, and the living room was only twelve by fifteen. Court turned on the overhead, and Travers began moving towards the sofa.

Court stopped him. "Not there. Sit on the mantel in front of the fireplace. Hands on your lap where I can see them."

Travers did as instructed. Court moved to the couch and, with his gun trained on the other man, yanked up the cushions.

The handle of a sheathed bowie knife jutted out of the corner where the springs met the side of the sofa.

Court pulled out the blade and tossed it on a side table. "You are just full of tricks, aren't you?"

"And you seem to know every one. Again, who the fuck *are* you?"

Court sat down in a wicker chair next to the sofa, ten feet away from the man seated on the hearth. He then lowered his neck gaiter and took his hood and his cap off his head.

"Sierra Six?"

"We both know what's about to happen."

Travers cocked his head. "Maybe you do, but I don't have a fuckin' clue."

"Sure you do. You're going to act compliant, wait for me to let my guard down a little, say a bunch of shit about how we used to be buds, and you're going to look for your opportunity. As soon as you see any chance, you're going to take it."

"Why would I—"

"Just know that I'm expecting it, and also know that as soon you fucking flinch, I'm putting three rounds through your heart."

Travers said, "I don't know why you think I'm going to attack you, and I sure as fuck don't know why you are pointing a gun at me."

"Because you're SAD, and you have orders to kill me."

"*Kill* you? What the hell are you talking about? I haven't heard your name in years."

Court was impressed. Travers did a good job selling his story.

"Bullshit."

"I swear it, man."

To that Court just replied, "Moscow."

"*Moscow?* What about Moscow?"

"Two years ago, a market a couple blocks away from where I was staying. I saw you with another dude, I didn't know him, but he was a Ground Branch–looking motherfucker. I followed you back to your hotel, the Hilton Leningradskaya, then watched you leave with your partner and four other guys. A full six-man element. I recognized Jenner. I figured him to be the team leader because he's been around since forever."

Court could see the wheels turning in Travers's brain, but to be fair, they turned fast. "Yeah. Okay, we were there. But it didn't have anything to do with you. Another op. Code worded, so I can't talk about it." He paused. Faked a little chuckle. "I didn't see you at all. That's a hell of a coincidence, I'll give you that."

"You're full of shit. You guys were on my trail. You ran a full monty surveillance op outside the place I was renting. Bad luck for you that I saw you first and left town before you got set up." Court smiled. "How long did you guys sit on the location before you realized I'd bugged out?"

Travers said, "Man . . . you're just paranoid. I'm not after—"

"I know about the shoot on sight. I know Carmichael has JSOC and SAD hunting me all over the world. I *know* that's what you were doing in Moscow. The longer you sit here and deny it, the more pissed off I get while pointing a gun at your face. Right now might be a good time to do things to minimize my anger."

Travers looked like he was going to keep up the ruse, but after a few seconds he deflated, his shoulders drooping. He gave a shrug and a nod.

"You win, Gentry." After another shrug he said, "If it makes you feel any better, I felt bad about it."

"That's a huge comfort," Court said, then added, "asshole."

"So? What are we doing? What do you want?"

"I want to know why. Why is there a shoot on sight out on me?"

Travers and Gentry made eye contact for several seconds, till Travers asked, "Why are you playing dumb?"

"Because I *am* dumb. I have a guess, but I don't know for sure. Tell me."

"*You're* the enemy of the state, not me. Don't ask me what you did."

"Come on. They told you why. What did they say?"

Travers heaved his shoulders and closed his eyes. In frustration he said, "Dude, why'd you come back here? What the hell are you trying to accomplish?"

"I'm trying to figure it out. To make it right."

"Make it *right*? Jesus H. Christ, you really do *not* know why they are after you!"

"Tell me."

Travers shrugged, and this gesture looked utterly real. "I don't know the specifics. Just that you were sent out on an op, you were given good intel and clear orders, and then went off script." Travers winced, like he didn't want to say it. "You killed the wrong dude, bro."

"What do you mean?"

"How else can I say it? You smoked the wrong guy. You capped a noncombatant. You fragged a friendly. You termed some innocent son of a bitch and fucked up the mission."

Court shook his head slowly. "No. That's not true. That must be disinformation Carmichael is using to get everyone on board with the term order. All my ops were solid. I never had an unauthorized termination."

Travers kept his eyes on the gun. "Court, I didn't get it from Carmichael. You think door-kickers like me hang out with Denny Carmichael?"

"Who told you?"

"Me and a lot of the guys asked for a full brief on the reasons behind the term order. We didn't like hunting one of our brothers, know what I mean?"

Yeah, Court thought. *I know exactly what you mean. You mean you want me to lower this pistol because I'm supposed to act like we're just members of the same big happy family.*

"We were briefed by Jordan Mayes and some big-shot lawyer from the Office of General Council. Chunky dude, German name, don't remember it. He wore this goofy bow tie, I do remember that. Anyway, he said you were derelict on a mission, but no one knew at the time. Years later intel filtered from some foreign service to Carmichael proving you zapped the wrong motherfucker. Bow tie dude told us Carmichael wanted you brought in for questioning. Your own task force was sent in to pick you up . . . and then you smoked them all." Travers hesitated before saying the last part, as if he only just understood the repercussions of having a killer of CIA officers sitting in his apartment with a gun pointed at his chest.

Court said nothing.

"You going to tell me that didn't happen, either?"

Court kept the gun up, but his body sagged a little. "They weren't bringing me in. They were sent to terminate me."

"*Term* you? Why would you be killed for schwacking an innocent person on a mission? Shit happens. You might have been cashiered from the Agency if the dereliction was bad enough, but they wouldn't *kill* you. Not for that."

Travers went on. "But once you killed your own guys . . . then it was on, bro. Denny has been after you ever since. You've done a hell of a good job hiding out, but if you kill me now, well, they'll just know you are here in town."

Court cocked his head in surprise. "Pretty sure they already know I'm here."

Travers rolled his head back as if he was looking to the heavens. "Well, I sure wish someone would have bothered to give *me* the heads-up."

"Look, you aren't going to believe me over this suit from General Council . . . but I was *not* derelict. I never fragged the wrong target. Not once. Not *ever*." He added, "And my team tried to murder me, not bring me in. I *had* to defend myself."

Travers nodded like he believed, but Court didn't think for a minute that he'd convinced him.

Travers said, "Okay. I guess they got it wrong. I'll let everybody know. That should fix things." It was sarcasm, brave considering Travers's situation, but it was clear to Court the other man wanted to show he was not afraid.

Court thought a moment. "AAP. Does that mean anything to you?"

Travers was taken aback by the question. "You mean that magazine for old people?"

"No, Chris. That's AARP. I am talking about the Autonomous Asset Program. Did this guy from General Council say anything about that?"

Travers shook his head. "I don't know what that is. He didn't mention it. Sounds stupid."

Court sagged low on the couch, frustrated and confused. But then he nodded to himself. Softly he said, "Carmichael needed an excuse to kill me, so he came up with a cover story. He had to erase the AAP. Terminate all the participants . . . But they couldn't breathe a word about it to anyone. They blamed me for some imaginary screwup."

"Whatever you say, dude," Travers said. He hadn't heard everything, because Court had been speaking to himself.

Court ignored him and stood up slowly.

"What are you going to do?" Travers asked, letting a little nervousness show in his voice now.

"I'm leaving. You are useless. You know even less about what went down than I do." Then he said, "Stand up."

Travers did so. Court reached into his coat and pulled out zip ties. The other man's eyes widened just a little, but he made no comment.

Court said, "Your lucky day, right? You know how to get out of these in five seconds. Put them on. Behind your back."

Travers followed Gentry's orders, confused. He *did* know how to defeat zip ties, even when his arms were fastened behind his back, but if Gentry knew this already, why was he using them?

When his arms were secured, Court walked up to him and spun him around. A second later Travers heard the sound of thick duct tape being pulled from a roll.

"You motherfucker," he mumbled. The zip ties were just to keep his hands down while Court restrained him in a way that would be much harder to defeat.

Five minutes later Travers's arms and hands were completely secured, from the shoulders all the way down to the fingertips, with an entire roll of duct tape. His ankles were bound with wires from two table lamps. He sat on the floor, arms outstretched behind him like a single wing, and his feet in front of him, lashed together.

Once Court was finished he knelt over the other man and surveyed his work. "You look ridiculous," he said.

"I've got to piss."

"Just think of that as additional incentive." Court patted the other man on the head. "Good to see you, Chris." He headed for the door.

"Fuck you. Seriously, how the hell am I supposed to get out of this?"

Court flipped off the overhead in the living room. The only remaining light was from the street, filtering in through the curtains. He said, "If this equation takes you more than ten minutes to solve, then you are a poor excuse for an asset." Court reached for the door latch.

Travers called after him. "Hey, Court?"

"Yeah?"

Travers paused, then said, "I'm going to tell you this as a friend. I really hope you'll take my advice. Run. Just fucking run. You had the right plan. Staying off grid, out of the States. That was working for you. There is no future to you sticking around here. Trust me on that. Now that you're here. Now that they know. They'll rain down on you with everything they have, and they *will* kill you."

"I suspect you're right," Court said, and he left Travers there, alone in the dark.

It was well after two a.m. when Court pulled into a little market and gas station a mile from his long-term storage unit in Columbia Heights. He'd been driving around for a while, rolling into, and then back out of, a half dozen other convenience store parking lots, because he was looking for a very specific setup.

He needed a place with poor CCTV camera coverage of the parking lot.

Court took it on faith that the U.S. government would have access to civilian CCTV networks here in the area. They would also have facial recognition software working to identify him as he moved around the city. While there was nothing Court could do to avoid getting picked up on cameras inside stores—he couldn't very well wear a ski mask as he shopped—he knew it was in his best interests to show neither his face nor his vehicle on camera.

Court could mitigate the risk to himself by never going to the same place more than once. By the time he was identified on camera and CIA or police arrived to investigate, hours would have passed. Court merely had to know better than to ever return. But if he allowed his image to be recorded and identified *and* he allowed his vehicle to be identified by parking it in view of a CCTV camera, then he would be screwed, because he couldn't very well change cars every time he went out into the city.

The parking lots of the first six late-night markets he pulled into had good camera coverage, with no place to park without exposing his vehicle. The seventh store, to Court's great relief, did have a couple of outdoor cameras near the pumps, but the store's owners were cutting corners and relying on the inside camera to film a portion of the lot near the window. Court only had to pull up to one side of the front window or the other, park in a space there, and then go inside.

Court stepped carefully into the Easy Market on Rhode Island with his head down. He lowered his hood, but he left his baseball cap on, low in front of his face. He moved slowly to the back corner of the establishment, far away from the register, and he pretended to look through the cooler for a drink. Soon he glanced up and around the little shop, scanning high and in the corners, searching for cameras.

And Court liked what he saw. Not only had the management here gone cheap with the cams outside; two of the cameras inside the market were hanging down with wires unplugged—clearly out of commission. A third camera was up to the right of the front register and facing down, but Court determined he could defeat it with his cap and by turning his face away from the proper angle needed for successful facial recog.

Within one minute of passing through the door, Court decided he would become a faithful customer here at the Easy Market on Rhode Island Avenue.

Court grabbed a few items off shelves—more duct tape, a few cans of food, a bottle of water, and a candy bar—then he carefully stepped up to the register at a forty-five-degree angle, with his head turned slightly to the left and the bill of his baseball cap slightly cocked to the right. A lone clerk stood behind the counter, watching his approach. She was mid-twenties, heavyset, and African American. Her nametag read LaShondra. When Court put his items up on the counter he glanced at her again and noticed she had a severely lazy left eye, with the pupil drooping down.

She looked tired, but she wore a kind smile. "Hey, baby doll, how's your night goin'?"

Baby doll? "It's goin'," Court said, looking to the left.

He paid for the tape, the canned food, the water, and the candy bar, and LaShondra put it all into a plastic bag. While he waited Court spent his time scanning reflective surfaces behind the woman, making sure there were no threats behind him. He glanced to his left, back out to the parking lot, and saw that it remained clear. He was careful, however, to avoid looking to the right, where the camera hung down pointing at him, just eight feet away.

As he left the store, careful to avoid looking up to the camera recording the front two aisles of the market, the clerk called after him, "You have a good night now, honey."

"You, too," Court muttered on his way out the door.

As he climbed into his car Court realized that he hadn't carried on such a pleasant conversation with anyone in a long time.

18

On most days of the workweek, Leland Babbitt left his Chevy Chase home around seven forty-five a.m. to make it into his office in the District by eight thirty. But this Monday morning his garage door hummed and opened at a quarter till seven, and Babbitt emerged behind the wheel of his silver Lexus and backed down the driveway out onto the street.

A black Lincoln Navigator sat parked in front of Babbitt's home, and inside it four men raised their hands towards Babbitt's car.

Babbitt acknowledged them briefly with a nod as he passed them by. He wasn't going to stop to chat with his home protection detail. He had somewhere important to be today—a clandestine rendezvous arranged with a high-profile official—so his attention was focused on beating the traffic and making it to his destination in plenty of time.

A half hour later Babbitt parked in the lot by the Capitol reflecting pool, climbed out of his Lexus, and pulled on a trench coat, and then he began walking west along the National Mall.

Leland Babbitt was director of Townsend Government Services, a private intelligence and security firm that worked on classified projects for the United States intelligence community. Townsend had been around for 150 years, making a big name in an extremely low-profile industry by employing some of the best headhunters in the world. Townsend had gotten its start in the old West when its investigators tracked down train robbers, bank robbers, even marauding renegade Indians. In the following century Townsend hunted Nazis and Russian spies, it helped catch Noriega and Serbian war criminals, and in the 2000s it had a hand in the capture of Saddam Hussein as well as many of the leadership of al Qaeda and other terrorist organizations.

But on its most recent mission Townsend Government Services had failed unequivocally.

Leland Babbitt and his company had been chasing the Gray Man for years on a cost-plus contract with the U.S. government. They'd come to within a hair's breadth of killing him in Brussels; Babbitt himself had been there at the scene during the gun battle. Unfortunately for everyone, Gentry had escaped, and in the process he'd killed some of Babbitt's men and wounded others.

The shoot-out in Brussels had been a major news event, of course, and although Babbitt had managed to avoid exposure in the media for himself and his firm, since Brussels, Denny Carmichael had treated Lee Babbitt like he had the plague. The Director of the National Clandestine Service had flatly refused every meeting, every teleconference, even private phone conversations with the director of Townsend since he'd returned to the U.S. Only a few clipped and businesslike e-mails had come from Carmichael to Babbitt, and these made clear that NCS was indefinitely suspending its contracts with Townsend and removing the private firm's access to classified material.

Babbitt understood Carmichael's frustrations in a general sense. For some reason Carmichael's involvement in the Gentry hunt was very personal, so after the debacle in Europe it was no surprise that the head of NCS would naturally try to scapegoat Townsend. But Lee Babbitt had grown weary of the cold shoulder, and he was determined to end his company's exile from clandestine work and get things back on track.

To this end Babbitt had e-mailed Carmichael over the weekend, insisting the two men sit for a face-to-face to put the matter to rest. Babbitt took into account the fact Carmichael was obviously trying to distance himself publicly from the happenings in Belgium, so he suggested an old-fashioned clandestine rendezvous. He gave Carmichael directions to a quiet location, told him he'd be there at seven thirty ready to do whatever he needed to do to end the rift and reboot the important mutual relationship between Townsend and the CIA.

Denny Carmichael hadn't exactly agreed to the meeting, but he had not expressly declined it either, and Babbitt felt like Denny would come to the realization that a continued partnership between CIA and Townsend Government Services was in everyone's best interests.

Denny would show, he told himself.

Babbitt had mentally prepared himself for a verbal beating from the grizzled spymaster. He knew his company hadn't done what the CIA had sent it to do, but he was ready to spin it by reminding Carmichael that he had gotten closer to Gentry than the CIA had, and Carmichael should simply send Babbitt back out after the Gray Man.

Court Gentry had lived out his nine lives. Next time they would get him for sure.

Babbitt walked directly from his car to the meeting site. He knew he should have conducted some sort of surveillance direction route, but this was the fucking USA, and he was certain nobody was tailing him. Plus, he was too angry and focused on returning his forces to the Gentry hunt to devote attention to anything other than getting to his rendezvous and giving the person he'd meet there a very measured dose of his rage.

While Babbitt walked to his destination, thinking about how much he wanted just one more opportunity to hunt Court Gentry again, the object of his thoughts was exactly one hundred fifty yards away, jogging along the National Mall, doing his best to catch up to the man in the Burberry trench coat before he lost him.

Gentry had been on the man's tail since just before dawn. He'd found Babbitt's home in Chevy Chase on USCrypto.org, and he'd parked his car in a little lot in front of a pair of tennis courts near a country club. He'd used the cover of the thick foliage on the edge of a golf course to get close to Babbitt's property, and then he'd spent a cold, miserable hour under a magnolia tree in a neighbor's yard surveilling the house.

Court hadn't been surprised to see Babbitt had a security detail at his place; he was, after all, president of a security firm. A black SUV with four men sat parked in front, and two more men wandered the acre of property.

Court stayed well out of sight of any curious eyes, just squatting there against the tree trunk, watching the house.

At six forty-five the garage door opened and Babbitt rolled down the drive in his silver Lexus. Court didn't stick around to see where he went; instead he jogged back across a golf course to his car. He had just climbed behind the wheel when the Lexus passed in front of him on Connecticut, and he fell into an easy tail behind it.

Babbitt drove straight towards the city, finally parking in a lot near the Capitol building's reflecting pool. He climbed out and began walking towards the National Mall.

Court was confused. He'd assumed the man would be heading to his office, which, Court knew, was in the Townsend Government Services building in Adams Morgan. But instead of this, Court now found himself scrambling to find a parking space and to begin a hasty one-man foot-follow operation.

Court found a spot for his Escort just south of the mall and jogged back to where he had last seen Babbitt. Using his binoculars he caught a quick glimpse of his target at a distance as he walked west along Madison Drive. Court picked up his pace to catch up to him—the area was full of early-Monday-morning joggers, so Court didn't stand out save for the fact he was wearing brown work boots—and slipped into a tailing position sixty-five yards behind. Soon Babbitt turned right into the Smithsonian Gardens Butterfly Habitat, a set of two footpaths that ran through a thick garden of various types of dense foliage.

Court doubted Babbitt was so into butterflies that he'd begin his work-week with them, so he presumed Babbitt was here for some sort of a clandestine meet.

Of course Court knew there was also a chance Babbitt was here for a Monday-morning hookup with a girlfriend, or a boyfriend for that matter, but the more Court thought about it, the more he wondered if the director of Townsend was here to link up with someone senior in the CIA.

Maybe even Carmichael?

It was almost too much to hope for, a lightly protected CIA exec, a man directly invested in the hunt for Gentry, out in the open where Gentry could bag him on just Gentry's second full day of his op here in the U.S.

But Court thought it was possible.

He knew Leland Babbitt ran a private military company here in D.C. They had been part of the chase and they had nearly gotten him in Stockholm and in Hamburg. In Brussels they had gotten so close Court now wore a bright red scar in the shape of a bullet hole on his right forearm.

Court wondered if Townsend was hunting him here in D.C., as well.

He found himself getting excited that Denny Carmichael might just walk up the narrow path any minute. If he did, Court would deal with whatever security force Denny had with him. This wouldn't be easy, but the opportunity would be too good to pass up.

Then Court would find a way to get Denny back to his car, take him to his storage unit, and beat the truth out of him.

"Settle down, Gentry," he said to himself. Bagging and zip-tying a nation's chief spook wouldn't be easy anywhere, not even in Paraguay or Namibia. Here in D.C. surely it would be virtually impossible.

Court forced himself to lower his sights a little. If Carmichael showed, Court would evaluate the situation. He doubted he could bag the man himself, so he'd just watch, listen in if he could, and wait for them to part ways. He'd stay on mission, following Babbitt back to his car and taking him at gunpoint as he climbed in.

Babbitt remained the target.

Court moved a little closer, then tucked himself into the foliage of the butterfly habitat and watched his target from behind and one hundred feet away. He placed the Walker's Game Ear behind his right ear and turned the volume up.

19

While Leland Babbitt sat on a bench in an outdoor butterfly garden near the U.S. Capitol building staring at his watch and wondering when the hell Denny Carmichael would show up, Carmichael was five and a half miles to the west, sitting in his seventh-floor office at CIA, sipping coffee and reading his morning Violator Working Group report.

The report started on a down note. There had been a grand total of zero positive IDs of Gentry the day before. Facial recog had gotten quite a few possible sightings, and analysts in the Violator task force were evaluating these hits now, but Brewer said she'd looked at all the images and to her nothing appeared terribly promising.

That was the bad news. The good news was that the facial recognition software had been tweaked and retooled overnight, using some newer images of Gentry taken from security camera images out of Belgium, and the technicians felt confident they would, sooner or later, pick him out from the millions of human faces from thousands of video feeds in the D.C. metro area.

Still, Denny had his doubts the Violator operations center would get much out of facial recognition. No, Gentry was too good for that. He would mask himself a dozen different ways to spoof the software.

Next in the report Brewer wrote that JSOC operatives were up and running in the city, ready to be vectored to the right location as soon as there was more information to go on. Two men were also over watching the home of SAD director Matthew Hanley, in the hopes Gentry would show up to question—or to kill—his former boss.

The report also confirmed that thirty contracted assets were on station in the area watching known associates of Violator.

This wasn't in the report, of course, but Carmichael also knew the Saudis would be deployed in the District. He hadn't spoken with Kaz since he'd left him in the Kimpton in Alexandria the afternoon before, but Carmichael knew Kaz would waste no time getting his operation in gear.

Carmichael was confident one of the myriad elements involved in the hunt would locate Gentry soon, but he also suspected the action would really only start the second Gentry did something to expose himself to the hunters. He would make his play, contact a known associate or show himself at a CIA facility, and CIA would be ready.

And while Mayes sent JSOC and other assets, Denny would send the Saudis to cover any escape.

Court Gentry was going to die here in D.C., Carmichael felt certain. The only real worry was making sure it happened without either the media or the Department of Justice finding out about it.

Just then his intercom beeped. His secretary's voice came over the speaker. "Sorry, sir, I know you asked not to be disturbed, but Department Director Hanley is here to see you."

Carmichael put down the report and pushed the call button. "I didn't see an appointment on the calendar."

"No, sir. But he is insistent."

Of course he is, Carmichael thought. "Prick," he said aloud, then he pushed the talk button again. "Send him in."

Matthew Hanley was a burly man, like a college linebacker who'd hit his fifties much harder than he would have liked, but still retained the ability to kick a much younger man's ass if it came down to it. When he entered through the doorway Carmichael noted the SAD director filled the door frame nearly as completely as he filled his gray flannel suit, and it wasn't until he stepped fully into the office that Denny realized Hanley had another man in tow.

Carmichael offered a fake smile, but he didn't stand or step around his desk to offer a handshake. "Morning, Matt. What is it that couldn't wait till you got on my calendar? And who's this?"

Hanley said, "This is Travers. He's on Jenner's team."

"Travers," Carmichael said, his version of a greeting, and he scooped up the paperwork in front of him, anxious to get back to it.

Hanley's voice was twice as loud as Carmichael's now. "Tell me you did *not* know Court Gentry was here in the city!"

Carmichael lowered his paperwork again and looked back up. Suddenly he found himself significantly more interested in this impromptu meeting. "You saw him?"

Hanley's jaw tightened. "Son of a bitch, Denny! You knew?"

"Shut the door and come in."

Hanley nearly slammed the door, then he and Travers stepped over to Carmichael's desk. Travers remained standing, while Hanley took the chair.

Before anyone spoke Carmichael hit a button on the console on his desk. "Get Mayes in here. Now." He turned his attention back to Hanley and asked, "What did he say?"

Hanley jerked his head to the man left standing. "Ask Travers."

Carmichael raised an eyebrow and looked to the younger man. "Talk."

Travers was clearly nervous standing in the office of the legendary Denny Carmichael, but he composed himself. "He got me at gunpoint last night."

Carmichael snapped back, "I thought you guys were supposed to be good."

Travers did not reply, but Hanley spoke in his defense. "Come on. It's Gentry we're talking about."

"Right," said Carmichael. Quickly he looked down to Brewer's report. On the last page was a list of Gentry's known associates that she had covered with watchers. There was no mention of Travers on the list.

He looked back up to the Ground Branch officer. "Did you two know each other?"

"Barely. I'd met him a couple of times. We'd trained together some at Harvey Point and at Blackwater, and I had the Golf Sierra team over to my apartment once after a funeral. That's how he knew where I lived."

"I see he let you go. Why do you think he did that?"

"Because I didn't have what he wanted."

"And that was?"

"Answers. Just answers. He wanted to know what he did to initiate the SOS. I told him what I knew. That he waxed the wrong target on an op and then killed his team when they tried to detain him. He said he didn't fuck up, and his team fired first."

Carmichael shook his head. "He knows what happened. He's here trying to get intel on the executives involved in his hunt. He'll target us, one by one, to exact his revenge."

Hanley asked, "How long has he been here?"

"Less than thirty-six hours. I'm confident we'll have him in hand soon enough. We have control of the situation."

"Undoubtedly," replied Hanley. "And by 'control' you mean Gentry is allowed to wander the city freely with a gun in his hand while he targets the homes of Agency employees. What's the game plan, Denny? You just trying to lull him into a false sense of security before you drop the cage down over him?"

Carmichael rolled his eyes. "He was your man when he went off reservation."

"And it was because of *your* order that he went off rez!"

Travers looked back and forth between the two men, his mouth shut tightly. Like most CIA officers he was good at keeping secrets, but he couldn't fucking *wait* to tell the other guys on his team about standing up here in Carmichael's office watching the old man and Hanley duke it out.

Jordan Mayes entered the room now, and Carmichael filled him in. As soon as he finished, Mayes turned to the younger paramilitary officer. "Travers, when you leave here I want you to go find Suzanne Brewer. Tell her every last detail."

Hanley was confused. "What does Brewer have to do with Gentry?"

Mayes replied, "She's running the TOC."

Hanley sighed. "Brewer from Programs and Plans knows all about this, but the director of the Special Activities Division does not? Why is that, Denny? Why am I not involved? If Gentry is a legitimate danger, then why wasn't I told?"

"Calm down, you've been protected."

"What the hell does that mean?"

"I've had a team of operatives watching your house."

"Without my knowledge?"

Carmichael just shrugged. "I've had a lot on my plate. I was getting to it."

"*What* operatives? You can't task my guys without informing me."

"They aren't your guys." Carmichael hesitated. "They are part of a special mission unit from JSOC."

Hanley looked like he'd been poleaxed. He leaned all the way back in his chair. In a nearly hoarse voice he said, "What in the name of God are you doing?"

"I wasn't planning on using SAD. I have sanction to pull certain military assets from—"

"Why?" Hanley quickly put a hand up in the air. "Why not tell me and call up Ground Branch assets?" He sat up straighter in his chair and raised a finger. "I get it. You are using me as bait."

Carmichael grinned like a cornered dog showing his teeth. "He'll try to make contact with you. You *know* he will."

"Meaning . . . you think he'll try to kill me."

Carmichael did not respond for a moment. Finally he picked up the report again. "You'll be safe."

"Despite your best attempts to keep me out of the loop, Gentry has made other arrangements. Now I am involved, whether you like it or not. I know what's going on here, and I know you are doing your best to keep this whole thing under wraps. For the sake of the Agency I hope you do keep a lid on it. If U.S. military forces go loud on the streets of Washington, D.C., some really curious folks are going to want to know why."

Carmichael replied, "I am well aware of that." He drummed his fingers on the table now. "I suppose some support from Ground Branch wouldn't hurt. Why don't you task a few elements to my Violator Working Group? We can involve them in the hunt, wrap this up even faster."

Matt Hanley shook his head with a laugh. "You've got some brass balls, Denny. Trying to suck me into your debacle in the making so I'll be invested in the outcome? No thank you."

"I will remind you that I am your superior. Your men are, ultimately, mine to do with as I see fit."

Hanley stood. "Can't argue with you there. My guys are at your disposal." He started to turn for the door. Then he stopped himself and turned back. "Of course, I can always drop by the director's office. On something this big, you don't mind if I check with him just to make sure everything is squared away."

Carmichael's jaw flexed. "On second thought, maybe SAD should sit this one out. I'm sure your operational tempo is keeping your forces busy."

"As a bee," said Hanley.

It was quiet now as two men who neither trusted nor liked each other squared off. Finally Carmichael looked back down to his paperwork and said, "Now, if you'll excuse me, I have a lot of work on my desk."

The meeting was over but, to the surprise of the senior executives, Chris Travers spoke up. "Sorry. Can I ask a question, sir?"

Carmichael looked up, annoyed. "What is it?"

"If Gentry really did what we accuse him of . . . why the hell would he come back, grab me like he did, question me like he did . . . and then just leave? I've been thinking about it all night. If he wanted to hunt down the people after him, why expose himself like that? He's too smart to give away a tactical advantage."

Hanley looked to Carmichael, his eyebrows raised, waiting to hear the older man's response.

Carmichael said, "I have stopped trying to understand all of Gentry's motivations. Did it make sense that he would eliminate his team and go on the run like that?"

Travers said, "If what he says is true . . . if they *did* shoot first . . . then, yeah, it does make sense. I love my team like brothers. But if they draw guns on me, I'm gonna do the same to them, and somebody's gonna die."

Carmichael said, "Son, you are not cleared for the op that got Gentry in hot water in the first place, so you are not cleared for anything that Gentry told you last night. That means the questions you are asking me are out of line."

Mayes took over now, ending the meeting by ushering Hanley and Travers towards the door.

As they walked off Hanley put an arm around his younger employee. In a voice loud enough for all to hear Hanley said, "Don't feel bad, Chris. I'm not cleared for it, either. Denny is the only one in the building with enough juice to know what Court did to put him in the CIA's crosshairs. I bet Mayes here is flying as blind as the rest of us."

The two men left the room. Mayes shut the door, then turned back to Carmichael. Carmichael said, "Don't worry about Hanley. Despite his posturing, he's in this as deep as me. If we leave him alone, he'll continue to play ball."

Mayes said, "I'm not worried about Hanley. He makes noise, but he always comes around. He knows you are the law around here, not the director. I am, however, a little concerned about this Travers. I could see him becoming a problem."

Carmichael nodded and said, "Agreed. He's unreliable. I don't want him operational until the Violator situation is resolved." Carmichael quickly put up a hand. "Belay that. I want him out. All the way out."

Mayes whistled. "Hanley is going to fight that tooth and nail."

"Come up with something. Unfit for duty. Sketchy psych eval. Doctored blood work. Whatever. Hanley won't be able to contest a positive drug screen."

The intercom buzzed again, and Carmichael's secretary said, "Sir, you have an urgent call from Leland Babbitt."

Carmichael rolled his eyes. "I forgot. That bastard e-mailed me on Saturday, basically demanded I meet him this morning."

Mayes said, "I don't want you leaving the building again unless it's to go to a safe house."

Carmichael chuckled without smiling. "I'm not going anywhere." He pushed the button for his secretary. "Put him through."

20

ourt Gentry stood tucked into the dense foliage of the Smithsonian's butterfly sanctuary, watching Leland Babbitt from a distance of one hundred feet.

His high hopes for getting his eyes on Denny Carmichael took their first hit of the day when he noticed Babbitt continually checking his watch. Then he began nervously pacing back and forth, and soon it became clear that whoever Babbitt was here to meet was late.

At eight fifteen Babbitt pulled out his phone and dialed a number. Court wouldn't be able to hear the conversation; his high-powered earpiece was picking up every bird chirp and passing vehicle so he turned it off, and instead he just stood there in the bushes, looking on.

eland Babbitt continued pacing, waiting for Carmichael to come on the phone. When he finally did, Babbitt looked up and down the path before speaking quickly and quietly, spending no time on pleasantries. "It's a quarter after eight, Denny. You were supposed to be here a half hour ago."

Denny Carmichael replied, "I didn't agree to come at all. I just said I'd think about it."

"Oh, come on, Denny. We *need* a face-to-face."

"No, we don't. You and I won't be doing any face-to-face meetings any time soon. I don't want you at Langley, of course, and I sure as hell don't want to set foot at Townsend in light of all the exposure you've had in the past two weeks."

Babbitt's voice rose and fell with desperation. "I get that. That's why I proposed off-site. A neutral location. You and me. We can put this to bed and move forward."

Carmichael said, "Lee. Let's give it the time it needs to die down."

Babbitt gritted his teeth. His fleshy jowls rolled with the movement. "You aren't going to leave me to swing in the wind on this."

"For now, Lee, that's exactly what I'm doing."

"You pulled our access to classified data. How the fuck are we supposed to stay in business?"

"I have no doubt that Townsend will be able to find lucrative security contracts in the commercial sector."

"We're American patriots! We're not *fucking* mall cops!"

Carmichael did not respond.

After taking a moment to calm himself, Babbitt said, "You aren't the only game in town, you know."

"Was that some sort of a threat?"

"It is what it is."

Carmichael growled, "Fuck you, Babbitt."

"No, Denny, fuck you. As a matter of fact, I think I'll do just that right now."

Lee Babbitt hung up the phone, stood up from the bench, and reached back like he was going to throw the phone into the trees. But he stopped himself, slipped it back in his pocket, and began walking up the path towards the National Mall.

Babbitt walked back out onto the road running alongside the National Mall with Gentry trailing two hundred feet behind, and while the butterfly sanctuary had been nearly empty, the road and the mall were chock-full of commuters, morning walkers and joggers, patrolling cops, and tourists.

Court wouldn't be pulling his gun on anyone right here, right now.

Babbitt walked right past his car in the lot at the reflecting pool and continued on.

Court stopped under a cherry tree, not yet in bloom, and he let Babbitt go. To Court's surprise, the big man headed straight towards the Capitol building.

Softly, Court said, "What the hell are you doing now?"

Babbitt disappeared heading into the East Portico, and Gentry headed south, back in the direction of his car.

As he walked he took his hand off the small Ruger pistol he carried in the left-hand pocket of his jacket, and he used the same hand to pull his baseball cap down lower over his eyes. His right hand remained in his pants pocket, which kept his sore arm from swinging while he walked.

He stopped at a hot dog cart on the mall, bought a bottled water, and drank a few sips while he stood there, allowing himself one last glance at the U.S. Capitol. This was his first real look at the building since he'd been back in town, the first time he took the opportunity to take in any of the sights here in D.C.

For five long years he'd been outside of the USA, and each and every day during that time he'd thought something of home. Now that he was back he couldn't allow himself the luxury of devoting any real time to enjoying himself, to relaxing, or to appreciating his triumphant return, such as it was. But for just this moment he gazed upon one of the greatest structures in America, and he felt the power of the symbol and the love for his country in his heart, deep in his bones.

He shook away the moment. Despite the emotions welling inside him, it would not do to stop and stare. He was in cover, and his cover wasn't some wide-eyed foreign tourist.

And if he blew his cover now, agents of the America he loved so much would find him and shoot him dead in the street.

But his cover was solid, because unlike all of his other operations, in this rare case his cover identity matched his true identity. He *was* American. He'd been gone for a while, but he was still American, and now he was home.

Court tossed the empty water bottle in a garbage can, turned, and headed back to his car, still wondering what the hell Babbitt was planning on doing in the Capitol.

Leland Babbitt stormed through the rotunda of the U.S. Capitol, his Burberry coat whipping along with his brisk gait. He waved his credentials to make his way towards the congressional offices. It was just after eight thirty a.m. and he had no idea who would be here this early, but Congress was in session, so at least legislators were in town.

His mind raced as he tried to decide where to go for help.

He knew Mike Avery, a Republican senator from Utah and the president pro tem. Avery was one of the most powerful personalities in Congress, and Babbitt liked the man. But Avery wasn't particularly interested in matters involving the intelligence community and Homeland Security, so Babbitt eliminated him from his list of potential recipients of his bombshell.

He also knew Joel Landers, the Democratic congressman from New Mexico who chaired the House Permanent Select Committee on intelligence. Landers was a firebrand, always looking for something to bitch about when it came to the CIA. Babbitt thought about everything he knew concerning Carmichael and his five-year-long hunt to kill an American citizen.

Yeah, Representative Landers would *love* to hear his story.

Of course, Babbitt knew what he was doing was professional suicide; he'd never get another government contract if he sold Carmichael out, even if Carmichael was led off to Club Fed in chains, but Babbitt knew he could still write books and give lucrative seminars on corporate security.

He'd never work in this town again, as the saying went, but he *would* find work, and, more importantly, he'd take down Denny Carmichael.

Babbitt continued towards Representative Landers's office. Even if Joel wasn't in yet, he could camp out in his outer office till he showed and ask for five minutes as soon as he came in, and in those five minutes Babbitt knew he would blow the congressman's mind.

He pushed through a group of legislative aides standing in the hall and found himself just fifty feet from the representative's office when a young man in a gray suit passing on his left in the corridor turned suddenly into his path.

"Sir, may I speak with you a moment?"

"What about?" snapped Babbitt.

"Director Carmichael has asked me to intercept you before you do anything you will regret."

Immediately Babbitt's pounding heart skipped a beat. His eyes narrowed. "You tell your boss that he had his chance to make this right. Now it's *my* move."

"You should tell him yourself. He'd like you to come to Langley. Now."

"*Would* he? I bet he would. No thanks. I—"

A second man appeared from nowhere; he loomed behind on Babbitt's left, put a hand on Babbitt's shoulder, and leaned in uncomfortably close.

"We can take my car. We'll have you right back here in no time."

Another hand squeezed his right shoulder now. Babbitt turned to look, and a third man had materialized from thin air. They were all under thirty, all wearing suits, and they looked at him with pleasant smiles that, Babbitt knew, would disappear quickly if he did not do exactly what Carmichael wanted him to do.

"Fine," he said, shaking the hands off his shoulders. "Let's go talk to Denny."

21

eland Babbitt knew relations between Townsend and the CIA had never been worse, but the fact that he was here, walking down the corridor on the seventh floor at Langley, meant he still had the juice, and this pleased him greatly.

The drive to McLean had passed in silence. For much of it *complete* silence, because the moment Babbitt pulled out his phone to call his office and inform them he would be running late, one of the young men sitting next to him in the back of the Yukon took Babbitt's phone out of his hand and said, "Sorry, sir. Operational security. No calls until we leave headquarters." The phone disappeared into the jacket of the helpful yet ominous CIA officer.

At Langley Babbitt was processed quickly and placed in an elevator that took him directly up to the top floor. As the elevator door opened he was met by Jordan Mayes, who shook Babbitt's hand as if today were just any other garden-variety day, and the impending meeting was nothing more than another discussion about contracts, fiscal year budgeting, or logistical allocations.

Babbitt waited in a conference room for several minutes; he and Mayes made a little small talk but there wasn't much to it, and then Denny Carmichael entered, wrinkled and rail thin, as always. Carmichael always looked to Babbitt like a combat-hardened Abe Lincoln, as if the sixteenth president had spent his twenties through his forties fighting in the Third World, as Carmichael had.

Regal yet menacing.

Patriarchal yet savage.

Denny sat down at the table, folded his hands in front of him. Babbitt knew he'd get right to it, because that was Carmichael's way.

The head of the Clandestine Service said, "Very well, Lee. You win this round."

"What does that mean?"

"I don't want you talking to Congress. Our temporary discord is not as important as the long-term headache that would create."

"So?"

"So, we'll fold you back into the hunt for Courtland Gentry."

Babbitt had wanted to hear just this out of Carmichael's mouth, but when he did hear it, he instantly became suspicious. "That quick? You went from 'fuck you' to 'all's well' just like that?"

Denny shook his head. "Negative. The 'fuck you' remains in place. Threatening to reveal intelligence pisses me off, but I'm nothing if not a pragmatist. I can't stop you with a stick, so I'll wave a carrot, see if that does the trick."

Babbitt had won, and he knew it. He fought a wide grin and a fist pump into the air by focusing immediately on the job at hand. "Excellent. Obviously I've been out of the loop for the last several weeks so I'll need to get back up to speed. Does the Agency have any new confirmed sightings of Court Gentry since Brussels?"

There was no hint of a pause from Carmichael. "No. None at all. Our analysts speculate he has melted back into Central Europe." Carmichael turned to Mayes. "How about it, Jordan? Any intel more current than that?"

Jordan Mayes shook his head, an expression of gravity and disappointment. "The trail is cold, I'm afraid. We certainly could use some help."

Babbitt appreciated the conciliation all around. He said, "Expect that to change in short order now that Townsend Government Services is back in action." He cleared his throat. "While we're all here together, let's go over my terms."

Carmichael's eyes narrowed. "Your *what*?"

"Terms . . . I want in. Back in on everything."

"What does that mean?"

"I want the suspension of all our contracts to be rescinded, our clearance to be reinstated."

"I'm fine with that."

"And I want to see submissions from you for new contracts. New opportunities on the horizon we can bid on. This Violator hunt isn't your only big operation."

Carmichael raised an eyebrow. "It seems as if you are trying to leverage your newfound position into increased government contracts."

Babbitt smiled. He was all smiles now. He had the CIA right where he wanted them. "Face it, Denny, I'm the only game in town."

"Of course you are."

The meeting lasted another ten minutes. Babbitt had expected it to go even longer, but Carmichael said he had another appointment that could not wait.

Carmichael and Mayes watched Babbitt leave the conference room with an unmistakable saunter in his step.

As soon as the door shut, Carmichael looked to Mayes and sighed. "He's got to go."

Mayes just nodded, knowing exactly what his boss meant by the statement. "I concur. And it needs to happen soon."

"How?"

Mayes had an answer ready. "Hightower."

Denny blew out a chest full of air while he thought. "Will he do it?"

Mayes said, "Back in the Goon Squad, Zack Hightower would do anything we told him to. He sure as hell looked gung ho yesterday."

"He did, didn't he?" Carmichael drummed his fingers on his desk. "All right. Turn him loose. But no blowbacks on us."

Mayes said, "Right." He thought a moment. "Denny, we might want to look at this as something of an opportunity."

"I'm way ahead of you."

"I had a feeling you might be. Hightower terminates Babbitt, we float the intel in-house it was Gentry."

"If nothing else it will light a fire under Suzanne Brewer and the targeting officers. Show them just how dangerous their target is." Denny picked up his paperwork and reached for his glasses. "Talk to Hightower."

Zack Hightower had spent the first part of the morning on the fourth floor of the Old HQ building, working with Suzanne Brewer on possible staging locations Violator might use here in D.C. Former haunts in the area, suitable locations to train and store materiel. They also discussed his knowledge of current and former SAD weapon caches on the East Coast, thinking it possible Gentry would try to raid a stockpile somewhere to acquire more equipment.

Zack had enjoyed this work for about half an hour, but since then he'd been bored. This was analytical shit, not his forte. He wanted to be out in the field, in the city, man-hunting.

At noon Brewer had a lunch of Chinese food brought in to the tactical operations center, and Zack was seated at a desk picking through his shrimp lo mein when Jordan Mayes stepped into the room and hurried over. "I need to speak with you."

Zack put down his cardboard carton and his chopsticks, stood smartly, and stepped into the hallway. Mayes looked back to Brewer as he headed out himself. "I'll have him for the rest of the day. Maybe tomorrow, as well."

Hightower fought a smile. "It's party time!" he told himself.

The two men went upstairs to Mayes's office. Once there, Mayes closed the door and walked over to a small sitting area. When he and Hightower were seated close together, he leaned closer still and said, "I have a problem."

Hightower always sat ramrod-straight, but he tightened his posterior chain muscles even more. "Not for long. I'll take care of it."

"You know a man named Leland Babbitt?"

"No, sir. I do not."

"He runs Townsend Government Services."

Zack nodded. "I know those assholes."

Mayes sighed, adopting a worried look on his face. "Babbitt has made himself a clear and present danger to our operation at the Agency. We have tried to dissuade him from this, but he persists. He has threatened to go public detailing some classified intelligence programs that, if revealed, would be devastating for our mission here." He shook his head, an expression of disbelief. "There is no question but that these revelations will put good men and women in the field at great personal risk. Frankly, Zack, at this point, we have exhausted all of our options."

Zack Hightower grasped instantly that he was being asked to assassinate an American citizen in the United States. He blinked hard at this realization.

But only once. "I'll take care of it."

"I need you to do this alone."

"Of course you do. Don't worry. I'll get it done."

"Denny and I are more than confident that you will. Of course I can help you with any equipment you might need."

Zack smiled now. "Mr. Mayes, this might come as a shock to you, but I've already got a couple of tools that should be suitable for the task at hand."

Mayes just said, "I had a feeling you might."

22

Raphael and his brother Raul had no clue their customer was going to murder them, not even when two of the customer's business associates entered their garage and pulled the bay doors down, cutting off any chance for their escape.

They had no real reason to be concerned. After all, the brothers had done quality work in the short time frame demanded by their customer, and he stood before them now, clearly more than pleased with the results.

Murquin al-Kazaz was the customer, and they had an inkling he was a dangerous man, but they couldn't have known he was a Saudi intelligence operative. Not that they would have really cared. The brothers ran a small chop shop operation just outside of Baltimore, so they dealt with all sorts of shady characters on a daily basis. They'd never done work for a foreign spy, as far as they knew, but they had no aversion to such a customer, as long as he had cash.

Their specialty was high-speed paint- and bodywork that could make a stolen car unrecognizable, even to its owner, along with changing out VIN numbers and tags. They offered other services, as well, for a premium, of course, and it was one of these special orders that would hasten them on to the end of their lives.

But for the moment they just stood there, nodded at the two new men who'd entered and closed the bay doors. Before they could ask what was going on their customer told the brothers that he and his colleagues just wanted to make sure no one on the street saw the three vehicles parked in the garage. Raphael and Raul did not protest, chiefly because they thought they were seconds away from making a lot of money from the man who now praised them while kneeling down next to one of the cars and running his hand back and forth over the blue decal that read Metropolitan Police, Washington, D.C.

Kaz marveled at the work done by the two Puerto Rican brothers. It wasn't just that they had turned three regular used Ford Tauruses into the spitting image of D.C. Metro police cruisers—it was that they had managed to accomplish this in only twelve hours.

Kaz had come up with this plan some time ago, long before he knew the Gray Man would show up in Washington, D.C. Two years earlier he envisioned a number of scenarios where he would need to move men, armed men in disguise, throughout the city on either direct action or counterintelligence missions. He had his agents travel to Ohio and purchase three lightly used late-model Ford Taurus sedans at auction, and then they brought the cars back to the D.C. area, where they stored them in a long-term garage just outside of Springfield.

The Ford Taurus was the same body style as the Ford Police Interceptor sold to the Metro Police Department, so Kaz purchased the cars with the intent to turn them into mock police cruisers.

After obtaining the vehicles, he searched the area via his deep back channels in the criminal underworld, looking for a person or business that had the high workmanship and low morals that he needed. He found these two brothers in Baltimore. Their chop shop had run below the radar of the local authorities, but one of the Saudi's contacts knew about them, and he passed the info on to Kaz.

Al-Kazaz bought the lights off of old junked police cars and he had all the decals needed for each cruiser created by a company in China off of detailed digital images his men had made of real D.C. police vehicles. He then had the decals brought into the U.S. via the diplomatic pouch.

After this, he waited. Kaz knew the minute he converted the three normal Fords into police cruisers he would be committing a serious crime, and he did not need them for his work immediately, so he decided it would be prudent to keep everything under lock and key until he had use for the cars. He stored the decals and lights and sirens on embassy property, locked in a storage room accessible only to intelligence officers. The three Tauruses remained in the underground lot, and the phone number of Raphael and Raul stood at the ready in his contact list.

Until yesterday afternoon.

Now Kaz rose up from his close inspection of the last cruiser with a smile on his face. "Gentlemen, I must congratulate you again on your incredible workmanship."

Raphael did the talking, because Raul's English wasn't good enough to understand the foreign accent of the customer. "No problem. Like I said, the paint and glaze run eighteen hundred total. The labor is three grand for each car. That's ten thousand, eight hundred."

Kaz nodded again, and he looked at both men. They stood right next to the rear of the third white cruiser. "A fair price, I am sure," he said. "Shall we all step into your office to complete the transaction?"

The office was above the garage, up a small set of stairs.

Raphael shook his head. "We don't leave the garage when it's open. Somebody could show up and steal something. You brought cash?"

Kaz said, "Yes. Of course." He backed away from the pristine white car a few feet, hoping the two Puerto Rican brothers would follow. Instead Raphael said, "Where are you goin'?"

Kaz made to reach into his coat. "Just getting the money. I want to count it, maybe the light is better here closer to the door."

Raphael looked up at the powerful lights illuminating the Ford Tauruses. "The light don't get no better than this right here. Just count out the money on the hood so we can all see it."

Kaz had been trying to get the men to step away from the car to avoid a mess, but now he just blew out a long sigh of frustration and looked to his two associates with a shrug.

Raphael said, "The money?"

"Oh, yes. Of course. I have it all right here." His hand disappeared into his coat and then reemerged holding a suppressed Walther P99 semiautomatic pistol. Both brothers raised their hands in surprise, but the Saudi shot them where they stood, dropping Raphael straight down to the floor with a shot to the head, and then spinning Raul twice with two rounds to the chest. The heavyset Puerto Rican slammed into the right rear quarter panel of the closest Taurus, and he died with his body draped over the trunk of the vehicle.

"*Waa faqri!*" Kaz shouted. *Dammit.*

He jerked his head to the dead man on the car and one of his two operatives stepped over to the body, pulled it from the back of the Ford, and allowed it to slide down to the floor of the garage.

A large blood smear remained on the vehicle.

"Clean it up," Kaz demanded.

Twenty minutes later three D.C. Metro Police Department cruisers left the chop shop hidden in a tractor-trailer the Saudis had had waiting outside. The big rig drove south to Virginia, where the Saudis dropped the trailer off in a leased parking lot in Rosslyn, a neighborhood of Arlington, just across the Potomac River from D.C.

A two-story gated home backed up to the lot, and this was owned by a shell company for Saudi intelligence. The property had been employed as a Saudi safe house for years, and the evening before, Kaz had moved his ten assets into the home to use it as a staging base for the duration of the Gentry operation.

Back when he'd bought the Tauruses and the decals for the vehicles, Kaz had also acquired a dozen police uniforms by having his agents purchase identical clothing and styles from uniform shops around the country. Shoes, utility belts, holsters, badges, buttons, and body armor were all purchased from various suppliers on the Internet.

The duty gun of the Metropolitan Police Force is the Glock 17, and at the same time he acquired the uniforms and accessories, Kaz also purchased a number of these handguns from a supplier in Riyadh who acquired them directly from the manufacturer in Austria, with one major change to the actual duty gun. These Glocks were outfitted with threaded barrels, which would allow a silencer to be attached at the end.

D.C. cops didn't use silencers—no regular police force on the planet did—but these were no regular police. They were assassins. Kaz knew this group of assets might need to keep the sound of their gunfire to a minimum, so he purchased the threaded barrels and suppressors to fit them.

All these were brought in via the diplomatic pouch as well, and then locked in the care of Saudi intelligence in the embassy until this morning, when they'd been handed out to his ten operatives.

Ammunition was purchased in a gun shop in Roanoke, and even here Kaz and his men strived for accuracy. They bought Winchester Ranger full metal jacket ammunition, similar to the duty ammo used by the MPD. While Kaz had been unable to obtain the exact Winchester rounds used by the police since it was only sold in bulk to law enforcement agencies, research into ballistics told him the civilian bullets he obtained would be virtually indistinguishable from the duty ammo when dug out of a body by a coroner or surgeon.

When Kaz and his men returned with the police cars, they stepped into the safe house and saw the seven other operatives already dressed in the full light-blue-on-dark-blue uniforms of the Metropolitan Police Department of the District of Columbia. It was an impressive sight, and Kaz knew they would look even more the part once they climbed into their cruisers.

Soon all ten men presented themselves for inspection in D.C. Metro uniforms. Kaz checked them over carefully, and he was pleased with what he saw. Some of these men spoke excellent English, and others struggled, but Kaz had no plans to have them interact with the public like real police officers. No, on the Gentry hunt they would be assassins, only moved into the target area when Denny Carmichael ordered them to a location to make the kill.

23

Even though Leland Babbitt didn't make it into his office till after noon, he still worked a full nine hours before knocking off for the day and returning to his five-bedroom house on Cedar Parkway in Chevy Chase, Maryland.

His four-man home security detail already sat parked out front as Babbitt's Lexus rolled into his driveway; the men worked a seven-to-seven shift, giving Babbitt's property coverage through the hours of darkness. The men alternated patrols, with two in the vehicle at all times and two standing on the drive, walking around to the back from time to time, and sitting on the patio furniture, periodically casting an eye out to the Chevy Chase golf course that bordered his backyard in case any threats approached his property from the first fairway.

Babbitt's wife didn't much care for the security and she felt they were only there because Babbitt thought it made him look tough to the neighbors, but she didn't fight her husband on it anymore, especially since one of their neighbors had her Porsche SUV stolen right out of her driveway several weeks back.

As he pulled into the driveway Babbitt acknowledged the two patrolling security officers there with a distracted wave. He closed his garage door a moment later, then climbed out of his car and stepped into his kitchen to find his wife waiting for him there.

"It's eleven, Lee. Eleven!"

"Sorry I didn't return your calls. Long day at work."

He passed straight into the living room, with his wife close on his tail.

"I made dinner, you know."

"I ate at the office." He said it without looking up, because he'd pulled a bottle of fifteen-year-old Macallan from his bar and was now concentrating on a two-finger pour into a leaded crystal rocks glass.

He turned towards the floor-to-ceiling windows in his living room, which gave him a terrific view of the golf course just beyond his ample backyard and a six-foot-high ironwork fence.

While Babbitt faced the window, drink in hand, his wife stood behind him near the stairs. She stared him down, waiting for him to answer for himself or to notice her. Neither of which he did.

Babbitt's two kids were in college, so they had the place to themselves, but since the kids had left for school they'd done little to take advantage of the privacy. Babbitt had been obsessed with Gentry since well before Brussels, but after returning from Europe, minus a huge contingent of his men and the Top Secret clearance that gave his company the access they needed to function, Babbitt had barely acknowledged the existence of his wife.

His wife, who was still behind him and still hoping for some reaction from her husband, just sighed and headed for the stairs.

Court Gentry moved his binoculars back and forth between Babbitt and his wife. To himself he said, "She's pissed, and he couldn't care less."

Neither could Gentry, actually; he was just trying to get an accurate accounting of who was inside the property.

By the time Babbitt arrived home Gentry had already been in place for hours. He'd climbed over the back fence just after eight p.m., after a one-hour reconnaissance spent up in an oak tree on the first fairway of the golf course, and now he lay flat on his cold and muddy belly in a thick corner flower garden that was not yet in full bloom, but nevertheless provided a fair amount of cover, as long as Court remained low.

He wore black Carhartt work pants, a black hoodie over a black thermal, and dark brown boots. His face was covered by his gaiter and his knit cap, and on his hands he wore black Mechanix gloves. His black backpack completed the theme to his ensemble. He wasn't invisible, but he was damn close. It would take both a keen pair of eyes and a direct hit from a flashlight to notice him here.

Court had spent the last two hours carefully thinking over his ingress to the target location. He saw several motion sensor lights closer to Babbitt's house, but he knew he could defeat them when he made his approach by simply moving slowly. All motion sensor equipment was calibrated to detect objects traveling above a certain speed, and Court had spent nearly twenty years of his life in work that, more often than one might imagine, required him to outsmart the little computer chip in a motion detecting light.

He also took care to identify the lines of sight from the different windows of the property so he could avoid advancing in view of anyone inside.

It seemed to Court like Babbitt put the majority of his trust for his family's safety in the hands of his goons in the SUV out front, and the foot patrol. The Babbitts didn't have a dog; this became clear when Court scanned the perfectly green back lawn. The only disruption in the grass was on either side of a paving stone walkway that circled the house, and from the foot patrol that began once Babbitt came home, it was obvious the two men walking abreast were the culprits.

The security officers looked competent to Gentry, but he knew they wouldn't be members of Townsend's A-team. No, these were static guards, well trained, but not to the level of the Townsend operators he'd squared off against in Belgium. And they were well equipped, but not as well equipped as the men he'd fought before.

That said, Court looked at their gear longingly. Each guard carried an HK MP5 nine-millimeter submachine gun hanging from a two-point sling around his neck, and wore a black Kevlar bulletproof vest under a light chest rig that carried three more thirty-round magazines for the sub gun, as well as two mags for the Smith and Wesson M&P nine-millimeter pistols that jutted out of the holsters on their utility belts.

Court thought about how much he'd like to take one of these guys down, drag him back into the bushes, and liberate him of all that good gear.

But that wasn't going to happen in any sort of low-profile way, so he pushed the fantasy away.

Now Court observed Lee Babbitt himself standing right in front of his huge back window, exposed to the world, and he noticed the relaxed nature of the man, as well as that of his protection detail. While Gentry scanned through his binos he thought about the lackadaisical attitude of the guard force, and he found it odd that the CIA had not told Babbitt to beef up his security profile yet. It made no sense to him whatsoever the man had not been informed that the person he'd chased all over the world was now on the loose in his own area code.

Court worried this could have been some sort of a trap, so he took a moment to lift his head and begin a 360-degree scan of the area. Behind him was the dark golf course—he could see it through the bars of the iron fence—and just beyond the grounds of the country club, the silhouettes of darkened office buildings rose three or four stories into the sky. To Court's left and right were other homes, and he'd neither seen nor heard humans nor dogs at either residence. And dead ahead was Lee Babbitt, his wife, and four armed dudes who didn't have a clue this evening was about to become the most interesting night of their careers as security guards.

Now Court just needed to sit here till Babbitt and his wife went to bed. Once that happened, Court would wait for the guards to pass on their lazy patrol, then he would move to the window. He had purchased a high-end glass-cutting tool at the hardware store that could get him through the sliding doors without triggering the home alarm, although Court knew it would take at least ten minutes to cut through both panes. He'd have to work a couple of minutes, then secrete himself from the strolling Townsend men behind some raised flower beds before returning to work as soon as they moved around to the front. Eventually he'd remove an eighteen-inch circle of the double-paned window, and he'd slip inside the home. As long as he didn't open the door or shatter any glass, the security alarm would not be triggered, and he'd be free to move around inside the home.

Just then, the two patrolling security men made an ambling pass through the backyard; a flashlight waved in front of them but didn't reach into the corners of the property. Within a minute they disappeared around the side of the house on their way back out front.

Court looked through the back window again, and he noticed Babbitt's wife had moved to the staircase and Babbitt himself had stepped over to his bar, facing the other direction. Court rose to his knees and began crawling through the garden, wanting to take the opportunity to cover as much ground as possible while no one was looking his way. This flower bed continued down the side of the backyard, almost to the back patio, so Court felt confident he could come close to within steps of the back door without risking compromise.

"Here we go," he said softly, and he began his slow progression through the garden.

W hen are you coming to bed?" Babbitt's wife asked. She stood at the top
of the staircase, a halfhearted attempt at a come-hither look on her face,
which was hard to generate, considering the person who generated it was
tired and angry and the person it was directed to had shown not a shred of
interest so far.

"Later," Babbitt replied without looking up.

"What about now?" she asked again, hoping the cajoling would at least
cause her husband to turn around.

"I'm on the scent of a new target, dear. Something big. You know it takes
all my energy."

"What energy?" She turned away. It was a rhetorical question. Before she
disappeared on the landing to the second floor, she said, "This time, do try
to go after someone you can handle." There was a mocking tone to her voice,
a small riposte to her husband's rejection. "Not like that target in Belgium,
I mean. All those funeral dresses I bought to wear last month went out of
fashion on the first day of spring."

B abbitt growled into his glass as he wet his lips with the Macallan. "Bitch."
He turned on the stereo, flipped to a classical station, and began
pacing back and forth across the living room, backed by Shostakovich's
Eighth Symphony in C Minor. His mind tuned out his wife's barbs, and it
went back to spinning with ideas and planning, logistics and tactics.

"Where the hell are you, Gentry?" he said softly, standing at the floor-to-
ceiling window now, looking out over his back lawn and garden and the dark
golf course beyond it.

Babbitt paced. Struggled with the mind-set of an assassin.

Gentry would have fled Belgium, for certain. The CIA thought he was
in central Europe, but Babbitt disagreed. Fleeing the continent was Gentry's
usual MO after a big operation.

But where would he go?

Latin America? No. That had been his last distant refuge. He wouldn't
go back, not yet.

Africa was out; he'd gotten himself into quite a bit of trouble there a couple of years ago. Of course, it was a big continent, but Babbitt just didn't see Gentry returning to Africa now.

Asia? Yeah, maybe.

Babbitt finished the last swig of his scotch, stepped back to his little bar, and made himself a third drink.

Returning to the window, he thought about Asia again.

"Asia. Yes," Babbitt said. He felt confident he was in Gentry's brain now. He knew where he'd go.

Immediately Babbitt pulled out his phone and began thumbing through contacts, looking for the number of his Hong Kong–based agent. It would be mid-morning there—he could reach his man and get him started on building an infrastructure for the hunt to come.

Absently, while he scrolled through his phone, he lifted his rocks glass to down a swig of Macallan. Just as he brought it up to chest height the glass cracked, broke apart, and fell from his hand, dousing his shirt and trousers with the tepid scotch.

Babbitt looked down at the mess, an expression of mild surprise on his face. He took a half step back, concerned he'd cut his hand on the lead crystal.

Then he saw the blood, and it wasn't on his hand.

A hole in the middle of his white shirt, just to the left of center, from which redness grew, expanding.

Leland Babbitt dropped his phone on the floor, brought both hands to his wound, realizing only now that he'd been shot. He was in the industry, so he recognized within another second that the shooter must have employed a suppressed weapon. He looked up to his sliding glass door, just five feet in front of him, and he saw the hole in the glass at chest height, and he looked beyond the glass and saw movement in his garden on the far edge of the patio. A dark silhouette appeared from his rosebushes, turned, and began running towards his back fence.

"Gentry?" It came out in a hoarse whisper, and then Leland Babbitt dropped dead in a heap on the floor.

Leland Babbitt was the first person, but certainly not the last person, to believe with absolute conviction that he had been assassinated by the Gray Man.

Court was on the move before Babbitt's face slammed down on the living room tile. He'd heard no gunshot, but the screaming bullet had zinged through the night air from behind him on his right, crackling by at high speed thirty or forty feet off his right shoulder, and then snapping through the window glass.

Gentry gave up stealth for speed in his race to leave the scene, because he needed to get the hell out of here as fast as possible. He had a litany of immediate concerns, and none of them would go away as long as he remained hiding in the garden bed.

He was worried about the sniper, of course—there was a guy out here with a gun and eyes on the back of the property, but he was several orders of magnitude more concerned about the armed assholes *on* the property. Court had closed to within twenty feet of the back door, and as soon as Babbitt's body was discovered the estate would be locked down tight, lights would turn on, and Gentry would be way too close to avoid detection.

Two members of Babbitt's security detail were somewhere walking the grounds. They carried HK submachine guns, and Court only had a tiny .380 to fight them off.

Court knew if they saw him it was going to be a *fucking* mess.

He ran to the iron fence, but he hesitated climbing over it, because he had no idea if the sniper was still watching. It occurred to him that since Babbitt's body had not yet been discovered it might be better if he stayed here, at least for a minute or two, to give the shooter time to break down his position and leave his sniper's hide, thus giving Court a better opportunity to—

Babbitt's wife screamed in the house, her cry loud enough to be heard easily here forty yards away, and certainly loud enough to alert the security officers.

Fuck, Gentry thought, and then he climbed the fence, careful to avoid using his injured right arm for weight-bearing duty.

24

Zack Hightower took his eye out of the scope the instant he saw his target drop. He knew Babbitt wouldn't be getting back up after taking a 168 grain, .308 caliber high performance boat tail round to his center mass, so Zack began his exfiltration process immediately after confirmation of his kill.

He had no need to scan around the property or to look for more targets. This wasn't combat. This was a sanctioned termination.

His target was down, and it was time to go.

He unscrewed the silencer from the barrel of his Remington Defense CSR concealable sniper rifle, then he unscrewed the carbon fiber–wrapped barrel from the receiver and slipped it into the oversize gym bag next to him. He collapsed the stock against the receiver, placed the gun and the silencer in the bag and zipped it up, and then moved in a low run back to the staircase. Thirty seconds later he exited the fire escape door of the three-story office building, and he stepped out onto a dark street in an industrial park that had long since emptied out for the night.

Zack was proud of his shot, though he acknowledged to himself 435 yards into a man-sized target was nothing for a man of his skill set to write home about, really. Still, he'd removed a bad actor off the stage, an enemy of U.S. intelligence and a threat to his brothers and sisters in the Agency.

He knew this to be true because his leaders told him it was true. He did not question; he did not second-guess. He did not hesitate.

That was not Zack Hightower's way.

As he began walking to the north he was surprised to hear gunfire behind him. But not surprised enough to go back and take a look. He assumed Babbitt's men had discovered the body, they'd freaked out, and then they'd found something or someone in the neighborhood to shoot at.

Good, thought Zack. Nothing like a little fog of war back at the scene to help him get clear of the area.

Court knew he'd been spotted running across the first fairway of the golf course because he'd been shot at already; a short burst from an MP5 had blown lily pads out of a water hazard to his left, and a longer burst kicked up fescue that ran alongside a bunker on his right. He continued running off the turf and up into the natural area that divided the first green from the eighteenth green.

His short-term goal was putting distance between himself and the shooters, because he knew the shortcomings of their weapons. The MP5 was an excellent submachine gun at submachine gun range. Certainly at targets under fifty yards it was first rate, and with careful, judicious marksmanship it was accurate enough at a distance more than four times that. But the Townsend men's weapons had no advanced sights, and they were firing the HKs in automatic bursts while pursuing their target, and this reduced their accuracy and enhanced Court's chances for survival, as long as he could keep those chattering guns far back behind him.

He caught a brief respite from the incoming fire when he entered the trees and the darkness there, but he didn't slow, because he looked back over his shoulder and saw the headlights of the Lincoln Navigator bouncing onto the golf course just to the north of Babbitt's home. The SUV charged onto the first fairway at high speed, just one hundred yards from Court's position.

Court's old Ford Escort was parked in a lot two miles to the north, but he turned to the south, because he knew there was no way he'd make it to safety before the SUV caught up with him. No, his only hope now was to run, to evade the Navigator by moving into and out of the natural obstacles here in the dark golf course, and to find his way back to his car at some point much later in the evening.

Court decided he'd do his best to stay in the dark and get out of the golf course onto one of the main streets, to try and steal a car or find some sort of in extremis hide site.

He rounded a large pond, his tactical brain still acutely aware of the location of the black Lincoln Navigator, which now barreled through the tree line and spun onto the eighteenth fairway, behind him on his right. Court dropped to his knees below the lip of a rise, hoping the vehicle would pass him by and continue to the south. But just as he lay on his stomach, a burst of fire came from the center of the first fairway on his left, and it sent supersonic rounds zinging over his head.

The Navigator must have dropped off at least one man there before racing ahead.

Court had Babbitt's street and at least one shooter to his left, a vehicle with an unknown number of shooters twenty-five yards to his right and passing to the south, and the one place Court could not go was back to the north, because his car was parked there and he could not lead his opposition in that direction.

Court drew his pistol, leapt to his feet, and ran to his right.

The Navigator passed him on the fairway. Court charged behind it as it roared by, hoping like hell they didn't see him running out of the rough in his dark clothing. He sprinted deeper into the golf course, racing for the tree line that separated the next fairway from this one, but he heard the SUV on his left slam on its brakes, tearing up the pristine wet turf as it slid to a stop.

He'd been spotted.

Court ran on, across a wide green, towards a thicker grove of pines, and just when he thought he'd make it to the trees without being shot at, the barking fire of two MP5s behind told him men had dismounted from the Lincoln and were well aware of his location.

As he entered the trees, thousands of needles exploded off branches. Bullets ripped through the thick grove, the pounding sound of metal striking wood and the smell of fresh pine prevalent in the cool night air.

A round whined by within a foot of Court's right ear and he dove forward and rolled at speed down a hill out of the copse of pines, end over end, tumbling down until he landed flat on his face in a sand trap, moist and sticky with nighttime dew.

25

Zack Hightower could no longer hear the gunfire. He sat behind the wheel of his F-150 pickup, heading north through Bethesda, listening to an overnight a.m. talk radio station. A man had called in to tell the host about his recent alien abduction, and Zack was already absorbed in the story.

His cell phone rang and he snatched it out of the center console and held it to his ear while he drove.

"Yeah?"

Mayes said, "You need to get out of there!"

Hightower made a face at the phone. "What are you talking about? I'm clear."

"Traffic on the Townsend inter-team radios claims they are converging on a fleeing subject through the golf course."

"It's not me, boss. I'm golden."

Mayes was confused. "I'll call you back."

"Roger that," Zack said, and he hung up the phone and turned up the radio.

Denny Carmichael had decided to spend another night in his office. He'd already changed into his nightclothes, but he'd remained at his desk, waiting to hear confirmation of Babbitt's death. He had Mayes listening in on the Townsend frequency in his office, and he had confirmed the kill just two minutes earlier.

Carmichael turned off his computer and stood up from his desk now, getting ready to lie down on the couch and turn off the lights, but his phone rang again, surprising him. He snatched it with irritation. "What is it?"

Mayes spoke in his clipped tone. "Townsend is chasing a man who was on the property at the time of Babbitt's shooting." He paused an instant. "I spoke with Hightower. He's clear."

Carmichael understood almost instantly. "Gentry."

"Who else could it be? I'll deploy JSOC."

"Do it. The local police will get there first, but if Gentry squirts out of the police cordon maybe they can get a shot at him."

Carmichael hung up and immediately picked his secure mobile off his desk. He sent a brief text to Kaz.

Violator spotted in Chevy Chase. Under pursuit by private security. Vector to police traffic in area.

It took less than a minute for the text reply.

Understood.

In Arlington, Virginia, three Washington, D.C., police interceptors raced out of a parking lot and headed north, taking similar but separate routes. At this time of the evening it would take them less than twenty minutes to arrive at the destination, not that they knew exactly where they were going at this point. They would listen to police bands during the ride up, however, so they hoped to have a good idea of the location of their quarry by the time they got close.

Court Gentry crawled back up to his feet in the bunker alongside the twelfth green, spit out a mouthful of sand, and looked around. He saw the far edge of the golf course and a low wall there, and beyond that the streetlights of a busy intersection. There were several closed businesses up and down the street, but on the corner he saw the bright lights of two that appeared to be open.

He told himself he had to make it to the street to have any chance of getting away from his pursuers.

He raised his little pistol and fired two rounds into the air as he ran for the wall and the street, hoping any dismounts behind him and in close pursuit would hear the gunfire and worry they were being targeted. It was a weak move, a Hail Mary that, at best, could buy him five seconds as the attackers dropped to the ground or ducked behind a tree, but until he got to the cover of the buildings on the other side of the street ahead he saw no other option.

He made it across the last fairway without getting shot at again, though he heard shouts far behind him. He ran onto the ninth green, close to the clubhouse, and sprinted down a gentle hill towards the intersection.

Another cycle of automatic fire erupted from back at the pine trees, bullets impacted the tall windows of the clubhouse restaurant a dozen yards from Court, and the glass of the massive wall of windows cracked and shattered.

He thought about seeking cover inside the dark building, but he knew the men behind would see him enter, and although he could probably hold them back a minute or two with his pistol, he certainly couldn't wait them out, because the police would just surround the building and fill it with tear gas and tactical officers.

Court ran on for the wall at the edge of the country club. When he arrived at the wall, he climbed over and dropped down on the other side.

He still wore his gaiter high on his face and his cap low, so he imagined he must have been an intimidating sight for the cars passing him on Wisconsin Avenue, even though he'd stowed his handgun before vaulting the wall. Looking to the left, he thought he might be able to find a vehicle moving slow enough towards the intersection on his right so he could stop them at gunpoint, but all the traffic he saw moving through the intersection was heading east to west at speed, and he was in the northbound lane.

Shouts behind him at the wall of the golf course told him the dismounted Townsend men were close, but he'd lost the Navigator somewhere back on the other side of the copse of pines.

He raced across Wisconsin Avenue, towards the lights of the open businesses, a McDonald's and a twenty-four-hour pharmacy. Bursting armed into an occupied commercial space was not his first choice, but to break into a closed building involved slowing to pick a lock, or stopping to find something to smash a window with, and considering the armed security men so close on his heels he knew he didn't have the time he needed for either.

As he entered the parking lot of the McDonald's he noticed a dark alley behind the restaurant, and beyond the alley was an eight-foot-high chain-link fence with a thick hedge on the other side. Court's spirits rose quickly when he saw this; he felt sure he could enter the restaurant to misdirect the men chasing him and then immediately exit at the rear of the restaurant. Once he did this he could climb the fence, push through the foliage, and find himself in a new neighborhood, where he had a chance to get away.

For the first time he heard the sound of approaching sirens. They weren't right on him, but they were close enough to where he knew this entire section of the city would be locked down tight within minutes.

Just before he put his hand on the door of the McDonald's he looked back into the intersection behind him. The black Navigator was there, approaching in his direction and slowing next to two armed Townsend men in the middle of the street, who kept running towards him as they pointed his way.

So much for ordering a chocolate shake and waiting this out, Court thought to himself. He heaved the door open and ran inside.

26

Court drew the Ruger from his front pocket as he entered the restaurant. There were only a half dozen or so tables occupied, and everyone looked up as the man clad head to toe in black raised a small pistol over his head.

He shouted in his most commanding voice. "Everybody out!" and for additional emphasis he fired one round into the ceiling.

Screams and squeals erupted from both the dining room and the three employees behind the counter. The customers all jumped up from their tables and raced to the back door of the dining room, pushing one another to get out the door. Some ran straight to their cars, others to the safety of the all-night pharmacy next door.

Court rushed to the counter now, yelling at the employees, ordering them to leave. A panicked young man in a mustard-colored uniform held one hand up in surrender and, with the other, pushed a button on his register, opening the till, just as Court stepped behind the counter.

Gentry slammed the drawer closed and grabbed the young man. "I said go, kid!" He shoved him towards the exit.

The teen followed his coworkers to the front door.

Court raced into the kitchen now, just as he saw the last cook run through the back door of the building and out onto the raised concrete loading dock in the back alley. Court charged to the back door himself, ready to make for the back fence.

He managed two steps out the rear door before the Navigator screeched into the alley on his left. Its headlights illuminated everything, and there was no way in hell Court would make it over the fence and into the cover of the neighborhood on the other side without being seen and engaged.

The cooks ran around the corner in the direction of the front parking lot, but the driver of the Navigator obviously saw Court, because he slammed on his brakes in the center of the alley.

Court stopped, turned around, and retreated back into the McDonald's, but as he passed through the door he fired a round into the exterior light over the door, blowing it out with a shower of sparks.

A man in the front passenger's seat of the SUV reached out with a handgun and raised it at Gentry, only twenty-five feet away.

Court dove for the hard floor of the kitchen as the pistol cracked loud in the alleyway behind him. The round hit the door three feet above his back.

He kicked the door shut, then looked around the kitchen, weighing his options. He knew going back out front wouldn't work; there would be at least two men there armed with submachine guns, possibly already inside the restaurant.

Court thought it possible the Townsend men would just cordon him off here and wait for the cops to arrive, but he also knew they would all be ex-military and sure of their martial skills. They would take it personally that, in their understanding of events anyway, the man in the McDonald's kitchen just murdered their employer on their watch, and that would piss them off to no end.

Court darted back through the kitchen, in the direction of the front counter, and as he did so he noticed a metal ladder fixed to the wall on his right, just next to a walk-in freezer. Looking up, he saw the ladder led to a roof access hatch.

Court liked having the option of escape from the kitchen, even if he wasn't quite sure what good this ladder would do him. If he made it onto the roof he'd be even more stuck than he was here, since at least here at ground level he had access to multiple exits.

Court stopped in the middle of the kitchen, trying to decide his next move. He had exactly five rounds of .380 ammo in his mouse gun. Whether it was the cops or the Townsend boys who eventually kicked in the doors of this Mickey D's, Court knew he was in serious trouble.

He looked at the back door again just as it began to open. Court ran around a stainless steel prep table in the middle of the room and slid on his butt along the greasy tile floor next to a row of griddles and three large fry vats, then he crawled forward, out of the line of sight of anyone at the open back door, which was only ten feet from where he knelt. He looked between a low open shelf of metal pots and pans below the prep table, and he saw one of the Townsend men enter, his submachine gun up at his shoulder, scanning for threats.

Court fired twice between the pots and pans, hitting the operator at the door once in each calf. The man dropped flat on his back, inside the door, screaming in agony.

Court fired three more times towards the dark opening of the back door, sure another man would be entering just behind his mate, because he couldn't imagine any scenario that had one guy hitting the building on his own.

He heard his second shot clang off of metal, and he thought he might have hit the MP5 in the operator's hand. He knew this would slow the man but not stop him, because the man would simply transition to his pistol and come through the door to the aid of his partner.

Court's handgun was empty now.

Quickly he rolled up to his knees, reached over to the stainless steel counter next to him, grabbed a fist-sized aluminum can, and threw it out onto the darkened loading dock.

As he did so he shouted, "Frag out!"

The can banged against the doorjamb, then bounced onto the concrete dock and clanged against a metal garbage can there. If the Townsend operator had military experience, which Court suspected he did, then he would naturally think someone had just tossed a fragmentation grenade just feet away from where he stood.

Court heard the sound of a man covered in metal and other gear clambering over an iron railing, and then dropping onto the asphalt of the alleyway four feet below with a loud crash.

On his hands and knees Court crawled to the back door and kicked it shut again, then he crawled over to the injured operator on the floor. The man had rolled up onto his knees, and he reached out for his weapon on the tile, but he sensed movement and he turned, looked up, and saw a man in black flying through the air at him.

Court tackled the wounded man back to the ground.

Straddling the security officer now, Court held his empty little pistol against the man's sweat-covered forehead, and the wounded man went still, his eyes crossed looking at the gun. Court didn't say a word. Instead he just pulled the Smith and Wesson pistol out of the man's drop leg holster, flicked off the safety, and fired four rounds into the front wall of the kitchen, hoping to discourage anyone with ideas about rushing into the kitchen.

Now Court tossed his empty Ruger to the side and shoved the hot Smith into his waistband, along with another handgun magazine pulled from the Townsend man's load bearing vest. He also removed the three long HK submachine gun magazines from the vest.

He waved the three mags back and forth over the face of the man lying on his back and bleeding from the calves.

Court said, "Listen up. I know you're hurting, but if I were you . . . I'd figure out a way to move."

Court stood, turned to his right, and tossed all three magazines, each loaded with thirty rounds of nine-millimeter ammunition, across the room.

All three plopped into one of the big vats of molten hot fry grease positioned against the wall.

"No!" the injured man shouted, his eyes wide with disbelief, and then he rolled over on his stomach and began crawling, using only his arms to drag himself across the floor towards the back door.

Court scrambled across the room to the walk-in freezer, entered, and yanked the door shut behind him.

It was silent in the kitchen, save for the grunting and groaning of the man on the floor, struggling to pull himself as fast as he could. He had just reached the back door, pulled it open with his arm, and rolled out onto the concrete loading dock when two Townsend operators, moving in a small tactical train, spun into the kitchen from the front counter area.

Both men covered a different section of the kitchen with their submachine guns. The man on the left traced the front sight of his weapon over the walk-in freezer, the cooler, and the dry storage pantry. The man on the right saw in his sector his wounded comrade rolling out the back door, the wash area for the mops by the door, and the main kitchen prep area with the stainless steel table, the grills, the ovens, and the three big fry vats.

Left called, "Clear!"

Right hesitated, then he shouted, "Get down!"

27

The operator on the right had seen the bubbling vat of grease spewing, and he sensed trouble, but not in time to avoid it. Just as both men looked to the right, the center vat popped once, spraying red-hot grease into the air. Neither man was hit by either a round or the burning liquid, but a second after this, just as both men turned away to run for cover, the remaining eighty-nine rounds of nine-millimeter ammunition cooked off nearly simultaneously. The cacophonous explosion blew fire, bits of metal, and hot cooking oil in all directions.

The bullets were not traveling through rifled barrels, so they were nowhere near as deadly as actual gunfire, but they were still capable of causing serious wounds. The brass jacketed projectiles, along with the scalding oil, cartridges, and bits of the metal fry vat itself, slammed into both men as they tried to run, knocking them back through the passageway into the counter area of the restaurant.

As soon as the boom of the explosion diminished Court exited the door of the walk-in refrigerator, grabbed the metal ladder on the wall next to him, and climbed up. It was hot with fry grease and slippery as hell, but he held on, fighting his way to the ceiling access hatch. He opened the door, rolled out onto the flat roof, and rose to his feet.

Court ran straight to the front edge of the building, hoping to somehow shimmy down to the parking lot, but when he got there he saw a half dozen police cars rolling into the lot from the intersection, their lights flashing.

Shit. He turned and raced along the roof in the opposite direction.

He stopped at the south side of the building now, hoping no one would see him here. He looked over the side, a dozen feet straight down onto asphalt.

He couldn't make that drop quickly without running a high risk of hurting a knee or an ankle, which would make his escape nearly impossible.

Court turned and rushed to the rear of the restaurant now, thinking the loading dock might be high enough for him to drop down onto. But quickly he saw that was no good, either. There were two Townsend men here, and although one man was wounded, both were armed, and the back door to the restaurant was open, allowing anyone inside a view of the loading dock.

Court ran to the north side, desperate for any option now. And an option presented itself immediately. As he ran he saw a Montgomery County Police Department SUV, its lights and sirens blaring, racing through the parking lot. Court knew where the officer was heading. He would be part of the cordon of the scene, moving to the alleyway to cut off any escape through the back door.

Court knew that this moving vehicle was his one ticket off the roof of this McDonald's. He turned and chased after the SUV, running for the back corner of the roof as fast as he could, knowing the vehicle would have to come close to the building here to pull into the alley to seal up the back exit.

It was all about speed and timing now, and while Court knew he had the speed, he couldn't see the SUV below the lip of the roof, so he had no idea about the timing. If he jumped too soon he'd land on the asphalt after a twelve-foot leap, and he'd probably also get run over by the officer in his sport utility vehicle. If he was too slow he'd just hit the asphalt behind the vehicle, and no doubt break a leg in the process and lie there till discovered by the cops.

Using the sound of the siren as his guide he ran on, then stutter-stepped near the edge to buy himself an instant of time. He launched off the roof, windmilled his arms and legs through the air, and pounded down feet first on the roof of the SUV, six feet lower than the roofline. His forward momentum propelled him off the moving vehicle, and the SUV's forward momentum, as it moved to Court's left, cartwheeled Court sideways. He spun in the air, tumbling down towards the parking lot. He landed on his feet but immediately crashed to his side, then continued his tumble into a forward roll off his right shoulder.

Out of the roll he snapped back up to his feet. This propelled him on even faster, and in just a few steps he was back in the air, leaping and then grabbing onto chain-link fence near the top. Hurriedly he climbed the rest of the way over.

The Montgomery County Police vehicle screeched on its brakes and the driver put the transmission in park and leapt out, but by the time he got around to the other side of his vehicle to pursue the dark figure who had just crashed down on his unit, the fleeing man had dropped on the far side of the back fence and pushed through a high hedge, and he was now running through the dark parking lot of a dentist office.

The two Townsend men were on the dock, but they'd missed the man leaping from the roof. By the time the uninjured security officer saw what was happening and tried to level his pistol at the movement, two police officers inside the restaurant saw him through the open back door and screamed at him, demanding he drop his weapon and raise his hands.

The young officer from the SUV watched the fleeing figure clear the hedge on the other side of the fence and run away. He reached for the radio on his shoulder, still not completely sure where the guy came from or whether he was involved in all the gunfire reported inside the building.

The cops dragged the two dazed and scalded armed men out the front of the smoke-filled McDonald's, and they found two more men, dressed the same as the others, in the back alley. One had been shot twice in the lower legs and was dazed by shock and blood loss, but the other operator was more coherent than his colleague, so he relayed a version of events that had all the cops at the scene scratching their heads.

The *Washington Post*'s lead national security reporter Catherine King reached for the vibrating phone on her bedside table. Looking at the screen, she recognized the number.

In a sleepy voice she said, "You only call in the middle of the night."

Andy Shoal's voice, in contrast to hers, was alert, almost excited. "Talk to my editor. I only *work* in the middle of the night."

Catherine asked, "What's up?"

"Another shooting."

She began sitting up. "Where?"

"Chevy Chase"—he paused—"and Bethesda."

Catherine said, "Two shootings, then."

"Sort of just one shooting. Picture a dead rich guy in Chevy, with four of the dead rich guy's security guards chasing the killer a half mile to a McDonald's in Bethesda."

"Wow. Did they get him?"

"He got away, right under the noses of two dozen cops."

"And I guess you are calling me because the CIA is there?"

"I don't see anyone who looks like those two from the other night. But the victim is a guy named Leland Babbitt, and on Google it says he is—"

King interrupted. She was wide-awake now. "I know who Lee Babbitt is. He runs a PMC and investigation firm. Government contracts with the intel community."

"Right," said Andy.

"And someone *murdered* him?"

"Shot him dead and then fled across a golf course. Got in a gunfight with Babbitt's security men in a McDonald's and then disappeared. I was wondering if you might be interested in coming over and checking it out. I doubt there's any relationship to the thing in Washington Highlands the other night, but considering the occupation of the victim, I thought this might be right up your alley."

Catherine was already moving towards her closet to get dressed. "I'm coming from Georgetown. Fifteen minutes to Chevy Chase. Text me the address."

28

Court moved calmly through the deep darkness at two a.m., avoiding the glow of streetlamps and the lights shining from porch lights and the occasional passing car. The streets were quiet here, a mile and a half from where the action went down an hour and a half earlier. Though he still heard the thumping of helicopters patrolling to the south, they weren't close enough to worry him, and he'd neither seen a police car nor heard a siren for the past thirty minutes.

He wore a different set of clothing now. An hour earlier he'd taken all the clothing he'd worn during the gunfight, every last stitch that had been visible to the shooters, the witnesses, and any security cameras, and he'd shoved them down a drainage culvert. Then he'd pulled a wad of clothing out of his backpack and dressed in a light gray parka, a gray thermal, a pair of black track pants, and a red baseball cap.

Now he was walking north on Rockville Pike, feeling good about his chances, but questioning just what the hell had happened back at Babbitt's house. The man had been assassinated, that much was clear, but Court could only make uneducated guesses about who might have been involved.

From the first moment it happened he felt like it must have been a CIA hit. The Agency knew Court was here in town, they wanted to get rid of Babbitt for some reason, and the symbiosis of these two things resulted in a shooter on a rooftop near Babbitt's house at the same time Court was ninja-crawling through the man's backyard.

Court knew he'd be blamed for the hit. Hell, he would have been blamed even if he *hadn't* been on the scene at the time, but the entire chaotic escapade with his exfiltration through the McDonald's just played even more into the CIA's plan to pin Babbitt's assassination on him.

"This night sucks ass," he mumbled to himself. He'd accomplished nothing this evening with the exception of getting a crystal clear under-standing that the CIA was going to fight his fire with fire of their own, and the objectives of the CIA were even murkier than he'd imagined.

Why the hell did they kill Babbitt?

Just ahead was an overpass that ran over the Capital Beltway. On the other side was an apartment complex and, next to this, a bus stop where he could take a bus that ran all night. Court knew this bus followed a route that would drop him within a few blocks of his car, about a mile away. He'd passed this stop this afternoon on a bus that got him closer to Babbitt's house, and noted this location as a secondary exfiltration route in case he wasn't able to make it directly back to his car for some reason.

His plan for the rest of the evening was simple. Pick up his car, take it back to his storage room, lock it up, then go home to his basement apartment at the Mayberrys'.

But everything changed suddenly when he scanned to his right. There, parked in the darkness of a private driveway, sat a Metro D.C. police cruiser. The vehicle itself was a little odd, as this was Maryland, after all, but the fact that at least two men sat in the dark car was more suspicious to him.

D.C. cops usually ride alone in their patrol cars.

Court began crossing the street, heading away. Behind him he heard the doors of the police cruiser open.

Court looked to his left and right for a place to run, expecting that at any moment the cops were going to call out to him, or else they were right now radioing for backup and within minutes cruisers, tactical units, and helicopters would surround him.

He looked on either side of the road and saw rows of adjoining houses. Short of kicking in a door or a window, he had nowhere to run.

"And this night keeps getting better and better," Court mumbled to himself.

Just fifty feet in front of him was the overpass; he knew he'd reach a decision point there. Either he'd turn and run into the neighborhood here, before he got stuck on the overpass; he'd try to run across the overpass and lose the cops on foot over there; or else he would slide down the embankment and into the traffic of the Beltway.

No option looked like a good one, but while he kept walking he couldn't help but wonder why the two cops, just fifty feet behind him now, hadn't challenged him yet.

The answer presented itself a moment later when two more Metro PD squad cars pulled onto the far end of the overpass and stopped. Car doors opened and four police officers poured out, fanned out away from the vehicles, and drew their pistols.

Time to run.

Court turned to his right and raced for the embankment. He had taken only a few steps in this endeavor—he was still twenty feet from the steep concrete slope to the Beltway below—when gunfire erupted in front of him.

What the fuck? Court thought. The cops were just gunning him down, not even giving him a chance to surrender.

Within the first five cracks of incoming fire, Court felt a sharp sting wide on his right rib cage. His gray parka ripped, and he doubled over while running. He stumbled almost all the way to the ground, to the point that his hands went flat on the street, but he kept moving, rose back up, and leapt over the railing of the overpass without taking time to look below.

Court dropped six feet through the air and landed on his right hip on a thirty-degree concrete incline. He rolled end over end several times, then righted himself and began skidding on his back, picking up speed towards the Beltway below. Above him the gunfire had stopped, but he had no doubt it would resume again as soon as this group of overzealous Washington cops got a bead on him from the overpass railing.

He made it to the bottom of the hill, staggered up onto the shoulder, and looked to the oncoming traffic.

An idea came to him quickly and he didn't pause to second-guess it. He timed his move, then jumped in front of a speeding semitrailer. He raised his hands, shielding his eyes from its headlights.

He knew the vehicle would not be able to stop in time.

The semi driver slammed on his brakes, the air brakes squealed and the tires burned and skidded, and the semi's load began to jackknife.

Court leapt out of the way, ran off the shoulder and several feet back up the concrete embankment. As he did so he felt blood on his stomach, soaking the elastic band of his warm-up pants.

As soon as the semi came to a complete stop Court drew his Smith and Wesson pistol, ran with the gun in his right hand and his left hand clutching his wounded rib cage, and reentered the Beltway under the cover of the overpass. Behind the semi trailer a maroon and white taxicab had slammed on his brakes to avoid a rear-end collision, and Court ran around to the driver-side window and banged on it with his pistol.

The cabbie opened the door and raised his hands. He screamed something in a foreign language. Court thought it might have been Swahili, but he wasn't sure.

"Out!" Court yelled, and the man seemed to understand because he complied instantly.

Court climbed behind the wheel of the cab, and threw it into gear. He lurched forward onto the shoulder, did a quick and dirty three-point turn, and then bounced into the grassy median between the eastbound and westbound lanes. He drove across to the westbound and entered the Beltway here, and he stomped on the gas, trying to get as much speed as possible before showing up below the far side of the overpass. He could only hope that the cops above him had not been able to see the carjacking or the maneuver, and that they would only find out about it as soon as they spoke with the furious cabbie.

His plan paid off, and within minutes he was miles to the west, clear of the area and hunting for a place to dump a stolen cab with blood all over the driver's seat.

29

Denny Carmichael sat at his desk, his head in his hands. He was back in his suit and tie now, though as soon as he got the energy he would again dress for bed. Two and a half hours ago he was moments from flipping off the lights and lying down on the couch, but then came the suspected sighting of Violator at the Babbitt home in Chevy Chase, so he stood by in his office. When the police were dispatched to the scene he'd received a call from Suzanne Brewer in the Violator tactical operations center on the fourth floor, telling him something he already knew, but he sold his surprise as genuine. He hurriedly dressed and rushed down to the TOC, and here he sat while Brewer and Mayes furiously worked their team of targeting officers. They sent the JSOC special mission unit into the area, but by then Gentry was long gone.

And then, an hour and a half after the assassination, Brewer and Mayes departed for the scene of a carjacking of a taxi a mile and a half north of Babbitt's house, thinking it possible Gentry was involved in this, as well.

Denny Carmichael had not heard a word from Kaz since sending the text ordering the Saudi kill team to the scene of Babbitt's killing shortly after eleven, and he had no idea if Kaz's men had gotten anywhere near Gentry, so he just sat here at his desk waiting, trying to get the energy to climb back to his feet.

His mobile chirped with the sound it made when an encrypted call was waiting. He glanced down at it and saw it was Kaz, and as he snatched the phone off the desk he found the energy reserves he was looking for.

"Talk."

Kaz said, "My men made contact with the target."

"When and where?"

"Forty minutes ago, about two kilometers north of the original event."

Carmichael knew this would be the carjacking Mayes and Brewer were en route to inspect.

He asked, "How did you find him?"

"Process of elimination. We saw where the police were focusing their attention. It was mostly to the west, because that was the direction he was last seen moving. But from the radio reports we determined Gentry originally tried to go south, but that was when he knew he was being pursued, so we felt he was leading forces away from his planned exfiltration route. That led us north. I positioned men in five choke point locations, and simply waited, thinking he might still be on foot."

"What happened?" Carmichael caught himself squeezing the phone so hard he ran the risk of breaking it.

"Two of my men saw a lone man fitting the general description. They stepped out to follow him. When my other assets arrived, the man began to run. We engaged and, I am told, there was blood at the scene. We are confident that we wounded him."

Carmichael snapped back, "But you didn't put him down, did you?"

"He managed to escape in a hijacked vehicle. Understand, Denny, this operation my men conducted was completely in extremis. If we'd known something about the person the Gray Man was targeting, this Leland Babbitt, we could have been in a much better tactical position."

Carmichael growled now. "We didn't know Gentry was after Lee Babbitt, either."

Kaz clearly did not believe this. "You contacted me within moments of the first shots being fired in Chevy Chase. The only way you could be so on top of the situation like this is if you had some sort of advance warning."

Carmichael could not tell Kaz the truth: that they had no advance warning, but had instead been targeting the same man and just stumbled onto Gentry in the commission of their assassination. Instead he changed the subject. "How badly was he injured?"

"My assets had to leave the scene before the police arrived. All I know is Violator has been shot."

"Very well. I'll try to do better next time with the quality of the intelligence. It would be helpful if your men do better next time with the quality of their marksmanship."

Kaz took his time before replying. "We remain at the ready."

Carmichael said, "Don't *remain* anywhere. Keep shaking the trees. He's out there, and he's hurt. He'll be easier to hunt."

Court lay in a shallow ditch on his left side, his ears tuned to the sounds around him so he could make sure there was no traffic on the residential road above. After a full minute like this he felt secure enough to proceed.

He used a small penlight to illuminate the right side of his rib cage. Slowly and gingerly he pushed his torn gray parka out of the way, pulled up his blood-soaked gray thermal shirt, and held the light a little closer.

He lifted his head to get a better look, then he dropped it again.

Court closed his eyes for a moment, willing away the sight.

He knew he'd taken a bullet, but he was hoping it was nothing more than a slight graze. He'd seen enough gunshot wounds in his life to know sometimes rounds could just barely break the skin if they traveled along at the right angle, and these types of superficial wounds could nevertheless be incredibly painful.

But now that he'd seen the result of his latest near-death experience Court realized that even though he would not die from this wound, it was no mere superficial scrape. The bullet had failed to penetrate his rib cage, but it had definitely ripped skin, muscle, and other tissue away, all the way to the bone.

It burned and throbbed and stung and ached all at once, and now that he knew what it looked like, it hurt even more.

Court made himself look again. A smear of blood covered the right side of his torso all the way down to his waistband, and with help from the flashlight he could see plainly the dull gray white of bone in the wound—one of his lower ribs was exposed in the seeping hole.

He spoke slowly and softly. "Fu-uck."

He couldn't stitch this up. A half-inch-wide and one-and-a-half-inch-long swath of skin and muscle was gone, so there was nothing for the sutures to hang on to. Instead all he could do was clean the wound and cover it with a sterile compress, and tape that down nice and hard so the bleeding would stop. The compress would foul with the coagulating blood and he'd have to peel it away a couple times a day to clean the wound, an excruciating process he'd have to keep repeating for at least a week.

He'd hurt from this, to be sure, but he'd survive, and he told himself this wouldn't slow him down. He'd compartmentalize the pain and keep going.

Court pushed it out of his mind now and thought about his situation. He had dumped the stolen taxi deep in the woods in Bethesda, near the Grosvenor metro station. It would be daylight before it was found; he was certain of this. Now he just had to get himself out of this ditch and make his way to an all-night bus stop, then use the mass transit system to get back to his Ford Escort.

His mind went back to the second shoot-out of the evening. He found himself astonished that a half dozen D.C. Metro police officers opened fire on him like that when he had no weapon in his hands, and without saying anything to him before the shooting began.

Cops don't do that, do they?

For a brief moment he wondered if those men might have been SAD Ground Branch paramilitary officers disguised as police. No, that didn't make sense to him. On occasion the Agency could be bold as hell when operating in other countries, but if they were chasing him here in the nation's capital, there was no way they'd be playing by a rule book that allowed them to impersonate police in the course of an extrajudicial assassination.

That was just too ridiculous to contemplate.

Court lowered his shirt, closed his jacket, and looked at his watch.

It was nearly three a.m.

He had to move, he had to get someplace to get the supplies he needed to treat his injury, and he had to get home before first light.

"Move your ass, Gentry." He said it to himself, and it worked. He pulled himself up into a sitting position and then, with one hand pressing on his right rib cage, he struggled to stand.

As a shock wave of pain jolted him with the movement, he managed to stifle a scream, but he could not manage to suppress a long low groan.

Once up, Court adjusted the position of the Smith and Wesson pistol in his waistband, slipped his backpack over his shoulder, and slowly climbed out of the ditch.

30

atherine King and Andy Shoal stood on the shoulder of the Capital Beltway under the Rockville Pike overpass. Two of the three lanes of traffic had been pyloned off for the police cars, ambulance, and wreckers, so even though the two *Washington Post* reporters had to park up on Rockville Pike and then scoot down the concrete embankment, once they were here, at least, they were able to walk around the scene and observe the two dozen or so Maryland State Police at work.

A helicopter circled overhead, its spotlight scanning around the Beltway below, and this, along with passing headlights, flashing red and blue lights from the officers' cars, and a burning flare in the road next to the jackknifed semi, gave a dreamy psychedelic feel to the scene.

The two reporters arrived directly from the scene in Chevy Chase twenty minutes earlier after being frustrated by police tape and unhelpful law enforcement there. They'd learned next to nothing about the murder of Leland Babbitt, but when Andy heard the call on his scanner about the violent carjacking on the Beltway, he gave Catherine his professional opinion that there was no way in hell both these things could happen in tranquil western Maryland on the same night without being related, so they set off for the second scene.

And here they'd had a little more luck getting information.

The semi was more than halfway off the road, with the front wheels of the cab in a ditch next to the shoulder. A group of troopers and other law enforcement officers stood around it. Andy didn't know these men; he visited three or four crime scenes a day, but always inside the borders of D.C. That said, he did know how to talk to cops, so he finessed his way through the tape and introduced himself to a young detective who helpfully mentioned that the troopers had found blood traces on the concrete embankment and on the shoulder of the Beltway. The CSI units were just now setting up lights and starting to crawl around, looking for more samples.

The cabbie sat in an ambulance, although he didn't seem to be injured. To Catherine's astonishment Andy finagled his way through troopers to the open back door of the ambulance and asked the witness for a description of the criminal.

The driver was from Mozambique, and his accent was incredibly thick, but he told Andy the man who'd jacked him had been white, in his thirties, carried a black pistol, and had driven off to the west.

Andy wrote the cabbie's name down, making him spell it out slowly and carefully, and then he made his way over to the driver of the semi, who had finished giving a statement to the police and was now waiting for his company to send a tow truck. From him Andy got essentially the same description, with the additional information that the man was wearing a red or burgundy cap and a gray jacket. He said the man came down the embankment, stood by the side of the road for a few seconds, and then purposefully leapt in front of the tractor-trailer.

Andy walked back over to Catherine, who had knelt down over a splatter of blood the troopers had already photographed and sampled. He stepped up behind her while she took pictures of the blood with her iPhone. He said, "Both witnesses report one male, thirties, clean-shaven."

"That's it?"

"That's it. Didn't remember the color of his hair or his height. Apparently the carjacker caused the cab of the semi to skid off the road, and its load blocked the rest of traffic from getting by. When the cab driver stopped his taxi behind the truck the armed assailant showed up at his window."

Catherine asked, "Did either of them mention the gunman being injured somehow?"

"No."

She put her phone away and motioned to the red splotches on the side of the highway. "Is that a lot of blood?"

Andy shrugged. "I've seen crime scenes with about five hundred times more."

"Sure," said Catherine. "But there is more blood over there, and CSI found drops on the pavement on the embankment."

"Right."

"And the Babbitt shooting happened a little after eleven."

"So?"

"So let's assume the shooter is the same person as the carjacker."

Andy smiled. "I'd stake my limited reputation on it."

"Well," Catherine continued, "I'm trying to picture someone bleeding like this for two hours."

Andy thought he understood. "You are saying you don't think the shooter was hurt during the shoot-out in Chevy Chase?"

"What do you think?"

Andy looked at the blood again, both here and on the embankment. "I'm not a doctor, but I've seen a lot of crime scenes. This isn't arterial spray, or anything like that, but this guy was most definitely draining blood. You're right. No way he bled like this for an hour and a half. He'd be dead, or at least unconscious."

Catherine said, "If neither witness said anything about the man getting hurt here, there must be a third crime scene somewhere, and *that's* where he was injured."

Andy said, "You're pretty good, Ms. King."

"I don't have all the answers," she said. "But I know where we can go to get them."

"Where?"

Catherine looked behind Andy, and he turned his head to follow her gaze. There, just climbing out of a black Suburban, were Jordan Mayes and Suzanne Brewer. They both wore black overcoats, and Mayes had two bearded bodyguards with him.

Jordan Mayes flashed his credos to the detective in charge of the carjacking scene and took the man aside. While the two of them stepped off beyond the jackknifed semi, Suzanne Brewer walked over to the truck driver and began talking to him.

"I'll be damned," said Shoal. "Are you going to ask them what they're doing here?"

Catherine said, "We both are. Divide and conquer. I'll take Mayes." She started to walk off, then she turned back to Andy. "Don't mention Brandywine Street. You're just here because this is a crime, and I'm just here because of the Babbitt killing nearby and his ties to the intelligence community."

"Got it," Andy said.

A s soon as Suzanne Brewer finished talking to the truck driver, Andy Shoal caught up to her. "Hello? Excuse me." She stopped and turned, extended a hand. Andy knew she thought he was a detective, and he was about to ruin her night. "Andrew Shoal from the *Post*. Can I get your name? Do you have a card?"

She pulled her hand away quickly. "No, sorry."

"Are you law enforcement?"

"Homeland Security," she said, and she turned away, making a beeline to the police tape around the blood spatter, thinking it would keep Andy back.

"Really? I just assumed you work with Jordan Mayes over there."

Brewer knelt under the tape, kept walking. After a few seconds she looked back and saw Andy had ducked the tape as well and remained on her heels. She said, "Sorry, I'm involved in an investigation here. Will you excuse me?"

"Any thought this might have something to do with the Babbitt killing on Cedar Parkway?"

"We are looking into—"

"I mean, it would have to, right? You've got bloodstains here. There was a lot of shooting at the other scene."

"I'm going to have to ask you to step on the other side of the tape." Her eyes flitted around, trying to find an officer close enough to help her.

Andy continued as if he hadn't heard. "But the weird thing to me is, there is a lot of blood here, especially considering the first event was an hour and a half before the second. No way some guy is going to bleed like that for that long. You have any information about another shooting? Something after Cedar Parkway, and before here?"

Brewer turned away from Andy, looked around at the scene, as if she was considering what the young reporter was saying. After a few moments her head seemed to clear, and she reached out and grabbed a passing state police officer by the arm.

"Yes, ma'am?"

"Is this reporter authorized to be inside the police line?"

"No, ma'am." He squared his shoulders at Andy. "Let's back it up."

Andy pulled out a card and pushed it into Suzanne Brewer's hand. Then he said, "Thanks for talking, Ms. Brewer. I've got plenty to run with for now. Call me if you want to talk more."

Andy turned away, ducked back under the police tape, and headed off to see if Catherine King had gotten any further in her interview.

Jordan Mayes finished with his briefing from the confused detective with a handshake. The man had no idea who Mayes was, but the federal credentials he presented trumped any reticence on the Maryland State officer's part, so he told the man everything he knew about the scene here.

Mayes turned around to look for Brewer in the large group of men and women working the scene here, but the first person he recognized was Catherine King from the *Washington Post*. He didn't know her personally, but he read her column and saw her on TV from time to time. He had a vague memory of King being pointed out to him at a cafeteria in the Green Zone in Baghdad years before, and he was introduced to her briefly in one of Saddam Hussein's palaces that had been turned into a coalition command center.

He didn't have a clue what she was doing standing under an overpass at three thirty in the morning.

"Mr. Mayes? Catherine King, *Washington Post*."

Mayes's defenses fired into high gear, but he was polite. "Ms. King? How are you?"

They shook hands.

"Please call me Catherine."

Jordan Mayes had two bodyguards within arm's reach, but they didn't have any clue that this small woman in an overcoat was a threat to his mission. Mayes was stuck talking to her, for a few seconds at least. "Sorry, I'm right in the middle of something."

"Wondering if you can tell me if you think this carjacking is related to the Babbitt murder."

"Too early to say. I was on my way there, and came over here, just out of curiosity. What brings you out tonight?"

"Same thing, I guess. I'd love to talk to you, off the record, of course. Can you tell me if you think Babbitt's murder was related to the work he did with CIA?"

Jordan Mayes frowned. "I think you should talk with the Maryland State Police. I can't possibly give you anything more than what they have. If you'll excuse me, that's all I really have time for right now."

Mayes felt a muscle in his left eye twitch, and he damned the movement.

Catherine saw Mayes's immediate discomfort, and she hesitated, unsure just how much she wanted to turn up the heat. Quickly she decided to go for broke. "I noticed you arrived with Suzanne Brewer. She is responsible for protecting CIA personnel domestically, isn't she? Obviously you must have concerns about Babbitt's killer targeting Agency assets."

Mayes held up his hands in surrender. "That's a lot of speculation there, Ms. King. Your readers would probably appreciate facts, not conjecture. Like I said, talk to the police."

Now she decided to drop the bomb. "Well, I would, but I doubt the Maryland police would have much information about that double homicide in Ward Eight the other night. Are you investigating the possibility of a connection to these crime scenes?"

"Ward Eight? I'm not sure I know what you are referring to."

Mayes was a good liar, but Catherine knew he would be.

"Washington Highlands. Saturday night. Brandywine Street." She smiled. "You know the one."

"I'm sorry, Ms. King, I'll have to break this off right there. If you want you can call Media Relations and they—"

"The Agency's media people won't be able to help me on my story. I am aware that you and Ms. Brewer went to the Brandywine Street crime scene the other evening, so I am speculating you had credible intelligence that event was related to a threat on Agency personnel. Then tonight, Babbitt is killed. He was closely affiliated with CIA. You are Clandestine Service, so I'm not sure what your interest in this is, but—"

Mayes turned and began walking back to the Suburban. His security men, late to recognize their principal's discomfort, began moving between Mayes and the middle-aged woman following him.

Catherine backed off with a pleasant "Good night, Mr. Mayes."
She received no reply.

Andy and Catherine found each other in the crazed lights of the crime
scene a minute later.

Andy wore an expression of frustration. "I didn't get a thing out of her."

Catherine smiled, satisfied. "I struck out, too, but I don't care. Most importantly, we shook the trees a little. I'll reach out to Mayes in the morning, ask for a meeting on background with him and Carmichael, and helpfully suggest I might just go to the director's office if I don't get anything from them."

"What will that accomplish?"

"Carmichael doesn't like the director. He doesn't like *any* director. He resents any oversight. My guess is the director is unaware Clandestine Service leadership is hanging out with the Maryland State Police.

"I surprised Mayes tonight with what I knew, I could see that. They are going to have to come up with some sort of story for me. It won't be the truth, but they think it will slow me down."

"But it won't?"

"No. Whatever direction they try to send me off in will be a feint, but it will show me to look in another direction. You and I need to keep pounding the pavement on this. It's just getting good."

Andy and Catherine began climbing back up the embankment to their car.

Andy said, "I need to file a story, you know. I'm not an investigative reporter. My editor wants the news, and he wants it now."

Catherine said, "File what you know, but not what you suspect. Don't mention CIA being here at all, but mention Babbitt's ties to the IC."

"But—"

"Don't worry, Andy. When I file a story, we'll do it together. Trust me, it will be worth the wait."

Andy smiled as he climbed.

31

It was just past four a.m. when Gentry pulled his gray Ford Escort into the parking lot of the Easy Market on Rhode Island. He was careful to park in the same spot as he did the last time he visited this store, and just as careful to pull his red ball cap down low and to walk where the cameras could not get a look at his face.

The same heavyset young woman with the lazy eye greeted him as soon as he came in the door. "Hey, baby. How's your night goin'?"

"It's goin'," he said. He held his right arm down tight against his parka, as much to hide the tear and the little stain of blood that he'd been unable to clean off as to put a small amount of direct pressure on his painful wound.

"You must work nights, too," she said, but she'd already turned her head back to the little TV behind the counter.

"Yeah," he muttered.

He headed to a back aisle and found a small section with simple first aid items. He picked up an ACE bandage and two rolls of gauze, some tape, and a single off-brand bottle of antiseptic. He then stepped back to the cooler, where he hefted a six-pack of beer off a shelf.

LaShondra called out to him. "Oh, I see. You need you some beer for a big party over at your place. Suppose my invite got lost in the mail, is that it?"

Court smiled, then he scooped up a can of ravioli, a loaf of white bread, and a candy bar, and he brought his food and beer up to the register along with the first aid. He fished some bills out of his jacket with his left hand. "Nah. No party."

"Mm-hm." She said it in a playfully suspicious tone.

Court hoped she would be too occupied with her TV show to pay any attention to the other items he'd brought to the counter.

"Oh, baby, you done hurt yourself?"

So much for that.

"No."

"Then what's all this for?"

"Just stocking up on my first aid kit. Going camping this weekend."

"*Campin'?*" she said, as if it were a preposterous concept. "I ain't never been campin'."

Court did not respond.

She began ringing up the items, scanning the gauze, the ACE bandage, the tape, and the antiseptic. Once she got to the canned ravioli she looked up at him again. Court kept his head turned from the camera on his right, pretending to be reading a newspaper on a rack to his left. The injury to his rib cage burned like hell.

"Hey, this ain't yo dinner, is it?"

Court shrugged. "Yeah."

She paused, stopped scanning the food, and Court glanced further to the left. He got the sense she was looking at his face.

She said, "You don't look good."

"I'm fine."

"Nah, you sweating. Your skin is white. I mean like *really* white."

"Allergies. Every spring."

"You need you some greens."

"Okay," he said, thinking her comment to be rhetorical in nature.

When she kept staring at him, he glanced up quickly into her good eye.

She said, "I'm for real. Go get you a can of turnip greens or spinach or something. Don't cost but two dollars, and you look like you need it."

Court did as instructed, following LaShondra's pointed finger to a shelf. He grabbed a can of turnip greens and brought it back to the counter, set it down, and went back to looking at the magazine rack.

"You know that's real good with some vinegar. You got vinegar at home?"

Court did not. "Sure do. I'll try it."

A minute later he was on the way out the door, a little stressed about the level of questioning from the woman but ultimately satisfied he'd not compromised himself in any way.

Court realized that people here in the U.S. were nicer to strangers than in the other places he'd traveled in the past five years—when they weren't shooting you in the ribs, that was. And while Court had no problem with politeness, for a man who lived his life moving through society without leaving a trace, this was problematic.

As he struggled into the driver's seat, the pain in his torso limiting his movement, he thought he might have to change his late-night shopping habits so he didn't get any more probing questions from the ultra inquisitive cashier. He suspected LaShondra was a level of chatty not common among most late-night store clerks, so he could just find another place to make his purchases.

Court found this unfortunate, because he liked the slightly annoying woman. When she called him "baby doll" the first time he had realized it had been a very long time since anyone had called him by an affectionate name.

Court pulled out of the parking lot, a sense of sadness creeping into his normally mission-focused mind.

LaShondra would have no way of knowing it, of course, but she had become his best friend.

Too bad he would never see her again.

A half hour later Court knelt in the alley that ran catty-corner to the Mayberry home on NW Quincy Street, and he eyed the area around his rented room. He'd been here for nearly ten minutes, watching the scene, his bags from the market by his side. It would be dawn in a little while, but he was using the security afforded by darkness to survey the neighborhood, making sure he had not been followed or his hide had not been otherwise compromised.

It had been a shitty night—his covert B&E had turned into a mad run for his life, a leap from a rooftop, explosions and wild-assed, trigger-happy police officers, helicopters, and even a gunshot wound thrown in for good measure.

Jesus Christ.

Court had planned it very differently, to say the least.

He checked his watch, looked to the sky, and told himself he needed to be in the room well before first light, so he stood and crossed the street. All the while half expecting the pops of guns or the wail of sirens.

The neighborhood remained quiet.

He entered his room at six, peeled off his clothes, inspected bruises and scrapes that would get no more attention, and cradled his forearm in his hand. He'd not rebroken it—he was sure of this because he knew exactly what it felt like when it was broken—but the tissue around the injury had not appreciated the way Court had decided to spend his doctor-ordered convalescence.

He wanted to jump into the little shower, but he fought the urge for a few minutes so he could restage his booby trap by the front door. Once he had his device assembled and set, he headed for the tiny bathroom at the back of the apartment.

Court took a hot shower. The water stung like hell in his gunshot wound but he powered through it, careful to make sure he washed out any foreign debris lodged deep in the sticky mess. He then toweled off as well as he could with the wounded ribs and poured antiseptic onto a thick wad of gauze. Carefully he placed it over his injury, and he used the ACE bandage to secure it by wrapping it all the way around his torso several times.

That done, Court re-dressed in a fresh set of dark clothing and put on a pair of black running shoes. He pulled the one tray of ice out of his little refrigerator/freezer, and he moved into the closet. Here he lay on his back, the Smith and Wesson on his chest, and his right arm resting on the ice tray at the point of most discomfort.

He fell asleep like this at six forty-five and he dreamed of killer cops.

32

Zack Hightower entered the Violator Working Group's tactical operations center promptly at eight a.m., clean-shaven for the first time in two years and professionally dressed in a blue suit with a regimental tie. He was feeling better than he had felt in a long time, because he was back on the job, part of the team, and operational. True, at this point he hadn't worked out his official status or even whether he would be getting a paycheck for his services, but he didn't care. Mayes and Carmichael knew what he did, and men like Mayes and Carmichael needed a man like Zack Hightower.

More work would follow; Zack was sure of it.

Hightower was not surprised to see Suzanne Brewer already hard at work in the TOC. She was that kind of executive. Hightower had seen the type a few times before, always from distance, because he was labor and they were management. Brewer would come early and stay late, and she'd make this operation her life for the duration of it, then she'd move on to something else. But wherever she'd go from here, she would always move up; she would always leverage her access and her associations to serve as rungs on a ladder.

She'd step on Zack's head to help her climb if she needed to, of this he had no doubt.

Brewer wasn't the type of person Zack looked up to, but he'd been around the Agency long enough to know a highflier with seventh-floor potential when he saw one.

That was who she was.

And, Zack being Zack, he couldn't help but think about getting her glasses off and her smart business suit wadded up at the foot of his bed.

He pushed the imagery out of his mind and went back to business.

He imagined Brewer was the type who would keep her nose clean at all costs, and that meant, he knew without having to be told, that she would know nothing of his extracurricular activities the evening before. She was in Programs and Plans, but she wouldn't dip her toe into non-sanctioned programs or plans such as an extrajudicial killing in the USA for all the money in the world.

"Morning, Ms. Brewer," he said as she hurried over to him.

Brewer wasn't a chatty person. She was all business. "Good. You're here. I need to fill you in on what happened last night."

"Please do." Zack feigned surprise and interest, and the two of them stepped into a small glass-walled conference room.

As she sat down she said, "Around eleven p.m. yesterday Courtland Gentry murdered Leland Babbitt, director of Townsend Government Services."

Zack just said, "I'll be damned." He smiled inwardly, thinking he deserved a fucking Oscar for his acting abilities. He wasn't surprised in the least that Gentry was getting fingered for the hit. Denny Carmichael was a crafty old fox, after all.

She continued, "Shot him in the chest, then led Babbitt's security detail on a chase across Chevy Chase and Bethesda."

He blinked. "Oh." Zack's surprise was authentic now. Apparently they had hard evidence Gentry was there at the scene. But Zack still had to employ his acting talents, because it was becoming clear Gentry had been in range of Zack's Remington, and Zack had failed to see him. "That is very interesting." He said it as slowly and flatly as he could. "Any idea where he went?"

"He was tracked from Babbitt's house, and was cornered for a short time, until he blew up a McDonald's."

"He did *what*?"

"Yeah. Tossed nearly a hundred rounds of ammo into a fry cooker."

Zack burst into laughter. "Holy shit. Kill anybody?"

"No, luckily. Two Townsend men are going to have some pretty bad sunburns for a while. Another security officer was shot in the legs."

"And then Violator just vanished?"

"For ninety minutes. He then turned up on the Capital Beltway, where he first caused a traffic accident and then carjacked a taxi. The cab was discovered just twenty minutes ago in Bethesda. No sign of Gentry, though there was blood at the scene of the carjacking, and significant blood in the vehicle."

Zack said, "So he's hurt, but apparently not so badly he can't ninja his way across the greater metro area."

"Exactly. Since about three a.m. we have been monitoring hospitals, all-night pharmacies, and minor emergency clinics, expecting him to show up for supplies. Nothing so far."

Zack shook his head. "He won't go to a hospital or a clinic. He'll treat himself. If he didn't already have wound management supplies, he'll get them at a grocery store or a corner market or a vet clinic because he'll expect you to monitor video feeds at pharmacies. There can't be more than a dozen that are open all night around here."

Brewer nodded thoughtfully. "That makes sense. Any other suggestions?"

Just then, Jordan Mayes leaned into the TOC. "Sorry, Suzanne. I'll need to borrow Zack for a few minutes. I'll send him back down when I'm done."

Zack followed Mayes up to seven, neither man speaking the entire way. The older man with the white hair looked exhausted, which Zack found hilarious, because *he* had been the one in the field the night before, not Jordan Mayes.

Zack was late forties, Mayes was just a few years older, but Mayes was a suit. Zack told himself he wouldn't let himself go to pot like Mayes when he hit his fifties; hell, not even when he was eighty-five.

They entered a small private conference room, and Zack expected to see Carmichael waiting for him. But the room was empty. Mayes motioned for Zack to sit, and Mayes then took the chair next to him.

Hightower understood now. Denny was using Mayes as a cutout. Mayes would provide a barrier between the shooter and the man who gave the term order.

He'd expected instant and profuse gratitude from Mayes for killing Babbitt, but what he got was something quite different.

Mayes began, "You had eyes on the rear of Babbitt's property. How is it you didn't see Violator?"

Zack wasn't ready to go on the defensive, so it took him a moment to answer. Finally he said, "I guess that's why they call him the Gray Man. He probably got into position before I arrived. He had a secure hide site. I was focused on the target, and the target's security."

"And after? Babbitt's men saw him. Why didn't you?"

Hightower's square jaw flexed. "After I smoked my target, I hit the bricks. Nobody said anything to me about Babbitt being a potential Gentry target."

Mayes sighed. "Still, you knew Gentry was on the streets. A little vigilance on your part and you could have killed two birds with one stone last night. This op would be over."

Hightower was no longer on the defensive—now he was pissed. No seventh-floor suit was going to tell him how to do wet work. "Look, if you'd integrated me into this op a little bit more, let me know about the connection between Gentry and Babbitt, whatever it was, I could have done your analysis for you." Zack shrugged. "You just brought me into this to be a trigger puller, so I just pulled the fucking trigger."

Mayes let it go. "Very well. Denny and I are satisfied with the Babbitt termination."

Zack wanted to say, "I killed the motherfucker for you, why *wouldn't* you be satisfied?" but instead he forced out a "Glad to hear it. Next time, send me after Gentry, and I'll get Gentry. It's as simple as that."

33

D enny Carmichael stared at his computer monitor, the thick worry lines in his forehead tight with concentration. He was reading the website for the *Washington Post*, and on it an article filed at six fifteen a.m. by metro reporter Andrew R. Shoal. The story laid out the bare bones of the killing of Leland Babbitt, the escape of the killer, and a carjacking ninety minutes later that, police were saying, might have been related to the earlier crime.

There was no mention of Catherine King in the article, and she was not included in the byline, but Denny had heard all about her surprise appearance at the scene last night and her proclamation that she knew Brewer and Mayes had been in Washington Highlands at the site of Gentry's first act in the area.

There was also no mention in the piece of the two CIA employees the *Post* reporters ran into at the carjacking scene, and while Carmichael was thankful for this, he presumed Catherine King would be working on that end of the story and he'd be forced to deal with her soon. Actually, he was certain of this, because shortly after eight a.m. the *Washington Post* investigative reporter herself had called Denny's office, asking his secretary for a meeting on background with the director of NCS.

Denny didn't know if King was just fishing or if she had some clearer picture of what was going on. The fact that she knew Mayes and Brewer had been in Washington Highlands Saturday night was a problem, because now there was no way he could claim the Agency's appearance in Chevy Chase was only a curiosity about Babbitt's killing and not part of something that they had known about for several days.

Carmichael's secretary came over the intercom, breaking his train of thought. "Sir, Suzanne Brewer of Programs and Plans is asking for five minutes."

He tapped the intercom button. "Send her in."

Brewer stepped into the office, and Denny found himself impressed with just how good she looked, considering he knew she had been wandering around murder scenes at three thirty that morning.

As always, she was all business. "I just got the preliminary autopsy report on Babbitt. It doesn't fit the witness statements at all."

She handed the paper over the desk, and Carmichael took it. He adjusted his reading glasses and began skimming it. While doing so he asked, "What do you mean it doesn't fit?"

"The coroner recovered fragments of a .308 round from Babbitt's lung."

"And?"

"That's a rifle caliber."

Carmichael looked over his glasses at the younger woman. "I am a marine, Suzanne. I know what kind of weapon fires a .308."

"Of course you do. Forgive me, I've been talking to analysts all week. You know that's a round commonly fired from a sniper rifle. Not always, but certainly it must be fired from a rifle. But the Townsend guards say they first encountered the masked subject in Babbitt's backyard, less than forty yards away from where Babbitt was shot. Certainly not a sniper's distance. Plus the subject was not carrying a rifle of any kind, nor was there a rifle found in Babbitt's yard. It's going to take a while to get ballistic results back, but when we do, I feel sure it is going to indicate the rifle was fired from somewhere else, meaning Gentry could not have been the shooter."

Carmichael took another moment to skim the report. While he read, Jordan Mayes entered the office. He and Brewer chatted softly about the coroner's finding.

Finally Carmichael looked up from the paper. "Apparently the security men were mistaken. They thought they saw someone on the property, but it wasn't until they were out on the golf course that they actually came across the fleeing suspect. According to reports he was wearing a backpack. Perhaps he had time to break down his weapon. Remember, this is Violator. He could probably do that in two seconds."

"I thought of that, but there is something else."

Carmichael's eyes flitted to Mayes, but then they rested again on Brewer. "Go on."

"Saturday night in Washington Highlands, our target risks life and limb to obtain a small-caliber pistol, killing two people in the process."

"So?"

"So does it make sense that Monday night he assassinates a man with a sniper rifle? Where did he get the gun? Did he have it Saturday?"

Carmichael shrugged. "Maybe you're overthinking it. We suspect he also took money from the Aryan Brotherhood dealers. Maybe he didn't need the weapon, but finding the little pistol was just a happy accident, so he grabbed it. He could have a weapons cache the size of a Walmart and we just don't know about it."

Brewer thought it over a moment. "True. But one other thing worries me."

Now Carmichael sighed audibly. "Let's hear it."

"The reporter from the *Post* pointed out all the blood on the Beltway and asked me if there was some other crime scene. He thought the shooter had been injured somewhere after the Babbitt killing, considering the fact he couldn't have possibly bled like that for an hour and a half."

"And what do you think that means?"

"I . . . I don't know."

"You have a lot of questions, but no conclusions."

"Agreed. I just feel like we are missing an important piece of what is going on here."

Denny said, "I don't mind you speculating, but your job is not to solve a murder, it is to prevent Gentry from threatening Agency personnel."

"I understand that, sir. But if there is more than one attacker, or if I am looking for the wrong man . . ."

"You are *not* looking for the wrong man. Gentry has killed Agency assets many times before. He has killed people here in D.C. this week, and I'm quite certain he killed Babbitt. Gentry, an assassin, arrives, and two days later the man formerly in charge of hunting him is assassinated. That's proof enough as far as I'm concerned. And there is no one else involved, because Gentry works alone. Trust me, I've been chairing the Violator Working Group for five years. You've been with us for less than three days."

Chastened, but clearly unconvinced, Brewer said, "Yes, sir. Of course you're right."

As soon as she left the office, Carmichael looked up to Mayes. In an accusatory tone he said, "You brought her into this operation."

Mayes said, "I did, and for good reason. Look, Denny, we hit a patch of terrible luck when Hightower and Gentry both went for the same target at the same moment. That complicates things in the short term, but it's nothing to worry about long term. Brewer will do her job. She knows she's not here to investigate a murder."

Denny let it go, rubbing his tired eyes. "Gentry has acted the last three nights in a row. Let's plan on being ready for his next move this evening."

Mayes nodded. "I've doubled the men watching Hanley's home. Two sniper teams now. Violator's other known associates are fully covered. He might be good, but he's not going to reach out to anyone here without us seeing him."

Carmichael said, "I hope you're right. What about this other problem?"

"Catherine King?"

"Yes. Should I meet with her?"

Mayes shook his head. "Put her off for a day."

"What will waiting one day accomplish?"

"Events are moving fast. If we bag Violator today quietly we'll tell her we thought there was a threat to the Agency in the city, so we naturally looked into the Babbitt killing. Turns out we found nothing."

"And if we don't get Gentry today?"

"Then we put a lure in King's article. Feed her something that will get back to Gentry, and make him think she knows what this is all about."

Carmichael screwed his face up. "And Gentry reads the *Post*?"

"It's Catherine King, Denny. Her articles get picked up all over. TV media will run with a story like the one we'll give her. Everyone will be talking about it. Trust me, if you tell it to King, it will go in Gentry's ears."

Carmichael thought it over, then he nodded. "I like it."

Mayes cautioned, "But give it a day before we go that route. We're not looking for publicity in this. That's a last resort."

"Agreed."

34

ourt slept in his closet until nearly noon, and then he woke quickly, snatched up his pistol, and looked out into his little room. It was still and quiet; dust hung in the small shaft of light coming through the high window.

He lowered his gun and groaned with the fresh onset of pain in his side. He touched the bandages on his rib cage and found them sticky with blood. He needed to change them, but before he did he left his closet bunker and sat on his little bed. He grabbed the television remote just as the noon news began, and he flipped around until he found a local station.

The first images on the screen were of a helicopter sweeping its searchlight over a residential street lined with large homes. Court immediately recognized the property of Leland Babbitt. It was surrounded by two dozen vehicles; Maryland State Police patrol cars, Bethesda Police, ambulances, and fire trucks.

The news anchor's voiceover gave context to the images, telling the viewers some things Court already knew, and telling them other things that surprised him.

"Maryland State Police released a statement this morning saying Babbitt had been shot to death, and the killer was then chased on foot by private security nearly half a mile before briefly holding hostages at a McDonald's on Wisconsin Avenue. He then managed to elude law enforcement and escape, and his whereabouts are currently unknown."

Court sighed. So much for accuracy in the news. There were two complete falsehoods in that one sentence, since he wasn't the killer and he'd held no hostages.

Then came the images of the scene on the Capital Beltway, and this time the anchor relayed a passably accurate version of the events there, including the jackknifed semi and the armed carjacking.

But Court found it extremely odd the report made no mention of D.C. Metro police encountering the suspect at that scene as well. Hell, he'd been shot, so they *must* have suspected him of being the man involved in Babbitt's murder.

This piece ended and a new story began, so Court flipped channels to CNN. After a few minutes he was surprised to see that they also ran a brief piece about the brazen assassination of a Maryland businessman and the audacious and violent escape of the assassin.

Court was national news.

He groaned aloud in anger and turned off the TV.

He stood and grabbed a beer from his little refrigerator. In the bathroom, he drank from the can while he changed the black and sticky dressing over his gunshot wound, tears of pain welling in his eyes.

Matthew Hanley had spent a large part of this Tuesday off-site, meeting with SAD Air Branch staff at Andrews to discuss the registering of some new aircraft with shell corporations so they could be used in an upcoming operation in Central America. Through a front company the CIA had recently purchased four very used and totally untraceable de Havilland DHC Twin Otters from an Indonesian air transport service that had gone bankrupt and then shipped the planes to the States for refitting and refurbishment. Once Hanley had the new paperwork complete, the aircraft would go to work in Central and South America, moving supplies and men to denied areas for the Special Activities Division.

They would be completely untraceable to CIA, but for now they sat at Andrews in a sealed hangar, and Hanley wanted to inspect them personally.

He didn't return to his sixth-floor office at Langley until three thirty, and when he did he found Suzanne Brewer waiting on a sofa in an outer office, working quietly on an iPad while Hanley's secretary talked on her phone behind her desk.

Hanley feigned a pleasant look upon seeing Brewer, but he had a ton of work to do and was in no mood to talk to Denny Carmichael's newest foot soldier.

She stood with a charming smile. "Hi, Matt. Suzanne Brewer. It's been a while."

"Of course, Suzanne. How are you?"

"I'm good. I'll be a lot better if you can give me ten minutes of your time."

Hanley replied, "Can you make it five?"

"Five is great. Thanks so much."

The two of them walked together into his office.

Hanley did not know Brewer well, but one couldn't be a member of senior staff here without hearing her name on a regular basis. Her career had been skyrocketing straight up since she'd joined the Agency, just after getting her master's at Villanova in International Studies. Hanley had seen her name tied to all sorts of successful programs, and she'd never spent more than two years at the same desk, instead working her way steadily up the ladder.

Hanley was still several rungs above her, but he felt sure he would top out long before Suzanne Brewer, who seemed to be just getting started. He could imagine her running the whole damn Agency someday, so he told himself he should go out of his way to curry favor with her on her way up, so hopefully she'd remember his actions later on when she had the power to make his life either a little more pleasant or a lot more difficult.

Hanley said, "So, I hear you are working on the Violator operation."

"That's correct. I was put in the Working Group when Violator showed up in D.C. I guess you could say this is my geography, considering I am in charge of domestic asset protection. So now I'm trying to guess Violator's next move and, since I'm new to all this, I'm having some difficulty."

"He's a hard target, no question about that."

"You heard about Babbitt, didn't you?"

"Saw it on the news. You're thinking that was Gentry?"

"Carmichael is certain of it."

Hanley shrugged.

Brewer said, "Townsend Government Services had contractors hunting Gentry in Belgium last month. He killed several of them, as a matter of fact. We think it likely Gentry learned Babbitt's name somewhere during the course of that operation, and that's why he targeted Babbitt here in the States as soon as he arrived. He thinks it will take some of the heat off of him so he can pursue whatever his objective is."

"That's a plausible theory, I guess," said Hanley, but there was no conviction in his voice.

She recognized his uncertainty, and added, "I thought the Babbitt killing looked like it had been carried out by more than one man, but Carmichael doesn't buy that. I also spoke with Hightower about this, and he backed Carmichael up. He said Gentry often operates in a manner to obfuscate the fact he is working alone."

Hanley's eyes went wide and he took hold of the edge of his desk with both hands. "You spoke with . . . *who*?"

"Zack Hightower."

Hanley put his big forearms on his desk now, then he leaned over them, nearly halving the distance between himself and Brewer. "What the *hell* are you telling me?"

Brewer was confused, and she did not hide it. "I'm sorry. I must have something wrong. I was told Zack Hightower worked for you on the Goon Squad . . . sorry, the Golf Sierra Task Force."

Hanley continued looming over her. "That is correct."

"Then . . . what is it you don't understand?"

"I don't understand how it is you spoke with him recently."

"Why not?"

Hanley sat back in his chair now. Gave a huge shrug to his big shoulders. "Because I went to the man's funeral five years ago."

Brewer herself sat back in her chair in surprise. "Well, I can assure you he is very much alive. He is no longer with the Agency officially but has come in to help me understand the tactics of our target."

Matt Hanley took out a handkerchief and wiped his ruddy face. "Okay. Zack's back from the dead to help you find the guy who killed him. Just another day in the office around here. I'm with you."

She said, "This isn't my first rodeo. I've run security at facilities where I couldn't know what was going on inside. I've protected assets and employees from threats that were unclear to me. But the capabilities of this threat and the importance of the people I'm being asked to protect in this case have me thinking I need to know more about what is going on here. I thought perhaps you might have some other advice for me since you worked with Gentry for several years."

Hanley said, "Suzanne, we don't know each other very well, but I hope you will take this recommendation as it's intended, just a friendly suggestion."

"Of course." She picked up the stylus for her iPad and touched it to the screen, ready to take notes.

"Your job is to fortify the gates of this institution. In my opinion, based on twenty-five years of experience around here, the greatest dangers to the institution are already inside the gates."

She did not reply.

He said, "Court Gentry is Denny's war. He's brought you in to help him fight it, but there is no future in it for you. Sure, maybe you'll kill your target, and that might be a little feather in your cap, but this isn't true Agency business, and someday Denny is going to crash and burn for all his extracurricular activities." Hanley spoke softly. "You are a winner, Suzanne. I see it. Don't follow Denny Carmichael down into the dirt."

Brewer smiled a little while looking down at her iPad. Hanley got the impression she was trying to extricate herself from what she saw as nothing more than a personal conflict between Hanley and Carmichael. She did so by ignoring his comments entirely. "I know Gentry killed several men in his unit when they tried to detain him. Can you tell me what he did before that? Why they were after him in the first place?"

Hanley saw Brewer wasn't going to listen to his advice. Denny was top dog, so she would do what he said, not follow Hanley, a topped-out and burned-out minion.

He said, "I don't know what Gentry did before he killed the other men on his task force. Whatever happened with Court Gentry five years ago, it hurt Denny personally or professionally, maybe both."

Brewer said, "CIA does not vendetta-kill our own because some exec is pissed off."

Hanley smiled at her. "If you think Denny Carmichael is just an exec, then you aren't going as far in this building as I thought you were. Denny *is* the CIA these days. He has the president's ear, because he kills a lot of bad guys, and the director fears him, because the director doesn't want to get any of Denny's blood on his own hands. In the history of this Agency there has never been a more powerful entity than Denny Carmichael. *Never.* Doing his bidding will help you move up to the seventh floor, but like I said, Denny's house of cards will tumble, and those left standing will sweep away anyone connected to the man. If you know what's good for you—"

Apparently Suzanne Brewer had heard enough. "Director Hanley, this has nothing to do with my future aspirations with the Agency. Violator is a threat to Agency personnel, and it is my job to protect Agency personnel. It is as simple as that. Take yourself, for example."

"What *about* me?"

"You have to know you are a potential target of this man."

"Of course I know."

"Then why don't you let me increase your security profile?"

"Carmichael and Mayes put a team of JSOC skull fuckers on my house. They are *hoping* Gentry comes after me."

"And that makes you feel secure?"

"Hell no! It makes me feel like a goat tied to a stick! I've got two of my guys riding with me and I've requisitioned an armored car. But it won't be enough. If Gentry wants me, he'll get me."

"Then let me help you. I can give you a full motorcade, a dozen security officers."

Hanley did not answer her directly. Instead he said, "Last night I walked out onto my back patio and talked to the trees. I figure that if Gentry is coming for me, he's probably back there somewhere waiting for me to go to bed."

"What are you telling the trees?"

Hanley laughed. "The truth. I'm telling them that all this shit is Denny's doing. Not mine."

"Aren't you just giving him an easy shot?"

"Gentry doesn't *need* an easy shot. Won't make any difference to him if he has to skulk into my house. This way my poor Ecuadorian cleaning lady won't have to wipe my brains off the wall, she can just hose it off the patio tile."

Suzanne Brewer stood. "I certainly hope that doesn't happen to you."

He stood as well, and they shook hands. "Yeah. Me, too. Somebody has to be left standing when Denny goes down. I'm hoping it's me." He shrugged, lurching his big shoulders up and down. "I'm hoping it's you, too."

"Thank you for your time today, Matt."

Brewer left the office, and Matt knew he had not managed to dent her thick armor at all.

35

Matthew Hanley sat in the backseat of an armored Toyota Camry, gazing through the tempered glass at the heavy evening traffic on Rock Creek Parkway. A flash of lightning illuminated the high hill to the right of his vehicle, thick with trees and shrubs. The director of the Special Activities Division took the quarter second of illumination as an opportunity to scan the high ground, searching for signs of a man there with an anti-tank weapon.

The darkness returned, and Matt closed his eyes.

Calm the fuck down. He's not after you.

Two Ground Branch paramilitary operations officers sat in front of him in the armored car, but they knew better than to disturb the silence. Jenner drove and watched the other cars on the road while Travers rode shotgun and watched everyone and everything that was not riding inside another vehicle. They kept their HK MP7s stowed below the dash and at the ready, and both men carried radios that would connect them with CIA security forces positioned in D.C.

Hanley did not usually carry a weapon himself, but an MP5 with a collapsible stock sat inside a briefcase on the floorboard by his leg.

Another flash of lightning gave him another chance for a quick scan of the road. This time a slight rumble of thunder worked its way through the bulletproof glass, letting him know the storm was moving closer.

This nine p.m. drive home from work felt to Matt like a movement in a hostile environment, and in a way it was, but Hanley was less certain of Gentry's intentions than anyone else at Langley, because Hanley knew something no one else knew. A year ago he had run into Gentry in Mexico City. Hanley had been a station chief at the time in Port-au-Prince, but the CIA had tracked the Gray Man to Mexico, and Hanley flew in to assist with the hunt.

A drug lord captured Gentry before the CIA got to him, so Carmichael ordered Hanley to render a positive ID of their old asset and then let nature take its course, meaning Hanley was to let the drug lord's henchmen kill his former CIA paramilitary operations officer.

Instead, Hanley saved Gentry's life, not because he particularly liked the guy, but rather because he disagreed with the op on principle. Hanley found the events in Mexico were so much against everything he stood for he could not sit by and watch Gentry die at the hands of the cartel.

Now as he rode in the back of an armored sedan, Hanley wondered if he should have just let Gentry get smoked by the Mexicans. He didn't know for sure. He did not for a moment think things were patched up or in any way simpatico between himself and Gentry, but he wasn't so sure the world's best assassin would put a bullet in his brain, either.

He put the chances somewhere around sixty-forty in his favor.

Still . . . *only* a forty percent chance that the world's best assassin was gunning for him didn't exactly fill Matt Hanley with serenity.

Hanley saw Gentry as a good man who'd been soiled and turned into something dangerous by his work. He was like so many others in CIA, but he was several cuts above the rest, because Court Gentry had just gotten so damn good at being so damn bad.

He looked at the two men in front of him in the car. Jenner was an SAD Ground Branch team leader, and Travers was his number two. Hanley had gotten an e-mail earlier in the evening from personnel requesting that Jenner's entire team come in for a drug screening tomorrow, but Hanley hadn't passed this information on just yet.

This happened from time to time, it was part of the work, but Hanley knew Carmichael had ordered the screen, because Carmichael was looking for an excuse to pull Travers. Some doctor working for personnel would do what Carmichael told him to, which meant Travers was twenty-four hours away from testing positive for some controlled substance, and this would derail his career.

Probably his life.

And Hanley didn't think he could do a goddamned thing about it, because Carmichael was the king.

Matt Hanley lived on 28th Street NW in Woodley Park, a tree-lined hilly section in northwestern D.C. He was a bachelor after a divorce twenty years earlier; both his kids were grown, living on the West Coast near his ex-wife.

Jenner navigated the Camry into Hanley's garage while Travers continued scanning the neighborhood, then both officers climbed out of the vehicle. While Hanley remained locked in the armored car the men checked his entire two-thousand-square-foot home. It took them fifteen minutes; they put their eyes on any possible man-sized space they could find. Travers crawled the attic, and Jenner moved paint cans in the corner of the basement to shine a light over every square foot where Gentry could possibly hide.

While all this happened Hanley waited silently. He had calls to make and papers to read, but he wasn't in the mood tonight. He just sat there in the armored car, thinking about nothing.

Finally Jenner opened Hanley's door. "The place is secure, sir, and it's locked down tight. Once we leave the garage, set your alarm. Nothing is getting in here."

"Okay," he said.

Travers asked, "You sure you don't want us to bunk here tonight, boss?"

"I could use the company, for sure. But no. You guys run on."

Jenner shifted his weight back and forth on his boots. "Violator is out there, sir. Got to say I find it a little odd you don't want the extra security."

"I'm fine."

With obvious reluctance, his two men pulled out of the garage and back out onto 28th Street NW. Hanley set the alarm, and then closed his garage door.

Once he changed out of his suit and tie and into jeans and a flannel shirt, he headed down to his kitchen, reheated last night's takeout from LiLLiES, an Italian bistro right up the street from him. Then he opened a bottle of Chianti, drinking it while scarfing down day-old penne alla vodka from a microwave-safe carryout bowl.

Matt ate a lot and he drank a lot, and when he wasn't working he did most of his eating and drinking alone. He took his time with his meal, enjoying every bite, but each time a flash of lightning brightened the backyard he glanced out of his kitchen, past his living room, and through the French doors, halfway expecting to see a man standing there, gun in hand.

He finished the last gulp of wine in his glass, then he tried to pour more, but found the bottle empty.

Looking at the clock, he realized he'd been sitting in his kitchen for an hour.

His mobile rang in the front pocket of his jeans, startling him, showing him just how on edge he remained, even though he kept telling himself Gentry probably wouldn't kill him. He chastised himself as he pulled out the phone and looked at the caller ID.

"Hello, Jenner."

"Just checking on you, boss."

"That's sweet."

"Seriously. Wanted to make sure you are okay. You watched the garage door till it closed?"

"I did."

"Okay." A pause. "Again, you change your mind, you just let me know. Travers lives ten minutes from you, but you know him, he'll be there in five. I'm twenty out, but I'll be there in ten if you need me."

"I read you five-five, Jenner. See you tomorrow."

Another pause. "You okay, boss?"

"Good night." Hanley hung up the phone.

Matt Hanley then stood, walked to the French doors overlooking the back patio, and looked out at the approaching storm. The wind blew the trees wildly, and the waist-high ferns in stone planters on his patio whipped around like mad dancing children.

Matt put his hand on the door latch, hesitated almost a minute, and then opened the door.

His home alarm began beeping, but he ignored it.

The smell of rain was strong, blowing into his living room with the wind.

Hanley spoke to the trees. "Okay, Six. Let's get this over with."

He stepped out onto his patio and pulled one of the smaller stone planters inside, then used it as a doorstop to keep one of the French doors propped open a foot and a half. Then he turned away, walked over to the security box, and disarmed the alarm.

He headed for the stairs to his bedroom.

Matt Hanley had spent many years intimately aware of the abilities of the assassin known as Violator, Sierra Six, and the Gray Man. He wasn't sure if Gentry wanted to kill him, but if he did, Gentry *would* get the job done.

Hanley knew, without any doubt, that if Gentry saw no way to walk right up to Hanley he could kill him from a mile away or even more if he wanted.

Hanley wasn't going to hide under a rock for the rest of his life.

Court Gentry might kill him, Hanley had decided, but he wasn't going to do it from distance. No thousand-meter shot through the heart.

No, if Hanley had to die, he would die deep in conversation with the Gray Man.

It was his only chance.

At the top of the stairs, Hanley felt a presence here in the house with him. His already pounding heart seemed to find another gear. He sniffed the air, thought he detected the odor of another body, the smell of the outdoors up here on the second floor.

But he could not be certain.

He looked behind him on the stairs, then he opened the door to a hallway bathroom. Another flash of light from outside revealed the room as if it were day.

There was nothing.

Hanley spoke loudly, almost in a shout. "If you're here, Court, I only ask for a moment of your time before you do whatever it is you came to do. You owe me that much."

No sounds anywhere in the home, only the pounding of the rain now, on the roof and on the windows.

Hanley turned and headed up the hall to his bedroom.

In his room he turned on the light by his bed, opened the drawer in his end table, and was comforted to see his old Wilson Combat 1911 .45 ACP pistol. He'd had the gun since he'd worn the Green Beret of U.S. Army Special Forces in the 1980s, and although it wasn't his only firearm, it was the gun he kept by his bed for things that went bump in the night.

He turned off his phone and laid it on his side table, kicked off his shoes, then turned off the light and lay on his back on the bed. Fully clothed, fully expecting no sleep at all tonight.

Matt Hanley's eyes opened and he sat up, unsure how long he'd been asleep, or even if he had dozed off at all. The thunder barked outside, the room was dark, but again, he felt someone close by.

He dropped his head back on the pillow.

"Jesus Christ, Court. If you are here, just fucking say something."

A new flash of light outside, at the same time as a thunderclap.

A man stood at the foot of Hanley's bed, head to toe in black, his face masked, his clothes dry.

"Jesus!" Hanley shouted, jerking back until his head slammed against the headboard. He grabbed at the stitch of pain in his heart.

36

ome on, Six! That's not necessary! You scared the piss out of me!"

There was no reply in the darkness for several seconds, only the rumble of distant thunder. Then a soft voice came from the side of the bed, ten feet away from where Hanley had seen Gentry in the lightning's flash.

"Which is it? Are you stupid, cocky, or suicidal?"

Hanley was still recovering from the fright, but he sat all the way up in bed now. "I left the door open because I wanted you to know I'm not trying to keep you away. I didn't want you to blow my head off from five hundred meters. I'd much rather we talk."

"And *then* I blow your head off?"

Hanley swallowed. "Hell, you almost scared me to death." He rubbed the top of his head where it had hit the headboard. "I can't stop whatever it is you are planning on doing, but killing me would serve nothing. Can we *please* talk?"

"I'm not here to kill you, Matt. I remember what you did in Mexico."

"Glad to hear that."

"But I'll warn you right now . . . that fancy .45 that was in your bedside table is now on my hip."

Hanley turned to look at the nightstand. He couldn't imagine how Gentry had gotten all the way up to his bed, opened a drawer, and retrieved a weapon without making a sound.

He said, "*Christ*, Court. I wouldn't have gone for my gun. I know you could kill me ten different ways before I got my hand on it."

"Of course you know. But now I won't have to."

Hanley changed the subject. "Did you see the snipers?"

"Yes."

Hanley said, "I don't know where they are, just heard JSOC had me covered."

Gentry replied, "One hundred forty yards east, rooftop of a four-story office building. Two guys. An AI .308 on the shooter, and an HK 416 with an ACOG on the spotter. And one hundred fifty-five yards northeast, two more, in a second-story apartment. Same sniper rifle, but the spotter has an M4 with an EOTech."

Hanley turned his head slowly, trying to identify the location of the voice, because clearly Gentry had moved again. He gave up and said, "You managed to ID the caliber of the rifles and the brand of optics from one hundred fifty yards away?"

Court said, "I got a little closer."

"You didn't kill them, did you?"

Court pulled a chair into a corner, Hanley could hear the movement, and when he focused his eyes on the location, lightning struck outside, closer than ever. With the flash through the curtains Hanley could just make out the silhouette of a man. On the man's right was the window that looked over the front yard. Even though it was covered with a curtain, Hanley saw Gentry had positioned himself so no one out there could get line of sight on him through the glass.

Court replied, "It's *me*, Matt. When have I ever killed a Delta operator?"

"People change."

"*Other* people change. Rules change. Loyalties change. *I* don't."

Hanley forced a smile. "You've been out of it for a while. They aren't called Delta anymore."

"No? What are they called now?"

"Can't tell you. Classified."

"That's cute." Lightning struck again and, along with it, a massive thunderclap. "So they've got you running SAD now."

"Can you believe it?"

"When I shot you in Mexico I told you it would be a perfect opportunity for career enhancement."

"Is this where I express my eternal gratitude for you filling me full of lead?"

Court did not respond.

Hanley said, "I am not going to have much information for you. I've got nothing to do with the Violator Working Group. Denny asked for Ground Branch guys to help target you, and I told him to fuck off."

"I'm not interested in who's after me now. I'm here to find out what happened five years ago."

"I know even less about that."

"Bullshit."

"It's Denny, man. He's been the one orchestrating it all from the beginning."

"I know that. I also know he told you *something*. He gave you a rationale for this. You may be Denny's bitch at CIA, but you are your own man, Matt, you always have been. You proved that in Mexico. Even if Carmichael twisted your arm to get you to come after me, he had a story to go along with it." Court leaned a little closer, but his face was still in darkness. "Tell me the story. That's all I want. You do that and I move on."

Hanley climbed off the bed and started over to a chair across from Court. He kept his hands away from his body, and he moved slowly. It was still nearly pitch-black in the room, other than the occasional lightning strikes that flashed through the curtained windows, and Hanley didn't even know if Court was holding a weapon on him, but he had been in this line of work too long to advance on a killer without making it plain he posed no threat.

He sat down in the chair. "Court, this road you are traveling doesn't lead where you want it to go."

"What's that supposed to mean?"

"It means, when all is said and done, you are going to wish you didn't go poking around D.C. to find out why everyone is after you."

"Why not?"

Hanley heaved a long sigh. He didn't want to say more, but he knew Gentry wasn't going anywhere unless he talked. "Because this whole thing is your fault."

A long pause. "No."

"Everything you think is just some terrible misunderstanding is *not* a misunderstanding. You are under lethal authorization because you *earned* lethal authorization. It sucks, and I've been against the sanction from the get-go . . . but it *is* a legit sanction."

Court shook his head emphatically. "Not true. I know everything that happened down at street level on my ops, and my conscience is clear. If something went tits-up on a mission it was strategic, not tactical, and I didn't have a damn thing to do with strategy. I'd fall on my sword in an instant if I fucked up, but I'm not taking the fall for someone else's mistake."

Hanley winced, feeling the pain of having to deliver bad news, but also the pain of having to deliver bad news to someone who just might kill the messenger of the bad news.

He said, "Carmichael called me up one day five years ago, back when I was running the Goon Squad, back when you were on the team. He said he had a new termination order for us. I said, 'Cool, we'll meet and wade through the intel, then go see legal and the director to get it approved.' He told me it was already approved by everybody. That wasn't how we did things, so I told him I wanted to talk face-to-face.

"He met me at a restaurant in Reston, and he brought Max Ohlhauser, the Agency's chief legal counsel. You know him?"

Court shook his head, Hanley could barely register the movement in the dark. "I don't hang out with CIA lawyers."

"Anyway, each time we got a term order, it had to be signed by Denny, Ohlhauser, and the CIA director, whoever was in the chair at the time."

"Okay."

"So Denny pulls out the order, all signed off on by the director and Ohlhauser, and then Denny signs it right in front of me. I looked down to see who we were terming. I figured it was some AQ guy, maybe Hezbollah, Al-Shabab. The usual suspects. But your name was on the order, Court."

"Why?"

"Denny wouldn't tell me specifics. It was a need-to-know thing. But Ohlhauser knew. And so did the director."

"How do you know the director—"

"Because I went and asked him. Personally. He wouldn't talk to me about it, he felt conflicted as hell, you could see it on his face. But he said if I had a term order with his signature on it, I needed to shut the fuck up and comply and to get the fuck out of his office." Hanley chuckled in the dark. "I'm not paraphrasing, that's verbatim."

"So Carmichael and Ohlhauser told you nothing?"

"No. They told me *something.* They told me which op you fucked up that earned you the sanction."

More thunder, the rain whipped in sheets on the window now.

"What op?"

Hanley did not reply.

"*What op?*"

Nothing.

"You gonna *make* me shoot you, Matt?"

Hanley said, "Operation BACK BLAST."

Court's eyes narrowed. The name meant nothing to him. He thought back several years, through so many operations. *Maybe.* He wasn't sure. "That first thing we did in Jalalabad?"

"No, man. That was BACKBEAT."

"That's right . . . The thing in Ankara?"

"BRAINSTORM."

"Sarajevo?"

Hanley looked at his former operator with bewilderment. "*Jesus*, that one was called AARDVARK SANDSTORM. Were you even paying attention during the briefings?"

Court shrugged. "I've had a pretty full plate recently. What the hell was BACK BLAST?"

"Trieste, Italy."

Gentry looked away a moment, thinking back. "The thing in Trieste had a name?"

Hanley nodded in the dark. "In your defense, it was kind of thrown together, wasn't it? But it *did* have a name. It's possible Hightower never read you in on the name of the op."

"But . . . what about it? That op was solid."

"Denny says it wasn't. He says you rogued it. Ohlhauser confirmed it, and the director seemed to agree."

Court stood from the chair quickly, startling Hanley. "That's a damn lie! I remember everything that happened in Trieste. A terminal sanction along with a personnel recovery. I wasted the bad guy and scooped up the good guy. Whatever Carmichael's real reason for wanting me off the table, it sure as shit wasn't anything that happened in BACK BLAST."

Hanley remained seated, but he put his hands up in surrender. "I only know what he told me, and he told me you were derelict on BACK BLAST. I fought him tooth and nail for more intel, and when he wouldn't give it up I just begged him to cashier you, or have you charged with something and pulled off Golf Sierra and thrown out of the Agency. But the term order was the term order, and that was that."

Court was barely listening now. He knew he'd done exactly as instructed on that mission, but there was one thing about Trieste that did stand out. He had been working with Zack Hightower's Golf Sierra Task Force at the time, but on that particular operation he'd been sent in alone due to operational requirements. Nothing had gone wrong on BACK BLAST, he was sure of it, but if it had, it would have been a mission where he was the only one who would have been blamed. Not the rest of Golf Sierra.

Court turned back to Hanley. "Do you know more than what you are saying?"

"Listen carefully, Court. Denny calls the shots at the Agency. He has more power than the director of the CIA. More power than the Director of National Intelligence. Denny is the king, and the king is after you. Better you just declare victory on this little operation. You came to D.C. to get intel on what went down. You got intel. You got me to tell you this knot isn't going to be unraveled. So now go, get out of the country, back into the Third World, and back to your life. You have one hell of a good business model. An assassin of assholes. You can be proud of that. Don't throw it all away because you are so naive to think you can come home and fix the goddamned CIA."

Court knelt down, right next to Hanley. It was the first time the director of the Special Activities Division had been able to clearly make out the face of his former asset.

Court said, "I'm not leaving till I clear my name. I'm dead otherwise, and you know it. Forget about BACK BLAST, this has to do with AAP, not some on-the-fly term and rescue I did in Italy."

Hanley said, "What's AAP?"

Court said, "It's the program I was part of before I worked for you."

Hanley gave Gentry a quizzical look. "I don't know anything about that."

"Exactly! No one does but those involved, and they're all dead. Carmichael wants me dead, too, before others find out."

Hanley shook his head back and forth. "I think you're wrong, buddy. I think you digging any deeper is just going to go bad for you." He hesitated for a moment, then said, "Six, I saved you in Mexico City . . . I can't save you here."

"I didn't come here to get saved."

"That's what worries me. You came back to go out with one last big bang."

Court said nothing.

Hanley put his hand on Court's shoulder. "Just remember why we got into this work in the first place. To help this country. Not to hurt it."

"Don't lecture me about the mission."

Hanley raised his hands in surrender. "You're right. You've done your part. There should be more guys like you, Court." He paused, gave a slight shrug of his shoulders. "Not many. Two. Three, tops. Doubt we could handle more than that."

Just then there was a loud banging on the open back door downstairs. A male voice called out. "Hanley?"

Hanley's own pistol appeared in Gentry's hand in a heartbeat, and he jammed it under the SAD director's thick chin.

"Who the *fuck* is that? You hit a panic button?"

Hanley answered back, his eyes shut tight because of the gun jabbed in his throat. "No. It's just Jenner. He didn't want me to stay here without security. He's checking on me."

Court said, "Say something to him," but he pressed the barrel of the weapon harder into Hanley's beefy neck.

Hanley shouted out of his bedroom and up his second-floor hall. "What the hell, Jenner?"

"You didn't answer your phone, boss. Your back door is propped open down here. You okay?" As the man spoke, it was clear he was moving closer. From the den to the stairs.

Hanley shouted, "I'll be fine when you get the fuck out of my house!"

"Just let me put eyes on you first. Make me feel better."

Court stood, began moving to the door, pulling Hanley with him by the collar of his flannel shirt. Court whispered, "I'll send you downstairs, but I swear if you say a fucking word I'll kill you both."

Hanley nodded, then said, "Six. The pistol. It was a gift from my dad."

Court rolled his eyes. "I'll toss it in a backyard flowerpot."

Hanley held a hand out for Court to shake, then Jenner called out again.

Court ignored the extended hand, spun his former boss around, and pushed him out into the hall. Hanley did not look back. He continued towards the stairs. Quickly he wiped nervous perspiration from his face, and he disappeared from Court's view. As he descended the stairs Court heard him speaking to Jenner, who sounded like he was halfway up the stairs himself.

"I'm sorry, boss, but *shit*. Why is your door open? And why are you dressed?"

"I needed some air. It's fine."

"You took a *walk*? With Violator out there?"

"Relax. Snipers are on every rooftop around here, anyway. Hell, they probably just watched me take a dump through my bathroom window."

The men kept talking, but their voices receded. Court waited another moment, then he left the bedroom, moved up the second-floor hallway past the stairs, and entered a dark guest room full of storage boxes. He felt his way to the window and raised the blinds. This was the southwest side of the house, the only portion Court knew was clear of surveillance.

Seconds later he was outside, using a copper drainpipe to make it down to ground level, struggling with dull pain in his right forearm and sharp pain in his ribs. In the backyard he moved low, placing the .45 pistol in an old wheelbarrow with a flat tire next to the back fence. He climbed the fence into another yard, and within minutes he was two blocks away on Cathedral Street making his way back to his car.

The JSOC watchers had no idea they'd missed him.

37

ourt drove through the trailing edge of the thunderstorm on his way back to his basement apartment, his mind twisted with plots, conspiracy, and guesswork. It was a bad time to think. It was midnight, there was a good bit of traffic even with the weather, and the old Fort Escort's wipers were shit. He struggled to see the road, and he found this even tougher to do than normal because his mind was near capacity processing everything Matt Hanley had just told him.

Again, much the same as in his conversation with Travers, most of what he'd heard from his former boss sounded like secondhand disinformation. Court felt certain Operation BACK BLAST was nothing more than a red herring. He remembered the op as a two-day in extremis rush job that took place at least a full year before the shoot-on-sight sanction came out for him. Court didn't think it was relevant to his problem now at all, other than the fact that Carmichael was using BACK BLAST as an excuse for the termination order, because he had to keep his real reasons under wraps.

If Denny wanted him dead for something that happened in BACK BLAST, why the hell would he wait a year to go after him?

No, Court's original theory still made the most sense to him. He was being silenced because he was part of the Autonomous Asset Program, an extrajudicial initiative that, for some reason he did not yet understand, could not come to light.

Court had learned one piece of actionable intelligence from Matt Hanley, though, and this was the focus of his attention now as he pulled off of Massachusetts and onto Rhode Island Avenue. Max Ohlhauser, a man he'd never even heard of, had apparently signed off on the termination order. Court knew his next step was to look into this guy to see where he was, and if there was some way he could get his hands on him.

The chief legal counsel for the CIA sounded to Court like someone high-profile enough to warrant at least perfunctory security, but it also sounded to Court like this would be a guy whose detail wouldn't be expecting their protectee to face an attack here in the city.

If he was even still the chief counsel, and *if* he was even still here in the city.

With all the obfuscation at every turn, Court felt his frustration growing. He didn't know what Ohlhauser would be able to tell him about the origins of Denny Carmichael's shoot-on-sight sanction, but at this point, Court found himself looking forward to the opportunity to extract any information he could get.

Court squinted through the water on his windshield and noticed a familiar sign just up ahead. He had no real operational reason to stop in the Easy Market on Rhode Island this evening. In fact, just yesterday he'd told himself he would never return. The woman behind the counter was nice but nosy, and although nice was good, his current situation couldn't allow him to hang around with inquisitive people.

But as he neared the market, he began to slow.

He told himself that he needed provisions, that there wasn't enough in his room at the Mayberrys' should the heat on him in the city get so intense he had to stay inside for more than a day or two.

But honestly he just felt like stopping in. He wasn't ready to go back to his tiny room; he wanted to prolong his evening, even if for just a couple minutes more, and he couldn't think of another place to go where he'd find a smiling face and sixty seconds of kindness without the risk of paying too high a price.

He justified his decision from a PERSEC standpoint. He had reconnoitered the Easy Market and he knew it was secure. Why go to some other shop or bar somewhere, and deal with new cameras and camera angles, new dark corners and blind spots, new personalities and unknown subjects?

Tonight Court decided he would just stop in here, grab a few more items to store at his place, listen to LaShondra talk for a minute, and then go home.

The rain remained steady as he pulled into his same spot in the parking lot, but it was no longer slamming down in whipping sheets. The loud thunder and lightning had abated as well, but he could still hear it rolling off in the east. He flipped the hood of his raincoat over his baseball cap, and he climbed out of the car.

As soon as he walked into the market he lowered his dripping hood, but he kept the cap down low. He knew the camera angles in here without looking, although he did perform a fast scan to make sure the broken cameras remained broken.

They hung there partially disassembled, just as before, so Court started for the refrigerated shelves.

He'd only made it a couple of steps before LaShondra called out to him. "Honey, ain't nothin' in this here place that's worth comin' out in this rain for."

"Yeah," he said. He walked to the dairy section with his head down, and he selected a pint carton of milk.

"You one of my regulars now. Three nights in a row."

"Guess so."

"I bet you came in just to tell me how good them greens were with vinegar. Ain't that right?"

"That's right," Court said. Then he added, "They were really good." In fact he hadn't even opened the can yet, but she was a nice lady and he wanted to make her happy, and this seemed like the easiest way.

She squealed in delight. "I done told you!"

"You did." Court smiled a little, glancing up at her over a low shelf of bread.

"You gettin' you some more?"

He hadn't planned on it. "Sure am."

Court grabbed two cans of greens and started to turn away, then he scooped a third off the shelf before he began heading up to the counter. His little kitchenette had only one small exposed shelf over the sink; now that shelf would be lined halfway across with turnip greens.

He grabbed a loaf of white bread and some packages of ramen noodles, and he turned for the front.

At the register he kept his face angled to the left to position it away from the camera. He repeated his now-customary ruse, pretending to look down to the newspaper rack.

LaShondra started ringing up his items, and she continued talking about what Court had come to suspect was her favorite subject. "They good for you. Make you feel better. Hey, you look a little better than you did last night."

"Feel a little better," he replied.

The door clanged open to Court's left, and a short man walked in wearing a thick black jacket over a dark gray hoodie. Court eyed him for a half second and saw he was way too young to be an operator or a cop. He was Hispanic, he might have been twenty, and he didn't even glance up as he passed by.

"Hey, baby," LaShondra called out to the man as he walked behind Court on his way to the back of the little store.

The young Hispanic made no reply.

Court put his change in his pocket while LaShondra bagged his groceries. She spoke softly to him. "Lots of folks 'round here don't speak no English." It was her explanation for why the man had not replied to her, as if Court were wondering.

He wasn't. The Hispanic went back to the beer cooler, and Court now had his eyes on two new people coming through the door. A male and a female, both African American, both in their late twenties. They were athletic-looking, and Court could imagine either one of them being undercover law enforcement or even FBI surveillance types, although he knew he was paranoid, and they could also be nothing more than civilians who liked to go to the gym.

Behind them a burgundy Monte Carlo rolled up and stopped at one of the gas pumps.

"What'chall doin' out in this rain?" LaShondra called out to the couple like she knew them, but this did little to allay Court's suspicions, since she had spoken to him the same way the first time she set eyes on him.

But the female spoke to LaShondra by name and with obvious familiarity, so Court relaxed.

LaShondra handed Court his plastic bag now. "Now you go home and get to feelin' better, you hear?"

"I will," he said with a little smile.

As he started towards the exit, he saw that two men had climbed out of the Monte Carlo and were approaching the store.

This market had been completely empty the first couple of times he'd been in, but those visits had both taken place later in the evening. Now, just after midnight, even in this storm, the Easy Market felt like Grand Central.

Court held the door open for two young men, both in their late teens or early twenties, just like the first guy through the door.

The young man in front was white and he wore a black skullcap and a black jacket. He nodded his thanks to Court.

The second man, on the other hand, looked at Court with rapidly blinking, searching eyes. He was Hispanic, his jaw was clenched tight, and he passed through without a word.

Something was wrong with this dude; Court saw it immediately.

Once the two newcomers were in the market, Court stood there an instant holding the door, then he stepped back into the store, walking a couple of steps to a magazine rack.

He picked up a copy of *Car and Driver*, but he didn't really look at it. Instead he remained tuned in to his surroundings.

That last guy's vibe was not good.

Not good at all.

Dammit, Court thought. *I don't need this shit.*

Court knew how to identify pre-assault indicators, and he'd seen clear examples of this phenomenon on the last man through the door. And, although he'd detected nothing out of the ordinary in the behavior of the nervous guy's partner, they were obviously together.

Now Court glanced up to the first young Hispanic to enter the market, wondering if he might also be with the other two, even though he had not arrived in the same car. The man in the gray hoodie was in the back corner, in the exact opposite end of the room as Court. But the man wasn't shopping. Instead he stood there, facing the entire room, looking over the shelves, his head moving back and forth.

Scanning. Another pre-assault indicator. Court now knew all three of these assholes were a team, and he was pretty sure they were not here for him. No, they were about to rob the convenience store.

Although he had an accurate headcount of the bad guys inside the Easy Market, Court knew there easily could be a driver, or a spotter, or both, outside in the parking lot. He glanced out to the Monte Carlo but couldn't see anyone else through the tinted back windows. Nor did he see any other movement in the rain-swept parking lot.

Court scanned again over the top of his magazine, up to the counter. The heavyset African American clerk was oblivious to everything happening around her. She had been chatting happily with the black couple, but they had moved away to choose some soft drinks from the cooler, not far from the gray-hooded man in the back corner. LaShondra had her good eye back on her little TV, and the two new men stood at her counter, pretending to look over some small shots of energy drinks on a rack. Casually LaShondra asked the men if it was still raining outside. She was just making conversation; she could see the rain through the glass if she just glanced back over her shoulder.

"Yeah," the white guy muttered, the one whose jaw didn't look like it was wired so shut he would need bolt cutters to speak. While Court focused on him this same man moved his right leg back behind him a little, and he turned his body at an angle to the cash register.

This was called blading, and Court knew it meant he probably had a gun on his hip and was about to go for it.

Fuck.

Court desperately tried to think of something he could do to ward off this impending event before it started. He tried to come up with a way to scare off the three robbers before they committed to their act, but he knew if he stepped any closer to the register he would show his face on the camera, and if he shouted out he would only draw attention to himself, ensuring all three guns would sweep in his direction first.

Short of drawing his own piece right now, Court didn't see any options.

Other than one. He knew he could simply turn around and push through the glass door. He could be in his car before this robbery began.

It was his only safe play, the one sure way he could get through this unscathed.

But Court Gentry stood his ground.

He looked the men over quickly, trying to figure out who would be the quickest on the trigger.

Determine the will—determine the skill.

He knew if any of these three young men pulled a gun, then all three of them would die. He wouldn't wait around to see if anyone wanted to drop his weapon and pray to Jesus for mercy.

Nope, if this went down, Court was determined to kill every threat in front of him.

Loud and messy.

He flitted his eyes up again to LaShondra, and he willed her to go ahead and pop open her register's till and hand over all her money to the two men standing there—*before* things turned violent.

But she just watched her TV while they pretended to shop.

The African American couple standing at the cooler each had a six-pack of soda, and the man selected a bag of potato chips. They had just turned to head up the aisle to the counter when the man in the back corner behind them began moving quickly towards them. Court couldn't see the man draw a weapon because of the shelves between his position and the back corner of the market, but the female's shout of alarm made it clear something was terribly wrong.

Court heard yelling at the front counter, then a flurry of movement there. The two men at the register pulled their knit caps down, revealing them to be ski masks, and they each produced a chrome automatic pistol from their jackets. The weapons reached out across the counter, nearly into LaShondra's stunned face. The third man racked a pistol grip shotgun he'd strapped to his shoulder under his black jacket and he held it high, then he shoved the couple away from the freezer and pushed them ahead of him to the front of the store. He forced them down onto the ground, and they huddled together with their hands on their heads at the opposite end of the front aisle from where Court stood.

Now gray hoodie pointed the twelve-gauge directly at Court, thirty feet away.

"On the floor!" he screamed, his Hispanic accent prevalent.

Court squared his body towards the man and he raised his hands. But he did not drop to the ground.

"Get on the floor!" the man shouted again.

The woman lying facedown on the linoleum just beyond the counter wailed in terror. Her boyfriend put his arm over her to both shield her and hold her there, lest the panic in her voice translate to the rest of her body and she try to run.

The two men at the counter kept their pistols on LaShondra. She stared back at them through her right eye, but she kept her hands down low, right in front of the cash drawer.

"Get down!" Gray hoodie shouted it again at Court, and as one, both men at the counter turned to look at the noncompliant man by the door.

The white gunman said, "Don't be a hero, man! Get your ass down!"

Court did not reply. He just began very slowly lowering to the ground. He kept his hands at shoulder height as he knelt.

Gray hoodie with the shotgun relaxed noticeably when he saw the white man across the room begin to obey his instructions.

His confidence was misplaced, however. Gentry had never willingly turned his back on imminent danger in his life, and he wasn't going to start by lying facedown and obedient on a dirty floor in a goddamned D.C. convenience store.

He'd go to his knees, but he'd keep his eyes on the three men. If it looked like they were going to murder him for refusing to lie flat, then Court would make a play for the Smith on his hip.

As Court made it down into a low squat his eyes flicked off the shotgun across the room, and onto movement ahead on his left. To his astonishment, LaShondra had taken advantage of all the attention elsewhere, and she had produced an aluminum baseball bat. It rose quickly above the counter.

Oh, hell no.

Court saw the bat before anyone else because all three armed men still had their eyes on him. But he knew in less than a second one of the three gunmen would notice the woman behind the counter, and then, even if she managed to crack one of these kids' heads wide open, she'd still die for her bravery.

Court was in a full squat with his left hand out in front of him as if to help him to the floor, the bag of groceries hanging from it. In full view of the three men he dropped the bag, fired his right hand down inside his open jacket, wrapped his fingers around the butt of the Smith and Wesson pistol, and began drawing it out of his waistband.

Simultaneously to this his legs spread a few inches wider and his knees softened, and he dropped to the floor in a kneeling position. As his pistol rose in front of him he lowered his body behind the gun.

The shotgun thundered, spitting fire and smoke across the front aisle of the market, over the backs of the prostrate couple. It sprayed hot lead the length of the room at a speed of 1,200 feet per second. The shot pattern expanded one and a half inches for each yard along its flight path, so when the buckshot reached Court's position they passed inches over his head in a pattern the size of a large pizza. The lead then exploded through the glass door just above and behind him.

Gentry knew gray hoodie would have to rack a new shell before he fired again, so he shifted his sights to the men with pistols. Both were swiveling their arms to get a bead on the armed man in the raincoat on his knees in front of the door.

Just as LaShondra hit one man in the shoulder with her aluminum bat, Court fired two rounds without pausing, one into the upper torso of each man, left to right. Then he swept further right to gray hoodie, and pressed off another round. His pistol rose in recoil and arced back to the counter in a blur and he fired two more shots, hitting the first man in the left temple as he dropped and spun and the second man dead center in his throat.

Court returned his aim to gray hoodie, who was stumbling backwards into the stockroom of the market with a nine-millimeter hollow point bullet lodged in his heart.

Court shot him again, this time high in the stomach as he tumbled back.

All three men lay still, but the six spent shell casings from the Smith were still moving, either in flight or rolling, spinning, and bouncing on the linoleum. The tinkling sound of brass was the only sound in the market for several seconds. Then the casings stilled and quieted, and their sound was replaced by an audible prayer from LaShondra, who had stood her ground by the cash register, her bat still high as if she were standing at the plate at Nationals Park.

Slowly the panicked sobs from the lady facedown on the floor grew, and then the sobs morphed into the same prayer LaShondra was reciting.

Court's ears rang. The couple on the ground climbed slowly to their knees. She wept openly now as she prayed, and he tried to comfort her. LaShondra lowered the bat and she turned, just stared at the man with the gun by the door. Blood and brain and bits of bone dripped off the rack of pastries next to her.

And Court just stood there. Taking it all in.

Loud and messy.

Without a word he turned and stepped through the shattered front door, his weapon high in front of him, his eyes flitting up and down, close and far, seeking the dark places on the street and between the other buildings, actively hunting for threats.

The maroon Monte Carlo squealed away from the gas pumps. Court watched it go, then he headed for his car.

38

Andy Shoal and Catherine King stood on the sidewalk in front of the Easy Market on Rhode Island Avenue, their umbrellas protecting them from a light rain. The lot and the market were blocked off with police tape Andy had not been able to charm his way through, but the two *Washington Post* reporters had managed to learn several things, even from distance.

Dawn was just breaking, but the lights on inside the convenience store made it easy to see two of the bodies on the floor, even from seventy-five feet away. Both men were faceup in front of the register; one man's leg was draped over the torso of the other. The glass front door was shattered, bloodstains around the counter were obvious, and Andy, whose eyes were better than Catherine's even though she wore her glasses, said he could make out the feet of another body halfway into the stockroom at the back of the store.

Detective Rauch was here and he confirmed three deaths, all young armed men, and all of whom, he said, were in the commission of a strong-armed robbery when a civilian shopper pulled his own gun and dropped them all. Rauch gave Andy the general description of the shooter.

Thirties, white, clean-shaven, nondescript.

Andy replied with a hopeful tone, "Sounds just like the perp on Brandywine street, and just like the Leland Babbitt assassin."

But Rauch, a man who'd not only seen a lot of crime, but had also seen a lot of reporters who were too quick to create a narrative that made a story more dramatic, threw cold water on Andy's supposition. "And it sounds just like tens of thousands of guys in the greater D.C. metro area. Should I start sending out paddy wagons to pick them all up?"

Andy put his hands up in surrender. "Fair enough. But what about the skill? Can tens of thousands of citizens do all this?"

"What do you mean?"

"On Brandywine Street you mentioned the shooter knew what he was doing. Any initial impressions about this scene?"

Rauch hesitated a moment. Finally he said, "I watched the security camera footage. It was beautiful."

Andy's eyes rose. "A guy uses a gun in your jurisdiction and you say it's beautiful?"

"You put that in your paper and I'll kick your ass, I'm not kidding. I don't condone it. I'm just saying the shooter was fast, sure of himself, and clean. Between you and me . . . four armed assholes walk into a building and only one armed asshole walks out. Around here, that doesn't sound like crime. That sounds like progress."

"Any chance I can watch the video?"

"Evidence, Andy. You'll have to wait for it."

Catherine King had remained to the side of this conversation, allowing Andy to work his magic with the police. But when Rauch headed back into the Easy Market to check on the progress of the crime lab technicians, she stepped up next to the young reporter. She said, "What do you think? Same guy as the others?"

Andy nodded. "Sure seems like it could be. But what I don't get is the fact that the CIA people aren't here."

Catherine had an answer for this. "I bet we scared them off. They won't be investigating the crime scenes in person anymore."

Andy nodded, and the two reporters started heading back to their cars. Andy said, "You know what's bothering me?"

"What?"

"This highly trained killer knocks off a couple of Aryan Brotherhood drug dealers in a shoot-out, but lets the others live because they stopped fighting back. Then he encounters an armed robbery here, and kills these bad guys."

Catherine knew where Andy was going with this. "Good against evil," she said.

Andy said, "Right. But that Babbitt thing doesn't seem to fit. Either Babbitt was a criminal and we don't know it, or the guy who did this and Brandywine Street didn't kill Babbitt."

Catherine said, "You are good at this, Andy. I think you are on to something."

"Enough to put into my article? I mean, I could just mention the difference in the victims."

"No. I'd leave Babbitt out of it for now. Mention the killing in the Highlands along with this event, maybe draw some parallels, but I think there are enough questions about Babbitt still to where you should not speculate."

Andy said, "You are working on your own piece about the CIA's involvement, aren't you?"

Catherine shook her head. "*I'm* not. *We* are. Trust me, when I get something ready I'm going to involve you, both in the work and in the glory."

Andy said, "You keep promising me that, but when?"

They were back at her car now. She fumbled for her keys in her purse, then pulled them out. "How 'bout I buy you breakfast and we get to work?"

Zack Hightower sat in front of a computer terminal in the fourth-floor Violator tactical operations center, his eyes fogged both from the early hour and from the steam pouring out of the coffee cup under his nose. The coffee had been placed in his hand a minute earlier by a young CIA analyst, and Zack had been put here—in front of the monitor in the TOC, that was—by Suzanne Brewer.

A half hour ago Zack had been snoring away in his McLean hotel room when a call came from Brewer informing him of a possible Gentry sighting in the District. Before he'd even processed this information she told him she was sending a car, and to be ready in five minutes.

Hightower shook himself awake and asked to be vectored to the location of the potential sighting instead of the office. Brewer wasn't using Hightower as a hard asset, however, so she didn't understand the request. No, she'd countered, he needed to come in and look at some video, to make a positive ID, and to let her know what he thought of the analysis.

Zack grumbled to himself but agreed, and now he sat here in front of a black screen, with Brewer standing just behind him.

When nothing happened on the monitor for several seconds Hightower took a sip of hot coffee and made a joke. "Inconclusive."

"It hasn't started yet," Brewer snapped back, and Zack realized his humor would fall flat on a bureaucratic automaton like Suzanne Brewer.

Soon the video began playing. It was security camera footage from a convenience store. Zack saw the time stamp and realized it took place less than three hours earlier.

"Where is this?"

"Rhode Island Avenue. East of Logan Circle."

A man in a black baseball cap and a raincoat entered the store, but the camera did not have an unobstructed view of his face. It only showed the bottom of the man's chin and the bill of his hat. He moved into the store, seemed to say something to the woman behind the counter, then headed to the back.

Another camera angle picked him up there, but it revealed even less than the first one. Only his back and a brief view of a portion of his chin.

Still, Hightower took another sip of his coffee and declared, "That's him."

"How can you be certain? His face is obscured."

"Ma'am, I spent the majority of a decade looking at this dude's ass as he ran point on my team. Most of the time his face was obscured then, too. Trust me, I know how he moves."

Brewer wasn't convinced. She remained silent so Zack could focus on the screen. The first Hispanic male entered the convenience store, wearing a gray hoodie. He was soon followed by an African American couple. The man in the ball cap stood at the counter, facing just slightly away from the camera above him on his right, while the cashier bagged his groceries.

A Monte Carlo parked out front in the rain. Two men climbed out.

Hightower watched all this quietly. Slowly a little smile curled on his lips. "Hot damn, there's gonna be some kind of a fracas, isn't there?"

"Just watch, please."

Zack did so. He saw the positioning of the three young men, the movement around the market of the African American couple, and the man in the cap at the magazine rack who could have just turned and walked out the door next to him, but instead squared off to the room.

When the man in the gray hoodie pulled the shotgun and pointed it at Gentry, Hightower just mumbled, "Last mistake of your dumb, short life, *ese*."

The next few seconds of video chronicled the shoot-out, beginning with the shotgun blast and ending when Gentry fired his sixth round from his handgun, the two men at the counter crumpled into their own blood splatter on the floor, and the gray hoodie with the shotgun disappeared, falling backwards under the camera's view.

The screen froze just after Gentry left the convenience store, three dead bodies in his wake.

Brewer sat on the edge of the desk next to Hightower and faced him. "Impressions?"

Hightower shrugged. "Boarding house rules."

"Boarding house rules? What are you talking about?"

"I'm talking about the shot sequence. Everybody gets a first helping before anybody gets seconds. It's textbook. Only a topflight close-quarters guy can cycle his weapon around a room like that, hit three guys center mass, back-stopping each one, and then recycle and shoot them all again before they hit the ground."

Brewer frowned. "One of the Townsend operators reported that Gentry stole his handgun at the McDonald's." She looked through some notes on the iPad in her hand. "A Smith and Wesson model M&P. It's hard to tell the weapon the man is using in the video due to the poor quality of the recording, but I had the analysts here look at the gun and they say it can't be the same gun, because the Smith and Wesson has an external safety lever on the side, and Gentry doesn't seem to take time to disengage a safety before he fires. What do you think of this analysis?"

"Ma'am, I think that analysis blows."

Brewer reacted with obvious surprise, and an analyst in earshot looked back over his shoulder at the big man, a scowl on his face.

Brewer asked, "And why is that?"

"Gentry wouldn't need to fan the safety off, because it would already be off."

"You're sure?"

Hightower snorted. "External safeties are for chickenshits and losers. I know that. Gentry knows that." He nodded his head towards the video. "Can we watch the video again?"

The recording played through a second time. Hightower viewed it with an unmistakable smile on his face.

"Enjoying yourself?" asked Brewer coolly.

"Professional respect. Gentry's still got the touch. It's obviously not the most impressive thing I've seen out of him, considering the low quality of the opposition. But he still possesses the speed and the marksmanship he did when he was in the Goon Squad."

"Why didn't he just leave the store when he had the chance?"

Hightower took a moment to select his words, so Brewer helped him out. "Let me guess. Because he thinks he's a good guy?"

Hightower countered, "He *is* a good guy. We're targeting him because of orders. We aren't vanquishing evil or any bullshit like that."

"But—"

"But nothing. You and me? *We're* the assholes in the mix. If we left Gentry to his own devices he'd be fine, and the world would be better off."

"I wouldn't let Denny hear you talk like this if I were you."

Zack shrugged. "I'm here to do a job. I don't have to like the job and I don't have to hate Court Gentry. I have my orders. I'll keep the Agency safe from him, I'll help you find him, and, if you let me, I'll kill him for you."

He gave Suzanne Brewer a little wink and a smile. "I don't mind being the bad guy. It's more fun."

39

S oft noises of the street leaked into the basement room from the outside as the city woke and began going about its day, but Court Gentry lay still in his tiny closet spider hole. His open eyes flitted about the darkness and his hand rested on his Smith and Wesson pistol on the floor by his side.

There was no great mystery as to why Court could not fall asleep this morning. The pain on the right side of his midsection and the worry and frustration about his confrontation with Hanley and the implications of the in extremis gunfight at the Easy Market all beat down on his psyche like a timpani drum, and the analytical side of his brain couldn't shut itself down before it evaluated and rehashed everything that had happened over and over till the point of utter confusion and mental overload.

After a massive bout of second-guessing, he was finally able to convince himself he had done a reasonable job eliminating the compromise from the gunfight. He'd done the obvious thing, anyway: he dumped his vehicle before returning to his safe house. He hated to do it; he needed a car, but the Ford Escort was compromised, and that made it useless to him. Even though he knew it had not been picked up on a camera at the market itself, after the shoot-out he was certain the police would begin looking at area traffic cam footage. In no time they would identify a gray Escort driving out of the area, and the time stamp on the video would match the distance from the crime scene and then the cops would draw the obvious conclusion that the driver of the Escort had been involved.

He didn't dare drive the car back to his storage unit to hide it, because he knew anyone monitoring traffic camera feeds could simply follow the Escort's route from where it was first seen all the way to the neighborhood around the storage facility. This would compromise the location, just as the car itself had been compromised. Instead, Court had driven the Ford to the east, obeying the speed limit and stopping at the necessary red lights, and then he parked the car in a dark lot on the edge of Howard University. He struggled to climb a rickety fence and then he dropped down on the other side. Once here, he was able to move out of the streetlights through residential backyards for a block.

When he stepped back out onto the street he wore a different cap, no raincoat, and a brown oversize thermal shirt; his backpack was under his clothing and hanging on the front of his body, giving him the look of an overweight man.

Twenty minutes later he sat on a bus alongside immigrant restaurant or factory workers either beginning or ending their workdays, and just before dawn he walked back up Arthur Mayberry's driveway with his keys in one hand and his backpack in the other. As he headed to his basement apartment, he glanced up into the windows of the two-story brick home and nodded a greeting to the elderly African American, who stood there watching from the second floor.

Arthur just eyed him suspiciously. He did not return the greeting.

As soon as he entered his place Court reset his defensive measures and then he went straight to the closet behind the door, lay down on his blanket, and rested his head on his go bag. His sticky bandages needed changing but he wasn't in the mood to play Florence Nightingale on himself this morning. He told himself when he woke up he'd clean up his wound, but it could wait a few hours more.

He thought he'd fall right to sleep, but that had been nothing more than wishful thinking. Instead his conscious and his subconscious mind both fought for his attention, making him unable to relax. With practiced discipline he pushed the action of the Easy Market out of his mind. This was replaced by places and faces and acronyms and operations that drifted to the forefront of his thoughts.

He tried to connect dots, to make the puzzle pieces fit into something that took shape. Hanley and Travers and Babbitt and AAP and Trieste. Carmichael and Ohlhauser and Golf Sierra.

He teetered somewhere between lucid thought and ethereal stupor for two hours, but by nine a.m. a light doze gave way to real sleep. Still, he did not find true rest. The pressures of his dire predicament filtered into his dream state. He thought of Delta Force snipers, of convenience store shooters, and of omniscient traffic cameras that followed his every move, but more than anything, he thought about an operation that had not entered his mind, either while awake or asleep, in a very, very long time.

Six Years Earlier

The commercial building on Norfolk, Virginia's Kincaid Avenue could not have looked more innocuous from the outside. A one-story red brick structure, it sprawled low and nondescript like an old factory, a few blocks from the airport and directly across the street from a small liquor distillery and a wooden pallet manufacturer. A Mexican fast-food restaurant was in walking distance, as well as a strip mall that offered both payday loans and Asian "foot" massages.

The sign in front of the red brick building read TDI Industrial Suppliers, which meant nothing to anyone, not even to someone in the industrial supply field, but buildings need a sign out front to look legit, so this place had one.

The looped razor wire rimming the high steel fence of TDI might have tipped off nosy neighbors that there was something inside worth protecting, but no one in a million years would imagine this to be the headquarters, op center, and team room of one of CIA's most utilized and proficient antiterror task forces.

Heavy snow had fallen all morning and traffic on Kincaid was all but nonexistent, but that changed when a black Yukon appeared out of the white and stopped at the guard shack in front of TDI. After a show of IDs the vehicle continued up the stubby driveway and parked next to the sign, and three men climbed out onto crunchy snow. They stepped up to the front door of the facility, stood under a metal awning, and waited a moment while shaking off their wool coats. Soon the door buzzed and one of the men pushed it open.

In the lobby their credentials were checked by a pair of security officers wearing plain gray uniforms. Once they were vetted they walked down a hall, passing empty offices and double doors leading to a warehouse full of Conex shipping containers, until they arrived at an elevator with a key card access lock. One of the men tapped his key on the reader and the doors opened.

The car took them down, past B1 where a team of analysts and communications specialists worked, and past B2, which was divided into a large storage area and a larger underground firing range with six shooting lanes.

They stopped at B3, and the door opened to a short, bright hallway. Two more security officers stood there waiting, as they had been alerted by the cameras that picked the men up when they were still out front in the driveway. The officers wore M4 carbines on their chests and Beretta pistols on their hips, but they were affable guys who recognized one of the three visitors and treated him as if he were a visiting head of state.

"Good morning, Mr. Hanley," the guard who looked over the IDs said.

"Morning." Matt Hanley did not introduce the two men with him or address the guards by name. Instead he handed over his badge and submitted to a wanding from the other guard. Seconds later all three visitors passed through a door. On the other side was a small room with a camera looking down on it, and yet another door, this one with a state-of-the art electromechanical locking system.

Hanley and the two others waited silently while the door behind them clicked shut.

On the other side of the electromechanically locked door, half a dozen men were spread around a comfortable team room the size of a tennis court. A projection screen TV took up a portion of one wall; a soft and worn sectional sofa was pulled apart and scattered around in front of it. Aluminum picnic tables with built-in benches were arrayed by a kitchen area, and high shelves of tactical gear and luggage jutted out from the wall to the left of the door. A row of three wooden workbenches covered with guns, tools, and cleaning supplies spanned half the length of the back wall.

The smell of gun oil, sweat, and spicy taco sauce filled the team room.

Unlike all the security personnel in the gray uniforms outside this room, the six men here were decked out in a haphazard mishmash of civilian clothing. Two wore flip-flops and shorts, two others workout gear, and two more jeans and sweatshirts. One of the men in flip-flops was shirtless with a wet towel wrapped comically around his head in a manner reminiscent of Carmen Miranda.

On an aluminum table near the steel door that led to the anteroom, a bank of tiny camera monitors gave the men a view to the outside world, but the closest man to the monitors wasn't paying attention to the screens right now. Instead, Keith Morgan sat at the table and looked into a small mirror on a stand, doing his best to adjust a contact lens. Next to him a bean bur-rito sat untouched on a wax paper wrapper.

Though he faced a wall he spoke loud enough to be heard by everyone in the room. "It's that grit and shit from Mogadishu. It's not the contact lens, the contact is fine. I think my fucking eye is jacked." He groaned as he took out the contact and looked closely at his bloodshot eye in the mirror. "I don't need this bullshit, I'm supposed to go see Springsteen tomorrow night at RFK."

Behind him on a piece of the sectional sofa that had been dragged away from the TV area, Paul Lynch sat with a canvas backpack in his lap and a thick sewing needle in his hand. He was working to repair a torn strap on the pack. None of the men in the room had been paying much attention to Morgan's play-by-play about how his eye was bothering him, but Lynch heard the last part. Without looking up he said, "If you've got a combat injury you can get Zack to put you in for a Distinguished Intelligence Cross. You can pin that shit on your shirt for the concert and pick yourself up some cougar tail." He chuckled to himself as he finished a stitch. "Cougars love wounded dudes."

In front of the TV, Dino Redus held his Xbox controller on his lap. He worked the buttons and levers frantically while he stared at the big screen in front of him. Despite his frenzy, his *Medal of Honor* match wasn't going his way, so he turned his attention to the conversation behind him and laughed at Lynch's comment. "Five, if Zack gives you a medal for getting sand in your eye, I should get a damn ticker tape parade for that time I got shot in Islamabad."

"It's not sand!" Morgan shouted back as he popped his contact back in. Then he blinked a few times and looked again in the mirror. After a moment he said, "Okay, maybe it *was* sand. I'm good to go." He reached for his burrito.

Sitting next to Redus on the couch, Ritchie Phelps spit tobacco juice into a plastic Gatorade bottle and adjusted the ice packs he'd strapped to both his knees with ACE bandages. Once he felt like he had them on the worst part of the swelling in his joints, he reached up and removed the towel from his head, then he shook out his freshly washed hair. "I'm the most busted-up dude on the team. If Five gets a medal and Three gets a parade, they need a marble statue of my ass right there by the bubble at Langley."

Across the room, sitting at one of the picnic tables and typing on a lap-top with a pen sticking out of his mouth, Zack Hightower shook his head in disgust and pulled out the pen. "You guys are the whiniest little bitches I've ever had under my command. Why can't you all be more like Six? Just do your job and stop griping about every little fucking scratch."

Keith Morgan was Sierra Five to Zack Hightower's Sierra One, but this was an extremely informal unit, so he had no problem talking back to his team leader. "Zack, the only reason Six doesn't complain about anything is because Six is fucking psycho." He had moved on from his worries about his eye, and now he took a big bite out of his burrito. With a full mouth he said, "Ain't that right, Six?"

Court Gentry sat at one of the workbenches on the back wall, hunched over a pistol he was buffing with an oil rag. He wore threadbare blue jeans, the sweatshirt of a college he had not attended, and a ball cap with the logo of a baseball team he knew nothing about.

Without missing a beat or looking up, Court replied, "Certifiable."

The room transitioned back to silence, other than the *Medal of Honor* match, as everyone returned to their individual projects.

This was an uncharacteristically lazy morning for the men of the Goon Squad. Hightower ran a tight ship on the Golf Sierra Unit, the informal banter notwithstanding. But he was showing mercy on his team today considering everything they'd endured over the past week. All six operators of the task force, Zack Hightower included, had been in Somalia since Sunday on a particularly dangerous and austere operation. They'd completed their job yesterday morning and then climbed aboard a company Gulfstream, flew for fourteen hours, and only landed at the airport here in Norfolk at one a.m. As soon as they deplaned they loaded their gear in a van and climbed into an SUV, and then they returned along with their equipment to the team room in the TDI building. They spent a couple of hours cleaning and refitting their kit in case they had another in extremis callout, then they crashed in their bunks for a few hours.

It was after eleven a.m. now, and Hightower knew his boys would be back at work soon enough, so he let them sit around and shoot the shit this morning while he filled out his after-action report on Mogadishu.

Keith Morgan took another bite of his lunch, then his eyes flitted up to the monitors in front of him. For the first time he noticed the three men standing in the anteroom, just outside the door. "Company."

All six men in the team room pulled firearms from holsters or grabbed subguns that they kept within reach. With the exception of Hightower everyone remained seated. Sierra One stood from the table and turned towards Morgan.

In the back Gentry one-handed an MP5 off the table, slammed a thirty-round magazine in it, and racked the cocking lever. He spun around in his seat and aimed the weapon at the door across the room.

"Who is it?" Hightower asked Morgan.

Morgan kept his eyes on the monitor for a few seconds, then he relaxed noticeably. "It's our fearless leader."

Hightower boomed back at him. "*I'm* your fearless leader."

"Hanley, I mean. He's got a couple of other guys with him."

"What other guys?" asked Hightower.

"Dunno."

"Operators?"

Morgan shook his head. "Nah. Look like a couple of brassholes from Langley."

Hightower headed to the door, surprised that his team's control officer was dropping in unannounced, with guests in tow.

But not too surprised. Even though Hanley didn't spend much time here, he occasionally stopped by after a successful mission, and Mogadishu had been nothing if not textbook.

Hightower said, "Unlock it," and he headed towards the door, but while he walked he looked over his team sitting and lying around the room. As if only noticing his motley crew for the first time, he sighed. "Straighten yourselves up. This place looks like a motherfucking soup kitchen."

A couple of men chuckled, but no one really moved but Redus, who stood at crisp attention and saluted, a sarcastic gesture that Hightower returned with a middle finger and an eat-shit look.

Morgan punched a button on a desk panel and the massive locks in the door released.

Dino Redus did a decent Matt Hanley impersonation, a little bombastic and just slightly patronizing. Before the door opened he called out to the room in Hanley's voice, "Hell of a job in Mogadishu, Golf Sierra! Welcome home!"

Morgan and Phelps both snorted out a quick laugh.

Hightower himself pulled the door open and bade the men into the lair of Golf Sierra. Hanley was first through the door; he shook Hightower's hand and then called out to the others. "Well done in Mogadishu, Golf Sierra! Welcome back!"

"Thank you, sir," said Hightower.

The two men with Hanley stood silently. One was in his forties with white hair, the other in his twenties, his hair black and slicked back. Both men wore heavy Burberry coats.

Hanley said, "Gentlemen, meet Jordan Mayes and David Lloyd. They're from the office. SAD."

The two suits raised hands to the men, and the men nodded back politely enough, but no one really tried to pretend like they gave a damn about a couple of suits.

Hanley, Hightower, and the two others stepped into the conference room, and the door closed behind them.

Keith Morgan mumbled to the others in the team room. "Son of a bitch. Hanley's sending us back out, I can fucking feel it. I had tickets to see the Boss tomorrow night at RFK."

"You mentioned that," said Lynch. Then he added, "Fifty bucks says somebody ID'd another number three in al Qaeda and we're heading back to Pakistan."

Redus turned away from his video game and looked to Morgan now. "Hey, Five, maybe Springsteen will play a gig in Peshawar and you can catch him during our op."

Morgan wasn't laughing. "Paid two and a quarter for those tickets. This is bullshit!"

Ritchie Phelps said, "Whatever is brewing, it's big enough for Hanley to come in person and bring suits along with him."

Redus corrected him. "Hanley *is* a suit."

"Yeah, now he is. He used to be SF."

Morgan snorted. "That was twenty thousand Big Macs ago."

The room erupted in laughter, and at the back workbench even Gentry cracked a half smile, but he didn't look up from his gun. He worked diligently, perhaps excessively so, on his new Glock 19. He'd finished cleaning it, and now he got to work adding a large front sight loaded with a vial of radioactive tritium gas that would ensure it glowed in complete darkness, giving the user the ability to line his barrel up on a target despite poor lighting conditions.

Court's last G19 had served him well, but he'd put seventy thousand rounds through it, and it was time to upgrade to the newest generation. He'd planned on taking his new piece upstairs to the range to test-fire it as soon as the adhesive in the screw on his sight dried, but now he figured he should wait around the team room to see what the hell Hanley had planned for the task force.

After Hightower and his visitors passed the one-hour mark in the conference with the suits, the speculation among the operators in the team room had transitioned from *if* they were about to get redeployed on a new op to *if* they would even have time to grab a burger and a beer before leaving the States again. They could imagine no other reason for the long meeting other than a mission, so amid the grumbles and bitching, the five men began packing deployment bags and double-checking weapons platforms.

A minute later the door opened and the four men reappeared. Hanley and Hightower came out first, then the other two CIA men. Gentry had already forgotten the young guy's name, but Lynch and Phelps had been talking about Jordan Mayes for the past hour. According to what Gentry overheard, Mayes worked directly for the head of the SAD, Denny Carmichael. Court didn't care much for office politics; hell, he'd only been to Langley once in his many years with the Agency. Most of his CIA career was spent in smelly barracks and team rooms like this, or else out in the field using a backstopped legend and pretending to be someone else.

After a wave to the six operators and Hanley's repeated congratulations for the success of the Mog op, the visitors left.

As soon as the door shut behind them, Hightower turned around to the room to face his team. All five paramilitary operations officers stopped what they were doing and stared back at him, wondering where they were headed, and if they would even get the chance to pass by a drive-through for tacos to go on the way to the airport, since by now nobody figured they'd even have time for a sit-down burger meal.

Hightower said, "Sierra Six. Front and center." Court Gentry stood and stepped forward. "Conference room," Hightower ordered, then he surprised the rest of the team when he said, "You other four lucky fuckers have seventy-two hours R&R."

Morgan pumped his fist in the air. "Hell, yes! The Boss is a go!"

Hightower opened the door to the conference room and held it for

Gentry, but he continued addressing everyone. "Don't forget, Monday at oh six hundred we're rolling in convoy down to the shoot houses in Moyock to run some CQB force-on-force evolutions."

Gentry looked around the team room at the other men. Confused. "Just me, Zack?"

"Yep. Don't you feel special?"

"My lucky day," he mumbled, and he entered the conference room.

Hightower followed him in with a whistle. "Kid, you've been hanging around these degenerates too long. Slowly but surely you're getting a fuckin' mouth on you."

"Sorry, boss."

Inside the conference room, Hightower and Gentry sat down at the table. Sierra One immediately got down to business. "Something different this time. A solo op. Real James Bond shit. Free tuxedo included. You up for it?"

Court nodded slowly.

Hightower glanced down to a small notebook in front of him. "Just kidding about the tuxedo. Local civilian attire will do." He coughed as he checked his notes. "Anyway, the Agency has liaison intel saying some Israeli deep penetration agent has worked his way into a cell of al Qaeda in Iraq. The cell is on a gun run in the Balkans, getting AKs and such from Serbian gangsters. They are meeting in a safe house in Trieste, just over the Italian border from Croatia.

"Unfortunately for this Mossad deep-pen agent, he's been compromised, and he doesn't have a clue. A group of Pakistan al Qaeda are meeting them in Italy, and shit's about to get nasty."

Court said, "*We* know the Israeli agent is compromised, but the Mossad doesn't know?"

"Affirmative. Like I said, another partner nation gave us the heads-up. We can't tell the Israelis, apparently, because we don't want to tip them off that we have a liaison relationship with this other nation."

Court asked, "Who is the other nation?"

Hightower made a face at Gentry. "If we were supposed to know that, Hanley would have told us."

"Right."

"Anyway, this entire thing in Italy is a setup to get this agent away from his area of operations, so he can be liquidated without it causing a rift between the two AQ divisions. The plan is for one of the Pak AQ operatives on the trip to smoke him in Italy, then blame it on the Serbs."

Court said, "And I need to stop that from happening."

"You are so much smarter than you look. Anyway, you'll be driven to Dulles within the hour. From there you'll fly commercial to Milan. In Milan you will take a train to Trieste."

Court wrote nothing down.

"You will ID the Iraqi guys when they arrive at the port, identify the Israeli asset among them, and follow them to their safe house. As soon as it's prudent get him out of there. Tell him he is compromised and take him to the train station. After that, he is the Israelis' problem. Remember, he must not know you are American. He speaks Hebrew and Arabic only, and you speak neither, so things shouldn't get too chatty between you two."

"Guess not."

Court still wondered why CIA didn't just pick up the phone and call Israel and tell them to rescue their own dumb agent. Seemed to him like the CIA could have just not revealed where they got their intel. But that was strategy, and that was above Court's pay grade.

As usual, Court just figured the graybeards knew what they were doing.

Hightower asked, "Any questions?"

"Just the obvious. Why me? Why solo?"

"Hanley's orders, but it looked to me it was Jordan Mayes's order, which means it was Denny Carmichael's idea. My guess is we're afraid Mossad will find out we are in the area if we roll in with the whole task force. I imagine the Israelis will have support personnel monitoring their agent while he's out of the Middle East. Hanley thinks you can get in and out low profile, stay fast and light if you don't have the high drag of moving with the Goon Squad."

Court just nodded. It wasn't how they normally operated, but whatever. "Got it."

Hightower said, "No kit but what you'll pick up in Trieste at a dead drop cache left by local Agency assets. They'll leave you a suppressed pistol and the image of the Israeli asset you've got to recover. Remember, this is simple if you *make* it simple. Your job is to go save some asshole who can't know who you work for. If anyone gets in your way, you are cleared hot to schwack them. We want you back in seventy-two hours, max."

Court nodded with earnest. "Roger that, One. I'll make it happen."

40

Jordan Mayes stood in his superior's office briefing the stone-faced director of National Clandestine Service on the early-morning convenience store shooting in the center of Washington, D.C. The killer had clearly been Gentry; no one had any doubts. From the description of events it seemed to Denny like Gentry had just happened to stumble upon an armed robbery and then do the only thing he knew how to do, which was shoot dead all the threats.

Carmichael didn't need to see the video. He knew his ex-operator's capabilities. A man of Gentry's caliber against untrained bandits was as sure as a knife cutting through butter.

When Mayes finished with the play-by-play of the Easy Market shootout, Carmichael asked, "What do we know about his escape?"

Mayes said, "Analysts monitoring traffic cams tracked a Ford Escort away from the scene. Lost it when it passed a neighborhood where the cams were down for repairs, but they found the vehicle this morning in a lot at Howard University."

"Did the cameras pick up anyone on foot leaving the area where they found the car?"

"Negative."

"Dammit." Once Denny realized the events of the previous evening would not lead to Gentry's imminent capture, he switched to the fallout. "How is the media reporting it?"

"Local PD has done a good job locking it down. You can expect them to squelch any 'good Samaritan with a gun' narrative since it happened in D.C. All guns are equally bad to them and, by extension, all shooters are equally bad. As long as the video doesn't get out this will probably get reported as gang v gang violence."

"Good," Denny said.

"There is one problem. The reporter from the *Post* published a story about it."

"Catherine King?"

"Not King. Andrew Shoal."

Carmichael said, "Is he looking to connect this to the others?"

"He put an article online forty-five minutes ago. He ties this shooting to the Brandywine Street shooting, but he leaves out Babbitt. I think we might have dodged a bullet with that."

"Not at all. Catherine King is cooking something up. She's probably scrambling all over, interviewing former intel officials, trying to get some kind of a guess about who is here in town that has us so interested."

Mayes said, "We can play it two ways. We can try to shut her down by saying all is well, or we can—"

Carmichael interrupted, "Or we can pitch her a story that has enough elements of truth to where Gentry knows she is getting intel about the hunt. If we do that I think there is a fair chance Gentry might try to make contact with her. We use her as bait, put a team on her, and then we terminate Gentry when he makes his play."

Before they could go any further, Carmichael's secretary came over the intercom, her voice agitated. "Sir, Director Hanley is here and he—"

Carmichael's door flew open and the large frame of Matt Hanley entered the office like a running back charging to the end zone. He stepped past Mayes without a glance and stared Carmichael down as he approached.

Carmichael yawned. He looked down at the papers in front of him, not at the intrusion. "Unless you are here to offer up Ground Branch assets for the Violator operation, I really don't have time for you today, Matt."

Hanley dropped down in the chair in front of Carmichael's desk. "You will never, *ever* guess who showed up at the foot of my bed last night."

Carmichael took off his reading glasses and looked up.

From behind Hanley, Mayes said, "Bullshit! Not possible! You were monitored by multiple teams."

"Gentry got past them. Even told me where they were and what kind of scopes they had on their rifles."

Carmichael tossed the papers in his hand across the desk. Another opportunity lost. "What did he want?"

"Same as with Travers. He's searching for answers. Court Gentry is a sad, lost guy, just looking for someone to tell him what he did wrong. CIA was his family, and he wants to know why his family doesn't love him anymore." Hanley added, "And he's got the skills to kill a hundred people to exact revenge, if it comes to it."

"What did you tell him?"

"I told him you want him dead for fucking up BACK BLAST."

"That's it?"

"That's all I *fucking* know, isn't it, Denny?"

"Did you tell him about Ohlhauser?"

Hanley didn't hesitate. "Not a word."

"Bullshit."

Hanley said nothing.

Carmichael growled. "You're lying. Goddammit, Matt! Whose side are you on?"

"When a trained killer is in my bedroom with a gun to my nuts, I am firmly on the side of my nuts."

Carmichael stared him down. Slowly he turned to Mayes. "We have anyone watching Ohlhauser?"

"He's a private citizen now."

"I don't give a damn. Put contracted security on him. Keep them back, but close enough to report contact if Violator turns up." Carmichael looked back to Hanley. "Gentry is lying. He knows what he did."

Hanley shook his head. A fierce look in his eyes. "Clearly he doesn't. He just wants this to end."

Carmichael sniffed. "He can end this by shooting himself in the fucking mouth."

Hanley stood back up from the chair. "From our discussion last night I take it he would not be receptive to your terms of surrender."

"Whatever, we'll get him, sooner or later. He's killed half a dozen people so far here in the U.S."

Hanley looked Denny over a long moment. Then said, "And he's just getting started."

The director of the Special Activities Division turned his back on the director of National Clandestine Service and headed out of the office, pushing by Jordan Mayes as he did so.

The sun pouring through the little window into Court's basement room created a narrow shaft of bright light that shone on his black wound. Court looked at it for a moment, poked and prodded it with his finger, and finally decided that, although it looked nasty, it didn't look any nastier than it had the day before.

It was shortly after ten a.m. Court had only been up for a few minutes but already he drank instant coffee while he worked on his dressings. Over his right shoulder as he sat on the bed the TV broadcast CNN's midmorning news hour. Court was using it mostly for audio; he'd only glanced around once or twice to watch the latest action in Syria between the Islamic State and the Syrian government. Court wasn't much interested in politics or international diplomacy, and he was no fan of war in most instances, but this was a war he could get behind, because he fervently wanted both sides in the conflict—despotic regime and nihilistic Jihadi alike—to kill the other.

The news went to commercial. He was only halfway listening when the CNN anchor came back on air.

"Welcome back. From the ongoing violence in Syria we are going to shift to a shocking display of violence at home. Two nights ago, the brazen murder of a Washington, D.C., businessman tied to the intelligence community has many wondering if an assassin is on the loose in the nation's capital.

"Joining us this morning from Miami is former FBI counterterrorism director and CNN contributor Greg Michelson, and from Washington, former CIA chief council and CNN contributor Maxwell Ohlhauser. Greg, I'll start with you."

Court spun to the TV and dropped his ACE bandage onto the floor. It rolled out across the little room.

A tan man with gray hair looked sternly into the camera on a split screen with the anchor. The anchor said, "Greg, two nights ago the killing of Washington private security executive Leland Babbitt has many inside the Beltway frightened. What are your sources telling you as far as who might be responsible?"

Court ignored his wound now. He just sat there and waited for the talking head, ex of the FBI, to finish pontificating about the all-points bulletin out for the vicious assassin and the probability that the hit man was either by now somewhere back home in the Middle East or hiding in a rat hole in the city waiting for the coast to clear.

Gentry drank his coffee and watched his television, wondering what made this ex-FBI guy such a shitty expert on the tradecraft of assassins.

The screen switched to a heavy man with a round face, dark hair, and a red bow tie. Under his image was the caption Maxwell R. Ohlhauser, Former Chief Legal Council, CIA.

"Now, Max, you were with the CIA, so you know what a dangerous job spy work is. But usually it isn't so dangerous here at home, is it?"

"Don, you are right about that. What we saw in Maryland two nights ago was no random act of violence."

"Son of a bitch," Court said. The man on television had been part of the small group of men that had sanctioned his assassination. And now here he sat, big and proud and famous, as happy as a clam to talk to the world about the CIA.

Court saw from the text on the screen that Ohlhauser was now a former employee of the Agency. He reached for his laptop, which lay on the bed nearby, and typed the man's name in Google. In seconds he discovered that Maxwell Reid Ohlhauser was now working as a private attorney here in D.C., with an office on K Street. There was a link to his Twitter account, and Court clicked on this. The most recent tweet from Ohlhauser announced he was due to appear on both Fox and CNN this morning in Washington, then he was looking forward to eating oysters for lunch at Old Ebbitt Grill with a good friend from college.

Well, that's helpful, Court thought.

He typed the restaurant into Google and pulled up a map to it. He found it just next to the White House, within walking distance to Ohlhauser's office on K. Also, the lawyer had helpfully added a link to the Twitter account of his lunch date, so Court could look into this man and gauge his potential as a threat.

Ninety seconds after first seeing Max Ohlhauser on the news, Court knew more than enough to find and fix his prey. He looked up from his laptop, a bewildered expression on his face. In his career Court had often hunted a single target for months before acquiring his location, and rarely had he discovered the exact place one of his targets would visit within days, or even weeks, of beginning the hunt. That Ohlhauser had been so accommodating to broadcast his day's to-do list almost made Court wonder if he was being led into a trap. But after another ten minutes on Twitter he saw that the fifty-five-year-old attorney had a huge social media profile, and for as far back as Gentry checked, the man told those who followed him on Twitter many of his most mundane of daily activities.

Court checked the time on the television. It was just after ten a.m., so he knew he had to get moving if he was to have any chance to get eyes on his new target by one. The restaurant was only a few minutes away by Metro, but Court couldn't go there directly.

First, he needed to go shopping.

41

Max Ohlhauser swallowed the remnants of his third martini and called for the bill, despite the sincere efforts of the Frenchman across the table to stop him. From as close as a few tables away it looked as if Ohlhauser's guest was fighting for the check, but nothing could be further from the truth. No, it wasn't that the Frenchman wanted to pay. Rather, it was that the Frenchman didn't want to stop drinking just yet.

The man sitting across the booth from Ohlhauser was a ruddy-faced ex-diplomat from Paris, here in D.C. this week for a conference at the Shoreham on nuclear disarmament. The two had gone to boarding school together in Switzerland, back in the late seventies when they were rebellious teenagers of wealthy parents; now they were both ex–government service types, living the last decade or two of their work lives raking in the big bucks, capitalizing on the access they'd cultivated while making peanuts employed in federal government jobs.

Of the two men, Max was by far the most successful. He was an attorney, after all—he could have been making bank without twenty-something years in the CIA—but with such an eye-catching CV he garnered some of the biggest international corporate clients in the USA. He spent his days either suing on behalf of his clients or lobbying on behalf of his clients, depending on the corporate legal strategy chosen.

The Frenchman was doing all right himself, but he'd been a foreign ministry official and an ambassador to Canada, so now he mostly served on corporate boards and spoke at universities. His speaker's fee was big money, unless you compared it with what Ohlhauser raked in each day he lunched with a congressman on the House Committee on Foreign Affairs and pitched an international treaty beneficial to one of his clients.

It was a quarter after two in the afternoon now; Ohlhauser and his guest had downed two dozen of the Old Ebbitt Grill's freshest Copps Island oysters and two orders of pan-roasted calf's liver, along with martinis before, during, and after the meal. The Frenchman could outdrink the American by a wide margin, but it had been thus since they were sixteen-year-olds sneaking out of their dorm to down beers behind the horse stables at their Montreux boarding school. Even back then the Frenchman was known for having the constitution of a water buffalo, and Max Ohlhauser was known as the brainy nerd who liked to wear red bow ties.

Much had changed in their lives in the forty years since, but some things had remained unaffected by time.

Max paid the tab, but only after the Frenchman ordered one more round for himself with plans of taking it to the bar. The American would have stayed himself, but he had to get back to the office. After a round of good-byes and au revoirs, Ohlhauser stood with barely a wobble and shook the hand of his old friend. He then headed for the exit, taking his coat from the hostess with a wink as he did so.

A well-dressed businessman sitting at the bar paid for his beer, left the second glass half full, and headed for the door, just a few seconds behind the dark-haired man in the red bow tie. The businessman collected his raincoat and his umbrella from the hostess, and then he stepped out into the afternoon gray, slipping on a pair of sunglasses because he saw a few others wearing theirs, and popping open his umbrella because the misty afternoon warranted it.

Pedestrian traffic was exceedingly heavy at the moment; in the District it was common for businesspeople and government workers to go to lunch around one, so now huge throngs of men and women in work attire walked along in all directions, returning to their offices. The White House was just a block to the west, and the adjacent Eisenhower Executive Office building alone accommodated hundreds of government employees.

The businessman turned to his right, in the same direction of Max Ohlhauser, and he began walking north.

Court Gentry had enjoyed his time drinking draft beer in a nice restaurant, but now he was back on the street, where he felt more comfortable. He adjusted his umbrella from his left hand to his right hand, and he picked his way through the crowd. As he walked he glanced up in the direction of the fifty-five-year-old attorney from time to time, but he didn't fix his eyes on him. There was some risk he could lose his target in the undulating mass of well-dressed humanity here on the sidewalk, but Court knew his main focus needed to be on the four men on the street who did not quite belong.

He'd noticed them within his first five strides out the door of the Old Ebbitt. There were probably 250 people in view on the street, but the four guys revealed themselves in seconds as a tail on Ohlhauser.

They did most things right, and that was their problem. Court knew better than almost anyone how to conduct a foot-follow, so he simply let his eyes travel to where his training told him he would position himself if he were tailing Ohlhauser, and there he saw the first pair of men. They were 150 feet or so back from their target, and their clothing was more rugged than the attire of the office workers around them. Court put them in their thirties—a prime age for this type of work.

He saw their tag-team partners a few moments later. They were also in their thirties, and just like the other duo, these guys were wearing comfortable shoes and raincoats from REI instead of Nordstrom or Brooks Brothers like most everyone else out here. They walked along behind Ohlhauser, on the same side of the street, just ahead of Court by fifty feet or so. They didn't eyeball the attorney, like the other pair; instead they kept their heads on swivels, scanning the crowd around them.

Court knew they were looking for him, but he knew they would never find him.

Court's suit and his glasses and his umbrella and the vague form of his body revealed through his black raincoat helped disguise him, but that wasn't the most important thing. No, Court walked with purpose, like he was a guy on his way back to work like most everyone else out here; like he belonged on this sidewalk and he wasn't doing anything shady or wrong.

The four watchers could look in this crowd all they wanted. Until Court actually made a move on Max Ohlhauser, they'd never spot him.

Court decided quickly that these four men weren't Delta, or whatever the hell the JSOC army-side special mission unit was called now. Delta was slicker and smarter than these four. And these guys sure as hell weren't SAD Ground Branch. Hanley had said SAD was not involved in the hunt for him, and although Court didn't know for certain if that was true, he did know SAD men working a foot-follow wouldn't be doing it while wearing 5.11 Herringbone Covert Shirts under their raincoats. It was a good brand, and low-profile enough to fool civilians, but Court knew a trained operator could ID the maker and the style, and he would know that the wearer of the gear would be in the same game as himself.

Court decided these guys were contractors, no doubt working for the CIA, no doubt involved in the Violator hunt, and no doubt armed. But they wouldn't work as shooters themselves, Court imagined. Instead they had been brought in to tail Ohlhauser, to use him as a lure. There would be shooters close by, and ready to swoop in, if this team spotted their target.

Court took a deep breath to center himself, then he picked up the pace, and began closing on *his* target.

He stepped up to the first major intersection since beginning his tail on Ohlhauser, and here, as he continued walking, he deftly moved his head to the right while turning his umbrella in a leftward angle that covered his face from the eastward-facing traffic camera there. When he got to the end of the street he quickly turned his head to the left and swiveled his umbrella a little to the right to cover himself from the northbound lane camera. He'd have to do this for the duration of his walk, and all the while keep his body language nonchalant and his eyes on Ohlhauser's tail.

Court continued closing on his target. He moved in stride with two women now, walking back to their jobs after lunch, and he positioned his umbrella over one of them without her even noticing. While doing this he passed the two followers, looking like he was with the two female office workers. The men in the REI jackets looked right through him, as he knew they would. When they turned to check their six, Court stepped away from the women and skillfully bladed his body to cut through a thick cluster of strolling businesspeople, and in seconds he was out of view from the CIA contractors.

Ohlhauser's office was on the corner of 12th and K streets, but due to the crosswalk signals not cooperating with his shortest route, Max walked east on G all the way to 12th before turning north. He was just about to pass the entrance to the Metro Center station when a man in a suit wearing a raincoat walking along next to him bumped him slightly on his left side. This jostled him closer to the escalators down into the Metro.

Ohlhauser felt a slight but unmistakable sharpness on his hip as he walked, and he looked quickly to the man, who was still almost shoulder to shoulder with him.

"Watch out," Ohlhauser growled.

The man pushed him forward with his shoulder, but he kept walking in stride, and he didn't even look his way. Softly the clean-shaven man said, "Hello, Max. In my right hand is a knife with a seven-inch blade. Keep moving along quietly or I'll drive it through your back and into your lung."

Ohlhauser's eyes went wide, and instinctively he slowed, but the man in the raincoat kept moving, nudging him onward through the lunchtime crowd with another bump of his shoulder. Ohlhauser started walking again, complying even if he did not yet comprehend, and he looked down at the man's right hand. It was mostly hidden by the cuff of his raincoat, but the glint of steel protruded just an inch between the man's bent fingers.

Ohlhauser said softly, "What . . . What do you want?"

"I just want to talk. Keep looking straight ahead. Not at me."

"Who are you?" Max's own voice had lowered several decibels, to match that of the man talking to him.

The man in the raincoat smiled a little. He seemed surprisingly calm as far as Max was concerned, especially considering the man was, apparently, executing some sort of an armed confrontation in broad daylight. Raincoat man said, "Tomorrow morning you'll be the biggest talking head on all the news shows, and this time you'll actually have something to talk about."

"I don't understand."

"You're a smart guy, Max. You'll figure it out."

Ohlhauser walked on a moment, still in the middle of the crowd, still with the raincoat man less than a foot away. After a wheezing gasp he said, "Violator?"

"Keep moving. There are four men following you. If they see me, I'm fucked, which means *you're* fucked, because I'll gut you like a fat fish. Got it?"

"Please. I want you to understand, I didn't have anything to do with—"

"Not now, Max. We're going to take the escalator down into the Metro. You go first, I'm right behind you."

Max Ohlhauser did as he was told, veering off the sidewalk and towards one of the entrances to the Metro Center station. Together the two men took the escalator down.

JSOC unit commander Dakota drove a black Suburban while his teammate, call sign Harley, sat in the front passenger's seat, hunched over a laptop displaying navigational information, as well as a constant array of images of the streets around them.

The twelve-man JSOC team was split up into two-man teams today. The two pairs who'd spent the evening watching over Hanley's house were sleeping off their long night's shift, which left four teams of two, each in a different vehicle, each in a different sector of the District.

Jordan Mayes had called Dakota two hours earlier and asked him to vector one of the teams closer to Max Ohlhauser's office, and to hold position in the neighborhood. Mayes didn't want anyone to actually tail the former CIA attorney. The head of the JSOC special mission unit cell immediately tasked himself to Ohlhauser's area, along with a teammate. It was a low probability callout because no one expected Gentry to be just idly wandering the streets outside of Ohlhauser's office, but until Suzanne Brewer and her people at the TOC got some better lead, Dakota figured he might as well give it a shot.

There were thousands of people walking and driving around the heart of D.C. near the White House, so it was a good thing Dakota and Harley didn't have to use their own eyeballs to hunt for the target. Instead they had mounted a state-of-the-art digital camera on the front grill of the GMC Yukon XL, and the camera scanned the entire street in a 120-degree arc, taking in all the facial recognition data it could pull from passersby, and feeding it into the computer.

While Dakota drove a crisscrossing pattern in a three-block radius of Ohlhauser's place of business, Harley's job was to sit in the passenger's seat and watch the laptop. Every second new faces were analyzed by the software as the computer searched the streets.

It was good technology under the care of hardworking and well-trained men, but even though they'd been at it for a half hour so far, they'd come up empty. They'd not had a single hit—not even a false alarm.

Dakota was frustrated, but he was committed to the search, so he kept his patrol up. He planned on making a right at the next intersection, then heading back in the direction of the center of his surveillance zone. Dakota and Harley both assumed Ohlhauser was sitting in his office in the center of their search pattern, and they had no clue he was, instead, walking down the street just in front of them as they headed west on G approaching the 12th Street NW intersection.

Harley had barely said a word in the past fifteen minutes, but he called out in a loud voice just as Dakota flipped his turn signal lever.

"Got a hit, boss!"

Dakota turned off the signal as he looked towards his partner in surprise. "Where?"

"Wait one." Harley looked away from the screen and out through the front windshield. After a few seconds to orient himself, to find a correlation between the frozen picture on the monitor showing Violator's image highlighted with a red square and the real world outside, he pointed towards the escalators ahead on his right. They descended down into the Metro. "Right there."

"I don't see him."

Harley checked the image again. A running digital timer in the upper right corner of the software told him how long ago the image was taken. It had just hit the ten-second mark. In the picture Violator was stepping onto the escalator. Harley said, "He's gone down into the Metro."

"Shit!" Dakota shouted, then he grabbed the walkie-talkie on the center console between the two men. "All elements, Dakota. Target acquired! He's heading into the metro station at Metro Center Square. Stand by." He sped the Yukon through the intersection and whipped into a parking space left vacant a second before by an Audi sedan. Looking again to Harley, he asked, "What's he wearing?"

"Black raincoat. Umbrella in his hand." Harley looked closer at the image in front of him. "Aw, hell! He's with that Agency guy, Ohlhauser!"

"Are you sure?"

Harley could see the right side of both men's faces in the image, because they had been moving perpendicular to the camera. "Fat dude with a red bow tie is right in front of him on the escalator. Looks scared shitless. Gentry's in contact distance to Ohlhauser. Might have a weapon in his hand."

Dakota spoke again into the walkie-talkie. "Consult your Metro maps and GPSs, and route yourself to nearby stations. Be advised. Subject has one hostage."

Dakota knew he didn't have enough men to conduct running surveillance in the Metro, so he pressed a button on his Bluetooth earpiece. Seconds later he relayed all the information regarding the facial recognition hit to Jordan Mayes. He expected this would get him more bodies to help with his hunt; either CIA contractors or regular D.C. police, whom the CIA could simply ask to be on the lookout for a man fitting Court's description.

And his call did bring out these forces, because Mayes immediately relayed his info to Suzanne Brewer in the Violator TOC, but Dakota had no way of knowing that Denny Carmichael would also receive word of the sighting within moments. Denny immediately contacted Saudi intelligence chief Murquin al-Kazaz. In minutes another force would be descending on the immediate area and conducting a hunt of its own, and if Dakota had only known what an absolute tragedy this would create, he no doubt would have kept word of the Violator sighting to himself.

42

Even though he'd had less than three hours to prepare, Gentry had planned this operation against Max Ohlhauser well, even to the point of buying two Metro Smart Cards, one for himself and the other for his hostage. He slipped the card into the older man's hand and together they went through the turnstiles. Feet away a pair of Metro Transit Police stood, the female officer holding the leash of a Belgian Malinois who looked only somewhat less bored than her handler.

The two men waited in silence on the platform, standing shoulder to shoulder, as per Gentry's instructions. Max's breathing was labored and sweat drenched his brow, but Court just stood there, his face placid and his eyes scanning the area around him calmly, not flitting back and forth.

They took a Red Line train heading to the northwestern outskirts of the metro area, but that was just because it had been the first train to arrive at the platform. Court wanted to interrogate Max while onboard the Metro, thinking it would make it tougher for the followers to catch up. Of course he knew at each stop he'd have a new crowd to look over, and it was possible the four CIA contractors up at street level had radioed to other units with instructions to be ready at every stop, but by making himself a moving target in a transitional area with spotty comms, Court was reasonably certain he'd bought himself at least ten or fifteen minutes in which he could squeeze Ohlhauser of intel free of danger.

Court led Ohlhauser to the back row of a car that was only about a quarter full and, as the train began to move, Court sat with his back to the wall and pushed Ohlhauser down into a seat where he faced Court and his back was to the car.

Court still carried an air of calm, and Ohlhauser remained petrified.

Court said, "Relax, Max. You and I are going to chat for a few minutes.

If you don't scream like a bitch, and if you don't try to make a run for it, I'm not going to hurt you."

Ohlhauser nodded. He didn't believe. But he nodded.

Court kept looking beyond Ohlhauser's right shoulder and down the length of the entire car. He'd slipped his knife back in its sheath inside his pants pocket, and formed a grip on the pistol inside the waistband on his right hip, shielded from view of the other passengers by his body. He said, "First things first: I did *not* kill Leland Babbitt. I was there. I planned on questioning him, but I didn't shoot him."

Ohlhauser gave another compliant nod that looked to Court like a man trying desperately to stall for a few moments until he could think of something to say that would get him out of this situation.

Court said, "I can see you don't believe me. If I let you go today, will that help convince you I didn't smoke Babbitt?"

Court saw a hint of optimism on his face. Then Ohlhauser nodded with conviction.

Court said, "Cool. Now, next item of business. The shoot on sight. You give me the truth, and you live. You bullshit me, and you die. What did Denny tell you that got you to sign the term order?"

Ohlhauser looked down at the floor of the train car for several seconds.

Court kicked his foot gently. "Talk. Don't think. *Talk.*"

"Denny said you assassinated the wrong man on an operation in Italy. You did it intentionally, in violation of clear and unmistakable orders."

Court did not react to this; he just kept scanning the car. A couple of days ago hearing this lie from Travers left him gobsmacked, but now he expected it. He simply replied, "Not true. Denny wants me terminated because of what I know about AAP."

Court glanced again at Ohlhauser and watched the man furrow his brow. Confusion on his face. Ohlhauser kept looking down at the floor.

Court said, "It's an old program I used to be involved in. Called the Autonomous Asset—"

Ohlhauser looked up and interrupted him. "I know what AAP is. Hell, I drafted the finding that sanctioned the program."

"What?" Court said. "You looked surprised when I mentioned AAP. Why?"

"I was only surprised that you think the shoot on sight against you has anything to do with that program. Why on earth would Denny term you for your *old* job?"

"I don't know why. All I know is that all the other operators from AAP are dead."

"Is that right?"

"Yes. I'm the last one. Denny needs to silence me. To remove the compromise."

Max rubbed his face. His eyes under his glasses. A nervous affectation. "Look, Violator, I hate to break this to you, but your theory doesn't make a bit of sense."

"Why do you say that?"

Another rub of the face. The skin of his thick cheeks reddened. "Because AAP is still up and running. Under another name. I mean . . . I've been out of the Agency for just two years, and it was going strong when I left."

Court sat back in his seat. The train came to a stop at the Farragut North station. Several people got on. Court scanned them perfunctorily, but his mind was on Ohlhauser's assertion. When it started rolling again, Court said, "I don't believe you."

Max shrugged. "Why would I lie about that?"

"But—"

"BACK BLAST, Violator. Denny came to me because of BACK BLAST."

Court shook his head violently. "Forget BACK BLAST, it's just a cover story Denny is using. I did nothing wrong."

Max sighed. "I just know what I was told, and I was told you took a payoff from the Serbs to kill the wrong man."

Court stared at Max. "The *Serbs*?"

"That's what Denny said."

"Then Denny is a *goddamned* liar. When I worked for the U.S. government I never took a cent from anyone *other* than the U.S. government."

Ohlhauser shrugged. "I guess Denny is the man you need to see."

Court's jaw flexed. "Don't worry. I'll be seeing Denny." Court took his eyes off the other passengers in the car now, just as it began to slow before the next station, and he looked at the man in the red bow tie. He got the impression the man wanted to say something, but was holding back. "What is it?"

"You say you did what you thought was right on BACK BLAST. If that's true, then the shoot on sight wasn't justified. But I did what I thought was right when I signed the shoot on sight, so you kidnapping me or . . . or worse. That's not any more justified."

"Spoken like a lawyer facing an armed man."

Ohlhauser shook his head. "Maybe you killed the wrong guy. Maybe by me signing that paper, I signed the death warrant for the wrong guy." He heaved his shoulders. "I'm truly sorry if I acted with bad information, but I did *not* act in bad faith. I did what Denny asked me to do. That is all."

"You were a rubber stamp for Denny Carmichael."

Max leaned forward. "You're damn right I was. And you were the tip of Denny's spear. We're the same, you and me."

Court just switched gears. He didn't want to hear anything more about Denny Carmichael and Operation BACK BLAST. He said, "This new iteration of the Autonomous Asset Program. Where is it located?"

Ohlhauser answered immediately. "How would I know that? I am out of the Agency, and even when I was in the Agency, I wasn't operational side."

"Did they move it? It used to be in a compound at Harvey Point."

"I'm telling you, Violator. I don't have a clue."

The train stopped at the Dupont Circle station. Court fought his anger and frustration at reaching another dead end, and he stood quickly. He just wanted to get back to his room, to regroup, and to come up with some other options.

He pulled Ohlhauser to his feet, turned him around, then pushed him towards the door.

They walked together in the station, just as they had ten minutes earlier before boarding the train at Metro Center. Court leaned in to Max's ear and said, "Go up the escalator to the mezzanine, then head to the escalator for the opposite platform. Take the train back to your office. We're done here." Max nodded without looking back, and Court leaned close one more time. "How 'bout that? You aren't dead. You're going to have to tell your friends on CNN that I'm not the monster they're making me out to be." Court immediately began lagging back a few feet. His plan was to separate from Ohlhauser here in the bowels of the crowded station and get up to street level, where he knew he could quickly melt into the busy neighborhood.

The crowd thickened on the mezzanine level at the top of the escalator, and Court drifted even farther back. He slipped off his raincoat, revealing his new black suit, and then he pulled off his suit coat and walked on in his shirtsleeves. He wadded the coats up into a tight ball as he exited the turnstiles to leave the station, and he crammed them both in a garbage can at the bottom of the five-story-high escalator that led up to Connecticut Avenue.

But as soon as he got on the escalator he saw them. Two D.C. Metro cops heading down the opposite escalator. They were checking faces, clearly looking for someone.

Court looked ahead and above him now. He could just barely make out the pale blue uniforms of two more cops at the top of the escalator, four stories up.

He turned quickly and began heading back down the escalator, pushing to the right of others on the stairs in hopes of covering his retreat. As soon as he got to the bottom of the stairs he hurried back along the mezzanine, planning on getting down one of the escalators to the platform level. From here he could jump on the first ride out of here in either direction.

He went back through the turnstile and walked a few feet, but there Max Ohlhauser appeared out of the crowd in front of him, along with four D.C. Metro police officers. The faces of the policemen did not register with Court at first. He just saw Max, the uniforms, and he started to turn away, hoping the fact he'd shed his jacket and his coat might disguise him to Ohlhauser.

But that had been too much to hope for.

"There! That's him!"

All four cops reached for their weapons, right in the middle of the crowded mezzanine of a subway station.

Court knew he could run, though his chances for escape weren't particularly good. There were at least eight cops in the vicinity and they all seemed to be hunting for him. Running would have long odds, although he'd certainly wiggled his way out of tighter spots than this. But, Court told himself, if he tried to make a break for it now, there was a chance one of these cops would open fire, just like they had done the other night, and there was no way they wouldn't hit innocents here in the busy metro station.

Reluctantly, Court raised his hands. Surely they wouldn't shoot him in cold blood with his hands up, he told himself.

Quickly all four cops stepped up to him, their guns still drawn, and they turned him around and walked him to a wall. They kicked his legs apart, pushed him till his hands slapped high on the wall.

Two men began frisking Court while the other two stood there, guns still drawn and pointed close at the back of his head. Passing commuters stopped to look, but only for a moment. This was a tight station and the mezzanine was narrow here. As the crowd backed up people coming up the escalators began pushing forward, and this kept the traffic moving, more or less.

The cops did not say a word, but Max Ohlhauser would not shut up. He told the police about how he was kidnapped and about the knife and the gun, and how he used to work for the government, though neglected to mention what agency. He told the four men, over and over in half a dozen different ways, that Court was some sort of a former Special Forces commando who was now a criminal, and he'd killed a lot of people, some of them this week here in the area. Court wondered if the big middle-aged lawyer was going to hyperventilate during his retelling of the events of the past fifteen minutes.

The cops for their part seemed oddly silent and unimpressed with this information, which frustrated Ohlhauser. They just continued their frisk. Court felt several hands upon him as his face was pressed hard into the wall. He had no wallet, only a phone, a cash-loaded credit card, a paper Metro card, and a thick wad of tens and twenties. When the cops finished frisking him and determined this for themselves, one of them said, "ID?"

Court looked back over his shoulder at the man. For the first time he noticed the man's darkish skin. He wasn't black; not Hispanic, either. Court said, "I beg your pardon?"

"Identification?" He spoke with a noticeable accent, but Court couldn't place it.

Behind the cops Ohlhauser said, "His name is Gentry. Courtland Gentry."

A couple of the cops looked at each other, then the other two handcuffed their prisoner. While they struggled to get the cuffs on, Court turned his head back and forth, looking back over both shoulders at the four officers.

Quickly he sensed his troubles were even greater than he'd realized.

All police everywhere are trained to interact with suspects using a tactic called contact and cover. One cop steps up to contact distance with the subject, converses with him, then frisks and handcuffs him if the decision is made to do so. The other officer remains far enough away to provide cover if things go bad for the contact man.

But these cops apparently didn't get the same training as every other police officer Court had ever dealt with. All four of them were close enough to touch Court—two of them *were* touching him, at the same time.

No. This wasn't right at all. These assholes didn't act like cops.

They spun Court around and started walking him to a nearby elevator that went from the mezzanine up to street level. This, Court knew, would let them avoid passing the police officers with the dog back by the escalators. He didn't know if the other cops were legit or not, but he was by now highly suspicious that these four guys were foreign operators, because in addition to their poor knowledge of police work, they all had olive complexions, and they had barely said a word.

It made Court think back to the other night on the overpass, when a large group of men in police uniforms tried to gun him down without any warning, and nearly succeeded.

Max walked along with the group now, as if Court was a trophy he wasn't ready to relinquish yet, and he stood there while Court and his captors waited for the elevator to come down from the street. Max pulled his phone out and tried to get a signal here, but he was having trouble doing so. Court suspected that, as soon as he made it up to street level, Max would be calling Carmichael or Mayes or someone else high up at CIA to let them know he had personally bagged the Gray Man.

The son of a bitch would probably be on CNN within the hour.

Court looked away from Ohlhauser and towards the uniformed man closest to him. His name tag read Stern, and his badge number was 99782. Court said, "Officer Stern, what's your badge number?"

The officer didn't hesitate, and he did not look down at his badge. In an accented voice he said, "Nine, nine, seven, eight, two."

Court smiled at him. "You must have stayed up all night to remember that."

Stern said nothing else.

The door opened and the cops pushed Court in, and the quiet men in uniform followed. Ohlhauser started to enter himself, but one of the cops held a hand up, keeping him out.

Max was confused. "Wait. I want to come, too. You have to be careful with this man. As I said, he is—"

"No. You stay."

Ohlhauser put his own hand out, holding the elevator door open. "Look, Officer Stern. This is a delicate situation. My former Agency is very interested in this man. They will be sending people—"

Behind Max Ohlhauser, three Transit Police officers appeared on the mezzanine. Their uniforms were a solid dark blue, in contrast with the cops in the elevator, who wore light blue tunics and dark blue pants.

The one female transit cop called out, "What you boys got?" The other two Transit Police shepherded the few straggling passersby along, clearing out the area in just a few seconds.

Max Ohlhauser, clearly still afraid the D.C. Metro cops in the elevator were going to abscond with his prisoner, put his foot in the door to keep it from closing.

After a look to his colleagues, one of the men in the D.C. Metro uniforms stepped out of the elevator and walked towards the transit cops. As he closed on them Court heard him speak. His voice was accented, but less so than that of the man with the Stern badge.

He said, "A man with a gun. We are taking him to station now. Everything is under control."

Ohlhauser took the opportunity to step into the elevator. Two cops were behind Gentry holding him by his arms, and one more was on his right, so Max stood to Gentry's left.

Court leaned over to him and spoke softly in his ear. "You don't want to be in here. These guys aren't cops."

Ohlhauser spoke back without whispering. "Don't be ridiculous. You asked the officer's badge number and he told you."

Outside the Transit Police continued speaking with the D.C. Metro cop. Court couldn't hear the conversation, but he could see a look of puzzlement on the face of one of the men wearing dark blue.

To Max he asked, "How long does it take you to remember a five-digit number?"

Another transit cop was turning suspicious. Court could see him cock his head and challenge something the D.C. Metro cop said.

Ohlhauser, also looking out at the exchange in the subway station, said,

"If it doesn't prove anything that he knows his badge number, why did you get him to tell it to you in the first place?"

Court rolled his head around slowly and brought his shoulders back, stretching the muscles in his neck and in his bound arms. He replied, less softly now. "Because I wanted to hear his accent before I killed him."

Ohlhauser turned to look at Court and, at that same moment, the dark man on the mezzanine wearing the D.C. Metro police uniform reached for the gun on his belt.

43

The transit cops had been suspicious of the man in the Metro police uniform, but not suspicious enough for their own good. They clearly did not think he posed a threat to them, because they were all slow to draw their weapons.

Court had the fastest reaction time out of anyone in the subway station. Before the foreign operator wearing the Metro PD uniform had even cleared leather with his handgun, Court slammed his head back hard into the nose of one of the men standing just behind him, then he spun around and jabbed the "close door" button with the index finger of his cuffed right hand. Facing the three armed men in the elevator, he saw the man in the middle had dropped to the floor after taking the back of Court's hard head to his face. His hands covered his nose and mouth, and blood dripped through his fingers.

Out of the corner of his eye, Court saw Max Ohlhauser drop to the floor himself, and then crawl out of the elevator to get away from the fight. But just as he did so, echoing bangs of pistol fire erupted in the metro station.

Court brought his right leg up, knee to his chest, and then he snapped out a vicious front kick into the face of the man by the wall on his left. This struck the man in the nose, and blood erupted from his face but he did not fall to the floor. He was, however, out of the fight, at least for the moment, so Court turned his attention to the man on the right. This fake cop had his gun out of its holster and high in the draw stroke, so Court sent a tight roundhouse kick from left to right, through the man's gun hand, sending the Glock pistol banging against the wall and falling to the floor of the elevator. He then rushed forward with his arms still secured behind his back, pivoted ninety degrees as he charged, lowered his body, and fired a shoulder into the man's chest, driving him hard against the wall. The fake cop wore a Kevlar vest, but the impact on both sides of his body as he was slammed into from the front and then, in turn, slammed back against the wall of the elevator stunned him soundly, and his legs gave out. He slid down to the floor and settled on his back.

The elevator door closed and the car began ascending.

The foreign operator on the floor in the middle of the elevator tried to get back up and draw his gun. Court kneed the pistol out of his hand, then Court spun behind the man, turned his back to him, and wrapped his handcuffs around the man's neck. He began to strangle him with the metal, shaking the man left and right to keep him off balance.

While this was going on, the operator on the far wall stood back up and fired a fist out, and it caught Court right above his gunshot wound on his right side. The punch hurt his ribs, but he knew if it had been two inches lower it would have sent him into jolting agony, and he might have been out of the fight.

Court spun away from a second punch, let go of the man he'd been choking out, then ducked down and rammed the punching man into the wall, like a bull slamming into a bullfighter. After regaining his footing from this dive, he continued using his feet, kicking the man in the groin, the chest, and finally the face as the man slid down in the corner of the elevator. Once he was on the ground fully Court used the heel of his shoe to stomp the man's face until he was completely unresponsive.

All three uniformed men were down—unconscious or dead, Court neither knew nor cared which. He knelt quickly, wincing with the pain in his ribs as he did so, and he turned around, away from the prostrate form of one of the fake cops. Reaching behind him, he fumbled with the man's utility belt. He felt his way around for a moment, then unhooked the handcuff key from a key ring.

Uncuffing himself was easy; he'd practiced unlocking handcuffs behind his back thousands of times, and had even done it in the field twice.

Court dropped the cuffs onto the still form of one of the men and scooped up a fully loaded Glock 17. This he shoved into his waistband, then he untucked his shirt and let it hang over the butt of the gun. He took his mobile phone, credit card, and cash from the front pocket of the man with the badge that read Stern, and in the man's pocket he felt something else that he recognized immediately. It was a silencer for a pistol. He pulled it out and dropped it into his own pocket, as well.

Just then the elevator jolted to a stop and the door opened, sending gray light and the smell of fresh rain into the elevator.

An elderly man stood there, and in front of him, his elderly wife sat in her wheelchair. They had called the elevator up, apparently oblivious to the throngs of panicked commuters fleeing the station from the escalators a half block away.

Court looked at the couple as he stood up fully. At his feet lay three bloodied, still forms of men in police uniforms, their arms and legs intertwined.

Smears of bloody handprints were on the walls.

Court shrugged. Said, "This isn't as bad as it looks." Then he took off at a brisk pace, moving past them without another glance.

Fifty yards to his left, Dakota, Harley, and three other JSOC men ran down the five-story-high escalator, guns drawn.

Court used Uber, an app on his mobile phone, to call a private car to pick him up at an address just six blocks from Dupont Circle. A Nissan Altima arrived in less than a minute, driven by a young Pakistani driver. Court asked the man to take him to a shopping center far north of his room in the Mayberrys' basement, which meant he'd have an hour-long walk this afternoon, but at least he'd be far away from the scene of the action.

As he rode in the back of the Altima Court wondered if Ohlhauser had made it out of the subway station with his life. The ex–CIA lawyer had obviously decided to put his faith in the odds of the three transit cops against the one foreign operator masquerading as a D.C. police officer. Court figured that, to Ohlhauser anyway, those odds looked better than taking his chances in the elevator, where one handcuffed man who had just kidnapped him was up against three armed foreign operators.

Court had no way of knowing for sure, but he had a feeling Max Ohlhauser had made the wrong call and was now lying dead in Dupont Circle station.

44

The action in the Metro had Denny in constant telephone contact with Suzanne Brewer in the TOC during the afternoon as the body count grew and the fragmented reports from Brewer's contacts at the scene radioed in bits of intel. But as soon as it became clear Gentry had managed to survive and escape the area, Denny asked Brewer to give him a few minutes to attend to other pressing matters.

He picked up his phone and dialed Kaz's number.

Murquin al-Kazaz seemed to be expecting the call, because he answered almost immediately.

"Talk," Carmichael demanded.

Kaz said, "Yes, I will get right to it. Violator escaped. One of my men died from gunshot wounds, but he managed to make it up to the surface before he bled to death. His body was recovered from the scene before he was compromised. Three more of my men were injured. Two will never work again."

Carmichael felt a tightening in his chest. Not for the fate of the men; rather for the fate of the OPSEC of his operation. "Captured?"

"No. Another group of my officers arrived in time to make it out of the area of operations with the wounded and dying before they were discovered by authorities."

Carmichael sighed into the phone. "That's something."

Kaz moved on from the talk of his men. "What can you do to make sure the recordings from the camera feeds at the station are lost or destroyed?"

Carmichael replied, "Municipal government mismanagement has seen to that. Our tactical operations center confirmed the cameras on the platforms were operational, as was the camera on the escalators going up and down from street level, but both cameras on the mezzanine level of the station were out of service."

Kaz said, "So Violator was seen leaving the train with Ohlhauser and going up to the mezzanine, but the incident itself was not recorded?"

"Correct. There may be questions about the D.C. police officers seen on camera entering the station, but as the elevator wasn't covered with CCTV, there is an explanation for their absence from the scene."

The two men spoke for several minutes, most of it consisting of Kaz relaying the after-action report of the least wounded of the three men beaten by Gentry in the elevator car.

As soon as Kaz finished the play-by-play, Carmichael asked another question, though he wasn't sure if he would get an honest response. "And Ohlhauser? Who killed him? Your men, Gentry, or was he caught in the cross fire?"

"The surviving members of my team did not see him killed and the only man on the mezzanine when Ohlhauser was shot said nothing before he bled to death in the back of an SUV. Ohlhauser was alive when the doors to the elevator closed. I gave my men no orders to kill him, so I can only assume he was simply caught in the cross fire."

Carmichael wasn't as disappointed with Ohlhauser's death as he might have been, because he saw an angle in it. A way he could leverage it to fit the narrative he wanted put out for all to see.

But he was worried about Kaz. As dangerous as it was for Carmichael to sanction a proxy force of Saudi Arabian gunmen in the capital city of the United States of America, he continued to see their value. While he had JSOC operators and dozens of CIA contractors hunting Violator, only Kaz's men had managed to wound him, and only Kaz's men had managed to get him in handcuffs. The fact that outside forces interrupted his killing was frustrating to Denny, but he wasn't ready to throw in the towel on the Saudi operators.

Denny's concern, however, was that Kaz planned on doing just that. He worried Kaz would just shut down his operation and try to forget he'd ever been involved in the Violator hunt.

Denny knew when to use a stick on Kaz to get him to work in the interest of the CIA, but right now it was time for the carrot. He said, "Look, I recognize this was a dangerous operation for you and your men, and your risk of compromise is real. I want you to know that if you will see this through to the end with me, I will be more amenable to your needs here in the U.S. than I have been of late."

The Saudi intelligence chief said nothing for a long time. When he did reply, it was clear he knew he held a temporary advantage in the relationship. "Specifics, Denny. I want to hear specifics before I subject my men to more jeopardy."

"All right," Denny said. "I know of your interest in our export of fracking technology to other Gulf states. You have spent a lot of time and resources trying to get intelligence on this."

"I will not deny that. We find it troubling that your partnerships with less stable oil producers have injured your relationship with our oil-producing sector."

"Cut the crap, Kaz. I'm not a politician, and neither are you. I'm offering you primary intelligence on the oil-production capacities and forecasts of our allies. Not everything. That would compromise me as your source. But good, actionable intel. From me to you. That ought to help your profile back in Riyadh."

Murquin al-Kazaz seemed to think it all over for a minute. Finally he replied, "Very well. Despite this difficult day for my operation, we will continue to hunt your target for you. We'll stay at it till the end."

"Excellent," Denny said. "As soon as I have something for you I will let you know." He hung up the phone, proud of his power to compel others to do his bidding.

In the Saudi Embassy on New Hampshire Avenue, Murquin al-Kazaz hung up his secure mobile and sat quietly, puffing his cigarette and drinking tea.

Slowly his face grew into a wide smile.

He'd not expected this. He'd suffered a flesh wound today with the death or disablement of four men, but he'd managed to avoid compromise, and he'd just been handed intelligence of the highest caliber on a silver platter.

And in trade he had conceded nothing, and he would offer nothing.

Murquin al-Kazaz and his men would not stop hunting Court Gentry until he was confirmed dead.

Nothing else mattered.

———————

Court made it back into his room just in time for the six p.m. news. He turned on CNN after resetting his booby traps, and while the show opened he gingerly peeled off his white dress shirt. He had a couple of new bruises, both of them purple-and-black and painful, but his main concern remained the GSW he caught three nights earlier. His bandages were black with dried blood, and a new rivulet of bright red blood had trickled down his rib cage, all the way to his underwear.

He wasn't bothered by the sight in the least, knowing just how close he'd come to real damage. He was lucky to have only sprung one small leak after what he'd just subjected himself to. He could clean this up and stop any more bleeding with little trouble, other than the searing, unrelenting pain.

Just as he expected, CNN opened live with a shot from Washington, D.C., with a stand-up report outside the Dupont Circle metro station. Court exhaled in frustration when the correspondent announced the shooting death of three transit officers along with one civilian, and the injury of four more civilians. The names were not being released so that next of kin could be notified, so Court didn't know if Ohlhauser had been among the dead.

Within forty-five seconds of the show's opening, the erudite and bearded anchor back in Atlanta asked the reporter a question Court had fully expected.

"Andrea, have police been able to determine if this shooting had any relation to the assassination-style killing of Washington area businessman and security consultant Leland Babbitt two nights ago?"

"So far police are not jumping to any conclusions, but they are speculating only that, due to the large number of victims in a public place, this looks like some sort of terrorist act."

Court closed his eyes. He was hoping against hope there would be something in this report about a group of Middle Eastern assholes dressed up like cops opening fire on Transit Police, but there was nothing of the sort. As the story progressed, he felt his heart sink, as it began to look as if the authorities were going to try to spin this as a lone attacker; the same lone attacker involved in Babbitt's killing.

Court kept listening for more details as he stripped down to his underwear and pulled a bottle of beer out of his little fridge. He headed back to the bed holding the cold bottle against the bruising just above the bandaged wound on his right side.

As the anchorman was asking another question he stopped speaking suddenly. Apparently he was listening to a producer in his earpiece. After a few seconds he said, "Just a moment." A pause. Then, "Is this confirmed? We need to be certain before we go live with this."

Court leaned towards the television. He feared what would come, but when it came, he found himself decidedly unsurprised.

"Ladies and gentlemen, we've just received word that one of the victims is someone known very well to our viewers and the CNN family. Police now confirm, officially, that CNN contributor Maxwell Ohlhauser was killed today in what appears to be a terror attack in the nation's capital. I've known Max personally for quite some time and . . . this is just an awful turn of events.

"On Monday night, the death of Leland Babbitt, who was also in the security and intelligence field, and now this on Wednesday afternoon. We just had Max on this morning to discuss the inherent dangers of working in government intelligence services, even here in the United States.

"We don't want to get out in front of the investigation, of course, but this obviously leads one to the inescapable conclusion that someone is out there targeting U.S. intelligence officials, or, in the case of Max Ohlhauser, ex-officials. Terrorism here in the streets of Washington, D.C. I fail to see how you could possibly characterize it as anything else."

Court put his head in his hands, his mind spiraling down into depression. He had come to America to clear his name, but so far, despite his best-laid plans, his arrival had had the opposite effect. Now there were more dead bodies that would be pinned on him, and he had no new plan to get out of the hole he'd dug for himself.

But through it all, one thing kept propelling him forward.

The firm belief that he had been set up, and he'd done absolutely nothing wrong.

45

The Mossad officer looked out the window through the early evening's haze to the twinkling lights of Tel Aviv and then beyond, into the vast blue of the Mediterranean Sea.

The man retained the clarity of mind to know this view was probably very beautiful, but he was not able to enjoy it as he should. He was a captive here in this room, and the big city, so close it looked as if he could touch it, just drew a deeper contrast to his predicament.

He understood his situation intellectually. The men and the guns and the orders to sit and wait made it clear he was a prisoner. But despite this difficult predicament, the Mossad officer did not understand what the hell he had done to find himself here in the first place.

Yanis Alvey had served in Israeli intelligence for twenty-six years, most of these as a member of Metsada, a paramilitary and direct action arm of the Mossad. He had been a shooter, then when he reached the age where he could not keep up with the younger men in his unit any longer, he graduated from black Nomex and balaclavas to an Armani suit and a BlackBerry. He became a coordinator for Metsada operations, overseeing logistics and planning of the unit's kill/capture missions all over the globe.

Life in the Mossad had been good to Alvey, until very recently that was, when he was shot during an in extremis operation in Hamburg, Germany. He spent most of the following month recovering at Tel HaShomer Hospital in Ramat Gan, a suburb east of Tel Aviv, before finally being released to go home for a lengthy convalescence.

After several weeks his wound had all but healed, and he was nearly ready to return to work. Then, just five days ago, he was called in to a meeting at Mossad's headquarters on the Coastal Highway north of Tel Aviv.

Here he met with a superior officer who asked him a question that tipped Alvey off he was in serious trouble.

"Yanis, yes or no. Did you, in any way, facilitate the escape of the Gray Man from Europe last month?"

Yanis Alvey had done exactly that, and he'd done it without authorization. That his superiors suspected likely meant that his career in the Mossad was in jeopardy.

But Alvey told the truth because he was a man of good character. "Yes. I alone helped the Gray Man leave Europe."

There were no more questions. He was told to stand and then he was handcuffed. It was done politely—no one thought the legendary Yanis Alvey was any sort of a threat—but he was restrained nevertheless. He was driven a kilometer east to Ramat HaSharon, a northern suburb of Tel Aviv, to a Mossad safe house on a gentle hillside. He'd visited here many times in his career, but this time, for the first time, it was clear he was a captive. He was uncuffed and led into a small apartment in the expansive home and told to remain inside. Security forces patrolled the garden and the driveway outside, and in the home outside Yanis's door, bored Mossad officers half his age sat around and smoked and watched TV, keeping one eye on the older man locked in the apartment.

They brought Alvey his food and a collection of daily newspapers, but he had no more contact with the outside world, and no information about what was going to happen to him.

After the first day Alvey demanded to speak with Menachem Aurbach, director of the Mossad, but Alvey's minders here had no way to make that happen, and to Yanis his handlers looked as if they had less of a clue about what was going on than he did.

So he just sat there, waiting for answers. He knew this strategy, of course. Aurbach was keeping him prisoner, softening him up, taking his time to allow Alvey to spend some time realizing the severity of his predicament and coming to terms with the fact his career, and his freedom, could be so easily threatened.

Late in the evening of his fifth full day here in the Ramat HaSharon safe house he sat looking out the window at the twinkling lights of Tel Aviv to the south and the water to the west. His near catatonic state was broken by some commotion outside of his room, and then the door opened.

Menachem Aurbach, the swarthy old man who ran the Mossad, stood in the doorway, along with two younger officers. In his right hand Aurbach held a thin blue file folder. He entered with a tired little smile and a nod to Alvey, and then with a wave of the folder he bade Alvey to follow him over to a small sitting area with a table in the corner.

Yanis did as his director asked, and soon the two men sat close to each other without a word, Aurbach calm and relaxed; Alvey tense and on edge.

The director of the Mossad waved his hand in the air and the two other men left the room. Only when they were gone and the door was shut did Aurbach speak.

"*Shalom. Ma nishma, Yanis?*" Hello. How are you, Yanis?

"*Tov, Menachem. Toda.*" Fine, Menachem. Thank you.

"The wound to your stomach has healed?"

"The wound is better. But I do not understand why I am here. I do not deserve this treatment from the service I served loyally for so long."

Aurbach looked around the little apartment. "Five days of house arrest. You are still young, relative to me, anyway. I can see how a few days locked in a home, even a nice home like this, could be a nuisance for you. Me? I'd consider house arrest a wonderful holiday." He laughed aloud and patted Yanis on the knee. "Why won't someone sentence me to a little vacation?"

Alvey did not smile. He leaned forward, feeling the pinch of tethered scar tissue in his midsection as he did so. The gunshot wound had healed, but the scar, like the memory of the pain, would remain with him forever. "I know why you put me here, but I don't know what I did wrong. I helped the man who saved our prime minister from assassination. How can that be bad?"

Aurbach put a cigarette in his mouth, lit it with a wooden match from a box he pulled from his pocket, then extinguished the match with a swirl of his wrist. As he blew out smoke he said, "You did it unilaterally, without telling your control. Without telling me. Why was that?"

Alvey spoke plainly and honestly. "Because the Americans wanted this man dead, and I worried you would give him to them. Your good relationship with the USA is a great benefit to this service and to our nation, don't misunderstand me. But your good relationship with them would have meant the death of Mr. Gentry, and I thought we owed him better after what he did for us."

Aurbach nodded. Clearly he couldn't have been happy with the explanation his subordinate had just given. The man was, after all, confessing to going behind Aurbach's back on an operation. But the old man did seem to appreciate the candor.

The seventy-two-year-old gently placed the thin blue file folder on the table between the men, and then he laid his rough hand on it. Patting it gently, he said, "I am going to tell you a little story, but before I begin the story, I will tell you how the story will end. It will end with you covering your head with your hands and begging forgiveness."

"Forgiveness for *what*?"

"Forgiveness for your complicity in allowing the Gray Man to live after what he has done."

Alvey just said, "Tell me."

"What do you know about a Mossad asset with the code name of Hawthorn?"

Alvey shook his head. "Nothing. I've never heard the name."

"Well, believe me, you know the man's work." The statement hung in the air a long time. It was all the more curious to Alvey because he never knew the plainspoken Aurbach to speak with such melodrama.

The younger man just replied, "Who is he?"

Slowly Menachem leaned back in his chair and puffed on his cigarette. "He was Iraqi. Hawthorn's father worked for us first. He was a pilot in Saddam's air force. This was the eighties, mind you, shortly after Osirak. We recruited the father while he was on leave in Cyprus. It wasn't an ideological recruitment; he was chasing money and girls, and we gave him a little taste, then offered him much more of both for helping us. He agreed. He wasn't terribly useful at first, he didn't provide us much in the way of intelligence about Saddam's air power capabilities, so we cut him loose, not wanting to throw good money after bad.

"We thought that was that, but after he left the military he became a pilot for Middle East Airlines, and we reached out again. MEA flew all over the region, so we thought he might be able to provide bits of intelligence for us here and there."

"Did he?"

Aurbach waved a hand in the air. "Nothing relevant to our discussion tonight, Yanis. We will talk about his son."

Yanis Alvey shrugged. "Okay. The son. Code name Hawthorn. We got him through his dad?"

Aurbach took another long drag from his cigarette. "The father relocated to MEA's home office in Beirut in 1990, and his eighteen-year-old son came with him. He went to the university there, got caught up in a student movement against Shia dominance of the government, and was arrested by the police during a peaceful sit-in.

"The police were controlled by Hezbollah, of course, so they threw him into a cell along with some of his friends. Beat them night and day. Hawthorn was the only student who survived the ordeal.

"We learned all this from his father, and with his blessing we made a soft approach. He agreed to work for us in Lebanon against Hezbollah, but within a few years he was informing against the more radical Sunni groups, as well."

"Sounds like a useful asset," Alvey said. Yanis Alvey was a commando, so he didn't run agents himself, but he certainly benefited from their intelligence product. He'd conducted countless operations in Lebanon, so he couldn't help but wonder if Hawthorn's product had served him and his various missions.

Menachem agreed. "He was one of my best agents, and he was good at his work, but I knew he could be even more valuable if we left him alone. I gave him the code name Hawthorn because it is a plant that grows here in the Levant. If raised in the wild, on its own, it bears plentiful fruit. My philosophy was to let him stay in Lebanon as our inside man, for the next time our army traveled north to clean the country of terrorists."

"But why did he agree to help us?"

"He hated Hezbollah, hated all the radical and jihadist groups, Sunni and Shia alike. He had no great love for Judaism or our state, but as Hezbollah took over Lebanon and al Qaeda began to grow in the Middle East, he saw the radical philosophies as insidious cancers, and he saw Israel as something of a surgeon, cutting away the bad."

Alvey understood. "I imagine as his case officer, you painted exactly that picture in his mind. You gave him a purpose. A reason."

"That is it, entirely." The old man smiled sadly. "And then came 9/11. And then came Iraq."

Alvey said, "We didn't share him with the Americans, did we?"

Aurbach shook his head, still smiling. "No. He was ours alone."

Alvey was not surprised. The Mossad was notoriously stingy with its intelligence sources.

"We sent him to the nation of his birth just after the invasion. He was on the ground during the insurgency. Doing enough to remain credible to the militias, but keeping us informed on developments."

Aurbach added, "This became a problem, though, when he was picked up by the U.S. Marines in Tikrit in 2006 and put in a prison camp. CIA sent his picture to us, along with hundreds of others, to see if we had any information about terrorist ties, or any interest in interviewing him ourselves. You can imagine how difficult it was when I saw the face of the man I had been running for over a decade, knowing he was rotting away in an American detainment facility, and was forced to tell the Americans I had no knowledge of or interest in the man."

Alvey said nothing, but he knew Aurbach well enough to imagine it wasn't very difficult at all for him to leave his man swinging in the breeze. Hawthorn was an asset for Aurbach, after all, not one of his children.

Aurbach continued. "I left him in detainment, said nothing to the Americans about knowing the man, unsure if he would ever see the light of freedom. Fortunately the CIA decided he possessed no value, and he was eventually released. As it turned out, his detainment was the best thing that could have happened to him operationally. He joined al Qaeda in Iraq with his newfound credibility, and he began passing us critical intelligence, some of which we traded with the U.S., some of which we used to influence matters in other ways.

"Soon the idea came to me that we should grow Hawthorn into a long-term deep-penetration asset of al Qaeda. To get him as close to the core leadership as possible. When much of AQ was rolled up by the Americans during their surge in Iraq, we protected Hawthorn."

Alvey was impressed. "Incredible. That was many years ago. How far has he gotten since then?"

Aurbach crushed out his cigarette in the ashtray, taking his time in doing so. It seemed to Alvey as if his boss was hesitating with his story. Finally the old man looked up. "Yanis, why, in God's name, are we not drinking?"

"I beg your pardon?"

Aurbach shouted to the men outside the room, surprising Alvey. "A bottle of scotch, please! Whatever you have lying around will do. And two glasses."

When the booze came, Menachem Aurbach drank, and while he drank, he told Yanis Alvey everything.

The director of the Mossad took an entire hour to finish his story, and then he went to the toilet. Yanis Alvey remained in his chair, his eyes unfixed, generally pointing to a spot on the wall, but focusing on nothing. After a long time, time enough for Aurbach to return and to light another cigarette, Alvey's head slowly collapsed down, like he was an inflatable doll with a leak. Finally his head settled, forehead down, on the table. He covered his head with his hands.

He spoke in a whisper. "I did not know."

"Of course you didn't. You can't know everything, can you? That's why there is a chain of command. That's why unilateral actions like the one you took are dangerous. Foolish."

"I am truly sorry."

Alvey sat up straight now, his eyes rimmed with red, glassy and blurring with tears of shame.

Before he could speak, Menachem said, "You are free to leave here. You will not be held, you will not be prosecuted. Just know that by your actions you have hurt your nation. You are a good man, so knowing this is punishment enough."

Alvey's water-rimmed eyes returned to the wall.

The older man stood. "Go home, Yanis. Take some more time off, look inside yourself. Try to put this behind you. After some period you and I together will decide if you can continue in your career in some fashion." He turned back to the younger man, still seated. "But know this. It won't be the same. Nothing will ever be the same."

Without another word the director of the Mossad left the little room, leaving the door open behind him.

Yanis sat still for a long time before he rose and walked through the open door.

46

As usual, the eight p.m. Wednesday night class at Georgetown Yoga had been a full house, and Catherine had been lucky to find a spot to lay her mat, arriving as she had at the last minute. She'd almost canceled her session tonight due to the Ohlhauser murder in nearby Dupont Circle, but after spending the entire day and early evening in her office, and the realization that she'd probably be pulling an all-nighter to get an article together, she gave herself permission to rush out for an hour and a half to attend to herself and make her favorite class of the week.

As soon as her hour-long practice was over Catherine rolled up her mat, zipped up her orange hoodie, and headed for the door. She didn't even bother to make small talk with the other ladies, the vast majority of whom were roughly half her age, and almost none of whom could perform a fore-arm stand scorpion pose half as well as she could. Catherine stood at the curb, hoping to catch a cab back to her office. Spying a taxi a block to the east she stepped into the street with her hand raised, but before the cab even saw her wave, a black Mercedes sedan pulled to a stop in front of her. An older man with a beard sat behind the wheel, and a young bald-headed man in a gray suit climbed out of the passenger's side, hurried around the front, and opened the back door, right next to Catherine.

With a pleasant smile he said, "Ms. King? How are you? I'm a big fan. Been reading your column since junior high."

She looked at the car and the beckoning open door, then back up to the bald-headed man. "Um . . . Thanks?"

Sheepishly he added, "I just had to get that out first."

"Before what?"

"I work for Denny Carmichael. He asked my colleague and me to come and collect you. He'd appreciate a brief moment of your time. For an interview, that is."

Catherine King took a half step back towards the sidewalk. "As happy as I am to hear that, I'd rather not just jump in a car and go. I could use a little time to prepare myself. If his schedule has an opening in the morning I can—"

"I'm afraid Director Carmichael will be very disappointed in me if I don't bring you right to his office."

She couldn't tell if the man was really as earnest as he appeared, or if this was all a ruse and she was about to be shoved into the car if she didn't comply.

"Well . . . can I at least change clothes and drop off my mat first?"

"You look fine, but if you insist, I can take you by your apartment to throw something on. You're up at Thirty-sixth and O, is that correct?"

Catherine swallowed. Of course the CIA knew where she lived. But having a CIA officer looming over her in the dark actually *admitting* he knew where she lived was more than disconcerting.

"I tell you what," she said. "I have a suit at the office. It's not far. Why don't you take me there?"

The bald-headed man blinked once, but his smiling face did not change. He just said, "I'm afraid not. The director wants to speak with you confidentially on deep background, and he'd rather you did not communicate with anyone before the meeting. Just a security measure."

"I see. Are you going to take my phone from me, too?"

"That won't be necessary."

Catherine King sat down in the back of the Mercedes. After the bald-headed officer closed her door for her, she had a thought. Quickly, she pulled her phone out of her purse. Holding it between her knees so the driver did not see her, she glanced down, then looked more carefully.

She was right in the middle of the nation's capital, one of the largest and most technologically advanced metro areas on planet Earth, but for some reason her phone's reception meter read No Service.

She dropped her phone back in her purse and bit her lower lip. As they drove in silence to her Georgetown townhouse, she tried to control her thoughts, so she could retain some control over the interaction that was soon to come, because she suspected the meeting between herself and

Denny Carmichael would be less of an interview and more of a chess match.

Catherine had visited the seventh floor of the CIA's Old Headquarters Building a few times in her career, but certainly never after normal business hours, and certainly never to meet with the director of the National Clandestine Service. Denny Carmichael had held the top operations job for several years now, and rumors that he would soon take over the directorship of the Agency itself as the first nonpolitical hire in decades looked plausible, as he clearly had the juice with the current administration, and the sitting CIA director had hinted in a recent interview that he wasn't exactly in love with his work.

She was taken into a conference room and was offered water and juice, but nothing to write on or with. She'd done background interviews with CIA personnel before, of course, and it was standard that she took no notes. Still . . . tonight's surprise pickup, the drive in the Mercedes, the sterile conference room on the legendary seventh floor . . . To Catherine this all had an air of stagecraft about it, and she wondered if the information she was soon to be given would be similarly manipulated.

Carmichael entered wearing a light gray suit and a burgundy tie. His tight face and his closely cropped salt-and-pepper hairstyle made him look to Catherine like a cross between Abe Lincoln and an emu. He offered a handshake but no smile, and she immediately detected a somber air about him. She wondered if he was going to speak about his close personal friendship with Max Ohlhauser. Catherine doubted the two men had been close; the rumors were that Denny didn't even really like his kids, so she didn't imagine he'd think much of some ex–chief legal council for his Agency, but from his solemn greeting she supposed he was here to talk about today's events with an eye for carrying the right tone of grief throughout the meeting.

Carmichael was not a charmer. He didn't ask about her at all, other than to open the conversation with, "You and I met once."

The two sat down at the conference table, with Carmichael at the head and King on his immediate left.

Catherine said, "That's right. In Baghdad. One of Saddam's palaces. You were having coffee with Jordan Mayes. I forced my way to your table and introduced myself. You were pleasant, but you couldn't wait to get away from me."

A nod from Carmichael, though she half expected him to deny the charge. Instead he said, "And here I am, summoning you to me tonight. Times change."

"I was told by the man you sent to collect me that you have agreed to my interview request. On deep background, of course."

"Yes. I don't usually do this, but events of the past few days warrant it."

"I think it's best for the Agency to get out ahead of the story."

"You've been tough on my Agency in the past, but fair. More or less."

She ignored the last part and replied, "And I assure you I will be fair now."

Carmichael nodded. "I know you were already working on a story about the death of Lee Babbitt, even before this dreadful thing happened this afternoon."

"That's right. Going back to the events last Saturday in Washington Highlands on Brandywine Street. This was curious to us, because it seemed as if CIA was interested in the homicide there, which happened forty-eight hours before the death of Mr. Babbitt."

"What do you know about the terrorist loose in the District?" Denny asked.

Catherine just smiled. "Sorry, Director Carmichael, but that's not really how it works, not even on background. I'm here to ask the questions." There was no way in hell she was going to divulge just how in the dark she and Andy Shoal were as to what the hell was going on.

Carmichael nodded gravely. "Very well. I'll tell you what we know. We received information recently. I can't, of course, get into sources on this, but suffice it to say that a reputable ally provided us primary intelligence indicating a personality already known to us was in the local area. We had already deemed him as a threat to the Agency, so we did not hesitate to follow all leads."

Catherine broke down Carmichael's intel speak and put it into plain speak. "You are saying that an ally told you a man you already knew to be trouble was here in town and you thought he might be dangerous to CIA employees."

"As I said."

"What tipped you off to the fact he was involved in the Brandywine Street attack?"

"Nothing, initially, and that's the truth."

Catherine wondered if this meant everything else was a lie, but she didn't ask.

Denny continued, "We were scrambling, looking for a lead. The shooting on Brandywine piqued our interest. We thought it possible this personality might be here without many resources, and we thought it likely a drug den like that would be a suitable place for him to find those resources."

"Money and guns?"

"Correct."

"The number six was left at the crime scene." Catherine stated it, not giving Carmichael a chance to deny it.

He seemed surprised she knew this, but he hid it well. "It's a symbol we've seen this man use in the past."

"What does it mean?"

"Unknown."

Catherine detected no deception, but she knew Carmichael would be good at hiding it. She said, "What is this suspect's nationality?"

Carmichael replied flatly. "He is American."

Catherine had not expected this at all. "This is some sort of homegrown terror scenario?"

"That, I'm afraid, is *exactly* what we are dealing with here."

Catherine looked into the director's eyes. "Is this someone who has, or someone who once had, a relationship with CIA?"

A shake of the head. "Only in his own mind. He's mentally unsound. A paranoid psychotic is our best estimate."

"Do you know why he is targeting the CIA specifically?"

"I can only guess. We are a symbol of American power. We make enemies, even at home."

Catherine did detect a little deception now, but certainly nothing she could pin down. She asked, "Can you give me his name?"

"I'm afraid I can't, only because we don't know it. We do know a little about him. Again, sources must be protected, so I can't tell you how we know what we know."

"I understand."

"He was born and raised in Jacksonville, Florida. He's in his thirties. White, male. A hair under six feet tall."

The Jacksonville reference seemed oddly placed to Catherine, coming even before his physical description and without any other references to his past. She stored this peculiarly positioned fact for later and said, "He's obviously had some training. I mean, some kook who thinks he is CIA but really lives in his mother's basement isn't going to pick fights with a bunch of drug dealers, police, and security contractors and live to tell about it."

Carmichael nodded again, even more gravely than before. "We think he's had training overseas."

"Where?"

"Again, unknown. A camp in Yemen, most likely."

Catherine was confused, and she didn't hide it. "Wait. He's a *jihadist*?"

"No, no." Denny put a hand up. "We don't think so. We just think he was deemed a useful tool for some group who had CIA in its crosshairs, so they recruited him for training. Probably off the Internet, as that's the way these things happen nowadays."

"What else do you know about him?"

"We think he spent time in Miami, Florida. Again, I can't tell you how we know."

Catherine did not pursue this; she wanted to keep Carmichael talking, not obfuscating. "So he killed Ohlhauser, Babbitt, the two dealers on Brandywine Street, and the three police today. Do you suspect him of anything else, so far?"

Carmichael hesitated a long time. Catherine was trying to draw him out, to see if he would mention the shooting the previous evening at the Easy Market. That shooting didn't fit the MO of the other events at all, and it didn't fit the profile of a paranoid psychotic terrorist, either. She told herself that if Carmichael did not mention it, it probably meant Carmichael was trying to control her story to portray the gunman in a way that benefited his narrative.

Denny Carmichael finally replied, "Nothing else. Not that we know of, anyway. Certainly nothing conclusive."

Catherine stored this information, as well. She then asked, "Is there anyone else at CIA specifically he might target next that you know of?"

"Yes."

"Who?"

"Me."

Catherine's eyebrows rose. "Do you know why he might target you?"

"No, but he's made threats."

"How does he know who you are?"

"Are you familiar with USCrypto.org?"

"Of course."

"Then you have your answer. It's a free country. Freedom to jeopardize my safety and the safety of my family rubs me the wrong way, but I serve America, so there are dangers I must endure."

Catherine got the impression that the big, tough, and dangerous Denny Carmichael was now looking for some sympathy, at least in this article she was working on.

More manipulation.

Catherine asked a few more questions. Carmichael answered them carefully, or deflected them fully. The *Washington Post* investigative reporter had conducted some tough interviews with some amazing spin doctors in her time, but getting information out of Carmichael felt like buying snacks from a vending machine. A big, silent source, with a very limited number of specific items available, pre-stocked by the supplier, and she had to push just the right buttons to get anything out.

Finally, when she felt like she'd emptied the machine of its limited contents she said, "Why Babbitt and Ohlhauser? What's the relationship between them?"

"Targets of opportunity, I guess."

Catherine, for the first time in the meeting, let Denny know she wasn't buying what he was selling. "No. There is something more. I can name two dozen ex-CIA people with higher profiles than Max Ohlhauser, and next to no one outside of the intelligence services knew about Babbitt's close relationship with the Agency."

Carmichael shrugged. "There is much we still don't know. I didn't bring you here to provide you with all the answers. Your article will just need to differentiate knowns from unknowns."

She chuckled. "It's *all* unknown, even after this interview."

"What do you mean by that?"

Catherine decided to lay her cards on the table. "What do I mean? I don't think *everything* you just told me was a lie, but I suspect the majority of it was. The death of Max Ohlhauser has scared you, not because you think you are in real danger, but because you worry that something is going to come out to the public about what's really happening on the streets of D.C."

Carmichael drummed his fingers on the conference table. Clearly frustrated.

Catherine continued, "My problem, Director Carmichael, is that I suspect my editor will want me to run with what you've told me, even though I don't believe it. A background interview with"—she made quotes in the air with her fingers—"'senior CIA officials' is too good to pass up in light of yesterday's events.

"So, you will get what you need out of this meeting. I will publish a piece that will tell the world what *you* want them to know . . . not what is really going on."

"Why don't you tell me, Catherine. What *is* going on?"

"I don't have a clue. But I intend to find out. In my job sometimes I reach into dark closets, not really expecting to take hold of anything. Now and then my hand wraps around something. I think I have something here, Director Carmichael. No way I'm letting go."

Carmichael said, "Sometimes in the dark the thing you're reaching for grabs *you* and pulls you deeper into the darkness."

That hung in the air for fifteen seconds. Finally Catherine sat back in her chair and crossed her arms. "I've been threatened by AK-waving Haqqani operatives. You don't frighten me."

Carmichael flashed a sly, charmless smile. "Give me the names of the Haqqani operatives who threatened you, and if they aren't dead already, just watch how fast I make them dead. You might construe that as a threat—please don't." His smile widened, but it was just as charmless. "I mean it as a government service."

Denny Carmichael is a weird man, King thought to herself.

Catherine stood, and Carmichael followed suit. She said, "I do appreciate your time. If you want to do another interview, one that isn't so obviously stage-managed, then I am always available."

Catherine King had only just stepped into the elevator with her control officer when Jordan Mayes entered the conference room via the side entrance. Carmichael relayed the major points of the conversation to his second-in-command.

Mayes followed with, "I'll put a team on her."

Carmichael shook his head. "That was my original plan, but she's a wily character. I underestimated her. She'll be looking for a tail at this point, and it will just make her think she's important, which will just make her think she's onto something."

"She *is* onto something," Mayes corrected.

"Something ephemeral. She is wandering in the mist. As she said, she will be forced to print what I gave her tonight. She might throw some disclaimers here and there in her article, but she will print the fact that CIA said they are looking for a man from Jacksonville who once lived in Miami. That is accurate, so Gentry will know she spoke with someone involved in the Violator hunt, and he will want to talk to her."

"But if we don't have a team of JSOC men ready to—"

Carmichael interrupted. "Put Zack Hightower on her. *Just* Hightower. She won't see one man as readily as she would see a team."

Mayes nodded. "Shall I give Hightower lethal authorization to target Gentry if he encounters him?"

Carmichael headed for the side door, on his way back to his office. Without looking back, he said, "You bet your ass."

47

The rain battered the tiny window high on the wall of Court's basement apartment. He lay awake in the closet, his bandaged ribs bare and his backpack under his head as a pillow.

His new Glock 17 pistol, now with the suppressor screwed on to the end of the barrel, lay by his side.

He hadn't left this apartment since he arrived home just before six the afternoon before; it was nearly three a.m. now, and he hadn't slept one damn minute of the past nine hours. He'd not accomplished much since watching the news and changing his bandages other than eating a dinner of bland collard greens and black beans, then washing it all down with tepid tap water and a pair of bottled beers.

After that, he vegetated, watching TV for hours.

The first half of his viewing was for purely operational purposes. He watched the major networks as they ran reports about the "terrorist massacre" in Dupont Circle. The faces of the reporters talking were different, but only a little. Their reports, on the other hand, seemed almost word for word the same.

After he couldn't take any more regurgitated information or uninformed conjecture, he switched off the news and began flipping through the entertainment channels. There wasn't much on that interested him, other than a comedy on basic cable about a group of guys who woke up with hangovers after a bachelor party in Las Vegas. Apparently this was the first film of a trilogy, but Court had never heard of it, and he wondered if watching all three would have increased his enjoyment. But despite the banality of it all and notwithstanding everything that had happened to him this week, Court caught himself laughing out loud at the absurd dilemma of the protagonists to the point his gunshot wound throbbed in protest at his enjoyment.

After the movie was over he turned off the TV, crawled into his closet, and assumed the awkward sleeping position he'd adopted since arriving here in the Mayberrys' basement. Like every night, he popped the Walker's Game Ear in his right ear, and immediately he could hear new sounds in the quiet neighborhood. A barking dog, the soft rumbling of a passing car, one of the Mayberrys leaving the kitchen above and walking up the staircase to their second-floor bedroom.

Now he lay here, fighting for sleep, moody and unable to find a way to shake it off. It grew from his utter frustration in his lack of forward momentum after the Ohlhauser meeting and the chaos that ensued from it. It was as if the wind had been pulled from his sails. He had no idea where to go next, and now he needed to find the momentum to regroup, to reacquire a target, and to reboot his operation.

He told himself he needed to work on his next move, which sounded good until he hit a wall the moment he tried to think. His original plan here in the D.C. area had been to talk to three men to get all the information he needed to determine his next course of action. Indeed, he had spoken with Chris Travers and Matt Hanley, but Leland Babbitt had been killed before he could interrogate him. And although Ohlhauser hadn't been on his radar at the beginning of this op he'd managed to talk to him before he, too, had been killed.

But now what? Court thought back to his conversations with the three men, trying to pull out some actionable nugget that he hadn't noticed before. Something that had eluded him.

Shit, thought Court. He was a shooter and a spy. He wasn't an analyst or an investigator. He wanted a mission, not a fucking puzzle.

Then it hit him. A way to reanalyze the problem. He asked himself, what one thing did all the men agree on? What was the continuum between all parties?

He knew the answer as soon as he posed the question.

Fucking BACK BLAST.

This was understandable, Court reasoned, because Denny had told everyone it was an op gone bad. It had been his justification to hand down the shoot on sight. Now, in the middle of the night, with nothing else to do and nowhere else to turn, he told himself he had no choice but to try to reach back into his memory banks somehow and to replay every minuscule aspect of this one op out of dozens in his time with the Goon Squad, and hundreds in his life as an operator.

The normal routine with the Goon Squad after a mission was to perform an immediate hot wash, an after-action review where all elements involved discussed the good, bad, and ugly. They did it while memories were still fresh. But BACK BLAST had been different because Court had worked alone, without a net, much as he had in the early part of his career, when he'd been a member of the Autonomous Asset Program.

After Trieste there had been no hot wash, no after-action review, literally no mention of the event ever again.

This made details very fuzzy after more than half a decade, but as Court lay in his long, narrow closet, his head next to his ersatz escape hatch to the basement proper and his booted feet pressed up against the wall, he committed himself fully to this endeavor.

He forced himself to do his best to remember an operation that took place a half dozen years ago.

Six Years Earlier

Court Gentry didn't mind commercial travel, not even in coach, because even a long-haul international flight over the Atlantic was far superior to any of the hundreds of trips he'd taken on Agency transport in his years with CIA. The majority of the time when he moved from one country to another it was in the ass end of a loud, cold cargo aircraft that smelled like jet fuel and BO. Even the Special Activities Division Air Branch Gulfstream that normally flew transport missions for the Golf Sierra unit was outfitted for function over form, and on the inside it looked nothing like what people assumed from its sleek and businesslike fuselage.

But tonight's flight from Dulles to Milan was something special, because by the time the SAD logistics staff bought Court's ticket coach was full, so he got to fly in business class.

And though he was the one man on his team who never bitched about the austere conditions that came with his work, Court *really* didn't mind sitting in a soft and wide business-class seat, either.

It wasn't lost on him at all that three days earlier he'd been lying on his belly inside a hot metal shipping container that had been left smashed on the banks of a levee somewhere on the outskirts of Mogadishu. With him had been Sierras Four and Five, and they had spent a day and a half waiting for the signal from Sierra Two that their target had been identified at the target location. Court's body armor, hidden under the rags the locals wore, pressed into him, his ammunition digging into his stomach while he swatted flies and did his best to ignore Keith Morgan's unceasing farts.

And now here he was days later, wearing a Tommy Hilfiger blazer and L.L.Bean khakis and sipping champagne from real glass barware while a drop-dead gorgeous English flight attendant went over his myriad options for dinner.

So much better than a Keith Morgan gas attack in all respects.

Sometimes Court's cover for action was a hell of a lot better than his real life, so he took advantage of it on these few missions with the Goon Squad when he got to play dress up. He felt weird not working with the rest of his team on this, but he'd spent the first several years in CIA doing singleton ops, so it was no big trick for him to operate alone.

Over Nova Scotia he dined on salmon pomegranate with Turkish pilaf, and he washed it down with white burgundy. He'd rather have a glass of Redbreast Irish Whiskey or Knob Creek bourbon, or just a bottle of cold Pacífico beer, but his cover for action was a mild-mannered American businessman who would know that white wine paired nicely with salmon.

After his meal, while his Virgin flight flew over Greenland, he opened up his laptop and began scrolling through satellite and street maps of his target location.

The woman in the seat next to him was Italian; she never looked over at his computer to see the map of Trieste, but had she done so, Court would have just said he was in the consumer goods industry and heading to several Italian cities to meet with vendors.

He looked like an eager businessman getting a jump on his trip by committing locations to memory, but in fact he was concentrating on the maps so he could pick out his primary, secondary, and tertiary ingresses and egresses to the target area.

He worked till late in the night, then caught a few hours' sleep before the end of the flight.

His plane landed in Milan before nine a.m., and Court breezed through customs using a CIA legend he'd been handed during the van ride over. With just his carry-on it was smooth sailing out of the airport, and he found himself in the train station less than an hour after touchdown.

The train from Milan to Trieste was six hours and passed first through Bologna. Court found his first-class compartment empty for nearly the entire ride, so he used part of his journey to continue working on memorizing the map of his destination city.

He arrived in Trieste just after four p.m. during a light February drizzle, and at a counter in the train station he rented a gray 2008 Peugeot four-door that looked like it would melt in nicely with the Italian traffic.

He found his safe house to be a one-bedroom apartment on the Via Valdirivo, just a few blocks from the port. The local station had prepped it for his arrival, apparently assuming he'd be spending some real time here. There was fresh milk in the fridge, along with meat and cheese wrapped in paper from the butcher. Court bypassed the niceties left by CIA station Italy, walked to the back bedroom, and saw a table, a bed, and a tall wooden armoire. He pushed the armoire away from the wall, just as he'd been briefed by Hightower the day before.

Behind the heavy piece of furniture he found a quality but nondescript briefcase. He brought it over to the bed, sat down, and opened it with a four-digit code—again, provided to him the day before.

Inside the case he discovered a small manila folder, which he placed to the side so he could see his equipment: a full-sized Beretta 92G semiautomatic pistol, an Advanced Armament silencer, three fifteen-round magazines, and a case of fifty rounds of expanding full metal jacket subsonic ammunition.

He was a fan of this brand and model of suppressor, but neither the gun nor the ammo were his top choices.

But they would do.

Court knew if Zack were here he'd bitch about the ammo, and maybe about the pistol, too, but Court was trained to see weapons as tools, nothing more. If the tool could accomplish the task, then it was the right tool for the job. He didn't need to wield a specific weapon to make a personal statement—it was all about the job.

Also in the case were a night vision monocle and a pair of small but high-quality binoculars. Court shoved these in the pockets of his blazer, then he placed the gun on the table. He stripped, reassembled, and function-checked it, determining it to be in good condition.

After charging the magazines with ammo and loading the Beretta, he slid the gun into a small plastic hook device that would hold it inside his waistband.

And only when all this was done did he open the manila folder. Inside he found an eight-by-ten surveillance photo of a man wearing a white polo shirt, sitting at a café table. The man smiled into the camera, well aware he was being photographed.

This was the man he was sent to rescue.

The Israeli agent had a trim black beard and he appeared to be in his mid-forties, but his deep-set eyes and high forehead were conspicuous enough that Court felt sure he could recognize him even if he was clean-shaven.

The picture had been taken on the street, somewhere in Jerusalem, Court saw immediately, due to the fact that he could make out the Tower of David in the background.

He folded the picture in fourths, then tucked it into his back pocket.

He then stood from the bed, leaving the case right there, and he left the apartment. The meat and cheese and fresh cream sat untouched in the refrigerator.

Gentry wasn't here for an Italian holiday.

Thirty minutes later he stood on the open fourth floor of an office building undergoing construction and he leaned into the late afternoon breeze coming off the Adriatic Sea. Through his binoculars he peered out over the Port of Trieste. Less than a quarter of a mile from shore, a small dry-goods hauler dropped anchor in placid water.

Court knew from his briefing the day before that the *Casablancan Queen* had left port in Nemrut Bay, Turkey, on Tuesday. On board, according to sources, were two al Qaeda operatives from Iraq, one of whom was actually a Mossad asset. They were here to meet five more AQ men from Pakistan, and then together open negotiations that AQ hoped would lead to a mutually beneficial weapons deal with Serbian gangsters. Court's job was to tail these men to the Serb safe house, obtain positive ID on the agent, and then, at the earliest possible opportunity, he was to make entry on the safe house and rescue him.

Forty minutes after the *Casablancan Queen* anchored, a launch went out to the ship, then returned ashore to deposit two bearded men. They were too far away for Court to make a positive ID but he was confident, at least, that he was looking at two males with olive complexions. They each carried a large backpack and a second handheld duffel bag, and they moved with confidence and purpose.

Court watched them walk directly to a parking lot near the dock, where they were met by a Mercedes van driven by a Caucasian man. In the back were several more men who appeared to be Arabs.

He'd missed it at first because it had been slowed by a stoplight a block to the north, but now that it caught up with the Mercedes van, Court quickly realized the Renault SUV with at least four more Caucasian military-aged males inside was part of this group. It pulled alongside the Mercedes, words were exchanged, and then the Mercedes led the way out of the port.

Court climbed into his Peugeot and headed off after them, intent on tailing his objectives to their destination.

He followed the two vehicles easily to the neighborhood of Barcola, also on the Adriatic and just north of the port, where they drove straight up the driveway of a large, walled villa at the end of a cul-de-sac. Court continued on, finally turning onto a road that wound its way inland farther up a hill.

Shortly after nightfall Court knelt in dense trees on the hillside overlooking the property, again holding his binoculars to his eyes. It was dark now; the drizzle had stopped but there were no stars or moon visible under the thick canopy of clouds above, and Court was invisible to all but thermal equipment in the darkness due to his black jeans, black turtleneck, and black ski cap.

Below him in the large, walled villa, Court eyed the Serbian security men guarding the property. He counted eight men in total strolling around the large main building, either on a second-floor walkway or down at ground level, and two more at the front gatehouse, all carrying stubby submachine guns. It didn't take him much time at all to determine these weren't the most skilled or vigilant guards money could buy. Through a set of French doors to the back garden Court could see into the large living room of the main building, situated towards the center of the structure. A television was showing a soccer match on the large TV, and some of the men designated to guard the perimeters of this villa actually lagged for long periods at the French doors and back windows that gave them a view of the action on the screen.

Inside the villa Court saw several of the al Qaeda men sitting with more Serbians, all in front of the television. They spoke animatedly, clearly focused on the game, and Court doubted anyone was getting much work done on anything having to do with illegal weapons trafficking.

This looked like some kind of fucking party.

Court focused on the match for a moment. He could not make out the names of the teams in the upper right corner of the screen, but from the uniforms and the players' actions on the field, he realized Red Star Belgrade had just kicked off against Partizan Belgrade. This was the biggest soccer rivalry in Serbia, and though Court didn't know which team these gangsters supported, he did know their focus would be on the match for the next two hours.

This would be the best window to make entry into this property without much chance of compromise.

But he wasn't going anywhere till he made positive ID of his target. PID was vital before he began his ingress, because he needed to know where the hell he was going.

Court decided to change positions to see if he could get more intel about the layout of the villa and the disposition of those inside. He moved twenty yards to the south on the tree-covered hill and found another suitable hide. He pulled out his optics again and, almost immediately, he found what he was looking for. A man sat in an upstairs bedroom, wearing a button-down shirt and tan slacks. He sat on the bed with a pen in his mouth as he read through some paperwork in his hands, and occasionally made notes on the pages. Two prayer rugs were rolled up on the floor by the wall.

Through the nine-power magnification of his optics Court recognized the face of the Israeli agent almost instantly. The man wore a full beard now, as opposed to his trim beard in the Tower of David photograph, but Court was certain he had the right man.

Now that he knew his destination, he looked back across the property and did some mental accounting. Including the men patrolling the grounds, he had the location determined of a dozen bad Serbs, five bad AQ, and one good Israeli. He was missing one more Arab.

Court immediately wished the entire Goon Squad were here. If that were the case Hightower would just put Redus and Phelps up here to snipe while he, Gentry, Lynch, and Morgan hit the building, liquidating everyone except their precious cargo.

Whatever, he said to himself. For some reason the Mossad couldn't know a thing about the help they were getting from the Americans tonight. Court stopped thinking about the what-ifs of the scenario before him, then he scanned the hillside with his night vision, looking for any sign of Israeli support operatives in the area.

Nope.

As Court did another head count, he couldn't help but wonder where the last AQ operator was. He wasn't downstairs watching the match, and up in the room with the two prayer rugs, Court had seen only one man.

Court did one more scan of the property with his night vision monocle, checking the outdoor walkway that circled the second floor of the villa, and he saw a pair of Serb guards standing close together, right above their comrades enjoying the match on the ground floor. These two men seemed to be more disciplined than their mates, because they were eyeing the side yard intently, their guns off their shoulders and in their hands.

To Court it looked like they might have heard or seen something that brought them up to the landing.

And then Court saw something that surprised him. On the terra-cotta tile roof of the villa, right above the two Serbs, his eyes picked up some movement in the dark.

Court lowered his binoculars quickly and then brought up his night vision monocle. Yes. Lying flat on the roof above the two Serbs, facedown and feet up towards the peak of the building, was a lone figure dressed in black.

Court squinted, trying to get better clarity. It seemed likely this might be the missing AQ operator, but it was difficult to tell. What was certain was the man on the roof just above the walkway was absolutely fixated on the two security men directly below him.

Court saw the glint of metal in the man's left hand.

And then it hit him. Court hadn't been the only one who realized the soccer match would be distracting the guards. An assassin wouldn't wait for the middle of the night to act, not when nearly the entire security detail was focused on the television in the living room.

The hit man was here, now, and he was on his way to take down the Israeli agent.

A loud cheer erupted downstairs at the television, a dozen men celebrating some play made by one of the teams, and, while this was going on, Court watched as two flashes of light on the roof signaled the firing of two rounds from a suppressed pistol.

Court did not hear a sound from the gunfire, but he saw the two Serbs crumple to the walkway.

Quickly the man on the roof slid around, dropped down next to the two bodies, and started dragging one of them to a nearby open door. Court recognized that the man planned on hiding them from anyone below who stepped away from the French doors and looked up to the second floor.

He realized it would take him a minute or two to hide the bodies, but after that he'd have a straight shot along the empty walkway towards the Israeli asset sitting alone in the bedroom at the back of the villa.

And Court knew it was his job to protect the asset.

He threw his binos into his pack along with his night vision monocle, and then he stood and pushed through the trees, closing on the villa below him with reckless speed.

48

Court scaled a back wall quickly and quietly, dropped down into a garden, then looked ahead. Directly in front of him was an open-sided shelter that covered a pair of speedboats on trailers, and to the right of the boats was a large garden with a fountain. Beyond both the garden and the garage was the main house of the villa, two stories high. The Israeli agent's room was on the second floor, right beyond the boat shelter. Court looked up and realized the window to the Israeli asset's room was open, although he could not make out the man inside from ground level.

He also saw two more Serbian guards. These men were on the sidewalk directly below the walkway and the second-floor window. They didn't seem to be on edge like the two who had just been murdered by the approaching al Qaeda assassin, but they also weren't goofing off around the corner watching the soccer match through the windows like the others.

Court knew he could take out these two men—just follow the lead of the other hit man in black here on the property and wait for some noise from the other side of the house, then use his suppressed pistol to drop them where they stood.

But he couldn't wait around. He knew the assassin on the second-floor walkway would be closing as quickly as possible on the man upstairs.

Court looked at the boat shelter next to him. He backed up a few feet, then used a palm tree that ran close enough to the shelter to brace himself on both the back wall of the structure and the tree's thick trunk, and he shimmied all the way up to the flat metal roof.

Once on top he quickly scanned all around. He knew he had no time to spare, because he couldn't see what progress the assassin had made in his effort to stash the Serbian bodies and make his way to his target.

The Israeli agent's window was right in front of the boat shelter, though it was separated by ten feet of air, because the two structures were not connected. The sidewalk below ran between them. Court watched from his new vantage point while the man inside the bedroom stood, walked to the window, and opened it wide. With a silver pen in his mouth he looked out into the night for a moment, then he turned around and returned to his work on the bed.

Court decided the best way to make it from the boat shelter roof to the bedroom without being seen by the Serbian guards below was to leap right over their heads. He knew he'd have to pull off an impressive ten-foot jump, then stick the landing on the second-floor walkway, then spring back into the air and vault through the window.

His ankles hurt just thinking about the gymnastics to come.

He rolled off his backpack and checked to make sure his pistol was seated in the retention hook so that it wouldn't come out when he landed, then he quickly kicked off his shoes. He rose to his feet and began running along the roof of the shelter as fast as he could, approaching the drop to the sidewalk below, aiming for a point on the second-floor walkway right in front of the open window.

Two long running steps before he launched himself into the air, he saw the bedroom door open, and he worried he would arrive too late.

Court leapt off the roof of the building, kicked his legs once while in the air over the Serbian guards, and arced through the dark night in perfect silence.

He landed perfectly on the walkway, letting his feet and legs absorb the first of the impact, then he rolled on his right shoulder, diminishing the force against his body even more as he converted his downward momentum into forward momentum. The energy from the roll whipped him back up to his feet and it propelled him up and forward; he leapt high again, and he hurdled through the open window into the bedroom, simultaneously ducking his head and lifting his feet, while drawing his Beretta pistol from his hip.

As he flew through the window Court evaluated the scene before him. The man in the white shirt was on his left and standing quickly up from the bed, the papers around him flitting through the air as they spilled from his hands. His hands were empty other than his silver pen, and his eyes were focused across the room on the doorway to Court's right.

And there the man in black had just entered, his gun arm outstretched, the silencer protruding, taking aim on the man in white.

Court landed flat-footed like a gymnast sticking his landing, and he saw the two men on opposite ends of the fifteen-foot space through his peripheral vision as both their heads swiveled towards his arrival.

Court pivoted on his right heel, swinging his gun in an arc to the right as fast as possible to get a shot off before the al Qaeda assassin killed the Israeli agent.

Downstairs a massive cheer erupted around the television.

When the front sight of Court's Beretta found the man in black, Court realized this man already had his gun up and pointed at Court's chest.

But the man in black hesitated an instant, then he shouted in Arabic. *"Istanna!"* Wait!

Court Gentry was not trained to wait. He was trained to act.

He shot the man once through the forehead. The cheer downstairs drowned out the muted thump of the gunfire.

The al Qaeda assassin's gun dropped from his hand and his head snapped back. He crumpled to the ground in the hallway just outside the door. Court rushed over, grabbed the body by its black shirt, and pulled it fully into the room. Closing the door now, he propped the dead weight against it as an ersatz doorstop.

Court spun to the other man now. He'd been told the Israeli agent didn't speak a word of English, only Hebrew and Arabic. Since Court knew next to no Hebrew at all and his Arabic was only fair, he realized communications between himself and the man he had been sent to rescue would be simple.

But this was a feature, not a glitch. Court didn't want to chat up the Israeli agent. He wanted to get the fuck out of here.

In memorized Arabic, Court said, "We go out window. Hurry."

The man stood there, his eyes wide, his hands in front of him, his pen still between the fingers of his right hand. In Arabic he asked, "Who . . . are . . . you?"

Court did not answer directly. He said, "Very dangerous here."

"Yes. Of course," came the reply, as the man recovered quickly. He slipped his pen carefully into his pocket, knelt, and began scooping together the paperwork off the floor.

If Court's mission parameters had included exploiting this site and getting an intelligence haul on this mission he would have helped the middle-aged man recover the documents, but he had no orders to bring out anything other than this Israeli agent, so he just grabbed the man by the collar, hefted him back up, and turned him towards the window. To Court's surprise and relief, the man gave him no problems.

Court pulled in front of the train station with his precious cargo after twenty silent minutes of driving. The only words exchanged had been a few sentences in Hebrew that Court did not understand, and to which Court did not respond. He heard "*shalom*" several times, but he ignored the man's thanks.

He stopped the car, moved quickly to the passenger-side door, and opened it up.

"*Imshi*," Court said. "Go away." Court's Arabic was limited indeed.

The man climbed out and, in Arabic now, asked, "Who are you? Who sent you?"

But Court just shook his head, pretended like he did not understand a word of it. The man nodded, then reached out with his right hand.

To move things along, Court took the hand to shake it, but the Israeli leaned forward and took him in an embrace.

"*Imshi*," Court said after a moment.

The man stood back with tears in his eyes, he said, "*Shalom*" one more time, then he turned and headed inside.

Court drove off immediately, heading for the highway that would take him north along the Adriatic coastline, and he pulled out his satellite phone. After nearly a minute establishing a connection, Zack Hightower answered on the other end.

"Hey, brother. How's the weather over there?"

"Nice and warm." It was a simple code phrase to indicate mission success.

"Good to hear that. Come on home. Don't dick around."

"Roger that."

Court drove the Peugeot through the early morning, returned it at the rental company's office at the airport in Bologna, then climbed aboard a morning train to Milan. He arrived back in the airport twenty-four hours and twenty-five minutes after he left, boarded the Virgin flight to Dulles with the rest of business class, tucked himself into his window seat with a rocks glass full of Maker's Mark, and fell sound asleep before the big Airbus leveled off over the German/French border.

Present Day

Court opened his eyes and found himself out of business class and back in his closet.

More than ever he was sure he'd done his *fucking* job on BACK BLAST, just exactly like he'd been told.

But it was no big mystery to Court as to why Denny Carmichael had chosen BACK BLAST to use to scapegoat him. It was the one op Court had performed during his Goon Squad years that hadn't involved the rest of the team. Denny could tell Hanley, Ohlhauser, and the director of the CIA that Court went to Italy on an op, that he took a payoff from the Serbs, that he let a bad guy slip away.

And he'd killed some innocent guy instead.

Court looked at the dark ceiling of the closet above him, and he felt weak, impotent, and low. He had no idea how to convince anyone he was innocent of the charge Carmichael accused him of.

He closed his eyes, telling himself he needed to sleep awhile to be able to think straight.

But almost immediately his eyes fired back open.

A faint noise, something indistinct but vaguely familiar, grabbed his attention. There was no way he would have heard it without the Walker's Game Ear increasing his hearing, but still, it barely registered.

While his brain was processing the origin of the sound, he heard it again. Soft but unmistakable.

A slight scratching.

A mouse?

No. *Yes.* He knew what it was now.

It was a plastic buckle, probably a FastTech, commonly used on tactical gear. Court had worn equipment adorned with FastTech buckles for the majority of his life, so he knew the sound they made when they touched other surfaces almost as well as he knew his own inner voice.

The buckle had brushed against the wooden wall on the little patio of his basement apartment, right next to the cement steps up to the driveway.

Now Court concentrated, listened beyond the ever-increasing sound of his own pounding heart, and he detected footsteps just outside his door.

He pictured the scene just six feet from where he now lay. A half dozen SWAT officers filed down the steps, then, one by one, they stacked up on the wall right outside his door. One of the men accidentally bumped his drop leg ammunition pouch on the wall as he moved into position, brushing the buckle against the wood.

Court reached for his gun.

49

Arthur Mayberry shook his head in disbelief, but Bernice Mayberry nodded her head as if she had known all along.

They both sat in plastic chairs in an all-night laundromat three blocks from their home. Arthur wore his pajamas and a blue jacket handed to him by an ambulance driver. He stared ahead, still unable to process what was happening around him, and Bernice sat next to him in her housecoat, equal measures scared and angry, but she had already professed herself to be wholly unsurprised by tonight's events.

Out through the windows of the laundromat law enforcement officers stood around, radios to ears. On the street ambulances and paddy wagons idled, and first responders waited for the order to roll forward.

Arthur and his wife had been roused by a phone call, just after three a.m., asking them both to very quickly and quietly come to the front door to speak with police officers. They'd complied, of course, and when they did they were told they needed to leave their home immediately. Bernice had demanded to know what was going on, and an officer said there was a chemical spill on the nearby train tracks, and everything would be explained at the command center. They were whisked away by a team of armed cops in body armor and taken here to the laundromat, where dozens of cops were already set up, and whatever they were planning on doing didn't look to Arthur like it had one damn thing to do with a chemical spill.

Guns, grenade launchers, night vision equipment, riot shields. Arthur hadn't seen so much military gear since Saigon in 1969.

He and his wife were led to seats near the front of the laundromat and, as a group of cops parted to let them through, Arthur saw a large photograph of his basement tenant posted on cardboard and leaning against the wall.

"Oh, *hell* no," Mayberry mumbled under his breath.

Fifteen minutes had passed since then, and now Arthur watched while the police looked over his hand-drawn diagram of his basement, including the corner apartment he built with his own two hands. He imagined when this was all over he was going to be in some serious trouble for all his building code violations, but he looked on the bright side . . . He sure as hell wasn't in nearly as much trouble as Jeff Duncan.

He'd done what he could to deflect blame away from the man in his basement. Jeff Duncan was probably up to no good, but the very idea the mild-mannered white man living on his property was some sort of a terrorist was asinine. Arthur had seen something on the man's face; a world-weariness, a hardened interior, maybe. But he wasn't as bad as all this, Arthur felt sure.

Bernice, on the other hand, kept muttering to herself that she knew Jeff Duncan was low-down and no-account, and she berated her husband mercilessly for not seeing this for himself.

The Washington Metro Police Department refers to its SWAT unit as ERT, the Emergency Response Team. The head of the ERT unit had sat down with Mayberry a few minutes earlier and asked, "You are *certain* there is no access to the house from the basement apartment?"

"Look, young man. I told the other officers. I built that place myself. You would need to knock a hole in the wall to get into the basement, and even if you could bust through, you'd be over there on the side with the furnace and the water heater."

Arthur had then drawn up the diagram, and although the police seemed to be very concerned about the man in the basement, Arthur could tell the Emergency Response Team captain was glad he wouldn't have to split his men and hit multiple entrances at the same time. They could, instead, enter the basement, and then, if the subject wasn't there, they could exit and reenter the home to clear it. Another thirty police officers were on the scene and charged with cordoning off the block to keep anyone from entering or exiting. If the cordon around the property was any good, and their suspect was inside, they'd get him, wherever they found him.

Now Arthur and Bernice sat quietly, waiting for the tactical officers to get on with their raid and remove their tenant from their home in handcuffs, so they could go back home and back to bed.

———————

Denny Carmichael awoke from a deep sleep on his sofa.

The phone on his desk trilled and he grabbed it, both surprised and hopeful.

"Mayes?"

"It's Brewer, sir." She sounded almost out of breath.

"Talk."

"D.C. Emergency Response Team has surrounded a house in Columbia Heights. They think they have the suspect from Dupont Circle holed up inside."

Carmichael clenched the receiver tight. "And *why* do they think this?"

"A Crime Stoppers tip led them to the area. Detectives came out and interviewed neighbors, showing them a picture taken from the Easy Market, and another taken at Dupont. They got a hit, apparently."

"And why are we just learning about this now?"

"We aren't monitoring tip line calls, there are a hundred every hour, most all of them useless. We only monitor the radio traffic of dispatched police units. This call went over a landline directly to a supervisor, and not out over the radio. He used his mobile phone to send out detectives, they weren't dispatched regularly. I guess they are suspicious a terrorist might be listening in to police radio traffic. When they decided it was a legit lead they called everyone out. We're a good twenty minutes behind the action."

Carmichael was furious the TOC hadn't accounted for the possibility the D.C. police would have a special protocol set up for Crime Stoppers tips.

"Where is JSOC?"

"En route, but they won't make it in time. ERT is going to hit that house any second."

"Give me the address, now!"

She did so, Carmichael hung up, and immediately he called Murquin al-Kazaz.

If ERT attacked, Court might die, but if he lived and escaped, the Saudis needed to put themselves in position in time to cut him down.

The worst-case scenario, for Carmichael anyway, was for Gentry to be taken alive by Washington, D.C., law enforcement. The thought of Court Gentry secure in a jail cell talking to a public defender made his stomach boil with acid.

D.C. Metro Police Department! Search warrant!"
Court opened the small hatch just as the shout came from outside his front door.

He knew the cops weren't going to wait for him to answer, and he was right. One second after the call came he heard a shotgun blast; a slug was fired into one of the hinges of the storm door. A second shot came one second later, and the door fell from the frame.

A battering ram would crash through the wooden door any second.

But Court wasn't waiting around for that. He had the hidden escape hatch door out of the way and he pushed his backpack through the hole, then he backed into it and reached for the hatch door to pull it back into place.

The battering ram slammed into the wooden door of his apartment as he did so.

The chair propped under the knob held for the first strike of the ram, and even the second, but as Court reseated the hatch and backed into the basement proper he heard the chair break fully and the door crash in, and then he heard another noise, followed by just exactly what he expected would come next.

He heard the screams of men.

The ERT team leader was fourth in the stack of eight men. He kept his M4 rifle high and his gloved left hand on the shoulder of the man in front of him. As the breach man smashed through the door with the battering ram and moved to the side, the first two shooters began pushing into the basement apartment. They had not made it fully inside the building before a loud rushing sound filled the patio, and then a massive orange ball of fire erupted out of the apartment, engulfing everyone in front of the door.

The three men exposed to the fire stumbled back, falling onto one another, finally getting themselves below the flame, which continued spraying straight out the door all the way up the cement steps to the driveway. As other team members grabbed the men and pulled them out of the fire, the team leader tried to understand what was happening.

All he knew for sure was that a massive cone of flammable propellant was spraying from the apartment through the doorway, and there was no way to make entry here. He had no idea if some sort of booby trap had been tripped or if the suspect was standing there with a *fucking* flamethrower, but he knew he had to get his team away from danger so they could regroup.

He called into his headset microphone. "Fall back! Fall back!"

Court crawled along next to the hot furnace on his elbows and knees, doing his best to ignore the agonizing pain from the old bullet wound on the right side of his rib cage. After several feet he was able to climb up to a low crouch. When he was up full and running for the steps out of the basement, he passed the home's main circuit breaker and he pulled down the lever, enveloping the entire home in darkness. He then ripped out all the fuses, dropped them on the concrete floor, and stomped them till they shattered. He imagined SWAT men would have NODs, night observation devices, but he also imagined they wouldn't have the newest models. Instead the cops would be looking through narrow tubes that would give them limited peripheral vision, and he hoped to use their weakness to his advantage. He then raced up the stairs, out of the basement, and into the kitchen, his pistol out in front of him.

Evacuating the sunken patio outside the basement apartment devolved into utter chaos for the ERT unit. The three men who'd been hit by flame were not seriously injured, but they did not know this yet. More than anything they were disoriented by the incredible light and heat that had encircled them moments before. The fact that the stairs to the driveway were right in front of the apartment door and therefore still involved in the fire meant everyone had to climb up and over the wall around the patio and onto the driveway, and this was hampered by the three injured men who needed to be helped out, as well as the difficulty in keeping rifles high and at the ready in case the fire stopped and Jeff Duncan charged out of the little room with a weapon in his hand.

After nearly forty-five seconds, though, all eight ERT officers were up on the driveway and to the side of the unrelenting exhaust of flame, and four of them covered the extraction of the wounded men.

More police ran up the driveway to help with the evacuation.

By the time everyone was off of the Mayberry property and positioned in the street, behind the cover of a pair of armored ERT trucks, the glow from the patio had finally died down.

There was concern for a moment as to whether the home itself might have caught fire, but when no evidence of either flame or smoke presented itself after five minutes, the ERT team leader called again into his microphone, "On me! We're going back in!"

The second breach of the basement apartment went much better than the first. The apartment was empty; that was determined quickly, but only after they entered to find a rolling propane tank with a toy airsoft gun mounted on top of it. A triggering mechanism with an electric lighter and a length of bungee cord completed the improvised automatic flamethrower.

The plastic gun had melted into the top of the tank, but the booby trap had proved effective in delaying entry. The propane expelled was primarily vapor, but the compressed gas in the airsoft gun had propelled it outward. The ERT leader couldn't figure out how the suspect could have left the apartment after having set the trap, but he didn't spend too much time thinking about it.

Instead he said, "He's not here. Let's clear upstairs."

Two teams of eight men each hit the house. Alpha came through the front door and Bravo came through the back near the kitchen.

After Alpha cleared the living room and dining room, they left a man in position to cover this area. Bravo cleared the kitchen, a laundry room, and then the basement. They left one of their officers to cover here. The rest of Bravo rallied at the bottom of the stairs with Alpha, who then left an officer here in the hall so he could cover the bottom of the stairs and remain in visual contact with both the man in the front of the house and the man in the back of the house. In this manner they formed a rear guard, in case an attacker had been missed in the cleared area or else found some way to double back past the main stack of ERT officers.

The remaining members of the two teams moved in a tight train up the stairwell, slowly and carefully, guns high.

The Bravo rear guard officer stood on the threshold in the kitchen that led down the stairs to the basement area. The lights were off all over the house, but he used his NODs to see around the space down at the bottom of the stairs. The full eight-man Bravo team had checked the basement, so he wasn't worried about anyone being down there. Instead he just turned away and kept his eyes up the hallway that led from the kitchen to the stairs, ready to train his rifle on any "squirters," or suspects trying to flee past the ERT officers still clearing upstairs.

This, as it turned out, was a mistake.

He never heard the man in stocking feet come up the basement stairs; he only knew someone was there when the pistol's barrel touched his left temple.

In a soft whisper he heard, "You make a sound into your mic and I'll blow your fucking head off."

The ERT officer made no sound. As he stood there, still looking up the hallway, he saw the two officers positioned with him on the ground floor look up the hall in his direction, as they checked to make sure he was covering his territory. The three men shared eye contact, but soon enough the others turned around and moved a few feet into the living room. They were unable to see the tip of the pistol barrel sticking out of the open basement doorway and pressing against the side of their teammate's head.

The Bravo officer was pulled by the neck into the basement, then stripped of his rifle, NODs, and communications gear. In the dark the terrified man heard the door next to him shut softly and a bolt slide into place, then he was directed by the barrel of the gun against the back of his neck to move down the steps. He followed the whispered instructions, walking all the way back in the direction of the furnace.

In the middle of the basement the suspect pulled the Bravo officer's pistol out of his drop leg holster. He then heard, "You have forty-five seconds to get everything off. Go."

———————

It was impossible for the ERT officer to get all his gear, his armor, his tunic, his boots, and his pants off in forty-five seconds, but he did his best. Court knew he couldn't do it, but he also knew he'd work faster with an impossible timeline.

While the man stripped, Court dressed, but he put the man's radio headset in his ear first so he could listen in.

Soon in a soft voice he heard, "This is Alpha One. Hold all positions. We've got a closed closet door in the master bedroom with movement indicated under the door."

Court now had a tunic, body armor, a balaclava, and night vision goggles on.

"Speed it up," Court whispered to the man as the cop fought to get his belt off.

A new call from upstairs came over the radio, asking all elements to report status before they confronted whatever was hiding in the closet. Court spoke to his hostage, who by now was down to his underwear. "Quick . . . what's your call sign? Think before you answer. If you're wrong, I drop you right here."

"Bravo Four," the man said.

Court zipped up the black tactical pants while the radio came alive.

"Bravo One, check."

"Two check."

"Bravo Three check."

Court clicked the transmit button, but he rubbed his headset mic against the stubble on his chin as he spoke to mask the sound of his voice. "Four check."

The next man on the team continued the roll call.

Court fastened the utility belt around his waist, not taking time to thread the belt through the loops. It was a little large for him, like the rest of the gear, but he made it work.

Court then cuffed the ERT officer to a pipe extending from the water heater, then he pulled a flash bang grenade out of the officer's load-bearing vest.

Alpha One stood outside the master bedroom on the second floor of the Mayberry home. Two of his men trained their laser aiming devices on the closet door at the far end of the room. Under the door, faint shadows moved back and forth at irregular intervals.

Alpha One shouted, "D.C. Metro Police! Come out of the closet! Hands high!"

There was no response then, nor when he repeated the command two more times.

Finally Bravo Six entered the room, moved to the side of the door. He let his rifle hang from its sling and pulled his pistol from his drop leg holster, then he used his free hand to reach for the door. Everyone else tightened for action, their laser pointers evenly spaced across the door as Bravo Six slid it open.

On the floor in the back of the closet, a flashlight stuck out of a woman's shoe. In front of this was a huge puddle of milk, and around the puddle, three cats moved around, lapping it up hungrily.

"Son of a bitch," the ERT man mumbled.

A flash bang grenade went off on the ground floor below them.

The four regular police officers watching the backyard of the house from the neighbor's yard saw the flash of light in the windows. The explosion broke glass in the kitchen that flew out over the patio. As they knelt behind a fence and watched, they heard in their radios the calls of the tactical team as they lined up on the second-floor stairs, ready to hit the floor below them from the stairwell.

It was clear they were missing a man, but these four in back understood why. A single tactical officer, his rifle in his left hand and his right hand clutching his left elbow, appeared in the side yard. The cops thought he might have come either from the front of the house or the basement apartment.

He ran up to them; clearly he was hurt, but at least he was ambulatory. While one of the cops made the officer-down call, the other three covered for the wounded ERT man as he ran past their position, all the way through the yard, and towards the street on the other side of this property. None of the men noticed the cop was wearing a backpack that was not police issue.

One of the officers started to run to help him, but he was called back by the other three. They knew they needed to hold their position in case the suspect appeared and tried to run after the fight inside.

Court ran to the street, where two police cars sat parked on the corner. The cars were both empty with their doors open, but four armed officers stood nearby, ready to block any traffic trying to get into the neighborhood.

"Ambulance is on the way!" one cop called out when he saw the tactical officer. "How bad is it?"

Court was all the way up to the two vehicles when he slowed and stopped. He let go of his arm now, and raised the rifle. "Show me your hands."

"What the hell?"

"Where are the keys?"

No one spoke; they were all clearly stunned. Court glanced in one of the cruisers and saw the keys in the ignition. "Drop your weapons on the street, kick them away."

All four did as instructed, and Court leapt into the cruiser, fired it up, and then raced off.

He knew this drive would be a short one. The helicopter pilot above would be informed of the situation in seconds, and it wasn't tough for a cop in the sky to track a cop car on an empty street.

He pulled under a covered parking space in an apartment complex just seven and a half blocks away, parked the squad car, and leapt out, leaving the rifle behind. Just as the helo above neared his position, he sprinted through the parking lot, then he climbed a fence and dropped down into a drainage canal that ran at the back of the apartment complex.

He knew where he was going, after having studied satellite maps of his neighborhood to plan for rushed escapes.

He raced along the canal, ran to a large culvert, and ducked in. As he moved through pitch-darkness he pulled out his phone to light his way, and with this he saw a smaller drain, waist-high and not more than four feet in diameter, that ran off at a ninety-degree angle. Water gushed down from it into the culvert.

This wasn't sewage; it was just runoff water from the streets, but there wasn't anything clean about it. Court climbed up and into the long, narrow shaft, and he knelt low. This killed his wounded ribs, but he ignored the pain and moved as fast as he could from the area.

He wasn't sure where the drain went—this wasn't on the sat maps—but he had a flashlight, and he had a sense that he was moving to the east. If he just stayed in here for a few blocks and climbed out he'd find himself some-where in the middle of the city, and from there he was sure he would be safe from the immediate threat.

50

Denny Carmichael opened this morning's copy of the *Washington Post*. DeRenzi had brought it in as soon as it arrived by courier, and Denny had been awake and waiting for it, even though it was only five a.m.

It took him no time to find the article he was looking for, just below the fold and taking up an entire half of the front page, as well as another half of A19.

Carmichael assumed Catherine King must have raced back from the CIA headquarters in McLean to the *Washington Post*'s office in D.C. to make her deadline last night. She couldn't have possibly filed the story before midnight, which meant the newspaper had done some impressive work to get the article in the edition that went to press just a few hours later.

It was all there, under the headline "CIA suspects D.C.-area shooter is 'known personality.'"

The description of Gentry was close to what Carmichael had handed King. She'd also reported the fact that he had spent time in Miami, along with information that he'd been trained, possibly by jihadists, likely in Yemen.

For some reason there was no mention about him coming from Jacksonville, Florida, but Denny wasn't too troubled by this.

Nor was he bothered by the fact that King's article clearly faulted CIA for not letting police know after the Brandywine Street incident that they had suspicions about who might be involved in the attack. Carmichael didn't care. After all, in one form or another, CIA had been blamed for everything bad that had ever happened since the 1950s.

Other than this small trifle, there was very little editorial comment from King in the piece, which greatly pleased Denny. She did add a small caveat at the end when she wrote that the investigation was ongoing and first reports, even from top government officials, often proved to be erroneous.

Carmichael shrugged. King thought she had couched her piece with skepticism, but she had done exactly what Denny wanted her to do.

She had published an article that would bait Gentry into targeting the writer of the article.

At any other time, the impenetrable blackness around him and the rainfall beating against the aluminum roof above him would have lulled Court into peaceful sleep. But his heart rate and the adrenaline pumping through him, even now, a full hour and a half after listening to the sounds of a tactical unit preparing to smash in his door, still prevented him from calming down enough to relax and doze off.

He sat Indian style in his small storage unit, his back to the concrete block back wall, his suppressed Glock in his lap, and his Yamaha motorcycle right in front of him for cover. He faced the closed metal sliding door, stared at the black in front of his eyes, and listened to the calming rain.

And he fully expected at any moment for the door to fly open and a team of shooters to rush in behind it with blinding lights and laser-targeting devices.

Court had made it to his storage unit over a half hour earlier, after running a short SDR by using two early-morning cabs and walking through back alleys and commercial parking lots. Once in his little unit, he checked the area around him before closing the door, then he used the light of his phone to find his second bugout bag here in his cache and to check the bike to make sure it was ready to roll.

Then he just sat down and did his best to relax.

He hadn't known who was hitting the Mayberry house at first, but after the engagement he determined they were a local police tactical unit. Their body armor said ERT, and while that was nothing conclusive—a gang of Arab goons had worn uniforms that proclaimed them to be D.C. Metro cops, after all—the tactical unit's movements confirmed to Court they were exactly what they purported to be. The cordon of regular patrol officers in the area around the Mayberry home only sealed Court's suspicion he'd been discovered in his hide site by local law enforcement.

That was a bit embarrassing for a tier-one operator like Gentry, but he'd known from the beginning he would be up against a lot of different opposition forces, and he'd be taking a risk operating inside the city.

If the cops hit this storage locker now he would lift the Glock and he would point it at them, but he wasn't about to kill a cop. He might squeeze off a couple of rounds into their body armor just to make himself feel good, but there was nowhere to run, so if the cops hit, he'd die right here, sitting Indian style and enjoying the sound of the morning spring rain.

But he wasn't just barricading himself here to die. Instead he was waiting a few minutes more for the early part of the morning rush hour, where he wouldn't be one of the only vehicles out on the street, and then he would climb aboard the Yamaha 650 and get the hell out of town.

But not too far. Despite this morning's setback, he still had work to do here in the District.

For now he just worked on calming his body, relaxing himself, and waiting for the right time to run.

Matt Hanley was the last to enter the conference room, and as soon as he did so he realized the meeting had begun without him.

Not that he cared. If he had his way he wouldn't be here at all, but he'd been summoned by Carmichael, and Carmichael was his superior, so he had no choice but to attend.

As he sat down at the table in an open wingback chair, he looked around at the attendees. Suzanne Brewer was in the middle of a presentation. She stood in front of a digital map of the city and addressed the room, perfectly coiffed and dressed.

Mayes and Carmichael were present, of course, as were many of the other Violator Working Group members, along with a team of techs sitting in chairs against the back wall.

And there was one more attendee. Down at the end of the conference table sat a big man with short blond hair, much of it turning gray. He wore a suit and tie, his face was cleanly shaved, and he had a small notebook in front of him.

But Hanley wasn't fooled—he knew a shooter when he saw one.

Hanley turned away from the man, presuming him to be a JSOC liaison or someone similar, but as soon as Brewer finished her presentation and sat back down, Hanley's head swiveled back to the man at the end of the table.

Matt hadn't seen Zack Hightower in five years, and he was almost certain he'd never seen him without a beard, so he forgave himself for not recognizing him. Calling out across the length of the table he said, "Morning, Sierra One. Welcome back to the land of the living."

Zack Hightower had worked for Matt Hanley for several years, till the day Hanley was told all the men in his Goon Squad unit were dead except for Gentry, and Gentry was the culprit for the deaths of the others.

"Hey, Matt," Zack said. He seemed embarrassed to be alive. He added, "Sorry about that." Zack then nodded over to Denny Carmichael, who was looking down at some papers. He shrugged. "Orders. You know."

Hanley just stared Hightower down and said, "Your funeral sucked, by the way."

Zack gave a half smile and looked down to his empty notebook, and one of the techs in the room, a man who had no idea what was going on, broke out in a surprised laugh.

The executives at the conference table, in contrast, remained silent, until Suzanne Brewer said, "Matt, you haven't missed anything, I was just getting started with the morning briefing. The short version is this: Gentry's in the wind. Again. Local PD had him, but they lost him."

Hanley asked, "How did that happen?"

"While forty cops cordoned off the neighborhood, two eight-man ERT units hit the house where he was staying. They engaged Gentry, but Gentry managed to get out of the building and past the cordon."

Hanley said, "Let's see . . . yesterday in Dupont Circle, Gentry brutally murdered several men. The death toll this morning *must* have been three times that, right?"

Brewer shook her head, not picking up on the fact that Hanley seemed to know the answer to this question already. "Surprisingly, no. Four men were injured, though no injuries were life-threatening."

Hanley glanced to Hightower, and he noticed his eyebrows furrowing slightly. But Zack said nothing.

Hanley next asked, "Could someone please tell me why I'm here?"

Carmichael spoke for the first time since Hanley had arrived. "Like it or not, Matt, it's in your best interests that we bring this episode to a close. Suzanne wants to know where Violator will go next for shelter. Today, we suspect, will be a repositioning day for him. He will find some new location, some new bolt-hole, and I'm going to venture to guess it will be outside of the District, some-place safer. You ran the man for several years, and he hasn't been back in the area since those days. We thought you might give us ideas about his possible new hide site."

Before Hanley could respond, Hightower raised a wary hand.

Brewer turned to acknowledge him. "Zack, it's not necessary to raise your hand."

"Sorry," he said. "Gentry will be south of D.C., in a remote location. Picture a covered ditch, a deserted cabin, a grain elevator on an abandoned farm. He will be very difficult to find once he gets there. Almost impossible. I feel our next moment of opportunity will be when he reengages us, *not* when we discover his hide."

Brewer said, "I understand why you think he will go somewhere more remote, but why south specifically?"

"He lived and worked in northern Virginia. It's more familiar to him. He might anticipate us making this assumption, but he is confident in his abilities to hide, especially when he knows the terrain."

Carmichael pointed to Hanley. "Your best guess as to his location?"

Hanley heaved his shoulders, not hiding his annoyance at it all. "I was management. Hightower was labor. Next to Court Gentry, Zack Hightower is the best operator I ever had working under me." He looked down the table at Hightower. "Before Zack's untimely death, he was also the best ground-level leader I'd ever seen. In your infinite wisdom, Denny, you've resurrected Hightower to sit him in a seventh-floor conference room, dress him in a suit and tie, and ask him questions about Gentry's new lair. Zack tells you the target has run someplace you'll never find him, so I defer to Zack's expertise. I guess you'll just have to wait for him to come back out to play."

Suzanne snapped back. "*Play*, Matt? Really? A veteran CIA official and three innocent Transit Police were murdered yesterday. I doubt their loved ones see this as a game."

Hanley sniffed. "Yeah, about that. Yesterday, a man with Court Gentry's abilities of escape and evasion was so backed into a corner in a location with a half dozen egresses that he was forced to murder three poorly armed and poorly trained transit cops in cold blood, in broad daylight, in a crowded location. And yet before dawn this morning, *sixteen* highly trained tactical officers raided his secure, defended ground, and in that instance Court only knocks a few heads together. Killing none. Zero."

Hanley was looking at Hightower now. "That is pretty damn curious, wouldn't you say?"

Despite Hanley's challenge, Zack did not say a word.

Brewer countered, "He did a lot more than knock heads together."

Hanley stood up from the table. "But he did a lot less than send a dozen poor bastards to the morgue! A cold-blooded killer is cornered like a fucking rat in a cage and he doesn't kill his way out?" He turned to Denny. "Not buying it. I'm not buying any of this bullshit. I'm walking, Chief. You have a problem with that, go to the director and have him remove me for insubordination. The way the walls are crumbling around here, you'd be doing me a favor."

Carmichael didn't stop Hanley from leaving, but Brewer chased him out and caught up with him on his way back to his office. "Matt?"

With a heave and a sigh he turned back to her. "Sorry, Suzanne. My comments weren't directed at you, specifically. They were directed at this entire operation."

"I understand. I just *don't* understand why you are in Gentry's camp the way you are. Hightower is the same way. Zack will do whatever we tell him to do, it seems clear he is a good soldier, but I don't get the feeling his heart is in this any more than yours is."

Hanley said, "Every day this goes on, Denny gets himself in deeper. I don't know what the fuck is happening out there, but the story he is giving you, and the story he gave the *Washington Post* yesterday, is just the story Denny needs us to believe. It's not the truth. I respect you, Suzanne, but when the smoke clears after this debacle, those of us who did what we could to stay outside of Denny's gravitational pull will not be able to do one damn thing to help those who got pulled down with him."

Hanley left Brewer there, standing alone in the hallway.

51

Court opened up the throttle on his Yamaha 650 as soon as he turned south on I-95. He wasn't sure where he was going, only that he needed to get the hell out of D.C., at least for the time being. He planned on finding a new hide, somewhere within a half hour to an hour's drive of the District, and someplace one hell of a lot more secure than Arthur Mayberry's basement apartment.

Although he wasn't sure where he was going, he wasn't exactly flying blind. He knew this stretch of highway, because the HQ of the Goon Squad had been in Norfolk and he'd lived in Virginia Beach, both just to the southeast. He'd driven up I-95 to D.C. from time to time on training evolutions, either to practice surveillance in Old Town Alexandria or around the National Mall near the Capitol building.

He passed Prince William Forest Park on his right, the marine barracks of Quantico on his left, and he continued another few minutes until he saw a turnoff for the Stafford Regional Airport. Instantly an idea came to him. Court had learned to fly light aircraft here, a long time ago, admittedly, but he remembered the facility, more or less. Security had been lax around the airport at the time, so he thought there was a chance he could hide out somewhere on the property, either in a hangar or a utility room, or perhaps even in the comfort of a private aircraft. It was a thin plan, because he hadn't visited the location in some fifteen years, but he knew if he continued on too much longer he'd be in Fredericksburg, and he had no intention of setting up his new hide in a developed area.

He exited I-95 and headed towards the airport.

As soon as he began riding along the chain-link fence to the airport property he decided his impromptu plan wasn't going to pan out like he'd hoped. It was a small airfield with only one runway and just a half dozen or so buildings, and security appeared much tighter than what he remembered. He knew he could wait till nightfall and gain access to the grounds, but it wasn't yet nine a.m. and he did not want to waste an entire day lying low, only to spend the whole evening developing a new hide. No, Court had things to do; he needed to find a new home right now so that tonight he could act.

Once he passed the airport he started to turn around to head back to I-95, but a lonely gravel road off to his right caught his eye. He didn't see a single structure on either side of the road, only oak and pine and thick brush, but he imagined the road led to someplace where no one would be looking for him, and for now, at least, that was good enough.

Court remembered flying low over these woods, all those years ago. His flight instructor, a retired Air Force jet jockey who taught single-engine piloting to CIA operators, had pointed out the roofs of a few wooden houses, far away from any noticeable roads. He'd told Court there had once been a Civil War camp in the woods, and a few broken-down battlements and other structures remained from that era.

Now Court wondered if he could find the old buildings and use them as some sort of shelter.

After only a few minutes of driving north on the gravel road the sky opened up and heavy rain began to fall again.

He saw a narrow gravel footpath that led off the road, and not a soul in sight, so he made the turn, driving deeper now into the forest. Another two minutes on the road and he found himself looking for any access into the dense woods so he could get under the protection of a tree and out of the rain. But as he peered deep in the woods he saw, on both sides of the footpath, low stone fences that looked like they were at least from the Civil War era, if not well before. He continued on because he wouldn't be able to get his bike up and over the stone barriers.

The path ran along a creek and then ended at the remnants of a washed-out wooden footbridge over the water. A sign on a pole told Court this was Accokeek Creek, and the 11th Union Army had spent the winter of 1863 camped nearby. Court's interest in the Civil War was surpassed by his interest in survival, so he worried he might have wandered into some sort of historic park that attracted visitors. But if he had, he was all but certain he'd come in through a back entrance, and he had the distinct impression there was no one around for miles.

Court turned off his bike's engine and rolled it to the creek's edge, then began pushing it upstream along the bank to get around the stone fence and find some cover from the storm.

He found the woods thicker here than he'd first thought, so he continued moving on the creek's edge, knowing he had succeeded in finding a remote location in which to hide, but wondering if he had overachieved by getting too far away from civilization to be practical. He'd been in search of a roof, and it seemed now he'd have to settle for a fallen tree or maybe just foliage with thick leaves.

His mood darkened with the frustration growing in him.

After a time he found evidence of an old set of stone stairs rising out of the creek and up a hill. They were barely visible under the brush along the creek bed, but it made him wonder if more development was close by. He pushed himself and his motorcycle up into the woods and away from the water.

As he climbed he saw that, although this path had long ago been cleared of trees, it had not been used in some time, and the farther he got from the creek, the deeper the grasses and foliage grew.

He'd gone no more than fifty feet when, ahead and off to the right of the overgrown path, he saw something big looming in the woods. He looked closer, then he rubbed rainwater out of his eyes to do a double take.

It was a two-story building, covered with vines and surrounded by oak trees. The first floor seemed to be made of stacked stone, and the second floor and the steeply pitched roof were wood plank, much of it bowed or rotten.

Court left his bike where it was and pushed into the trees to investigate the building.

The door had a lock on it, but that wasn't going to slow Court down, because the door was lying on its side on the porch, ten feet from where it had once been affixed in the doorway.

The stone steps up to the porch were covered in vines but good and solid. Not so the porch itself, which sagged down several inches when he stepped on it. He moved along the edges until he found a crossbeam under the rotten wood, then walked along this like a tightrope to the door.

He stepped through the doorway and into a large, dark room.

This was an abandoned grain mill; he could tell from the setup. It was at least as old as the Civil War battlements supposedly out here in the forest, but probably unrelated to the 1863 encampment of Union forces. The big, dark room was open to the elements because of all the windows and the missing door, and he could hear dripping rainwater here inside, but the roof high above him seemed mostly intact.

He pulled his flashlight from his pack and walked the beam all along the inside. A small amount of graffiti on the wall and the beams above, and a larger amount of twentieth-century trash, told him he hadn't discovered anything that had not been discovered hundreds of times by others, but he had serious doubts anyone happened by here with any regularity.

It was a roof over his head, and it was nothing if not secluded, but this wasn't going to be comfortable, at least not until he scrounged up a few more items.

He looked at his watch. It had taken him a little less than an hour to travel here from D.C., which made this a suitable location as far as he was concerned.

This was now home.

He dropped his pack against a wall and changed into dry blue jeans and a mostly dry dark gray thermal shirt. He didn't have any more socks other than the ones he was wearing, which, like his tennis shoes, were soaking wet, so he just told himself to forget about any real comfort and be glad for what he had.

When he was settled in, meaning sitting on a raincoat with his back against the wall, a tiny fire for warmth in front of him, he pulled out his smartphone and began calling up CNN and a few newswire services on the Internet.

It took him fewer than five minutes of surfing to come across the *Washington Post* article purporting to have information about a homegrown terrorist targeting the Central Intelligence Agency.

Court almost ignored it, thinking it was going to be nothing more than a bunch of bullshit conjecture, just like everything he'd seen during the daytime hours of CNN and the other cable networks. A bunch of people who knew nothing about the event pontificating just to fill airtime. But quickly he realized the writer of this article had spoken with CIA personnel. *Key* personnel, in fact.

Soon Court was certain Denny Carmichael had been involved in the background interview the reporter cited as her principal source.

He read through to the end of the article, and now Court's jaw muscles tensed and he looked up from his screen, furious.

They were making him out to be nothing more than a delusional psycho who held an imaginary grudge against the CIA, who then bumbled over to the Middle East for training and support before returning home to begin his reign of terror.

Court scrolled back up to the top of the article looking for the byline. Catherine King. An e-mail address and phone number were listed as well.

Court decided he wanted to talk to King to find out about the access she'd been granted and the people she'd interviewed. This might help him learn of others involved in his situation, someone he could target next.

But Court knew something else, as well. The CIA had planted intel in the article so that he would do just that.

Court shook his head in disbelief. All these years, all this cat and mouse, and Denny Carmichael still thought Court was just some knuckle-dragging door-kicker, not smart enough to see he was being set up.

Court smiled a little and decided he wouldn't go after Catherine King. No, not yet.

He would, instead, go after whoever it was tailing Catherine King, hoping it would be the same group of Arabs he'd been up against since at least the night he witnessed Leland Babbitt's murder.

If the CIA was using foreign operatives here in the U.S., Court felt they would be at the center of the reasons behind his targeting. He'd love to get hold of some of these men after him, to squeeze them for intelligence, because they would surely have the answers.

He'd speak with King later if he needed to, but for now, he would seek out the hunters on his trail, because in Court's long career, he had learned one lesson above all: it's no big trick to turn a predator into prey.

52

Catherine King parked on the cobblestone street just steps from the front door of her O Street two-story Federalist home and climbed out of her bright blue Prius. She retrieved her purse, her briefcase, and her yoga mat from the backseat, then she headed inside without a glance at the street around her.

Zack Hightower watched her through the Leupold scope affixed to his collapsible sniper rifle. Once she was inside her front door, he scanned the length of O Street, looking for any idling vehicles in the area. Seeing nothing of interest, he began training his optic on the lighted windows in the nearby apartment buildings.

Zack had no trouble admitting to himself that the Georgetown neighborhood of Washington, D.C., was a shitty place to set up a sniper's hide, but he was confident he'd found the absolute best location to secrete himself. He was on the roof of Gaston Hall, part of a massive neo-Gothic seven-story structure that served as the focal point of Georgetown University. From here he had a perfect vantage point for two hundred yards down the length of O Street, as well as many portions of various cross streets in a four-block area.

Eighty feet off his right shoulder was the clock tower of Healy Hall. The tower was several stories higher than his position here, and he could have made his way up there to set up his operation. It would have given him sight lines on more rooftops, street corners, and windows, and with any other target Zack would have plopped his ass right in that tower so he could have as many opportunities to see his target from distance as possible. But not today. No, right now he was hunting Sierra Six, and Six was the smartest prey Zack had ever tracked. The clock tower was an obvious place for a sniper to position himself, and Six would see it the second he arrived in the vicinity of Catherine King's home. Six would spend as much time as he needed hiding out, using all sorts of gadgets and tactics to get a look up at the obvious hide site, and if Zack put himself in the clock tower Six would know it and Zack would be dead fucking meat.

Zack liked his chances here on the rooftop. This building was attached to Healy Hall to make an L-shaped structure the width and length of a city block. There were hundreds of square yards of territory up here, much of it steep, but there were also standing seams and walkways, far enough back from the building's edge to allow him to avoid silhouetting himself, and there were dormers and crosses and antennae and satellite dishes and other bits of cover and concealment available to where Zack felt he was completely invisible from ground level.

Zack agreed with the assessment of Jordan Mayes: Gentry would come for Catherine King, looking to find out just who she'd spoken with and just what she knew. And at the speed Gentry's operation had been progressing, Zack could well imagine he would make his move tonight. If that happened Zack put his chances at nearly one hundred percent that he'd see his target from this position. He knew how Gentry thought and how he moved, and he was damn certain he knew where Gentry would go, even to the point of which backyards around here he'd skulk through on his way towards his objective.

And Zack and his rifle would be ready.

He didn't feel any better about taking out Court Gentry now than he did when he told Brewer that she was playing for the wrong team in all this, but that wouldn't slow Zack down for an instant. If he saw his target he would put a bullet through it, just the same as he would if he were taking potshots at the practice range.

He had been using the streetlights to see around O Street, but now he decided to dig deeper with his optic, to look into the recesses of alleyways and shady door stoops, to check blackened buildings and dim rooftops. He reached into his big backpack and pulled out his universal night sight. Made by FLIR Systems, it attached just forward of his regular optic on the rail of his rifle. After turning it on he simply looked through his Leupold day scope, and a television image of the scene below him enhanced all the light in the area so he could see deep into the darkest shadows. He had to avoid pointing the night sight at the bright lights on the street, but for the areas away from lights, the device was ideal.

Zack scanned the rooftops of the neighborhood carefully. It was still early, probably way too early for Gentry to move, but he had wanted to arrive here in his position well before employing his weapon. He needed time to memorize the surroundings, to take a mental snapshot he could refer to at any point during his hunt.

He'd finished a narrow scan of O Street and had just begun to move away from the rooftops on 35th Street NW when he noticed a faint flash of light coming from a building on the southwest corner of 35th and O. Everything in the area, save for the streetlights and a few windows, was dark or close to it, so the flare had stood out, especially since it seemed to come from the roof of an otherwise blacked-out building. Zack angled his scope down to street level so he could see what type of structure he was looking at and saw the building housed a coffee shop, which was closed for the evening.

There. Another faint flash. He could tell it was definitely coming from the flat rooftop above the coffee shop. Like the last time, it was gone just as soon as it appeared.

With his nine-power scope he couldn't see the exact source of the light, but in his pack next to him he carried a pair of one of the best binoculars on the planet. He reached in quickly, retrieved his Swarovski Optik SLC 56, and brought the long binos to his eyes. He steadied them by resting his elbows on the standing seam roof below him, and brought them into focus on the corner of O and 35th Street NW. Through the fifteen-power magnification he scanned the rooftop of the coffee shop where he'd noticed the light before.

Another flash, just to the right of his field of view. He shifted his binos to center them on the location.

What the hell?

He could just barely make out a smartphone, lying by itself, faceup, on top of the roof, slightly angled up towards Zack's hide.

In seconds he saw another flash, and realized the intermittent lights were due to incoming text messages.

He sighed. He'd gotten his hopes up for nothing. It looked like some asshole had thrown the phone from the street up onto the roof, God knows why, and now someone else was texting the owner.

Zack started to put his binos up and return to the search, but he paused a moment. Inside his pack he put his hand around his spotter's scope, already affixed to a tiny tripod. On a whim he pulled it out, set it up next to his rifle, and peered through it. It took him several seconds to line it up with the rooftop, and then zoom its variable 125-power magnification to the smartphone, but when he did, it was like he was looking at the screen from a distance of only one and a half yards. He realized he'd be able to read any more texts that came through.

Just then, the phone flashed. Hightower squinted into the eyecup of his spotter's scope, straining to see the text message.

How's it hanging, Zack? You still got that obnoxious 125x scope?

Slowly Zack Hightower pulled his eye out of the cup of the spotter's scope, and he placed his forehead on the cold metal roof. "You're right up here with me, aren't you, Six?"

From ten yards behind him Hightower heard a voice he knew well. "Figured I'd find *some* asshole up here. Can't say I expected you. Thought you were dead."

Zack's elbows were tight under his body, his forehead still lying flat on the roof. While keeping his arms perfectly still, he moved the fingers of his right hand under the collar of his black tunic. He took hold of a throwing knife attached to a necklace, but he did not pull it free from its sheath. Zack said, "Just up here hunting old ghosts, bro."

"Me, too," replied Court. "I've got a gun on you. In case you've forgotten, I don't miss very often. Whatever you are thinking about doing, just know that."

Zack nodded to himself, then he said, "I figure I've got a fifty-fifty chance."

"You give yourself too much credit."

Zack shrugged, then he launched his body to the right by pressing his left arm and left knee into the roof with all his might. Court fired a single suppressed round, and the bullet slammed into the midsection of Zack's Kevlar chest protection just as he rolled onto his back. Zack's right arm shot down from his neck. In one motion he yanked the folding knife free of the scabbard, the scabbard itself opened the blade, and he hurled it across the dark roof in the direction of the flash of gunfire. Zack saw his target react, contorting his body to the left, and the spinning knife flew just past Court's face, missing him by less than a foot.

Zack absorbed the baseball bat punch to the solar plexus from the round hitting his Kevlar, and he snatched his HK pistol out of the drop holster on his right hip. He brought it up to fire on his target, just in time to see the dark figure tumble backwards, down onto the tiles of the roof. He heard the pistol bounce along on its own, clanging down and then off of the seven-story building.

But he didn't know if Gentry himself had fallen down the sloped roof.

Zack sprang to his knees, keeping his pistol trained on the last place he'd seen his target, and he moved laterally a few yards, careful to not appear over the roof's edge exactly where Gentry would expect him. Slowly he moved to the end of the flat standing seam and looked down at the angled tile roof. It was dark below; he could make out little other than the trees in the courtyard at the back of the building. Right in front of him, just as the roof began to increase in pitch, was a small platform for a satellite dish, an old VHF antenna, and, alongside the VHF, Zack saw a curious-looking metal bar that came up from the platform with wires attached to it. The bar went up about one foot, then bowed down and angled out of site, down the side of the roof.

Zack took one more step forward to look on the other side of the platform, his gun up and ready, in case Gentry was hiding there.

He wasn't. Zack then looked farther down the steeply angled roof. There, ten feet below him, he saw a figure lying against the tile. He held something in both hands.

At the exact same instant Hightower realized Gentry was holding on to the long radio antenna, bending it down at an impossible angle, Gentry let go, and the bent metal aerial torqued upwards at high speed. After a brief whipping sound the antenna smacked Zack Hightower right between his eyes, sending him flying backwards, end over end, tumbling along the flat part of the roof. His HK sailed from his hand as he continued back, until he landed flat on his face on the eastern angled portion of the roof.

Here he slid down several feet, then stopped when his boots arrested his fall.

He tried to get his arms and knees underneath him to push himself back up, but his arms and legs gave out. His eyes and nose stung, his mouth bled, he was stunned and disoriented, but he knew Gentry was still somewhere up here with him.

He told himself he had to shake off the hurt and find his *fucking* handgun. He *had* to get back into the fight before the Gray Man closed on him and shot him dead with his own weapon.

Letting go of the antenna that was keeping him from falling off the roof solved one problem immediately; it knocked the shit out of Zack Hightower and removed Court's imminent threat of being hosed with lead. But letting go of the one thing keeping him from falling off the roof did create an obvious inconvenience. Now Court found himself sliding slowly but surely down the steep and slick tile to the precipice. The roof ended twenty feet from the tips of his shoes and, after that, it was a five-story drop straight down to the tree-filled Dahlgren Courtyard behind Healy Hall.

He flattened himself as he slid down, tried to get as much contact surface against the tile as he could to increase the friction, and while doing so he looked around in all directions, hoping for something to grab on to or even leap for.

There. At the very edge and eight feet to the right of where he was sliding, Court saw a decorative peaked dormer protruding out of the roof. He pushed himself up while he slid down, then fired off his feet, launching into the air to grab hold of the protrusion.

Court landed flat on the top of the peak of the dormer, nearly knocking the wind from him, but halting his downward slide.

He didn't hang around here for long because he knew Zack would be regrouping above. He immediately began climbing the roof again, careful to keep his body low and his weight and momentum both pushing forward.

On the flat center of the roof he looked for Zack, and he found him, thirty feet away. Hightower had just made it back onto the flat roof and into a standing position himself.

Hightower's nine-millimeter Heckler & Koch handgun lay between them, ten feet from Zack and twenty feet from Court. Right in the center of the flat portion of the roof.

Hightower did not move. His body leaned towards the pistol, his hand reached out for it, but his eyes were on Court Gentry. Gentry stood still himself, knowing his only play here was to beat Hightower to the gun. He prepared himself to dive for it if Hightower should move a muscle.

Zack said, "I know what you are thinking, Six."

Court was nearly out of breath from his ordeal on the steep roof. Through gasps he said, "Is that a fact?"

"Affirmative. Right now you are thinking about how you always were just a little faster than me."

Court kept his eyes on the gun. "You're right."

"But don't forget one thing, bro. I was always a little smarter than you."

Court glanced away from the pistol and up to Zack now. "You're going to *think* that gun into your hand?"

"There are a lot of variables in this equation in front of you. I'm closer, you've just climbed up here, then you tumbled back, then climbed back up. You might not have the speed and strength you think you do."

It was quiet on the roof a moment. Then Court said, "Anything else? Or is that all you've got?"

Zack shrugged, still leaning towards his HK. "That's pretty much it, I guess."

Court took two quick steps, flung his body forward, and dove with his arms outstretched. He landed on the metal roof and slid several feet. He snatched the weapon cleanly and brought it up towards his target.

Zack Hightower had not even tried for the gun. He barely moved, except to raise his hands. He said, "Damn, dude! It's always fun to watch you work! Great to see you again! I've fuckin' missed you!"

Court ignored the joviality, which seemed ridiculously incongruous to the present circumstance. "You were up here ready to blow my head off if you saw me. Why the hell wouldn't I shoot you now?"

Zack shrugged. "I'll be honest, bro. Can't think of a single reason."

Court climbed back up to his feet and leveled the pistol at Zack's face. "Me, neither."

"Unless . . ." Zack said, still holding his hands up in surrender, "you were interested in how I got here. Who's benefiting from this. The list of everyone who is involved. That sort of thing. If any of that shit matters to you, then I guess I'm more useful to you alive than dead."

Court kept the weapon pointed at Zack's face for another fifteen seconds, thinking over the situation. Slowly he lowered the weapon. "Bastard."

Zack grinned from ear to ear. "Good decision. We've got some catching up to do. How 'bout we go get a beer and some wings. I'm buying."

"Shirt off, pants to your ankles," Gentry ordered.

Hightower said, "Woah, Nellie! We're movin' this relationship in a new direction, aren't we? Maybe *you* should buy *me* dinner."

"Do it."

Zack whined a little more, but he knew the protocol for taking any prisoner into custody. Court just wanted to see if he had any tricks up his sleeve, or down his pants.

By the time Hightower got his Kevlar vest, tunic, boots, and black dungarees off, another folding knife, a can of pepper spray, a leather sap, and a pair of brass knuckles were scattered around the roof. Court then ordered Zack to pack up his gear in the Osprey pack and step away. Court hefted the pack onto his own back, ordered Zack to put his clothes back on, and then, when both men were ready, Zack led the way to a fire escape running down to the courtyard at the back of the building.

Court kept the HK pistol trained on Zack the entire way down, and in the courtyard he found the suppressed Glock that had fallen off the roof. He scooped it up, removed the suppressor, shoved both items into the big backpack, then followed Zack back to his truck, parked in front of a late-night watering hole two blocks north of the university.

Zack again offered to buy beer and hot wings, but Court had something quite different in mind for the evening.

53

The red Chevy Silverado pulled off the main road near Stafford Regional Airport, its headlights off and its brake lights extinguished, thanks to a few pulled fuses. Court drove the truck slowly, but with no lights, and on a cloudy night, this would have been impossible without the infrared device he'd found in Zack's bag. He held the device just in front of his face awkwardly while he drove with the other hand, and although this wouldn't have worked at all if anyone had been chasing him, it was a hell of a lot better than driving blind out here in the woods.

Zack wasn't here with him in the cab. As soon as the two men arrived at Hightower's truck at the bar in Georgetown, Court hog-tied his old boss with a long length of quarter-inch jute rope he found in the bed of the pickup, then took a shorter length of rope and looped it around Zack's mouth before cinching it behind his head. Lastly, he blindfolded him with a T-shirt. Once he was secure and silent, Court rolled Zack facedown in the truck bed and flipped the hard shell bed cover over him to keep any larger trucks on the road from looking down and seeing a prostrate form in the back of the pickup.

After several minutes of slow going on the dark gravel road to the north, Court pulled the vehicle off the road, just before they got to the Civil War–era stone wall. He forced it deep into the brush, finally parking it some forty feet from the footpath that lead to the creek.

It wasn't invisible here from the footpath, but it was nearly so, and it *would* be invisible from the air.

Court climbed out of the Silverado, hefted Zack's heavy pack, and then walked around to the back.

He cut Zack's gag and leg bindings free, but he kept the big knot of jute rope on his wrists, secure behind his back. Zack struggled to climb down from the back of the truck bed. When he finally did so Court pushed the barrel of the HK into Zack's forehead for a moment, then told him to turn around and start walking up the dark road.

"I can't see where I'm going, genius," Zack complained.

Neither could Court, so he flipped on a flashlight to direct himself forward, covering all but a thin shaft of light with his hand. He then said, "Go straight ahead till I tell you to turn."

Zack headed off up the path, and Court followed him twenty feet back.

After less than a minute Zack said, "Six, are we in the forest? I smell trees and shit. Where the hell are you taking me?"

"Just walk."

Zack stopped. "You could do us both a favor and shoot me here, if that is your intention."

"Yep. I drove an hour just to smoke you in the woods. Walk!"

Hightower mumbled to himself, but he started walking again.

They came to the washed-out bridge and Court took Zack by the arm and helped him along the edge of the creek. Another five minutes found them on the stone path steps on the hill that ran away from the creek. The darkness was impenetrable here beyond the flood and throw of Court's partially covered flashlight, but he pushed Zack up, deeper into the dark, and he followed behind.

Soon they arrived at the abandoned mill. Here Court pulled Zack's T-shirt blindfold off and crammed it into his own pocket.

It took the big man several seconds to adapt to the little light out here and, even in the glow of the flashlight, Zack didn't notice the mill at first. When Court told him to move into the trees, Zack turned around and faced him.

"What's in the trees?"

Court took his hand from the face of the light and shined two hundred lumens on the building now. "My humble abode."

Zack looked back. After taking a few steps he saw the mill looming large and dark in the trees, just twenty yards ahead. "Oh *hell* no. I'm not goin' in there."

"Scared?"

"You better believe it."

"Move," Court said, and he stepped up and kicked Hightower in the ass. The big ex-SEAL stumbled forward. Court added, "Don't worry, I'll protect you."

"Then I guess I'm fucked."

Both men stood on rotten floorboards inside the mill. Zack's wrists were still tied behind his back, and Court had also used a length of the jute to affix Zack to a heavy weight-supporting beam on the outside wall. Court stood a few feet away, leaning against a stone column around a wooden vertical stabilizer that went up to the roof.

Court didn't bother to build a fire. Instead he left his flashlight on and put it on the floor between them, with Zack's T-shirt draped over it to diffuse the powerful glow. It was enough for the two men to see each other here inside the mill, but from the air no one could possibly detect any light.

Court said, "I want to hear what you have to say. You were out there tailing Catherine King so you could get a shot at me. Is that it?"

Zack shrugged in his bindings. "I wasn't enjoying myself, if that makes you feel better."

Court just shook his head. "You do remember what happened the last time we saw each other, don't you? I saved your stupid life."

"And you remember what I said back then. I told you that if you saved me, I'd just come back and kill you. I was working for Denny. Denny calls the shots. Not me."

"Well, Denny is full of shit. I haven't done anything wrong."

Zack licked blood off his lips and spit on the floor. "Tell that to Ohlhauser."

"If I killed Max Ohlhauser I would only do it because I had reason to. And if I had a reason, I wouldn't hide it. I'd be proud."

Zack just eyed Court with mistrust. He leaned back against his tied hands on the beam.

Court said, "I didn't kill Max. I didn't kill Leland Babbitt. I didn't—"

"*I* killed Babbitt," Hightower replied casually.

Court cocked his head. "You *what*?"

"Jordan Mayes said Babbitt was threatening to go public with critical classified material. He had to be taken down. As in immediately. As in permanently."

Court thought about this. "He had been targeting me in Europe. Maybe Denny cut him out because he failed. Maybe he was going to talk. Shit, Zack. You just fragged an American citizen because Mayes told you to?"

Another shrug by Zack, like it was no big deal. "That's about the size of it."

"You know the CIA isn't supposed to do that without presidential sanction."

Zack winked. "Good thing I'm not CIA. I'm freelancing."

Court just mumbled, "There's a lot of that going around these days."

"Is that right?"

Court retrieved the Glock 17 pistol he had taken from the phony police officer with the Middle Eastern accent. He held it up, close to Zack's face. "Take a look at this."

Zack gave it a half-second glance and then shrugged. "Is it show-and-tell time, bro? That's a G17, threaded barrel. What do I win?"

"Tell me where I got it."

Zack just shrugged.

"I took that off a D.C. Metro police officer."

The man tied to the beam gave Court a double take. "Bullshit."

Court held up the silencer, as well. "This, too."

"Why would a D.C. cop have a suppressed pistol?"

"He wouldn't. Yet this was being carried by one of the four guys with shitty English dressed as cops in the Dupont Circle metro station. Those were the guys who *did* kill Ohlhauser."

"That doesn't make sense," Zack said softly. His veneer of self-assuredness had slipped. Then he said, "Hanley."

"What about Hanley?"

"This morning, in the conference room. He had some song and dance about how you didn't frag Ohlhauser. About how the evidence didn't fit."

"Well then," Court said. For the first time since he'd arrived here he felt like he just might have *someone* on his side. "Matt's right. I didn't do it."

"Who were the guys dressed as cops, then?"

Court said, "A foreign unit. Good, but not great. Middle Eastern. Gulf state is my best guess from the accents, but I could be off on that."

Zack was still not sure about this strange claim. In a doubtful tone he said, "They were Muj?"

"Sure looked like it. Whoever they are, Zack, you can be sure they are working for Carmichael."

Zack shook his head. "Denny's not going to contract Muj to proxy for him. Especially not in the middle of Washington, D.C. The director would hang him by his nut sack."

"Zack, think about it. Those guys would only be involved in the hunt for me if Denny wanted them here."

"I don't know," Zack said. "But I do know that doesn't have a damn thing to do with me."

"Okay," Court said. "Why *did* they bring you into this?"

"Because I told them I'd help them bag you."

"And here we are."

Zack looked around. "Here we are."

Court waved the Glock towards Zack. "It's time you think about your predicament."

Hightower looked again around the filthy old mill, and he licked at the dried blood caking his lips. "Really? Do tell."

Court said, "If I let you go, you will need to carefully consider your next move. If you run back to Carmichael and say I disarmed and disabled you, then took you someplace for an interrogation, he will know you aren't good enough to go toe-to-toe with me, and you are not reliable enough to keep in the fold because I might have gotten inside your head. You will be damaged goods to Carmichael, and you know what he does with damaged goods."

Court saw on Hightower's face that he understood completely. Gentry could let him walk, but if he did, Zack couldn't go back and report on anything that had happened tonight.

Zack gave a half nod, unwilling to give Court the satisfaction of knowing he had checkmated his former team leader. "What do you want?"

"I want you to talk to Matt. Tell him about the Middle Eastern assholes working for Denny."

"Look, Six. Hanley might be in your corner, but Hanley isn't the boss. Carmichael is."

"I know that. And I also know you only respect authority, and you only want back in the Agency. That's all you think matters in your world. But know this: I'm not going to stop until I knock Carmichael off his tower, and I am hoping I can get Hanley to help me. Think about how desperate Denny must be if he's using foreign assets right here in the U.S. You might want to think twice before hitching your wagon to his."

"Obviously, Six, you don't know jack squat about currying favor with the important people at Langley. I have a hard time taking advice from you in that department."

Court wasn't going to waste any more time with Hightower. He pulled Zack's T-shirt out of his pocket and retied it over the big blond-haired man's eyes.

"What are you doing?"

"I'm giving you time to think about it. I'm going to rest for a while, then I'm taking you back to D.C. You just sit there quietly or I'll shoot you in the baby maker."

For the return drive into the city Court did not throw Hightower back in the truck bed; he let him sit in the passenger's seat, but he blindfolded him and bound his arms together all the way behind the seat. It would take a contortionist to get out of the bindings, and even though Zack tried his hardest to work on the knots with his fingertips during the drive, he couldn't quite reach them, so he remained secured to his seat.

Court drove for ninety minutes on I-95, first to the south, but then he pulled off the interstate and jumped right back on the onramp heading back to the District.

He made his way into D.C. along with the first of the morning rush hour, and he drove to a parking lot a few blocks from where he'd left his bike. He parked Zack's Silverado under a tree, far away from any streetlights.

Leaving Zack in the passenger's seat, Court rolled down the windows and climbed out of the vehicle. He walked around to the other side, reached in to Hightower, and pulled off his blindfold.

Once Zack got his bearings he said, "What the hell are you doing?"

"Leaving your ass right here. Think about what I said, Zack."

"Where's my gear?"

"You mean your gun? You think I'm going to hand you back the rifle you were going to use to blow my head off?"

Zack did not respond.

Court added, "That baby's *mine* now. Thanks." He tossed Zack's keys into some low bushes nearby.

Hightower was more focused on his immediate predicament. "Wait. How the hell am I supposed to get my hands untied?"

"Easy. Just scream like a little girl when somebody passes by. Sooner or later someone will come to your rescue."

"C'mon, bro. Unnecessary. We're on the same team now, remember? You, me, and Hanley are going to smoke out those Muj Denny has tracking you."

Court just laughed. "I remember I *asked* you to join my team. Don't remember you giving me anything like your full-throated support."

Zack was pissed. The prospect of having to call out to a civilian for help was almost more than his bravado could bear. "You son of a bitch. I swear to God when I—"

Court interrupted. "It's this or shoot you dead in a ditch. I thought I was doing you a favor, but if you prefer . . ."

Zack slammed his head back against the headrest. "Just go, asshole!"

Court chuckled again. "If you want I can make this look like some kind of kinky S&M scenario that got out of hand. Might help with your cover story."

Zack pulled even harder on his bindings. "I swear if you fuckin' touch me, dude, I'm going to rip your head off and shit down your neck."

"Say hi to Matt for me. Tell him I appreciate his support." Court left Zack in the passenger's seat of his truck, struggling against his bindings.

54

The fallout from the previous day's article in the *Washington Post* had been immediate and intense. The D.C. assassination story was the lead news item all over the USA, after all, and Catherine King's piece had been the first and only one to provide something that looked, to the layman anyway, like an explanation as to what was going on. That Catherine herself remained wholly unconvinced she was reporting much more than official government spin had been irrelevant to America, even though she tried to relay her misgivings in her article as clearly as possible without pissing off the managing editor of her paper.

She'd been careful to throw in a disclaimer, even going so far as to say much of her information came from unnamed CIA sources who were government employees with their own version of events. Still, despite this proviso, as far as Catherine was concerned, the only thing she'd done this week was scratch the surface on a huge story, then get a completely bullshit version of events from a key player who had his own ax to grind.

And then she reported the false version.

She felt dirty.

Many times in Catherine King's illustrious thirty-year journalistic career she'd landed a big story ahead of her peers, and each time it happened it played out much the same way. Forced into a victory lap by her paper, she was paraded around other media venues like a trophy.

And today had been just this sort of event for her. She'd done two segments each on CNN and Fox, and one each on CBS, ABC, and NBC. She'd fielded calls from her colleagues at the wire services and National Public Radio, each time talking about what she knew about a madman on the streets of Washington killing two of our nation's Intelligence officials.

And through it all Catherine saw herself as a phony, because she knew she was profiting off a version of events that was probably far from accurate.

Between each interview, however, often while sitting in a makeup chair, she worked her phone, pumping and prodding all her contacts in the U.S. intelligence community, trying her best to get more information about what the hell was going on over at Langley. She had over fifty feelers out, and she would have had more, but her exhausting schedule of media appearances kept her from doing as much as she would have liked.

In contrast to Catherine, twenty-eight-year-old Andy Shoal was having a hell of a good time. He'd been given the night off of his evening duties as a cops reporter so he could spend the daytime hours in studios and on the phone, making a dizzying series of local and secondary radio and cable shows, talking about how he and his "partner" Catherine King had stumbled onto a terrorist assassin being hunted by the CIA on America's streets. He talked about the Washington Highlands shoot-out, about Chevy Chase, Dupont Circle, and Columbia Heights, and he made it out like he was Bernstein to King's Woodward.

In each interview he hinted there were more big revelations to come about the assassin only known as Jeff Duncan, but at this point he was pretty much relying on his senior colleague to make that happen.

Catherine did have a couple of potential leads. She had been checking her e-mail just before seven this morning, filtering through the messages she could put off till this whirlwind of publicity passed and trashing the items from the usual suspects of nut jobs who sent her long missives any time she posted an article. During this morning's scroll through her messages she held on to five e-mails that looked like they needed her direct attention. Three were from intelligence community contacts of hers offering context about her most recent article, although none of them promised very much. Indeed, they looked more like people trying to get on her bandwagon this week by getting mentioned in a follow-up article, and less like people who had significant information to offer.

The other two e-mails were from unknowns. One claimed to have intelligence about the people killed on Brandywine Street, insisting they were not, as she and Andy had reported, Aryan Brotherhood drug dealers, but rather NSA technicians operating some sort of illegal domestic listening post.

This sounded like complete nonsense to Catherine, but the sender of the e-mail seemed intelligent enough. She decided she'd feel him out with a few follow-up questions before deciding whether or not to set up a phone interview.

The fifth potentially promising e-mail to arrive this morning, however, had her especially curious. It came from an address that looked randomly generated—all numbers and letters—and the sender's message was both specific and compelling.

> Ms. King, I read your article regarding the death of Lee Babbitt and Max Ohlhauser, and want you to know the intel you received from the Agency is a lie. I am a former Agency support technician in the SAD, and familiar with the case. Your obvious source was D/NCS Carmichael, but you may have also spoken to others, such as Jordan Mayes, Carmichael's second-in-command in NCS. CIA has its own agenda and is using you to promote it. I am prepared to establish my bona fides via e-mail by telling you nonclassified information regarding the Agency and its activities, as well as specifics of the actions that have taken place since the man being sought arrived in D.C. Saturday evening last.
>
> After I satisfy you that I am familiar with the parties involved in your investigation, however, I will require a face-to-face meeting to provide you with more information. To put you at ease, you are welcome to choose the time and place of this meeting.
>
> Respectfully, A friend

The sender of this e-mail knew Carmichael's name, which meant he might well have been an Agency employee, although this was out in open sources if one knew exactly where to look.

But what most interested King about the message was the sender's understanding of the protocol of the tradecraft she used when interviewing sources in the clandestine world. Asking for general nonclassified information was exactly how she would initiate a conversation with someone claiming to work in a top secret position, and getting specifics about the event under investigation was her way of establishing relevance.

She decided quickly that "A friend" warranted an immediate response.

Below the message were a phone number and a URL link, and when Catherine clicked on the link it took her to a secure mobile messaging service called RedPhone. This told her the sender knew his stuff, as Red-Phone was one of only a very few off-the-shelf communications systems available that were, at least according to the experts she'd spoken to, completely secure.

She already had RedPhone on her mobile, ready to use any time a source demanded it, so she opened it up and typed in the number.

She sent a text first, asking a few follow-up questions, and she received a reply within seconds. When she was satisfied the other party was, in fact, familiar with the workings of the CIA and not just some kid in Cincinnati wasting her time, she called the number.

A man answered with a relaxed and pleasant enough voice, but the conversation was stilted, chiefly because it was clear the person on the other end did not want to be talking on the phone at all. She asked him two questions about the chain of command on a CIA Special Activities Ground Branch support unit, and he answered both with ease, even giving her information she didn't know, but could readily accept as accurate.

She then offered to meet in a public place with the former CIA technician, and the man on the other end agreed, but as he did so he told her something that made her blood run cold.

"We'll have to be very careful. I'm not supposed to be talking to you, and Denny Carmichael is having you followed."

"*What?* How do you know?"

"Last night I saw your tail when you came home."

"How do *you* know where I live?"

"There is an article about you on a local health and fitness website. It says you never miss Thursday night yoga in Georgetown." He paused. "And you didn't."

She knew the article. It had seemed harmless enough when she gave the interview a few months back, but now she realized how foolish she had been. "You followed me from yoga?"

"Just for a bit. I wasn't the only one. You can assume that is still the case." The man spent the next five minutes giving her a dizzying array of instructions. How to initiate her surveillance detection route, what trains to get on and off of, where to rent a car without using a credit card, and other means by which to shake the tail he claimed was on her.

He also told her she needed to fight the urge to look for her followers, because that would only ensure they took more care to stay invisible.

The man set a meeting for two p.m. at a restaurant in Union Station that specialized in salads, and then he hung up.

She looked at all the notes she'd written down about the route to take for the meeting to come. This wasn't the strangest bit of tradecraft she'd employed to meet with a source, but it was truly one of the most ingenious. Even though she was always suspicious to the point of being doubtful about any new source—so few of them panned out into anything worthwhile— the fact that this man knew his tradecraft down cold like this made her more optimistic than usual.

Catherine sat for a CNN live interview during the lunch hour and then immediately headed to the street to catch a cab. Following the mysterious man's instructions, she went by her bank to withdraw some cash, then headed to a metro station and took the subway to Petworth. From here she walked to a car repair shop, where they rented her a beat-up Honda Civic in exchange for two hundred dollars, plus a one-thousand-dollar cash deposit. She was made to show her ID to a man who made a copy of it, but he did not put it into any computer system, so there was no electronic record of the transaction.

The car smelled old and moldy, but the engine fired right up. She put her purse in the passenger's seat and then, almost as an afterthought, she pulled her six-million-volt stun gun from her purse and wedged it between the passenger's seat and the center console.

First-time clandestine meetings with CIA employees were usually the same. The man would want to make certain she wasn't making audio or video recordings of the proceedings. He'd ask to check her phone and to look through her purse, and the sight of the stun gun had turned off more than one contact. It wasn't worth the hassle, she decided, so she just pulled it out now while she was thinking about it.

Catherine drove to the station and parked her rented Civic on the roof of the parking garage on 1st Street NE, then she climbed out into the sunny afternoon. She still had twenty minutes before the meet, so she thought she'd employ her own tradecraft by walking around the station to make sure no one was following her. But as soon as she turned to close her door, she felt a presence close, right at her side. Thinking she had accidentally stepped in front of someone passing between cars, she tried to move out of the way, but the figure slipped between her and her car door. She looked up to see a man wearing a hoodie and dark sunglasses, but before she could even focus on his face he took the keys from her hand, quickly but gently. He pressed the button to unlock the passenger's door and walked her by the arm around to the front passenger's seat.

As he did this he only said one thing to her, but he said it over and over, in a tone that was both quiet yet commanding. "Look straight ahead, not at my face. Look straight ahead, not at my face. Look straight ahead, not at my face."

She complied, and she didn't call out for help only because he seemed so matter-of-fact and sure of his actions. Before she even had time to feel scared she found herself sitting in the passenger seat of her rental.

The lump in her throat grew as the man sat down behind the wheel. She looked up at him but he said the same sentence once again, and she complied instinctively, turning to look straight ahead. As she did this she asked, "What is happening?"

"You are fine. You are safe. Don't worry. These are standard operational security measures."

He adjusted the seat and the car rolled forward while, out of the corner of her eye, she saw the man adjusting the rearview mirror to match his height.

Catherine's hands began shaking once they were moving and the reality of what was happening began to catch up. She got the feeling that she must have looked at this man at some point when he came up to her, but now she had not the faintest recollection of what he looked like.

"You are the man from the phone?"

"Yes."

"But I said I wanted to meet in public."

"Sorry. My rules today. You wearing a wire?"

"No."

"What about a GPS tracker?"

"What? No. Why would I?"

He pulled out of the parking garage and turned right.

She said, "I . . . I didn't see your face. I swear to God."

"I know." His reply was confident. He sounded so . . . normal.

"People know where I am right now."

It wasn't true, and he had to have sensed that, but his reply did not contradict her.

"I'm not going to do anything to harm you. I promise."

Catherine said nothing, but she shifted in her seat slightly, and while she did so, her hands clutched her purse. The man behind the wheel reached over, took the purse from her, and then gently placed it behind him on the rear floorboard.

She did not protest.

They drove in silence for a full minute, heading north. Catherine kept her eyes straight ahead, her jittery hands on her knees. Finally she said, "You said you were ex-Agency. Was that true?"

"Yes."

"And you know the man they are looking for?"

After a slight pause he said, "I *am* the man they are looking for."

She closed her eyes hard. Furious with herself for not suspecting this from the beginning.

Her eyes reopened, and then her left hand slid back into the tight space between the center console and the seat. She started to turn to him to see if he was looking her way. But just as she began to look up he said, "Eyes out front."

She locked her eyes forward, but her fingertips walked their way back a little farther, to the item wedged tight between the seat and the console.

While she did this Catherine asked, "What do you want?"

"The same as you, I guess. Information. Answers."

"Answers? If you are who you say you are, you are going to have a lot more answers than me."

"Don't be so sure. I haven't had the opportunity to interview a bunch of CIA execs on background."

Catherine corrected him. "Just one."

"Carmichael."

Despite herself she nodded a little.

"Had a feeling."

Catherine's hand found what it was looking for. The plastic grip of her heavy stun gun.

Her kidnapper turned the vehicle off North Carolina Avenue and onto Lincoln Road NE.

"Where are you taking me?" she asked.

"I'd like to just drive around for a bit, if that's okay with you. We can talk."

"Sure," she said, doing her best to force calm into her voice. In fact, her racing heart beat faster by the second, and she steeled herself for what she was about to do.

And her mind raced along with her heart. When was the last time she had charged the stun gun? The packaging claimed the batteries would hold a full charge for six months. Had she even touched the device in that time? Yes, now she remembered. She charged the gun in early January, less than four months earlier. It should be ready to go.

Although she'd never used the weapon on another person, according to the packaging, it was quite simple to employ. One touch to the skin of the man beside her, ideally in the neck or low back near the spine, would fully incapacitate him for a minute or more.

Catherine tried to appear as nonchalant as possible. "Your name isn't really Jeff Duncan, is it?"

"What do you think?"

"No. What should I call you?"

"Call me Six."

Her breath quickened. This confirmed him as the man in Washington Highlands. She said, "The house on Brandywine Street. There was a number six left there." That had not been reported. The man said nothing. "Was that so the CIA would know you were here?"

"They already knew I was here. It was to show them I wasn't running." A pause. "Not anymore."

They approached a four-way stop. He said, "If you try to bail, I'll just stop you. Understood?"

Her thumb flipped up the security cap over the stun gun's actuator. Thinking quickly, she said, "*Bail?* I'm fifty-four. I'm not sure I ever knew how to bail. But even if I did, those days are firmly behind me."

Out of the corner of her eye she saw the man chuckle at this, as if he was completely comfortable snatching an innocent woman off the street.

A large black work truck rolled up to the intersection on the left of the old Civic.

Catherine squeezed the handle of the stun gun so hard it hurt. Her thumb hovered over the red actuator.

Six started to pull forward, but the work truck on the left began rolling out of turn, so he was forced to brake abruptly.

Catherine took her opportunity. In one motion she lifted the device up, spun towards the man behind the wheel, and plunged the metal tips into the right side of his throat, which, due to the black hoodie, was the only exposed skin showing around her kidnapper's neck.

She pressed the button and an electric clicking sound filled the air. It seemed impossibly loud and violent here in the small cabin of the Honda Civic.

The man behind the wheel cried out as six million volts coursed through his body.

55

Owwww!" His right arm swung up in a blur, and his forearm connected with the stun gun and knocked it hard, sending it flying into the backseat. It banged against the rear window and skittered to the floor.

"Are you *fucking* kidding me?" the man shouted now, his face a mask of pain.

But he did not go down. He did not collapse, faint, or appear, in *any* way, incapacitated.

Instead, he just seemed furious.

Catherine covered her face in her hands, cowered into a ball by her car door, and she readied herself for the killer's retaliation.

"Jesus, lady! That hurt like hell!" The car began rolling forward. She heard him moving in his seat, and thought he was checking his neck in the rearview mirror.

When she realized he wasn't about to hit her, she spoke. Almost to herself she said, "That was supposed to disable you for a full minute."

The man behind the wheel yelled back at her. "Well, it didn't!" he shouted, irritation strong in his voice. Then he said, "Those gadgets are overrated. Listen, lady, I've had a really shitty week. If you have any more dirty tricks I'd appreciate it if you'd just let me know."

"No, sir. Nothing else. I'm sorry. I'm just very frightened."

"You don't need to be scared. Hell, *I'm* the one who just got zapped." He seemed to take a moment to get control of his emotions, although he continued to cuss under his breath and feel at the spot on his throat where she'd shocked him. Finally he looked at her. "Sit up, please. I can't talk to you like that."

Slowly she did so, straightening her outfit and returning to her fixed stare through the windshield. They drove in silence for another block, and then she said, "This isn't my first time."

"First time for what?"

"I've been kidnapped before. 2004. Quetta, Pakistan."

"I'm not kidnapping you."

"I'm free to go, then?"

"In a little while."

"Not now?"

"Not yet."

"I don't want to get pedantic, but I think that means you *are* kidnapping me."

"I'm *not*. I'm offering you an exclusive interview. In exchange for me answering your questions, I'll need you to answer some of mine. Deal?"

Catherine said, "I must respectfully decline. Can I go now?"

The man who called himself Six just exhaled slowly. "All right. You win. It's a kidnapping."

"Glad we agree," she said. Then, "I guess I'll interview you then."

They arrived at Glenwood Cemetery and Six pulled through an entrance that led him to a series of winding roads through rolling hills dotted with trees and tombstones. They passed a mausoleum on the left. There were a few cars parked here and several people dressed in formal attire, some carrying flowers. Catherine wondered if she could just open her car door and roll out. This would alert the dozen or so by the mausoleum, but she didn't know if the man driving the car would just hurt them along with her if she tried this.

She stayed still, and soon they were driving around a quieter part of the cemetery grounds.

Six said, "I can't say I've ever given an interview. How do I start?"

"I need you to prove you are who you say you are. How do I know you didn't just read my article and snatch me like this as part of some delusional fantasy? You could be pretending to be involved in all this."

To Catherine's surprise, the man reached to his waist and hefted both his hoodie and a long-sleeve thermal he wore under it. Lifting both up high enough to first expose the butt of a pistol on his right hip, and then a heavily bandaged area on the right side of his rib cage. Dried black and dark red stains covered the beige compression bandages.

"What is that?"

"It's a gunshot wound. I can unwrap it if you really want to see it."

"I'll take your word for it. What happened?"

"I got shot the other night. Up in Bethesda."

"Is it . . . serious?"

"It's not much fun."

Catherine nodded slowly. "That's *one* way to prove your involvement."

"Are you satisfied?"

"Yes." She looked back at her purse behind her. "Is there any chance I can take notes for the interview?"

"None whatsoever."

Catherine did not push it. "You said you have been running from someone. Who? The CIA?"

"Yes. Among others."

"For how long?"

"Five years."

"And before that?"

"I was an employee of the Central Intelligence Agency for over a decade."

Catherine asked, "In what capacity?"

"SAD. Deniable special missions."

"That's a unit name?"

"A job description. My group didn't have an official name."

"It's the government, Six. Everything gets a name."

A pause. "They called us Golf Sierra. It was a call sign. But that wasn't exactly on the phone extension list at Langley."

"You were SAD black operators?"

"There are black units, and then there are the guys who walk in the shadows cast by the black units. That was us, I guess."

Catherine wondered if this could all still be just what Denny Carmichael had asserted in his interview. A figment of the imagination of an insane person.

"Do you have some proof?"

"Proof of?"

"What you did while working for the Agency."

"You think I walk around with a stack of Polaroids? I don't have any proof. You'll just have to determine for yourself if I'm a crackpot."

"That's fair. Why are you doing this? Why now?"

Six turned up a long, hilly road that undulated through hundreds of tombstones and crypts. He drove incredibly slow. He said, "I have been out of the country for five years. I found a way in, so I came back to end this."

She hesitated. "By killing people?"

"Of course not. I didn't come here to kill anybody."

"What about in Chevy Chase?"

"That wasn't me."

"You just said—"

"I was there. I was shot. But I didn't kill Babbitt."

"What about Dupont Circle?"

"Not me. Again, I was present, but I didn't kill Max Ohlhauser or the transit cops."

"What about Washington Highlands?"

It was a long time before the reply came. "*Those* guys I did kill."

"And the Easy Market shoot-out?"

The man in the hoodie and the sunglasses exhaled. "I assume you saw the footage, so I assume you know I *had* to do it."

"I didn't see any footage. Just bodies."

Six shrugged. "Yeah, I killed those guys. Believe me, they had it coming."

"So . . . you say you aren't here to kill anyone. Yet by my count eleven people are dead in four incidents, and though you admit to being present at all four incidents you are copping to just five of the killings. In my business that calls you something of an unreliable witness."

He shrugged. "I only killed the bad ones. That's kind of my thing."

"Who killed the rest, if not you?"

"People following the orders of Denny Carmichael."

She let that statement hang in the air while they drove for a moment, then asked, "Why does the CIA want you dead?"

"The CIA doesn't want me dead. Carmichael wants me dead. I don't know the real reason. I thought I did, but now that I'm here, I'm more confused than ever."

"What is his stated reason?"

"Some operation that happened six years ago. Something that went off without a hitch."

"But if it went off without a hitch, why does Carmichael want you—"

Six interrupted suddenly, as if something had just come to him. "Do you have contacts in Israeli intelligence?"

Catherine nodded. "Yes. Of course. Well-placed ones, as a matter of fact."

With excitement in his voice, he said, "Six years ago, a Mossad penetration agent in al Qaeda in Iraq traveled to Trieste, Italy. He was compromised and burned to the opposition but didn't know it. An al Qaeda assassin showed up to kill him. Before he could act, an operative arrived and rescued the Mossad agent."

King just said, "I've never heard of this incident."

"Doesn't mean it didn't happen."

"How do you know all this?"

"I was the operative. I termed the al Qaeda gunman and—"

"You did *what*?"

"Terminated him."

"Oh. Go on."

"And I got the Mossad agent to safety. Everything went off the way it was supposed to, but six years later I find out Carmichael is using this old operation as justification to term me." Court stopped the car in the middle of the little tree-lined road and turned to her. "If you can go to the Israelis and confirm any part of this event in Trieste, make it public, then Denny will have no alternative but to rescind the shoot on sight."

"Shoot on sight? That sounds like something from a bad movie." Slowly she looked up at him. This time he didn't order her to turn away.

He looked crestfallen suddenly. "You think I'm making this entire thing up, don't you?"

"People lie. Even the legitimate ones enhance their stories sometimes. In my work I see it every day."

Six rubbed his eyes under his sunglasses. She could see fatigue and frustration on his face, even if his eyes were obscured by the dark lenses.

She softened a little. "I believe you are who you say you are. But some men . . . some women, live and die for their country, and never receive any recognition. They come to me with an exaggeration, an embellishment, something to boost what they've accomplished."

The man behind the wheel all but recoiled. "Seriously, lady, do you really think I want recognition? Do you think any of the boys in SAD are looking for shine time? If I had my way no one on earth would ever know I existed. What I'm doing here, with you, this isn't about me. This is about finding the truth so I can expose Carmichael's hunt as an illegal operation. I just want to come home without all this hanging over me."

Catherine looked hard at the man in front of her. She thought he might have been in his early thirties, but she could not be sure. He was of average height and she caught sight of wisps of brown sticking out of the hoodie. His skin was relatively fair; he had some stubble on his face, but it looked like he'd shaved in the past twenty-four hours.

He was normal. Regular. Utterly nondescript. She wondered if she'd be able to pick this man out of a lineup an hour from now.

That was, of course, if he planned on letting her go at all.

Quickly she said, "You want me to contact someone in Israel?"

"No. I want you to *go* to Israel. Talk to people you know, but also talk to someone I know."

"And who is that?"

Six drove out of the cemetery and into the thickening afternoon traffic. "I don't have a name. He used to be a commando, but now he is working as some kind of a coordinator for their paramilitary units. He helped me get here to the States. He might be able to help you."

"I'll need more information than that if I am going to track him down."

Six thought it over. "He was in the hospital recently."

"How do you know that?"

"Because I shot him."

Catherine leaned back in her seat, rested her head against the door window. "And he's *helping* you?"

"We made up."

"Right. What else do you know about him?"

They spent a few more minutes, he giving her information about the Mossad officer who helped him escape Europe and get into the USA, and she doing her best to remember everything he said while simultaneously trying to regain her composure and understand her situation. After a while she forgot this had begun with a kidnapping. Six seemed to be no threat to her. Instead he presented himself as a man who felt like the world was against him, but nevertheless refused to turn and run away. Whether or not his assertions were true, she still had no idea, but she did not doubt for a minute that Six believed everything he was saying.

Finally he said, "I guess I just have one question for you before I say good-bye. Is there anything else you can tell me about your conversation with Carmichael? Anything else he might have said that stands out?"

Catherine thought a moment. "Maybe so. Were you, by chance, born in Jacksonville, Florida?" She saw no reaction on the man's face, though she looked hard for one.

"Why do you ask?"

"It seemed to me that Carmichael wanted me to put that in the article. I don't know what it means, but he said the man they were after was from Jacksonville."

"Why didn't you use it?"

"You say you are being played by forces bigger than you." She sighed. "Sometimes I feel the same way. I don't particularly like it, either."

Six drummed his fingers on the steering wheel. "I don't know what that means. I was born in Dayton, Ohio." He looked to her. "Please don't print that."

Catherine said, "Other than the fact that you kidnapped me, and the circumstances around that, there isn't much here that I can print. I can't talk about this Israeli connection without catching a lot of heat, and all I'll get from the Agency will be denials."

As they pulled up to a red light, Six surprised her by smiling. "You don't need to report it. Not till you have the proof you need. Carmichael has convinced everybody at Langley I need to die for a mistake I never made. You find out what happened in Trieste, you will see I am telling the truth. Then you'll have your story."

Catherine took offense to the man's insinuation. "The story isn't the only thing I care about, you know. I'm American, just like you. I want what's best for this country."

"Okay."

"Now it's *you* who doesn't believe *me*."

Six shrugged. "You are an investigative reporter."

"True, but I'm more than that."

"What does that mean?"

Catherine King shook her head slowly. "You didn't kidnap me to hear my sob story. Let's just leave it like this. If Denny Carmichael is doing what you say he's doing, I want to put a stop to it."

"Then let's work together. Look into Trieste. You can contact me through my RedPhone number."

And then, with a quick nod, he pulled the car over to the curb and opened his door. He stepped out and walked between two cars parked in the next lane, and she lost sight of him for a moment.

By the time she climbed out of the passenger's seat and looked around, he was gone.

Court walked for only a few minutes before arriving at his motorcycle locked to a rack outside of the Rhode Island Avenue Metro.

He slipped on his helmet, revved the engine, and began heading west through the city.

He was hopeful something would come from Catherine King's investigation of Operation BACK BLAST, but he couldn't allow himself to focus on that right now.

No. Now he had a new problem. He had to go back to his hide site in the middle of the forest, grab as much of his and Zack's gear as he could fit into a small backpack, and then go purchase another vehicle.

It didn't have to be anything fancy. It just had to get him to Florida.

Despite what he'd told the *Washington Post* reporter, Court was not from Dayton. He was indeed from a small town on the highway between Tallahassee and Jacksonville, and the fact Carmichael had dropped that little tidbit into the conversation, Court knew, was either meant as bait or as a threat.

If it was bait, then Court would be in real danger heading down to Florida.

But if it was a threat, if there was *any* chance at all something might happen to his father, his only close living relative, then Court knew he had no real alternative but to get involved.

He had to go.

He wasn't worried that the CIA was going to hurt his father. But the other group out there, this mysterious proxy force of Middle Easterners; what was to keep Carmichael from sending them down to Florida to hurt his dad, to punish him for the actions of his son in some way, or to hold him hostage?

Court didn't think much of his father. They hadn't spoken in nearly twenty years. But his dad was his dad, and Court couldn't let the same group of killers who murdered Max Ohlhauser get their hands on him.

56

A middle-aged secretary called for Denny Carmichael as he sat on the sofa outside the office of the director of the Central Intelligence Agency. "The director will see you now."

Denny walked into the office of the D/CIA, a seventy-three-year-old former congressman and senator from Alabama who had also served in the directorships of Homeland Security, Defense, and even Energy. The man's political career began in the state house in Birmingham, and it had never stopped, covering a period of fifty years.

Carmichael saw D/CIA as an intelligent man, but ultimately nothing more than a carpetbagger, a pol who took the reins of U.S. intelligence only because it was considered by others to be a coveted position, and his friend the president asked him to do so as a personal favor.

Despite the negative view the director of the National Clandestine Service held for the chief of the CIA, the man had left Denny alone, having gotten the hint from the former director of intelligence that the less one knew about the inner workings of Denny Carmichael's NCS fiefdom, the better for one's own tenure. Denny got things done . . . no need to dig into just how he accomplished this.

But now, as the two men shook hands perfunctorily and Denny sat on a sofa across from the handsome septuagenarian in the four-thousand-dollar suit, he worried that was all about to come to an end in the director's mind, because D/CIA was finally getting serious heat from those above him.

The director said, "Not sure if you've heard yet, but I'm heading to Capitol Hill tomorrow morning for a closed-door session. I'm going to have to talk about this mess going on in the District. And I'm not going to get away with saying I don't know a *goddamned* thing, even though the truth is that I really *don't* know a *goddamned* thing."

Carmichael said, "I understand, sir. Please know, I kept this situation off your radar for your own good."

"I'm sure you did, and nine times out of ten I need you to do just that. But this time my willful ignorance has bit me in the ass, because I don't know anything more than what I've seen on TV and read in the papers."

"Yes, sir. Unfortunately, the enemy gets a vote, and this personality we are after has proven extremely difficult to remove from the chessboard."

"Cathy King over there at the *Post* says it's a homegrown threat. That true?"

Carmichael heaved his shoulders. "More or less."

D/CIA cocked his head and looked at Carmichael through narrow eyes. "More? Or less?"

"He used to be one of ours. Former SAD Ground Branch."

D/CIA winced as if he'd just put his hand on a hot plate. "Don't tell me it's the Gray Man."

"I'm afraid so."

"My predecessor told me about this one. He's on the presidential kill list. Number one target, from what I remember. Is that right?"

Denny corrected him gently. "Actually he's the number one target who is also a U.S. Citizen. He's number nineteen on the list overall."

"Right," D/CIA said. "You know, I get to claim some plausible deniability with you and your exploits, since the president has supported your work for so long. I mean, hell, when POTUS is also president of your fan club, I can let a lot of things slide. But not this time."

Carmichael said, "If you can run interference with Congress and do your best to keep the DOJ away from this, even for just a couple more days, then I give you my personal guarantee that we will terminate this individual, and there will be nothing more to do but handle a little after-action fallout."

Carmichael expected D/CIA to open his drawer and pull out a bottle of Maalox. He wasn't suited for this type of work. But the next thing the man from Alabama said surprised him greatly.

"What alternative do I have? I can already hear them in the congressional inquiries. Carmichael's *your* top spook, they'll say . . . This happened on your watch. Hell, the Republicans are already plucking the chickens and heatin' up the tar."

Denny said nothing. Must have been some sort of Alabama reference, he assumed.

D/CIA said, "I can take some heat and buy you some time. But not much. What else can I do for you, something that might make killing this man easier?"

Carmichael blew out an inward sigh of relief. Then he decided to press his luck. "There is one other initiative that might be helpful, sir."

"Let's hear it."

"Unmanned aerials."

"Unmanned aerials? You mean drones?"

"Small ones. No more than three up at any one time. Crisscrossing the District. We have the best facial recognition suites known to man, but this personality has gone to great lengths to defeat them. If we were able to find, fix, and finish him from the air, then we could end this situation in short order."

"Finish." D/CIA said it softly, a statement, not a question, weighing the import of that word.

Denny nodded slowly. He had expected some shock from the man, but the older man showed nothing to indicate this was unexpected.

"You are asking for armed drones, then?" the director asked.

Denny replied defensively. "There are weaponized platforms that are extremely discreet. Virtually undetectable, and fundamentally no chance for collateral damage considering all the fail-safes and controls we have in place to prevent accidents and overkill."

The silence in the room hung over both men. Until: "Just one perfunctory question, Denny."

"What's that?"

D/CIA leaned forward. "Have you lost your *fucking* mind?"

Carmichael sighed. Clearly, he would *not* be getting his armed drones.

"I'm not putting fucking remote-controlled killing machines in the airspace over Washington, D.C.!"

"I understand, sir. We'll proceed without them. I just thought you understood how dangerous a situation we have here, from a political perspective, if nothing else."

D/CIA snorted out a laugh. "There is one thing you are not taking into consideration, Carmichael. One thing that makes me very different from you."

"And what's that?"

"I don't really give a damn about your Gray Man. I hope you get him before he murders more of our good people, but this really isn't *my* fight. And I don't care about politics. Not anymore. CIA won't be my last job, but it sure as hell will be my last government job. I'll be a college president three weeks after walking out the door here, and no one at UCLA or Duke is going to give a rat's ass that a rogue assassin rampaged around in D.C. for a few days shooting fascist spymasters before he was shot dead."

Neither Ohlhauser nor Babbitt were fascists, nor were they spymasters. But Denny got the point.

"I understand, sir," Denny said, but it wasn't true. He was tired of kissing this man's ass. It hadn't won him what he wanted. So he changed gears. "You don't want to be involved, I get it. But understand this. I *will* get what I need. Even if I am forced to pursue other avenues."

"You mean you're going to go to POTUS."

"I haven't ruled it out."

The director said, "*I'm* the goddamned director of the CIA. You report to me."

"And I have reported."

The seventy-three-year-old fumed. "You see yourself as the king here, Carmichael. The master of all you survey. You don't think you can be stopped, do you?"

A small snicker from Denny now. "Not by you, sir. No."

D/CIA rose to this challenge. "I might not be a killer like you, but by virtue of my title and rank, you know I have access to people who can stop people like you."

Carmichael just smiled. "You have *direct* access, of course. You just call me up, and I arrange it. Which means, I have access to the same assets as you."

"That a threat?"

Carmichael shook his head. "Nothing of the sort. I am just reminding you that I serve as a buffer between you and the elements out there that could be harmful to you." He paused. "Politically. I am speaking in purely political terms. Don't get dramatic."

"Get out of my office."

Denny stood and turned for the door. Then, just as Denny knew he would, the director blinked.

"Carmichael?"

Denny turned. "Sir?"

"Go back to your cave. Kill this man who's causing so much trouble. I'll give you a lot of latitude, just like you were going after some high-value target overseas. But I'm not giving you killer robots."

"Very well, sir."

He turned to leave again, but once more the director called out. "They tell me you have been sleeping in your office for the last week."

"Well . . . I've been working."

"I'll abide a lot of your extreme actions, Denny, but not that one. Not even considering your situation. Sets a bad tone for the younger generation when we old folks don't behave with the proper decorum. You're a divisional director, for God's sake. Start acting like one. This isn't a boardinghouse."

Carmichael blew out a hidden sigh of frustration. "Sir."

Carmichael stuck his head in Suzanne Brewer's TOC just five minutes later. Brewer had been leaning over one of her analysts while he checked a possible Gentry sighting in Foggy Bottom. It wasn't Gentry, the two of them decided almost immediately, so Suzanne was just about to head back to her office when she looked up to find herself facing the director of her division.

"Sir?"

She'd grown accustomed to Denny's clipped voice.

"I need a safe house, stat. You keep the TOC running here, but I need to get away from the Langley Campus to work without the director's interference. I want to be linked to you with a dedicated umbilical, not out in the boonies, but close by."

Brewer thought a moment. "Springfield Twelve has all the coms you'll need."

Carmichael shook his head. "Alexandria Eight has better security, I'll go there."

"We haven't used Alexandria Eight in years."

"It's a fortress. I want a fortress."

"Yes, sir. I'll get a team there stat to sweep and clean, and pull tech staff to get everything online. I'll oversee it personally. Give me a little time to prep and we'll schedule a movement to your new facility by the end of the day."

"Good," Denny said, then he disappeared from the doorway.

"Sir?" she called after him, and he returned. He looked annoyed. "Zack Hightower isn't answering his phone."

"Don't worry about it. He's doing something for Mayes. You might or might not get him back."

"But—"

Carmichael interrupted. "Alexandria Eight, Suzanne."

"Yes, sir."

57

Catherine King pushed right through the closed door to the office of the executive editor of the *Washington Post*. She got away with doing this sort of thing because she'd known the man since the late seventies when he had been her professor. The two had worked together at the *Post* since soon after, they'd become close friends, and they had developed an informal rapport that stunned some of the younger reporters.

But the other five men and women who came in behind Catherine all felt a sense of panic and dread when she ordered them to follow her in with assurances that all would be forgiven once she told the executive editor what had just occurred. While Catherine took a seat, her four-person investigative team, as well as metro reporter Andy Shoal, all lined up against the wall, most looking at their shoes or at books on a bookshelf, because no one wanted to make eye contact with the man behind the desk.

No one else in the room knew the subject of this impromptu confab except Catherine herself, but her excitement put everyone on notice that something big was about to be revealed.

Ten minutes later everyone, including the executive editor, knew what they had to do. The dramatic but simple narrative the paper had advanced in the past few days—that a psycho with a gun was terrorizing intelligence officials—had suddenly transformed into a multilayered story of international intrigue and government cover-up. No one knew what was true, but these were journalists; so the knowledge that they had to find the answers quickly meant everyone crammed into the office felt like a sprinter in the starting blocks, ready for the gun to go off.

And the executive editor pulled the trigger.

"All right. Catherine is on the first flight to Tel Aviv. Tonight. This story is moving too fast to wait around till this shooter turns up dead and no one gives a damn anymore."

Eager nods from everyone save for King, who did not like the thought of the death of the man she'd just met an hour earlier being discussed as if it were a fait accompli.

The executive editor continued, "The rest of you get to work on all our contacts in Israel. Hell, talk to anyone you know who has contacts over there in intel circles. We have a date where a man entered a hospital with a gunshot wound to his stomach. Could be a civilian or a military hospital. Talk to other Mossad people and find out the protocol for treating a Mossad man injured on the job."

Catherine added, "He said the shooting took place in Hamburg, Germany, so maybe we extend the range by a few days in case he was hospitalized there first. And check hospitals in Hamburg."

The EE agreed. "And when we find anything about this patient, we'll go to work on figuring out his identity. It doesn't matter if we can't dig into his government file; we just need to know where he lives, so when Catherine lands in Tel Aviv tomorrow she can hit the ground running."

"We don't know he'll know anything about the event in Trieste," one of the other reporters said. "We just know he helped Six."

"That's true," Catherine said. "And from that we know he has goodwill towards Six. If he doesn't know about Trieste, maybe he can help us find out who does."

Andy was the most junior reporter in the room, so he was surprised when the editor pointed to him. "Shoal, I want you to go back to Chevy Chase and to Dupont Circle. I want you interviewing everyone who lived or worked in the immediate area, as well as first responders and commuters who passed by at the time of the shootings. I want you digging even harder for evidence than the cops dug. Find somebody who saw something other than this guy named Six running around."

"Yes, sir."

"And Catherine." The executive editor turned to her. "While you're on that plane I want you e-mailing every government official. Call in every favor. Don't bring up the fact we are going after this wounded guy the suspect named, but do ask for comments about an Israeli asset rescued by American intelligence in Italy six years ago. I don't care if they won't speak on the record. I want to know what they *don't* say just as much as what they *do* say. If you get a lot of 'No comments,' or denials that sound like they are coming out of an official echo chamber, then we'll know we're on to something."

"Will do."

The huddle in the executive editor's office ended by four, and Catherine ran back to her desk, threw as much into one of her roll-aboards as would fit, and then rushed to the elevators.

Five minutes later she was in the back of a hired car booking a six ten flight to Tel Aviv from Dulles while the driver wove through D.C. traffic.

Court looked down at his watch as he passed the sign announcing he was leaving Virginia and entering North Carolina. It was seven forty-five in the evening; he'd been on the road less than two hours.

This meant he had another nine to go, and with that realization he reached down into the cup holder of the big pickup truck and lifted his massive cup of coffee. Half empty, half cold.

It was going to be a long, long night.

Court drove a 1992 Ford Bronco that showed just about the same amount of rust as it did its original blue and white paint job. He'd bought the vehicle two hours earlier for $1,900 at a "tote-the-note" used car dealership in Richmond, telling the salesman he needed something that could get him as far as the West Coast. The salesman proudly showed him the Bronco's 87,000 "original" miles, which to Court meant the odometer had been rolled back, but he inspected the truck inside and out and he decided it would get the job done.

He could have spent a lot more—he still had over seven grand from the money he took from the drug dealers last Saturday night—and he could have bought something more obviously reliable, but the moment Court saw the Bronco he knew it *had* to be his transport down to Florida, because it reminded him of some of his better memories of his youth. He'd driven an '87 blue and white Bronco around central Florida as a teenager, and it just felt right to him to return home driving virtually the same vehicle he'd used back then.

He told himself he needed to stay productive on this long drive, and he had two objectives: One, to come up with a plan about what he would do when he actually found his father. And two, to come up with a plan about what he was going to do when he got back to D.C.

But he really had not yet begun to tackle either of the two problems, because he still had other issues running through his mind. Namely Catherine King, and his desperate hope that she had believed enough of what he had said this afternoon to where she would do what he had asked her to do—fly to Israel to find answers about Operation BACK BLAST. As long as he was occupied on this side trip, this errand a thousand miles from where he needed to be, the reporter for the *Washington Post* was his only hope at getting any closer to a resolution to all this mess.

He put his chances for this at fifty-fifty; meaning he thought there was just as much possibility King would rush onto the set of Fox News to talk about her harrowing kidnapping ordeal at the hands of a maniac as there was she would fly to Israel and run down a vague lead about a wounded Mossad officer who might know something about an old asset who had once been rescued from the clutches of al Qaeda while on a trip to Italy.

It was all so tiring to think about, and he had to concentrate on staying awake.

He continued down I-95, passing through the town of Rocky Mount, North Carolina, and here his head instinctively turned to the left and looked off into the dark. He knew the exit here onto I-64 well, because he had spent some of the most intense years of his life less than one hour directly to the east, beyond the coastal plain and all the way through the swamps at the edge of the Atlantic Ocean.

Back before 9/11, when Court was just a trainee working to become a singleton operator in the Autonomous Asset Development Program, he spent two years in a sequestered set of small buildings just inside the protected area at the military and intelligence installation known as the Harvey Point Defense Testing Activity. Here he'd learned tradecraft, foreign languages, survival skills, hand-to-hand combat, scuba diving, and dozens of other talents and trades, all of which turned him into one of the CIA's best "one-man bands" of espionage. He'd been in his early twenties when he graduated from and left the compound at AADP, but he'd been back to other facilities at Harvey Point many times throughout the years. Each time he drove onto the grounds he looked off towards a swamp to the right of the road, and he'd wondered if back there on the other side of a thick copse of cypress, more young men were going through AADP training, hidden even from the rest of the men and women with Top Secret clearance allowed onto Harvey Point.

He'd heard the Autonomous Asset Program had been disbanded and he'd thought himself to be the last surviving operative from the program, but Max Ohlhauser had told him the day before that AAP had been rebranded somehow, and that it remained operational.

He wondered if the answer to all his questions was out there beyond the cypress trees and swampland, but he pushed the thought out of his mind and kept driving south, doing his best to instead brainstorm his operation to protect his dad. He began thinking back to a time long ago when the roads and farms just west of Jacksonville, Florida, had been his stomping ground. It would be surreal to be back on those roads, and he wasn't looking forward to it, but he worried Denny Carmichael would stop at nothing to end this, and he wouldn't think twice about sending foreign killers to target Court's father.

Think about something else, Gentry, he told himself, desperate to find a topic to concentrate on that wouldn't wear his mind out for the next nine hours.

For the first time on this drive, he reached to the knob on the radio, and he flipped it on. The speakers in this twenty-four-year-old truck were shit, and it took him several seconds to find an FM station that played something he could listen to, but as soon as he heard an old Allman Brothers tune, he stopped turning the dial, and he cranked up the volume as far as it would go.

"Midnight Rider" was just about the perfect song for tonight. He wished he could just play it on a continuous loop until tomorrow morning.

Court wore a green Caterpillar cap and a denim jacket; other than his Virginia drive-out tags he looked like a farmer or factory worker in any of the towns here in the Carolinas or northern Florida, his ultimate destination.

This was nice, he told himself. His cover legend, for maybe the first time in his operational life, felt exactly like the original Court Gentry. He'd operated undercover as a dockworker in Ireland and a financial analyst in Singapore and a commercial diver in Brazil. He'd played the roles of a light-skinned Masalit tribesman in Sudan and a Canadian businessman in Italy and an Iraqi nomad in Syria.

He'd played one hundred roles, easily, but he'd never once played the role of a hick driving his V8 beater and wearing a Cat hat and soiled denim, listening to Southern rock as the miles rolled by under his big tires.

No, he'd never played that role. But he'd lived it.

Despite the worries on his mind stemming from what he'd left behind in D.C. and the concerns he had about what he would find when he got where he was going, Court Gentry couldn't help but feel good right now.

He felt real. He felt American.

He was hours from home still, but somehow it was as if he'd already arrived.

58

Matthew Hanley had spent most of the day out of the office, working in a conference room at Andrews Air Force Base. His Air Branch was still working on getting the four de Havilland Twin Otter aircraft upgraded and registered with a CIA shell company. Hanley didn't have to spend his day at Andrews to help with the minutia of this—it was work beneath his rank and he had administrative people who did this sort of shit all day—but he had just wanted to get away from the campus at Langley for the afternoon, so personally attending to some of the intricacies of turning used turbo-prop puddle jumpers into hi-tech CIA transport aircraft had proved a good excuse to do just that.

Around eight p.m. he piled his large frame into the back of his armored Camry and began the movement west back to his home in Woodley Park. Jenner was at the wheel, as before, but Hanley had given Chris Travers the rest of the week off. Travers had been suspicious, of course, had asked his boss what was up, and Hanley thought about lying to his man. Instead he went the opposite direction: the cold hard facts. Hanley told Travers Carmichael was trying to get him booted from the SAD, probably by ginning up a positive drug result. He promised to fight for Travers but insisted Chris go home and make himself scarce for a few days.

If they couldn't find Travers they couldn't take a sample of his piss, Hanley explained, and, without a sample to taint, they sure as hell couldn't frame him for abusing drugs.

With Travers out a young Ground Branch paramilitary named Paladino rode shotgun in Hanley's car, but it wasn't just these two men in the Camry anymore. Now a Chevy Tahoe followed chase on Hanley's vehicle, with four more armed SAD officers inside, and all six men would stay at Hanley's house until Gentry was either captured or killed.

Hanley was no longer worried about Gentry killing him, but he'd bumped up his detail anyhow. It was his way of giving the middle finger to Denny Carmichael. Denny had JSOC men following him, so Hanley surrounded himself with Ground Branch boys to keep the army-side goons far enough back to where he wouldn't have to see them or deal with them.

He recognized how silly he was being, but he didn't give a shit.

A half mile from his home Hanley asked Jenner to divert to an Italian tratorria on Connecticut. The two-vehicle convoy did as instructed, and Hanley dropped in to the half-empty restaurant and took a small round table in the back. He'd asked Jenner and the boys to sit and eat with him, but even though he was their boss, they declined.

It was their job to keep him safe, they explained, not to pass him the garlic toast and listen to his old war stories about the Grenada invasion.

Matt Hanley ordered raw oysters and a rare fillet, along with an entire bottle of Chianti for himself, and he sipped his wine and slurped his oysters, all the while sitting there and humming along to sad Dean Martin songs playing softly over the restaurant's speakers. His men stood near the exits, their eyes out the windows and doors.

Shortly after Hanley's steak arrived, Jenner approached the table, his MP7 obvious under his suit coat.

The director of the SAD said, "Sure you won't join me for a drink?"

"No thanks. Boss, there's somebody here that wants to talk to you."

Hanley just looked up from his plate. "Well, who the hell is it?"

"It's that asshole TL from the Goon Squad. Forgot his name. The guy who died a few years back."

"Zack Hightower," Hanley said. And then, "It's fucking magic, huh?"

Jenner just shrugged. "It's the fucking Agency, sir."

Hanley chuckled, wiped his mouth, and took another sip of the Chianti. "Send him over. Maybe I can get the dead guy to drink with me."

Hightower appeared at the table and stood across from Hanley. He seemed nervous. "Uh, sorry, boss. I just wanted to apologize in person."

"Pop a squat," Hanley said, and Hightower sat down at the table while Hanley signaled the waiter. "Bring my old friend here . . ." He looked at Zack now. "You didn't quit drinking, did you?"

"Hell, no, sir. I was just fake dead, I wasn't really dead."

"Bring him a Stoli on the rocks." And then, "A double."

"Thank you, sir."

"You've put on a few pounds since I saw you last."

"And a few years."

"Same here on both counts," Hanley said. He still seemed more interested in his fillet than in his company. "So . . . what's the deal? You are Denny's personal direct action arm now?"

"No, sir. I was brought in to help them locate Violator."

"And you missed him, but you sure found Lee Babbitt, didn't you? One round center mass. Three hundred fifty meters."

Hightower didn't say anything. In the awkward silence his drink arrived. Hanley's knife and fork scratched his plate.

Eventually the director of the Special Activities Division looked up. "How did I know you zapped Babbitt, you ask?" He took another bite. "I didn't. It was a guess. You just confirmed it with your non-denial." He followed this with a healthy gulp of Chianti.

Zack said, "I was told Babbitt was a clear threat to Agency operational security, and he was unwilling to—"

Hanley interrupted, "Babbitt was a piece of shit. Fuck him. You did good." Then he pointed his steak knife across the table. "But Gentry . . . Why are you after Gentry? Back in the day that kid would have died for you, no questions asked."

"I'm starting to ask myself the same question, sir. I had a little run-in with him last night."

Hanley smiled while he cut another piece of meat off his fillet. "I'm still trying to get my blood pressure down to normal from his visit to my place. He get the drop on you?"

A pause. An embarrassed "Yes, sir."

Hanley shrugged. Not surprised. He was halfway through his dinner now. "What did he tell you?"

"He doesn't believe he did anything wrong on BACK BLAST."

"That's it?"

Hightower shook his head. He drank a third of his vodka in one gulp. "Sir, are you aware of any foreigners involved in the ideal hunt for Sierra Six?"

Hanley looked at Hightower with genuine surprise. *"Foreigners?"*

"Affirmative. Like, Gulf Arabs. Here in town. Part of the same operation."

"Of course not. I'm not involved in this hunt, but why the hell would there be Arabs in a CONUS agency op?"

"I don't know, sir. Gentry is alleging the men who killed Ohlhauser were part of some Muj unit."

For the first time since Hightower sat down, Hanley put his fork on the plate and leaned back from the table. "I know Denny is using a JSOC unit."

"Gentry would know Delta guys from Gulf Arabs."

"He would, indeed." Hanley shrugged. "I don't have a clue who they could be, but if Gentry says he saw them, then he saw them."

"I feel the same way, sir. I thought I'd start looking around while I'm out on the streets."

"I'd be interested to know what you find out."

"Of course, sir."

Hanley seemed lost in thought now, so Zack finished his drink quickly and immediately stood up. "I appreciate your time."

Hanley reached into his pocket and took out a pen. He took the damp beverage napkin from under Zack's empty glass and he wrote down a phone number. "Any time, day or night. This is me. No one listening. No one recording." He looked up at Zack and extended his hand with the napkin. "Just me."

"Understood, sir."

"You know, Zack . . . I told Court I couldn't help him, and I can't. But I sure as hell am not going to help the other side. When things settle after this, there is going to be a reckoning." He picked up his steak knife and pointed with it again. "You'd do well to remember that, Sierra One."

Hanley watched Hightower leave, then he called for the check.

59

The Central Intelligence Agency's Alexandria safe house, dubbed by the CIA Alexandria Eight, wasn't a house at all in the conventional sense. It was so much more.

On a fenced property that covered nine acres of grass-covered hills along North Quaker Lane, the main structure was a twenty-five-thousand-square-foot brick mid-Atlantic Colonial building. Built as a school of divinity in the 1850s, it had remained a college campus for seminarians for nearly a hundred years before slipping into private hands. In the 1960s the CIA bought the property, which had by then fallen into disrepair, and with money earmarked for overseas Cold War operations they rebuilt it as a veritable fortress, to be used as a safe haven for top CIA personnel in the event of an attack on the CIA HQ in nearby McLean, Virginia.

The building was never used for its original purpose, but over the years it had been employed on those few occasions when both a large and secure safe house was needed in the Washington, D.C., area.

There were twenty-six rooms on the property in total, spread across a north wing that was lightly protected with secure locking bolts on the doors and windows, a main central building with a dining hall, facilities for conferences and other common spaces, and a south wing that had all the security of a bank vault.

The wings were two stories tall with long, low attics, and the central building was three stories, with a large open clock tower in the center that stood over the main atrium and a spiral staircase that rose from the atrium to the conference rooms on the second and third floors.

As impressive as it looked on the outside, it was dramatically less so on the inside. During the War on Terror, the facility was all but mothballed, and large parts of the property had not been renovated since the early 1970s. Dark stained-wood paneling in the main hall and yellowed wallpaper in the bedrooms dated the facility, and it had the smell and feel of an old public school. Industrial antiseptic cleansers and many corners that were never dusted, and other than a few bedrooms and common spaces that had been used in the past few years a handful of times, most of the furniture dated back to the 1960s and early 1970s.

Even though the decor and furnishings weren't up to today's standards, the entire building retained a network of antiquated but robust security measures. All the locks were pneumatic and controllable from a security room. In the event of an attack on the property, steel barriers could be lowered behind the doors and windows to seal in the occupants in the south wing, which had its own dedicated air supply, its own long-term food storage, even its own water tower that was protected in a small rear courtyard.

Suzanne Brewer thought Carmichael's decision to utilize Alexandria Eight was over the top, even considering the threat from Court Gentry, but Carmichael insisted, so she personally toured the location and oversaw bringing the pneumatic security system back online, and she ordered technicians to augment the property with more cameras, communications gear, and high-tech security measures.

Carmichael arrived via motorcade at nine p.m. and he went directly to one of the bedrooms on the second floor of the south wing. This room also had an outer office he could use while here, as well as a huge adjacent conference room with a twenty-seat table, so the entire Working Group could begin holding their evening meetings here, instead of at Langley.

With him here at Alexandria Eight Carmichael had DeRenzi and his entire twelve-man personal protection detail, along with another sixteen CIA security officers pulled off of static safe house work in the area.

Carmichael toured the entire south wing and spoke with Brewer about adding a few more details to make the facility safer. Once satisfied all protective measures were in place, the director of the National Clandestine Service determined that, while there was no place safer than the CIA's HQ, running a close second now was Alexandria Eight.

Jordan Mayes arrived at Alexandria Eight a half hour later in the center of a three-SUV motorcade, feeling like the nucleus of an atom with eight bodyguards serving as the electrons. Together all nine men rolled up the long, straight driveway towards the massive building, checking in with a pair of parked Yukon XLs that blocked the drive halfway up.

Everyone knew Jordan Mayes, of course, but he still had to show his ID to gain access, as did everyone on his security team, and a pair of German shepherds sniffed under the SUVs to make sure Gentry wasn't riding below, holding on to the underside of one of the vehicles like a cartoon ninja.

The three SUVs finished their journey up the driveway and arrived at the front door of the massive building. Here they passed four more guards, each one armed with an assault rifle, and they entered the grand hall of the former seminary. More guards here looked ready to deal with any trouble, but they were professionals, and they were also in the presence of the number two clandestine services executive in the Agency, so they merely checked his ID perfunctorily and pointed the way up a winding staircase to the right that led to the south wing.

Mayes looked around as he headed to the open staircase that rimmed the grand hall. This place was a fortress, but he had expected nothing less as far as security. Suzanne Brewer had set up the defenses for Carmichael's stay here, and she was nothing if not good at her job.

Mayes climbed the stairs with four members of his detail, and at the top they passed through a wide doorway that opened into a hall that led north and south. Mayes knew from a phone call with Brewer that the door from the staircase into the hallway was iron and several tons in weight, and it was controlled by pneumatic pressure and flow-control valves so that it could pivot shut remotely and lock with wide internal iron bolts that could withstand a round from an Abrams tank. The entire south wing, in fact—doors, windows, even the walls themselves—were either steel-reinforced or protected by the pneumatic emergency security system, and the twelve rooms inside the protective cocoon could all go from wide open to locked tight in just seconds.

Carmichael's suite was at the end of the hallway. He was protected by DeRenzi and two more guards here, but when Mayes stepped into the office outside of Denny's bedroom, D/NCS told the security officers to wait outside. DeRenzi and the others stepped out, and Carmichael shut the door and locked it.

Carmichael was just finishing up a phone call with Brewer, who was on her way to D.C., where she had been summoned to the JSOC safe house to speak with Dakota, so Mayes took a moment to look around. The windows to the outside were tempered glass; not bulletproof, but they did not need to be, because iron slats could fall into place at the touch of a button. One exit out of the office led to the bedroom, a second to the hallway that served as the spine of the south wing, and the third to a narrow inner hallway that led past a narrow staircase, which ascended one flight to a locked door. The other side of the door was the south wing attic, which itself was secured from the outside and shut off from the other parts of the building. Beyond the stairway in the narrow hall was a bathroom, and then a large conference room.

As soon as Denny finished his call he looked at his watch. "It's ten p.m., Mayes. Trouble?"

"We have a problem."

"Talk."

"Catherine King. I gave Zack Hightower the day to recover after he watched her house all night long. I put four cars on her tail. She ran around doing press all morning, just what you'd expect to see from her. She's all over the news with the story you fed her. But then, just after noon, she started running an SDR."

"You're sure?"

"Yes. A good one, too, from the sound of it. Our surveillance people stayed on her for the first half hour, but she slipped them. She was in the wind from about one fifteen p.m. till almost two forty-five, at which time she returned to her car parked at the CNN building. She took that back to her office at the *Post*, arriving at three fifteen p.m."

Carmichael said, "From the look on your face, I assume there is something more."

"There is. At four twenty p.m. today she bought a ticket on a six ten flight to Tel Aviv."

Carmichael's razor-tight face stretched tighter as he scowled. "Son of a bitch. It's Gentry. He got to her somehow."

Mayes said, "It's possible."

Carmichael just said, "Gentry told her about BACK BLAST. He's sending her to Tel Aviv to find out details from people she knows in the Mossad."

"What can they possibly tell her?"

"Details, obviously."

"Details even I don't know?"

"Don't start, Mayes. We've been through this." Mayes didn't push it, and Carmichael thought a moment. "I want surveillance on her e-mail and phone within the hour."

Mayes nodded.

"And the other reporter working with her. What was his name?"

"Shoal. He's not an investigator, he's just—"

"I don't care what he is. I want a full surveillance package on him. Phone and e-mail as well."

"I'm on it."

Carmichael added, "And get some more assets to cover Gentry's father in Florida. Catherine King might have passed on the fact we were looking for someone from Jacksonville. He will read that as a threat."

Mayes said, "More assets? *Who*, Denny? We don't have SAD men we can call up, remember. The JSOC forces are deployed here in the District, and contracted security have proven themselves unable to go up against him. Who are we going to send down there other than the case officers already watching him?"

Denny Carmichael thought it over, then a thought came to him. "Harvey Point."

Mayes cocked his head. "What about Harvey Point?"

"There is a training evolution going on down there right now, isn't there?"

"Yes. Twenty-five case officers from Europe are down at the Point taking a class in defensive driving. One of Suzanne Brewer's initiatives to improve security at foreign postings." He shrugged. "But . . . what about them? Those folks aren't shooters. They are just case officers. None of them have fired a gun since the Farm. You want to send a bunch of cocktail circuit spooks out to capture the Gray Man?"

"They don't have to capture him. Send them down there immediately, *all* of them. Get them to lean on his dad, to see if he's been in contact. They will be able to detect deception in him. Put them on the street corners, in the grocery stores, flood the zone. If Gentry goes down there and they get wind of it, we can fly shooters in from Bragg in a couple of hours."

Mayes said, "I'll get them moving down."

60

Suzanne Brewer pulled her BMW 535i into the garage of the JSOC safe house three blocks from the U.S. Capitol. She was annoyed to be here; she'd rather be either back at the TOC at Langley running down the latest leads, or else curled up in her bed at home in Springfield, desperately trying to catch one of her all too few three-hour cat naps. It was ten-thirty p.m., after all; she had been on her way home for a break when she diverted all the way into the District, and since the last spate of Violator sightings were eight hours old she doubted she'd be needed back at Langley until the morning.

But she was here because Dakota had called and demanded a meeting.

The JSOC team had done everything she'd asked of them as they'd been sent on one chase after another over the past few days, so she gave in to his demand without putting up much of a fight. She knew they'd be tired and angry for being spun up again and again, often getting to locations where facial recog hits were too old for them to do more than wander around with only faint hopes their target might just be loitering in the area reading a newspaper.

The most recent callout of the JSOC team had taken place near Union Station around two p.m. Brewer's team at the TOC had caught the facial recog hit, and Brewer herself had double-checked it within five minutes of the image being captured.

The image was of a man, very possibly Violator, walking into the large parking garage just to the west of the massive train station in the center of the District.

Another image showing the same man was captured inside the garage just a minute later, and it had him walking up a ramp towards one of the higher levels. This photograph did not contain a good view of his face, but with the first image to go on, Suzanne decided to deploy Dakota and his men.

The full twelve-man JSOC team arrived, followed shortly behind by CIA assets, and they all searched the entire area.

But no sign of Violator was detected, and the analysts at the TOC were unable to find any images of him leaving the area. The interior of the train station was virtually enveloped by camera coverage, and the lack of any computer matches there led Brewer to the conclusion her target had simply vanished.

Suzanne then sat down at a monitor in the TOC and individually checked the image of each and every vehicle that left the parking garage from the moment Violator entered until four hours later, long past the time JSOC had ruled out Gentry still being in the area, because she worried they might have missed him. Early in this slow, laborious endeavor she thought she detected the problem. She noticed an issue with one of the cameras covering the garage. The angle at which the sun's rays hit the windshields of the cars leaving the H Street NE exit from one forty-five to two fifteen p.m. caused a large flashing glare on each and every digital image, and even by going manually through all the images time-stamped during this period, Suzanne could barely make out the drivers of any of the cars and trucks. If Gentry had left by this exit, inside a vehicle, within a half hour of when he arrived, it would have been almost impossible to identify him.

For a brief moment Brewer wondered if her target could have possibly been so thorough in his skills to have known that the sun would hit windshields at that time, in that location, at that angle. But she dispelled this notion.

Sure, it was possible to be that lucky, but Court Gentry could not *possibly* be that good.

Could he?

After the JSOC team got no joy at the garage, Dakota and his men raced around the station until nightfall, and then they spent another few hours widening their search area to include virtually all of central D.C., but now they were back in their safe house, waiting for the next sighting to be reported at the TOC and, Suzanne presumed by Dakota's tone when he called her cell phone forty-five minutes earlier, they were angry with her for the goose chase.

Her plan was to throw some compliments their way, take any grief they wanted to give her about the lack of a target, and then go home.

Now she sat in the living room of the house. Dakota was alone with her while the other men either bunked out, ate, or relaxed in the other rooms.

Catherine had declined the JSOC officer's offer of tea, but he poured a cup for himself and stirred a sugar cube into it slowly.

Impatient, Brewer started the conversation. "Look. I'm tired, and I know you are, too. But honestly, if you felt the need to browbeat me for not getting you a target after five days of hunting, you could have just done it over the phone."

Dakota took a sip of hot tea. "No, ma'am, that's not it at all. I've been in the army too damn long to get pissy when something doesn't pan out. Bad intel is the rule, not the exception."

"Then what am I doing here?"

Dakota wasn't happy with the flavor of his drink, so he tossed another sugar cube in, but he didn't bother with stirring this time. "Coming from the army, I always did have a pretty fair understanding of whose side I was on. I'm getting worried that something's gotten lost in the shuffle on this op, so I'm hoping you can help me sort it out."

"I'm not holding anything back from you. Just tell me what you want to know."

"I want to know the identity of the other bozos we keep running into. The other team involved in the Violator hunt."

Brewer furrowed her eyebrows. "I don't know what you mean. It's you guys, Agency support personnel, and contracted plainclothes security. I told you this already."

"That's not all the pieces on this checkerboard, Ms. Brewer."

"Look, we're doing our best to keep PD and DOJ out of this, but Gentry has stirred a hornet's nest. Shooting up subway stations and convenience stores and taking down SWAT teams draws the attention of law enforcement, as you can imagine. Obviously local PD was in Columbia Heights yesterday morning, and I'm sure they're looking as hard as they can for the same target we're looking for, but we aren't coordinating with them."

Dakota drank more tea, looking over the rim of the cup at Brewer with a skeptical eye.

The CIA Programs and Plans officer leaned forward in her chair. "If you have something to say, just say it. Otherwise, I'm going home."

"There's another group out there. Foreigners. They are being sent where we're being sent."

Her eyes narrowed. "Foreigners? Bullshit."

"No, ma'am. The only bullshit is that the Agency is farming out this job to some overseas actor. You folks can get yourselves thrown into prison for that, you know."

"I don't have a clue what you are talking about."

"Maybe you don't. Maybe you do. Maybe somebody is keeping you in the dark, same as us. But they are out there. We saw them yesterday morning when we got to Columbia Heights. A couple of unmarked cars, multiple individuals in each one. A couple of motorcycles that didn't look like they belonged. We got close to them, and they bugged out."

To Brewer this did not sound particularly conclusive.

Dakota continued, "And today at Union Station. Four more two-man tag teams wandering around inside the mall. I don't mean contractors or Agency spooks, I mean foreign actors of some variety."

"*What* variety?"

"They are Middle Easterners, that's for sure. Otherwise I don't know. It's not my mission to unravel that mystery, I only kept an eye on them to make sure my guys stayed safe, and I only bring it up with you so you know that's not the way we operate. I know there are one hundred thousand things you can't tell me, and to be honest I don't give a damn about any of them. But I demand to be told who else is going to be running around armed in my area of operations!"

Brewer was thoroughly confused, but she did not want to reveal that to the man who needed to follow her instructions. Instead she promised to speak with her higher-ups to see if they could clear her to reveal more information about the operation.

A few minutes later she was back in her car, but her plans to return home to Springfield had changed. Instead, she'd go back to the TOC. She told herself she'd sleep when this was all over, but until then, there were too many balls in the air for her to worry about her own needs.

61

By the time dawn broke over the tiny town of Glen St. Mary, Florida, the roosters on the farm just north of Claude Harvey Road had already been crowing for hours.

Court had known they would be. The ancestors of those roosters had been screwing with his sleep for as far back as he could remember.

To call this a farm at all was putting it charitably. It was fifty acres of mostly hard-packed sandy dirt, covered in trees and shrubs on the edges and flat as a pancake. There was a pond and a double-wide and a detached garage made of corrugated tin, and there were a few chickens in a coop and a few goats in a pen, but that looked like the full measure of the place if you were driving by on Claude Harvey, the only paved road in sight.

But a passing motorist wouldn't be able to see the largest structure on the farm from the road. It was back behind the trees, two hundred yards off Claude Harvey, just this side of a fat man-made earthen berm that had long since become overgrown with thatchy privet and wild oak.

The structure was a two-story shoot house, a firearms training center, constructed like a fort out of railroad ties, old tires, plywood, Conex boxes, and other rusted metal. At over nine thousand square feet, it was massive, although it had never been fancy and had fallen into disrepair in the past fifteen years. Next to the old wooden structure, several firing ranges could still be detected in the underbrush, and old rusted steel man-shaped targets leaned haphazardly against the berm.

The owner of the farm and the shoot house was a sixty-eight-year-old native Floridian named James Ray Gentry. Gentry had served as a marine in Vietnam, a small-town cop, a large-city SWAT officer, and his department's lead firearms instructor, and then, when he was still in his early thirties, he quit the force and opened his own private tactical training center for state and local law enforcement agencies. This was the early 1980s, when Florida's cocaine wars put armed bad guys with automatic weapons on the streets, in the bars, and in the boats offshore. Cops and deputy sheriffs all over the state needed to learn how to transition from the days of six-shooters and minimal chance for danger to fighting protracted street battles with heavily armed men with little reluctance to kill or die to protect their millions in product.

And James Gentry taught most of the state's SWAT teams right here on Claude Harvey Road. By the nineties he was training federal law enforcement and even some CIA units, as well, all of whom knew he had the abilities to show them how to clean and clear houses without subjecting large portions of their units to near-certain death.

James's wife died back in the eighties, but not before she gave him two healthy boys. Courtland, and then two years later, Chancellor. Chance seemed destined to follow in his father's footsteps from birth. He always wanted to wear his father's police gear, or dress up like the Lone Ranger.

Court was night and day different from his little brother; he was obsessed with Indians as a child, he was more interested in horses than in police cars, and Court became the Indian outlaw to Chance's U.S. Marshal. They chased each other all over the farm in character. Chance versus Court. Cowboy versus Indian. The good guy versus the bad guy.

The father's son, and the rebel.

Both boys assisted their dad in his business, first by helping to pick up spent brass around the ranges and shoot house, then by cleaning the training weapons each night while the SWAT teams sat in meeting rooms, going over the day's actions.

Even as a small boy Court had been a mascot of the school. Though he didn't have his brother's obsession with guns, he'd been a natural with firearms, even better than his brother, and students from all over the country training at the school would bet handfuls of ammunition they could outshoot the ten-year-old son of the legendary James Gentry.

The older Gentry took all their bets, and invariably he'd end up with more loaded ammo to throw into his oil drum full of Court's winnings.

By the time Court was fourteen, he and his brother had found themselves at the center of the family business. Their dad would let them play hooky from school so they could serve as opposition forces pitted against visiting SWAT teams, waiting in the dark for cops to come into the shoot house with guns loaded with paintballs.

Often the Gentry boys would take down full eight- or twelve-man units without so much as a single splatter on their own bodies.

And more often than not furious police captains screamed red-faced at James Gentry, insisting the training was rigged against his men, because no one could believe a couple of teenaged brothers, one short-haired and personable, the other long-haired and reserved, could wipe out well-trained tactical units of veteran cops.

James Gentry sometimes allowed the captains to make the rules in the next drill, to stack the deck in favor of their own men, and often the result was the same.

But Court's rebellious nature grew exponentially in his late teens and he ran afoul of his taciturn father. Though Chance did his best to keep the peace between them, Court and James were two stubborn personalities, and conflict between them became the norm.

Court drifted away from Glen St. Mary as soon as he turned eighteen, and he ended up in Miami. There, looking for work, he took a job in security for a shady businessman and, with no clear understanding of what he was involved with, he slowly realized he had managed to become a henchman for a drug dealer. This career lasted exactly two months, and it ended abruptly when an attempt on his boss's life at Opa-locka Airport caused Court to pull out his Micro Uzi and open fire.

In five seconds three men were dead, and in thirty seconds more, Court was on his knees with his hands in the air, complying with the orders of the undercover DEA officer who stared him down over the barrel of his shotgun.

The fact that the dead men were all Cuban assassins did not get Court off the hook and, by age nineteen, it looked like he'd spend the rest of his life behind bars.

But a CIA officer who'd once taken a weeklong course at the tactical training center in Glen St. Mary found out about the older Gentry brother's misfortune, and he sent recruiters to the penitentiary where Gentry was serving time.

Accommodations were made, his record was expunged, and soon Court Gentry was in training at the CIA's facility in Harvey Point, North Carolina, to become a singleton operator for the CIA.

He never looked back, and he never returned to north Florida.

Until now.

Court lay prone under a pine tree, eighty yards from his father's drive-way. Through the scope of Zack Hightower's rifle he had line of sight on the front door of the double-wide, and he could see all the lights were off in the windows inside. He'd detected no sign of surveillance, and an F-250 pickup truck was parked in the drive just exactly at the angle his dad had always parked his car, so he thought the odds were good his dad was home.

As the sun came up a little more and the light grew, he took in more of the property.

Court saw his old beloved Bronco sitting up on blocks next to the garage. It was half-hidden by the weeds and covered in grime from twenty years of accumulation from the crab apple tree above it.

He'd come to rescue his dad, but for a moment he thought about saying "Screw it," leaving his father to the enemy, and just rescuing his old truck instead.

But not for too long. By eight a.m. he saw the first movement of some-thing larger than a rooster on the property—a new gray Chrysler 300 rolling up the dirt road towards his father's farm. It looked like it was probably a rental car, but after it stopped and two men climbed out, Court knew in a heartbeat these guys were either FBI or state investigators, or perhaps CIA officers posing as law enforcement.

Court lowered his eye back into the rifle scope and tracked the men carefully as they parked by the F-250 and headed up to the front door of his father's old trailer.

The door opened after a few knocks, and Court put his eyes in his bin-oculars. His father answered, and he stood there in worn boxers and an old gray T-shirt with the logo for the NRA on the front.

Court zoomed his binos in on his father's face.

"Jesus, Dad. You got old."

Court chastised himself immediately. The last time he'd seen his father's face, James would have been in his late forties. Court himself had been a teenager, and since then his life had been hard lived, to say the least.

He figured if anyone looked twenty years older than the last time the two had spoken, it would be Court.

The three men on the little wooden porch talked for over a minute, and

Court couldn't hear a bit of it. The Walker's Game Ear was in place, and he could clearly hear their voices, but with the ambient sounds of a steady breeze and the clucking chickens it was hard to make out much of the conversation.

Finally Court heard one word, spoken by his father, in a surprised, questioning tone.

"Breakfast?"

These goons were asking to take Court's dad to breakfast on this fine Saturday morning.

And this told Court exactly where they were heading.

He wanted to back away right now, but instead he waited, and he was glad he did, because James Gentry invited the men inside, presumably so he could change clothes. As soon as the door closed, Court began a quick but careful egress across a small field till he got to the higher brush near the pond, and then he stood in a crouch and began hurrying back to his Bronco.

As soon as he made it to his vehicle, he pulled out all the clothes in his backpack and began digging through them. He wanted to pick just the right attire to wear for the surveillance he had planned.

Five minutes later Court had already changed clothes, and he was pulling out of the trees and onto a dirt road.

There wasn't just one diner that served breakfast in Glen St. Mary. There were two. But as long as Court could remember, his father had only gone to one of them.

Court pulled into Ronnie's dressed in jeans, work boots, a canvas jacket, and a baseball cap. With these clothes and the three-day growth on his face he looked like every trucker, every farmhand, every male for ten miles in any direction.

He was the Gray Man—he knew he could remain invisible, even to the government types palling around with his father.

Court was already sitting at the counter, a cup of black coffee in front of him and a plate of toast and eggs on order, when his father entered with two men in suits. The elder Gentry wore jeans and a Carhartt pullover, a Caterpillar baseball cap, and Roper boots, and he nodded to the young waitress behind the counter. She greeted him by name and gave a quick but curious glance to the two men, as did another table of old-timers, but no one looked Court's way, not even his dad when he passed within feet of him on his way to his favorite table, a booth in the back corner.

Court had his Walker's Game Ear in his right ear and he had turned it up before the trio arrived, so when his eggs came he was able to position the hearing enhancer perfectly in line with the booth on his right while he ate.

In this way he could hear every word the men said.

"Again, Mr. Gentry. The two of you haven't had any contact in how long?"

Court listened to his dad sigh. He thought the old man sounded much older than he remembered him sounding, and his voice was slow, slurred a little.

Court had the impression his dad was drunk.

"I told you this morning, and I told your coworkers the other day when they came by."

"Sorry, Mr. Gentry, but we need you to tell us again."

"You fellers want to write it down this time? Might help you remember."

"Please, sir. How long?"

A sigh. "It's been nineteen years, give or take."

Court bit into his toast, and he heard the pages on a notepad flipping over at the corner booth.

"What do you do for a living, sir?"

"Social Security. I had a stroke a few years back. Can't work."

"Sorry to hear that."

"Shit happens," James said.

Court wanted to look to his father, but he fought the urge. He ate his bacon and looked at his plate, finding himself relieved the man was not, in fact, drunk.

One of the men said, "You had another son. Chance. He was a police officer for the City of Tallahassee."

A pause before the elder Gentry responded. "That's correct."

"He was killed in the line of duty."

"Are you asking me, or telling me? Because I already know."

Court knew about his brother, but it still hurt to hear his dad talk about it. He chanced a half glance to his right, but still kept his ear turned towards the booth. He saw his father looking out the window now.

He looks so damn rough, Court thought.

"So . . . you are saying Courtland missed his own brother's funeral?"

Gentry looked back to his breakfast. He waited to hear what his old man had to say about that.

"It's crazy," James replied. "The whole time that funeral was going on, I kept expecting Court to pop his head out from behind a tree, like he and Chance always did when they played cowboys and Indians as kids."

"How did that make you feel? Losing your son like that?"

"Chance died serving his community. You go into police work knowing that's on the table."

Court heard his father trying to be stoic, but Court wasn't buying it. Chance's funeral had probably just about killed him. It easily could have led to his stroke. Court felt like shit for not being there, but his access to the United States had been limited at the time, to say the least.

Court knew that if he had come to his brother's funeral, he probably would have been shot through the head by a Delta Force sniper and dropped into the hole meant for his brother.

Killed while in the service of his community.

The other goon took over now. "One thing is troubling me, Mr. Gentry. I've got to admit I think it's pretty interesting that you haven't asked us anything about your son. Aren't you curious as to why we are here? Don't you want to know if he's in some kind of trouble?"

James Gentry laughed boisterously, causing Court to flinch in his seat because the sound was so loud in his earpiece. Court caught himself in mid-flinch, then he looked into his coffee, hoping like hell no one had noticed his action.

His father did not reply to this for several seconds. So long to where Court almost gave in and looked over to his right to see if something was wrong. But he fought the urge and concentrated on his coffee.

Finally his father spoke again, but he sounded different. More slow, more measured. "I didn't ask if he was in trouble, because I *know* he's in trouble." He lightened a little. "C'mon, gents. I was a cop for a long time. Sharp-dressed assholes like you don't show up at my door to tell me my son has just won the Publishers Clearing House Sweepstakes."

Court fought a smile.

"You boys haven't asked me what I'd tell my son if he did show up down here in Glen St. Mary."

Court glanced at the booth quickly, pretending he was just looking out the window at the little parking lot. He saw the two strangers looking to each other—clearly the question wasn't important to them.

But James Gentry answered anyway. "Well, I'll tell you what I'd say. I'd tell him to turn his ass around and go back to wherever he came from. There ain't nothing for him down here at home but problems."

"Problems?"

"Yeah. I don't know what the hell he's gotten himself into this time, but this isn't the place to come looking to get away from whatever's after him."

Court slowly turned his head in the direction of his father now, and he saw that his father was looking right at him, all the way across the room.

The older Gentry continued, still looking directly at his son. "All over this place there is trouble. Everywhere. I'd tell him this town is virtually crawling with it."

His dad was making himself clear. He'd recognized his son and he was tipping him off. The area was under surveillance. Not just these two guys. The fact that Court hadn't identified anyone else just yet made him wonder if there were cameras, drones, or other measures out there he couldn't possibly see, or if his dad had noticed the arrival of other new faces to town, faces Court would not realize did not belong.

One of the men asked, "Why is it you think he might come back?"

"Oh, I'm not sayin' he would. But if he did come here, the only reason in the world would be because he thought maybe something he did might put me at risk. He'd feel responsible, I guess, and he'd come here to try to help. But if that should happen, I would just tell him that I was fine, as long as he wasn't here, because I'd be worried about him here more than anywhere else."

"Why would he come here to help you out? You said you two have been estranged for nearly twenty years. What makes you think he gives a damn?"

The senior Gentry seemed to think about this a long time. He'd turned away from looking towards Court, and now he looked at the two men in front of him. "I always figured he didn't care. But maybe I'm wrong. Maybe he grew up between the old days and now, and just maybe he understands that both of us said and did things we regret, so it's better we both forgive each other, because we're all the family we have left."

The two men looked at James Gentry, and then at each other, confused by the softening change in their interviewee.

Gentry continued, "Who knows? I guess if he did show up here, I would know all that was true. I'd like that, to tell you the truth, but then, like I said, I'd tell him to turn his ass around and get the hell out of here."

Court caught himself staring right at his dad, and his dad stared back at him while he said the last part. It was a terrible piece of tradecraft from the younger Gentry, but he'd been that focused on his father's words.

Court reached for his wallet, paid his bill with a twenty, then stood up from the counter.

The waitress picked up his check and the cash. "Let me grab your change, hon."

"You keep it."

"Well, you have yourself a good day, y'hear?"

"You, too."

He fought the urge to chance one more look towards the booth in the corner as he walked out the front door of the café and climbed back behind the wheel of his old Bronco, because he thought it highly unlikely he would ever see his father again.

62

Catherine King landed at Ben Gurion Airport after fourteen hours from Dulles through Zurich. She was tired from the flights, but as soon as she made her way through customs and pushed through the crowds to find the hired car waiting for her, she powered up her international phone and dialed a number back in the States.

It was nine a.m. in Washington, and Catherine thought Andy Shoal might be sleeping off a long night of work, but to her surprise he answered on the first ring. "Shoal."

"Hey, Andy, it's Cathy. I'm surprised I reached you so early. You up already?"

"Never went to bed. I spent all night in Chevy Chase trying to find new witnesses. I struck out. I got to Dupont Circle a couple hours ago and, so far at least, I've got nothing to show for it here, either."

"Keep plugging away," she said.

"How about you? Did you contact anyone while flying over?"

"I did. I exchanged e-mails with three former Mossad officers. Men I trust implicitly. They told me they know nothing about one of their assets being rescued in Trieste six years ago."

"And you believe them."

"I do, and that's what makes this interesting. All three of these men, after first saying they didn't have a clue what I was talking about, came back to me a couple hours later asking where I heard about this thing in Trieste. All three conversations turned threatening. Accusatory, even. It was surreal."

"Somebody got to them after they dug around for information."

"That's it exactly. Mossad knows what I'm after, and they are getting prickly. Not sure why, but it's curious."

"What's your plan now?"

"I'm heading to my hotel, but I'll call the other investigative reporters and see if they've got any leads on the injured Mossad officer. Maybe this guy will be a dead end, too, but I've come all this way."

"Is there anything you need me to do over here?" Andy asked. Catherine could hear the hopefulness in his voice.

"You are already doing it. Keep pounding the pavement. We have to find something that makes Six's story about what is happing in D.C. plausible. Even if I find information over here about Trieste, that doesn't mean Six is innocent of all those murders."

"Okay," Andy said. "But if you need anything at all, you don't have to bother your regular team. I'm sure they've got a lot to do. Give me a call and I'll jump on it."

"I know you will," she said.

Andy Shoal hung up the phone and went right back to work. He told himself he was working harder than anyone else on Catherine King's much higher-paid and much higher-regarded investigative team, and this was probably true. He'd already spent ten hours in Chevy Chase and Bethesda looking for any witnesses to the events that transpired there the previous Monday night.

Undaunted after a long night with nothing to show for it, this morning he arrived in Dupont Circle. He'd spent the last two hours—minus a twenty-minute break to step into the nearby Krispy Kreme for a breakfast of coffee and donuts—interviewing anyone who would talk to him about the event in the metro station here on Wednesday. He was looking for someone who could say they saw Max Ohlhauser before he was killed, or identify anyone else at the scene who had been part of the melee. If this mysterious Six's story was to pan out, if it was true he did not shoot Ohlhauser or the cops, then someone in this area just might have seen other people running around with guns.

He'd met several individuals throughout the morning who had been here during the shooting. Most lived in neighboring buildings or else they were employees of the bars, restaurants, and little shops around Dupont Circle. A few people confided in him they'd seen nothing, and others greatly exaggerated their access to the events in question.

One, a bartender at a Mexican restaurant who was getting ready for the brunch crowd, had, at first, seemed like he had a real contribution to make. He claimed to have seen wounded people being hauled out of the handicap elevator, just across the street from the window in front of his bar. Andy pulled out his notebook and started asking him follow-up questions.

"The injured. How bad were they?"

"They were bad off. Covered in blood, all three of them."

"What did they look like?"

"Like regular cops, I guess."

Andy cocked his head. "Cops?"

"Yeah. A couple of Metro police cars pulled up, and one group of cops loaded up another from the elevator."

At this moment, the *Washington Post* reporter knew this bartender was lying. No cops had been injured. All three of the Transit Police had been killed down below in the station, and Andy had been on scene before the bodies had been collected. On top of that, they had been loaded in ambulances, not squad cars.

Andy thanked the guy perfunctorily, although he wanted to punch him in the face for wasting his time, and he moved on, looking for someone who wasn't full of shit.

By eleven a.m. he felt ready to call it off. All the Red Bull and coffee in the District couldn't keep his mood up after so many fruitless conversations, and just the same as in Chevy Chase, the only people who had been around at the time of the event that Andy found had said they'd been standing around the police cordon filming after the shooting. He'd even watched a few examples of footage, and each time it was useless to him. Even if the recordings had been made early on, while events were still unfolding belowground, the only thing captured had been screaming and stampeding civilians and a few beat cops yelling for everyone to get the hell back.

A middle-aged Chinese sandwich maker at a chain sub shop at first didn't seem interested in talking to Andy, but after he ordered a foot-long pastrami, she was stuck chatting with him while she prepared it.

Andy said, "A lot of people out on the street are still talking about it."

"Yeah," she said as she squirted mustard and mayo on his bread. "It was crazy. Everybody running every way. Somebody said there was bomb."

Andy shook his head. "No bomb. A man with a gun."

"Yeah. I saw some people bleeding." She added, "I was just getting off work, walking to the Metro, when everybody started running out. I took some video, but I didn't see nothing important."

As she rang up his sandwich, he felt obliged to ask her what, specifically, she had recorded. "You don't have to show me—in fact, I have to take my lunch to go—but can you just briefly describe what you saw?"

She waved her hand away dismissively. "Nothing, really. Just the police taking the wounded cops off the elevator. Putting them in the car and driving off. That's all."

Andy cocked his head. He didn't think for a second that was what the woman had actually recorded, but there must have been some real confusion to the scene, considering the fact her story matched closely with what one of the other witnesses had said. "On second thought, can I take a look?"

It took the lady a minute to get her plastic gloves off and retrieve her phone from her purse in the back, and another minute to pull up the clip. She played it while holding it for Andy at first, but about thirty seconds into the video, he ripped it from her hands.

Then he said, "What the hell is this?"

It wasn't high quality by any stretch, but the video showed enough for Andy to realize he was seeing something that no one in the local police had admitted. These were clearly wounded D.C. Metro officers, three of them being helped out of the elevator and placed into a pair of cruisers. All three men bled from their faces, and two of them were all but dragged by their colleagues. Just as they finished loading them, the elevator door opened again, and another cop staggered out and fell into the arms of his colleagues. This man looked as if he was bleeding profusely from multiple gunshot wounds. He was placed inside one of the cruisers himself, and the cars rolled off, east on Q Street NW.

Right before the video ended, the squad cars rolled right by the woman holding the cellphone that made the recording.

When it was over, Andy looked up from the phone at the Chinese sandwich artist.

"Did you show this to the police?"

She shook her head and looked down. Andy had met enough foreigners in the District to read the signals. She didn't have papers to work legally here, so she kept her contact with authorities to a minimum.

He stopped the video and pushed it back a few seconds, then let it play again. The woman offered to sell him the entire phone for $500, but he declined, gave her a hundred bucks for her time, and e-mailed the video directly from her phone to his *Washington Post* e-mail account.

A minute later he was seated at a table in the restaurant, and the Chinese lady was looking at him like she thought he might try to steal her cell phone. Instead he pulled out his own phone and called a buddy in the D.C. Metro Motor Pool, an old cop who used to work out in District Seven but was rewarded with a cushy desk job for the last few years before retirement.

"What can I do for you, Andy?"

"I'm trying to find some cops, but I don't know their names, only the numbers of their squad cars. If I give you the numbers, can you tell me who drove them on a particular shift?"

"I could tell you what police district they were assigned to and what PSA—that's police service area. You could call somebody at that PSA and get more info. Who was behind the wheel depends on who was assigned to what unit that day. Bunch of variables."

Andy read the number on the first cruiser to the sergeant. As soon as he finished the sergeant said, "Nah, you're one number short."

"No, that's it. That's the entire number on the cruiser."

"Sorry, Andy. We haven't used that number since . . . well, let me look it up. Since nineteen ninety-seven."

Andy quickly read off the next number. It was six digits long.

The sergeant looked through his computer while Andy waited. "Okay. Yeah, that's a Chevy Tahoe, over in PSA four oh three. Actually . . . it's here in the motor pool for repair. It's been here for almost a week waiting on a new oil pump."

"You're sure it's not a Ford Taurus that was in Dupont Circle on Wednesday?"

"Sure as I can be, kid. Dupont is PSA two oh eight. Somehow you screwed both vehicle ID numbers up." The sergeant laughed. "It's all them nights, Andy. Get you some sleep, kid."

"Will do. Thanks." Andy hung up the phone and slipped it back into his pocket, certain now that he was sitting on the biggest story in America.

Fake cops involved in a shoot-out in the middle of Washington, D.C.

While Tel Aviv would be Catherine's ground zero for getting to the mystery of the story about Six, Andy's ground zero was right here, just a mile away from the *Washington Post*'s headquarters.

"Oh my God," he said to himself, but he knew there was much about this he didn't understand. He worried that if he called Catherine King right now with what he knew, she'd just pass on his information to her investigative reporters. In fact, he was certain of it.

No, Andy told himself. He'd dig into this even deeper, connect the dots, and only go to King when he had done the investigative reporting himself.

He looked up at the woman behind the counter. "Do you guys sell coffee?"

63

Jordan Mayes arrived at Langley at eight in the morning and then, after dropping off his coat and briefcase on the seventh floor, he attended a few meetings he had scheduled with staffers who were working through the weekend. Just after noon he took the elevator down to four to visit the Violator TOC. He was surprised to find Brewer out of the office. But he'd just poured himself a cup of coffee when she entered, briefcase and travel mug in hand.

She looked like she had just changed into fresh clothes. Mayes wasn't a particularly kind man, although working his entire career next to a frosty personality like Denny Carmichael made him appear that way sometimes. But still, he found himself pleased to know Brewer had scheduled a break to rest and attend to herself.

"Hope you had a chance to recharge your batteries," he said as he held up the pot to refill Brewer's cup.

But she shook her head and took him to the side of the room. "Actually, sir, I've been up all night. Most of it here. I had a change of clothes in my office, but I haven't been home in over forty-eight hours."

Mayes was about to order her to leave the TOC for four hours to go home and catch some sleep in a real bed, but she took him by the arm and led him even farther away from the group. "Sir, I'm glad you are here. I need you to see something."

For the next five minutes Brewer showed Mayes a collection of images from all the Violator sightings of the past week. Specifically, these images were of a group of Middle Eastern–looking men who showed up either during or just after several of the sightings.

"What made you look for these men in the first place?"

"Dakota, the JSOC operative. He and his team had noticed these unknown subjects at multiple locations."

Mayes was as confused by this as Brewer, and he told her so, but he got the impression she did not believe him. When he asked her for her conclusions as to who these individuals were, she seemed to weigh each word carefully before it came out of her mouth.

"My conclusion is, either someone working here in the TOC, or someone in a leadership role who has access to real-time TOC analysis, is sending this proxy force out into the field to assist with the Violator operation."

Mayes said, "That leaves someone in this room"—he looked around and counted twelve analysts and technicians, all of whom he had known for some time—"including yourself, myself . . . and Denny, of course."

Suzanne Brewer agreed. "I recognize the fact I might not be read into everything going on, but I can't help but think some of my concerns earlier in the week that I was missing part of the puzzle might make a little more sense now."

"You thought Gentry did not shoot Babbitt or Ohlhauser, and you thought Gentry had been injured somewhere other than in Chevy Chase."

"Yes, sir."

Jordan Mayes was confused, and didn't know what to make of all this, and this made him feel both impotent and angry. He took it out on his subordinate. "Well, Suzanne, what do you want me to say? These images are indeed troubling, but I don't have the answers for you. I can assure you Denny and I aren't running these personalities ourselves. If your operation here is tainted, you need to get a handle on it posthaste. We have enough problems without a group of unknowns shadowing our movements."

"Yes, sir," she said, and Mayes saw in her face she wished she hadn't brought it up at all.

He returned to his office and had just sat down when he received a call from one of the electronic intelligence technicians he'd assigned to the Catherine King operation the evening before.

"Mayes."

"Sir, it's Kevin Morvay calling from the fifth floor, Signals Intelligence. You asked us to notify you if we found anything of interest in the e-mail of Andrew Shoal at the *Post*?"

"I'm listening."

"Uh . . . would it be possible for you to come up to my cubicle? I think you should see this in person, and I don't really want to forward it."

Court did not leave Glen St. Mary immediately after seeing his father. Instead he drove into the woods behind his old high school, parked his Bronco, and slept for over three hours. He woke just after noon, feeling surprisingly good, and then he made his way back to I-10, which would take him west to I-95.

He'd only driven a few minutes when he saw the sign for the Econo Lodge just off the road in Macclenny. On a whim he pulled off the interstate, then rolled into the parking lot. He checked the tags on every car in the lot, looking for D.C., Virginia, or even Maryland plates. These would either be CIA or feds, down here hunting for him. His father had hinted that the area was crawling with people who didn't belong, so Court expected to see cars belonging to the surveillance members.

But he saw nothing at all other than local vehicles, and a few from nearby Georgia.

It was the middle of the day, so he wondered if all the CIA vehicles were now deployed out on the streets. With a shrug he started to head back to the interstate, but then he noticed a Travelodge Suites, just across from the Econo Lodge. It looked dead over there—only a dozen or so vehicles were in sight—but he drove over anyway and began checking license plates on the cars parked at the small two-story property.

In the front of the building he saw no cars with tags that aroused suspicion; so he turned around the side of the building and headed into the back. Immediately he was surprised by the number of vehicles. While only a dozen cars had been parked out front, there were twice that number in back.

Court passed them by, careful to keep the bill of his ball cap low.

He thought there was a good chance he would find Virginia plates, making it likely they were CIA, but instead he found tags from Florida, Georgia, and Alabama. Four more vehicles, all large sixteen-passenger vans, were parked at the end of the row, and all four had North Carolina tags.

North Carolina? The first thing that came to mind was Fort Bragg, home of JSOC. Court couldn't really picture thirty or forty Delta Force or SEAL Team 6 shooters rolling down in a bunch of passenger vans, but he couldn't rule it out.

Curious, but just barely, Court committed two of these tags to memory as he passed, then he returned to the street.

He drove back to the Econo Lodge and parked. Then he pulled out his smartphone. He surfed the web to a site that offered registration information about license plate numbers to anyone who paid a ten-dollar fee.

Court pulled out one of his prepaid credit cards and typed in some numbers, then he put in the first tag number.

The page thought for nearly a minute, then it spit out a few lines of information.

The car was registered to a corporate fleet in Perquimans County, North Carolina.

Court's blood ran cold.

Harvey Point was in Perquimans County.

Quickly he typed in the second tag number and found it was registered to the same fleet. These were CIA vehicles, Court had no doubt, and they'd come from the Point. Court only knew two ground unit divisions of the CIA that were permanently billeted at the Point. One was the Special Activities Division; they had a Ground Branch installation there. The other was the Autonomous Asset Program.

Matt Hanley had told him Ground Branch was not involved in the hunt for him. That left AAP. Court wondered if Denny had them taking part in the hunt.

Court all but burned rubber getting back on I-10. He had a mission now, a place to go. He wasn't sure he could pull it off, but he had every intention of infiltrating Harvey Point and going back to where it all began.

Jordan Mayes drove alone through the gates of Alexandria Eight. He wasn't supposed to go anywhere without his bodyguards, but he'd slipped out without letting the security logistics office know, and he'd taken his own car, which had been parked in the lot at Langley for the past week.

Here at the safe house he stopped halfway up the driveway, showed his credos to the guard force positioned there, and then continued on to the front door. He climbed out of his car, pulled out a briefcase, and walked into the building. In the large great hall he was checked and wanded and his briefcase was opened and looked through, and then he walked alone up to the second-floor south wing doorway.

He crossed the wide and high south wing hall into the large conference room, made a right, and entered the narrow hallway there. This led him past the bathroom on his left, and then, also on his left, the stairs up to the attic. Beyond this Mayes found DeRenzi and two other security officers standing in the open doorway to Denny's office. The men parted with a nod to let the second-in-command of the National Clandestine Service through, and then Mayes found Denny sitting at a table by the window and working on a laptop.

Denny looked up. "What is it?"

Mayes said nothing.

Carmichael looked to the security team. "DeRenzi. Step out."

"Yes, sir." The three men left and shut the door behind them.

"Talk."

Mayes walked over to the table, and he stood over Carmichael. "Your attempts to play this entire hand so close to your vest that even I don't know what you are doing have failed you, Denny."

"Meaning what?"

"Meaning this." Mayes opened his briefcase, took out an iPad, turned it on, and offered it to Denny. Confused, Carmichael took it.

Carmichael saw a film waiting to run, so he tapped the "play" icon with the tip of his finger.

It was the video Andy Shoal had obtained from the woman working in the sandwich shop that morning.

Carmichael watched the entire video without comment and without emotion. When it was over, he simply handed the device back.

"Where did you get it?"

"Out of the e-mail account of Andrew Shoal, the *Washington Post* reporter. It came from an account belonging to a woman who works at a fast-food restaurant in Dupont Circle. So far Shoal hasn't sent it anywhere else. I had the tech alter the coding of the video, corrupt it, which just means if he tries to send it now it won't play. But he's seen it, he obviously gave some import to what he saw there, and the woman who recorded it presumably still has it on her mobile device."

Carmichael looked out the window. "What do you think you see there, Mayes?"

Mayes couldn't believe the question. "Obviously, Denny, it shows a bunch of wounded cops who I seriously doubt are cops. One of these men looks like he probably died within minutes. Nothing like this was reported by Metro D.C. If this gets out, the press will—"

Carmichael shouted, tension in his voice, "It won't get out!"

"Tell me what is going on, Denny."

The older man rubbed his face in his hands a moment. After some delay he nodded, looked back to Mayes, and softly said a name.

"Al-Kazaz."

Mayes cocked his head. "The Saudi intel chief? I know you are old acquaintances. What does this have to do with him? These are his men?"

"You might say, for purposes of the Violator operation . . . these are *my* men."

Jordan Mayes started to sit down in a chair at the table, but it was as if his knees gave out suddenly near the end of the movement. He dropped roughly into the chair.

"Mother of God."

Over the next thirty minutes, Denny Carmichael told Jordan Mayes everything about Gentry and the Saudi relationship to him.

Not just their service in the Violator hunt—but *everything*.

When Carmichael finished, his second-in-command looked out the window to the southwest. A thick bank of clouds grew low, gray, and ominous, approaching like a wall closing in on Washington, D.C. After a moment Mayes just said, "Jesus Christ, Denny."

Carmichael kept his eyes on Mayes's face. "Of course, you see the problem here."

Mayes nodded distractedly. Then, "Of course I do. Why didn't you—"

Carmichael interrupted. "Anything I did or did not do is all water under the bridge now, isn't it? Could I have managed this better from the beginning? Absolutely. I acknowledge that. But you see I had to make a series of on-the-fly critical decisions. Some I got right. A great many, as a matter of fact, but they have been eclipsed in importance by the very few decisions I got wrong."

He shrugged. "And here we are today. You are now in the fold, and I need to know that I can count on you for the good of the future of this Agency."

Mayes finally looked away from the window and towards his superior. "You just told me all this so I would know the stakes."

"I just told you because you asked me to tell you."

"Bullshit. If I turn and walk away, you'll send Hightower or someone else to term me."

Carmichael's face was impassive. "Of course not. Jordan. That's ludicrous. We've been together for twenty-five years."

"We have . . . and that's the first time you've ever called me Jordan." He stood and headed for the door on shaky legs.

Carmichael followed him. "You walk out on this and you know what this will do to the Clandestine Service. You *have* to see this through now. Court Gentry must die, because if he reveals what he knows, our human intelligence operations will be set back a generation."

Mayes thought about everything Carmichael had just told him. It was true. Right or wrong—and right now this all seemed so *fucking* wrong— Gentry had to be terminated. If not, Carmichael's assertion that CIA covert HUMINT would suffer for a generation seemed, if anything, like an understatement.

He said, "This is a lot to take in, Denny. I just need to go home. I just need to think."

Carmichael's severe face hardened even more. Mayes had never seen colder eyes in his life.

Carmichael said, "Think all you want, Mayes. But do your thinking alone, and in silence."

"Yes, sir," he said, and he left through the door to the narrow hallway, passing DeRenzi and his men without a word.

64

The café on Tel Aviv's King George Street offered outdoor seating that afforded a nice view of Meir Garden, but Mossad officer Yanis Alvey wasn't taking in the view. He sipped his espresso at a small table outside, but mostly he just sat there, looking at nothing and no one. A smoky bus thumped by, and other patrons at the tables around recoiled or covered their noses.

Alvey just ignored it, lost in his melancholy.

The sun had set an hour earlier, and the evening air cooled more and more each minute. Alvey wore a short-sleeve shirt with a light cashmere vest over it, not enough to ward off the April breeze, but he wasn't thinking about the cool air, either.

He sensed movement in front of him and he looked up in time to see a middle-aged brunette with a small backpack hanging off her shoulder standing at the foot of his little bistro table. For an instant he thought she looked familiar, but he could not place her. She looked down at him, though, like she knew him well.

An uncomfortable feeling for an intelligence officer, to be sure, especially when he recognized the person, but he did not know from where.

"Mr. Alvey?" she asked.

English. That caused him to refine his hunt to put a name to the face. A name was on the tip of his tongue for an instant, and then it melted off. No.

"Who are you?" he asked. Refusing to confirm his ID before getting more information.

"My name is Catherine King. I am with the *Washington Post*."

Instantly he knew exactly who she was; he'd seen her on television, and he'd read hundreds of columns she'd written over the years. He began to stand to leave. His eyes flickered all around, hunting for a suitable escape route.

"Please wait. Sit down with me a moment. I'm not going to ask you anything. Not yet, anyway. I need to tell you something. After I tell you, if you like, you can get up and walk away, and I promise I will not pursue you."

Alvey kept the nervous furtive eyes, but he lowered back to his seat.

The waiter came and she ordered an espresso. Alvey declined her offer to buy him another.

Soon she said, "A mutual acquaintance of ours told me this story. It's a good one. I speak to liars with depressing regularity, but I believe this man believes what he is saying. That doesn't make it true, mind you. I'm just letting you know I am normally quite skeptical of tall tales."

"Who is the acquaintance?"

"He wouldn't give me his name, but you know who he is."

Alvey smiled. Bemused. "Without his name, I highly doubt that. I know a lot of men."

"Yes, but how many of them shot you in the stomach in a Hamburg stairwell?"

Alvey measured his breathing carefully. Intent on not giving any of his emotions away. "Not so many."

"I presumed as much. Well, this man is in serious trouble. He thinks just maybe you might be able to help him."

The muscles in Yanis Alvey's neck twitched. "Help him, Ms. King? *Help* him? If he were sitting where you are sitting right now, I would dive across this table with this butter knife and stab it through his heart. I don't want to help him. I want to kill him."

Catherine King had not expected this at all. "But why?"

"Because he is a bad and dangerous individual. Dangerous to my nation, the nation I have sworn to protect with my life. Yes, I helped this man in the past, but that was before I knew the truth."

"He tells me he is innocent," she said, her voice unsure now. Then she said, "Why would he send me all the way over here to prove he was innocent if he wasn't?"

Alvey seemed to think this over for a moment. Finally he nodded. Said, "The reason is obvious. He has no idea what he has done."

"Will you tell me?"

"Why should I talk to a reporter?"

"Because I have information, too, Mr. Alvey. Perhaps you are curious. And perhaps . . . the both of us can piece some things together that might be interesting."

Alvey looked away. "I'm not curious at all."

King persisted. "You have seen the news from Washington. Our mutual friend is the one at the center of this. The one being blamed for everything. Perhaps you think he's done something wrong, and that's why you would wring his neck if you got the chance, but can you really say you believe he is crisscrossing D.C. on a mass murder spree?"

Alvey looked back to the woman from the *Post*. "No. I don't believe he would do that."

"Then the CIA is after the wrong man. If you can help them with your information, wouldn't you? Together maybe we can figure this out."

Slowly Alvey stood from the table. Catherine thought he was going to walk away without another word, but instead he surprised her. "We can take my car. We will talk while we drive. A running meet, we call it. A café like this is not safe for such stories. Not even stories from long ago."

Catherine stood and followed.

Andy Shoal had spent all of Saturday afternoon in his apartment in Arlington, sitting on his couch with his notebook computer on his lap.

He'd begun working on a new story without telling anyone what he had, for one simple reason. He needed to *know* what he had, and he was confused by how today's evidence fit in with everything else he and Catherine had learned in the past week.

On his notebook computer in front of him he had a hundred or so data points—all the reporting that had been done in the past full week. Beginning with his first conversation with Detective Rauch, just after midnight on Sunday morning in Washington Highlands, and ending with the discovery that a group of armed men dressed as cops and riding around in fake squad cars had been wounded in the shoot-out in the Metro that killed former CIA chief council Max Ohlhauser.

He thought back to all the blood on the ground in Bethesda. He and Catherine had decided it couldn't have come from someone who had already been bleeding for hours. He also thought about the vigilante nature of the shooting on Rhode Island Avenue, and about how much it contrasted with the other attacks of the past week.

It was as if there were different groups operating at the same time, in the same places, and now he had evidence that proved this to be true. These ten men in the video from Dupont Circle—Andy counted four wounded and six others—were some sort of hit team.

He was so worried that these men might be American spies that he didn't want to contact the CIA to ask for a statement, and he was too early in this even to contact Catherine. If he was going to make it into the ranks of King's investigative team, he would need to show he could do more than pound pavement and get people to talk. He needed to put puzzles together himself.

He closed his laptop and rubbed his bloodshot eyes. Leaning his head back against the back of his sofa for a moment, he realized he needed some caffeine to keep going.

At six p.m. he went downstairs to the tiny convenience store in his building, planning on buying some protein and a Red Bull to help him power through for just a few hours more.

He was the only customer in the shop; the nice Indian lady who nearly always worked the two p.m. to ten p.m. shift was the only other person in sight. He gave her a tired smile as he passed her stacking cartons of yogurt in the front cooler.

In the back he snatched up a cold Red Bull, then he grabbed a roast beef sandwich nearly the size of a football that was wrapped in microwave-safe plastic. Heading back to the front he heard a noise and looked up. Three men in black raincoats filed into the market, moving purposefully.

The Indian clerk said, "Can I help—"

And then she stopped talking. She backed up into the stacked crates of yogurt, knocking them all to the floor, and then she tumbled over on top of them.

Andy thought she had just been clumsy, so he rushed to help her up, but only for a few steps, because now he saw the guns. Two of the three men in raincoats had pulled silenced pistols, and they raised them out in front of their bodies.

Andy dropped his sandwich and his can of Red Bull and he stood there. A deer in the headlights as he stared down the barrel of a long black gun.

While one of the Saudi assets raised his Glock and fired at the primary target, a second asset eliminated the bystander by firing several suppressed rounds into her head.

The third asset did not even draw a weapon. Instead, he walked directly to the counter, stepped behind it, and located the security camera Blu-ray recorder. He popped out the disk running in the machine, and he slipped it into his pocket. He then turned the Blu-ray player off, giving the impression it had not been running today at all.

By the time he finished he heard the last cries for mercy from the man on the floor. The asset behind the counter did not even pause to look at the target. Instead he just went to the front door and held it open for his two colleagues, who both slipped their weapons into their raincoats before calmly walking out into the late afternoon.

The third asset followed.

After only thirty seconds inside the convenience store the three Saudis were back on the street. An old van with stolen plates pulled up to the curb, and the three men climbed in, barely breaking stride.

65

ourt slept four full hours at a rest stop just south of Savannah, Georgia, then he woke up as refreshed as he'd been in weeks and pulled back onto the highway. His meeting with his father—actually, he knew he couldn't really call it that, considering there was no conversation between them—had left him feeling settled in a positive way that felt foreign to him, but it was a good feeling, and it had helped him push through the miles heading back north.

Music had propelled him on, as well. On the radio he'd found a station here in North Carolina that played a good mix of Southern rock, the stuff he and his brother grew up loving.

An old Tom Petty tune was playing now and Court had the volume up as loud as it would go. He was enjoying the rock and the old Ford Bronco. He was still tired, the wound in his ribs still hurt, and his future was still very much in doubt, but all things considered, he wasn't having a bad day at all.

He realized he'd been driving along for the past few hours without checking his phone, so he lifted it from the center console and looked at it.

His RedPhone app showed four missed connections. He'd also received a text.

Driving along at seventy miles an hour, he opened the text.

Crucial that I reach you. Call me, no matter the time. —Cathy

The text and the calls that preceded it had been received about an hour earlier, and it was now nine p.m., and this disappointed Court greatly. Not because he'd missed the calls, but rather because, due to the seven-hour time difference between the East Coast and Israel, the calls and text had begun around four a.m. in Tel Aviv. Court doubted Catherine would be calling him in the middle of the night her time, which meant she probably had not gone to Israel, after all.

He assumed she was still in D.C.

Still, he punched his code into the RedPhone app, then he typed in her number.

The phone rang twenty times before he gave up and disconnected the call.

He listened to the last few bars of Tom Petty's "Rebels," and then he turned off on Highway 64, heading east.

Court stopped at a twenty-four-hour Walmart in Rocky Mount, and he bought everything he needed to conduct the operation he had planned for this evening, but he also bought a lot of things he didn't need, so as better to obfuscate his plan. It wasn't as if he thought the cashier was going to turn him in to the CIA thinking he was about to perform a solo frogman raid on a secure military and intelligence installation, but Court knew there was a possibility the cameras in the store would pick up a usable image of his face, and if this happened, he wanted to minimize any chance Agency analysts would be able to determine just how, in fact, he planned on going about his operation.

He hoped the camera feeds this far away from the District weren't being pulled into the dragnet for evaluation by the NSA's facial recog computers. If they were, he had to just pray no one would expect him to go to Harvey Point, or if they did, that they didn't expect him to get the materiel necessary for such a high-risk clandestine operation at a twenty-four-hour Walmart.

After he loaded up his purchases he drove east for most of an hour, until he could see water on both sides of the road. He made a left on Osprey Drive and took it till the road ended, and here he turned south onto an unmarked road. Of course he would be significantly stealthier if he went lights out on this drive, but Court understood enough about his opposition on this mission to know that it didn't really matter. The entire guard force at the Point operated with night observation devices, so they would see him anyway, and if they saw a truck rolling down the road with its lights extinguished, they would presume the occupant of that truck was up to no good.

Court knew it would be much better if he just operated like he belonged right where he was.

He stopped when he ran out of asphalt; right in front of him he saw water. He stood on Drummond Point, still a few miles to the southwest of Harvey Point, which lay on the opposite shore of the Yeopim River.

Court climbed out of the Bronco, ran around to the back, and opened the swing-out tailgate. He retrieved his newly purchased gear, then he changed clothes, going head-to-toe in dark brown, with a black watch cap on his head. He then donned a black rain suit, covering his body in light-weight waterproof lining. He cinched short lengths of bungee cord around his waist, his ankles, and his wrists, to further waterproof his outfit, and he used black silicone waterproof tape down the middle of the rain jacket to seal it more, even wrapping a long strip around his neck.

Court had no scuba gear, nor did he have a boat, but he had spent literally hundreds of hours in the waters of the Albemarle Sound, an estuary that led to the Atlantic, and the Yeopim River, which flowed into the sound. And he knew how the currents moved here. All he would need to do to get where he was going was to stay relatively buoyant and to float out into the river, let the water take him east, and then work his way across to the other shore.

The rain suit wouldn't remain perfectly watertight, but the air pockets created by it would increase his buoyancy markedly.

He only needed to float past the security fence that cut Harvey Point off from the mainland, avoid the Coast Guard and base security patrol boats, and make his way to land. From there it would be a long walk through cypress swamp woods to the road that led to the CIA's Special Activities Division Autonomous Asset facility.

Court loaded his suppressed pistol into a small waterproof backpack, along with his cash, wallet, phone, a flashlight, and other small odds and ends. After he sealed the bag up, he slung it around on his chest, and then he walked down to the water's edge at the tip of Drummond Point. Looking at his watch, he saw it was eleven p.m.

He waded out until he felt the current, then he knelt down and began swimming along with the natural flow of the estuary, drifting him east-ward, as the brackish water attempted to return to the sea, carrying along with it broken branches, trash, and a lone man with a vague mission to find out why his past was trying to kill him.

Suzanne Brewer left the exit of the Old Headquarters Building at eleven p.m., rushing through the south lot to her car.

It had been a long day that was, ultimately, just the most recent in a string of long days, but a new lead had presented itself, and she decided to go check it out personally.

She hadn't planned on going alone, but she was having trouble getting in touch with Jordan Mayes. Carmichael was at his safe house in Alexandria, of course, and Brewer had just called looking for Mayes, but Carmichael said he wasn't returning his calls to him, either, and a security team had been dispatched both to his house and to check the route from Alexandria to Langley.

She arrived at her BMW and put her hand on the door latch, unlocking the doors because her Bluetooth key fob sent an unlocking code to the vehicle letting it know it was in the possession of the person at the driver's door.

"Suzanne?" She jumped when she heard her name called. She turned around to find Jordan Mayes walking towards her in the parking lot. He was alone, which was odd, because this was the first time she'd seen him without the security men since Violator had arrived in the States.

Brewer said, "I've been calling you for the past hour. So has Denny." His tie was loose and his eyes were wide and rimmed with red. Everyone in the Violator Working Group was utterly exhausted, but Suzanne got the impression Jordan Mayes was more than tired; it appeared as if he had been drinking. "What's wrong?"

He walked around to the passenger's side of her BMW. "Let's go for a ride."

Brewer looked around in confusion. "Where are we going?"

"Nowhere specific. I need to talk to you."

"If it's confidential, why can't we just go back in the office?"

Mayes just shook his head.

After a moment Brewer understood he did not want to talk inside the building. She did not understand, but she climbed behind the wheel nevertheless.

Mayes reached into his coat and pulled out a case just larger than a cell phone. Suzanne recognized it immediately. It was a Faraday cage, a protective case that blocked radio frequency waves. Placing a phone or other device that emitted radio signal inside would make the device untraceable. The CIA used Faraday cages for smartphones, primarily, which had difficult-to-remove batteries.

He handed her the small case. "Put your phone in this."

"Come on. Really?"

"Really."

She took the case, locked her phone inside, then placed the case in the storage compartment under the armrest between the front seats. Mayes questioned whether she had an iPad or other device with GPS enabled in the vehicle. She knew her BMW itself surely transmitted location info through its computer, but she didn't mention this.

With a hint of sarcasm she said, "We're off the grid, Jordan. What's up?"

"Just drive."

No words were exchanged while they left the lot, because Suzanne's focus was on evaluating Mayes's condition, but as soon as the BMW began heading east on Dolley Madison Boulevard, she knew she needed to hear what he had to say, because she had other things to deal with. "I am heading into the District. One of Dakota's men is sitting on a house where a possible sighting was called in. I was trying to find you because I wanted you to come along, anyway. What is it you need to tell me?"

When he didn't answer immediately, she looked at him. His head lolled a little to one side, then popped back up. Catherine was sure now that the number two man in the National Clandestine Service was drunk.

Mayes spoke softly. "He's using a foreign kill squad."

"*What?* Who is?"

"Carmichael."

Suzanne Brewer did not speak for a moment. She realized she didn't want to hear any more, but she also realized there was no way she could shut Mayes down. She asked, "What makes you think this?"

Mayes's head lolled over in her direction now, and he said, "Because he told me!"

"Christ," she whispered. "Who are they?"

"They are Saudis. Working for Murquin al-Kazaz." Now he looked up at Brewer with suspicion. "You knew! Did you know?"

"Of course not. The JSOC team leader asked me who else was involved. He had some suspicions, so that made me wonder. But I knew better than to bring it up with Denny." She shrugged. "Or you, for that matter."

Jordan Mayes shrugged. "Good for you. I *didn't* know better. I confronted him when I saw the video."

"*What* video?"

"Saudi gunmen in D.C. police uniforms at the Dupont Metro."

Suzanne knew nothing about such a recording. "Where is this video now?"

"Morvay in SIGINT has it. He showed me. He took it off of Andy Shoal's e-mail account."

Brewer's stomach turned. She grabbed onto the wheel as hard as she could. She closed her eyes slowly for a moment while she drove, then she opened them again. "You don't know, do you?"

"Know what?"

"Andy Shoal was murdered two hours ago."

Jordan Mayes looked at her, then he dropped his head into his hands, doubling over in the seat. "He'll kill me, too."

"Carmichael? Don't be ridiculous. Odds are it was Violator who killed Shoal. He was out looking for more evidence in the assassinations."

"Bullshit. I doubt Gentry has killed anybody this week. Sure, Brandywine Street and the Easy Market, those were him. The rest were either Hightower or the Saudis." He looked at Suzanne, terror in his eyes. "It's all a big wall of fun-house mirrors, Suzanne. Denny is controlling it all, but it's gotten too big for him to manage. He'll *have* to kill me to protect himself now."

Suzanne still didn't believe there was any chance Denny Carmichael would kill Jordan Mayes, and she told him so.

"You don't know everything I know, Suzanne."

"You just told me. Or have you forgotten?"

"What I just told you barely scratches the surface of what's been going on."

Suzanne Brewer slowed her BMW, and then she pulled into a convenience store right before the on-ramp onto the George Washington Parkway. Here she bought Mayes a large black coffee.

Five minutes later the two of them sat parked under a streetlight in the parking lot at Fort Marcy Park, just off the parkway. There wasn't a single other vehicle in sight.

"I want you to tell me everything, Jordan."

"You aren't cleared for everything."

"If you really feel Carmichael might come after you, does it scare you that you are the only one who knows?"

This sank in a moment. Mayes took a gulp of molten coffee. "Okay. I'll tell you. But then we **go to Justice** with this. I'm not going down on a sinking ship."

Suzanne said, "And neither am I. If what you tell me warrants it, you're *damn right* we're going to DOJ."

Mayes nodded, relaxed markedly, and said, "Do you know anything about Operation BACK BLAST?"

Suzanne Brewer shook her head. "Never heard of it."

So Jordan Mayes told her.

66

Suzanne Brewer looked at her hands folded in her lap, and she realized they were shaking. Perspiration formed on her temples, and her mouth was dry.

She and Mayes were still sitting in her BMW in Fort Marcy Park. Blustery rain pelted the side of her car now, and the light from the streetlamp above them was at times blotted out with the movement of the tree branches. Mayes had been talking for most of the past hour, but not all of it had been productive. On the contrary, eighty percent of what Mayes said had been, as far as Brewer was concerned, the ramblings of an inebriated man who, for the first time in his life, felt free to let years of suspicion flow about his superior. He'd produced a flask filled with scotch, and it loosened his lips even more. He needed to talk, so she let him, but after she learned about Operation BACK BLAST and Denny's involvement with the Saudis here in the U.S., she had stopped listening, and she had begun thinking about what she would do next.

The information she possessed could certainly put Denny Carmichael in prison, and it could conceivably destroy CIA clandestine ops. But it was even bigger than that, as far as she was concerned. Once she got over the shock of it all, she realized this was a watershed moment in her career, in her life. The decision she made now, right this minute, would set the course for her future.

Mayes looked her up and down through eyes at half mast. "Right now you are at the point I found myself in this afternoon. I'd asked for an answer, and when I got it, I really wished I didn't know. Now we both know, so now we have to end this. I am friends with Juan Ferreria, the deputy director of the FBI, we can go to his place in Tysons right now, wake him up, and get the ball rolling with DOJ."

Suzanne hesitated. "I think we need to think carefully about our next move."

"What do you mean? We said we'd take this to Justice."

But Suzanne wasn't thinking about justice, duty, or even right and wrong. She was thinking about leverage. In her meteoric career she would never have more power than she had at this moment. She didn't want to dispel that power by telling the FBI what she knew.

She didn't want to destroy the CIA.

She wanted to *run* the CIA.

Suzanne started her car and pulled back out onto the George Washington Parkway, heading in the direction of Tysons Corner. There was some traffic out at midnight, but she was able to move along at the speed limit. She would play along with Jordan, just to buy some time, but she would spend the fifteen-minute-long drive trying to talk him out of revealing anything to the Department of Justice until they knew exactly what they were doing.

She said, "You and I need to make sure we won't get caught up in the fallout of all this."

"We are the ones going to the feds. I'm not worried about getting indicted. I'm worried about getting killed!"

Suzanne said, "In light of this information, I agree Denny is compromised, and I agree he might become desperate. But I don't think you have any reason to worry."

"Yeah?" Mayes said, clearly not buying what she was selling. "Why is that?"

She pulled into the right lane. Her BMW hummed along at sixty miles an hour without any effort at all. On her left a motorcycle with a passenger riding behind the driver kept pace with her. It was an unusual sight in the heavy rain, but she was focused on the road ahead and on the man sitting to her right.

She said, "Think about it, Jordan. You two have worked together forever. Say what you want about Denny Carmichael, but he's a pragmatist. He knows he needs friends in that building right now, and you have shown yourself to be a faithful—"

Suzanne Brewer noticed new movement on her left now, out her driver-side window. Through the rainfall she saw the motorcycle encroaching into her lane. At first she thought he'd just drifted over to the right accidentally, but it took less than a second for her to realize that the passenger's arm was outstretched, towards her window.

In his hand was a gun, pointed nearly at contact distance with the glass inches from her head.

She only had time to tap her brake pedal, barely slowing the vehicle, before the flash of light assaulted her eyes and the pound of a gunshot rocked her eardrums. Her windshield exploded in her face, and to her right she heard the passenger-side window shatter.

She felt the glass in her hair, blood at her hairline and on her left cheek. Somehow she kept her BMW on the road, so she stomped on the gas now, and the six-cylinder engine accelerated.

She had the wherewithal to drop her right hand from the wheel and punch a button on the center console of the vehicle, shifting the BMW into Sport Mode. Her head slammed back into the headrest as the car launched forward, her suspension stiffened and improved markedly. Her luxury sedan was now a sports car, racing ahead and surprising the assassins on the motorcycle with its power.

She centered her car on the white dashes on the road and weaved right between a pair of vehicles taking up the two lanes in front of her, and then she jacked back to the left, pulling in front of the motorcycle as it went left around the car in the left lane. The bike was forced to brake to avoid rear-ending her, but when she looked in her rearview she saw two more bikes race past the first. Both of them had riders on back as well, and she knew this was far from over.

The sound of their engines came through the shattered window by her face, along with the cool rain.

For the first time since the gunshot she looked over to Jordan Mayes. He hadn't made a noise, so she expected to find him slumped over in his seat dead, but instead he just held his hand against the lower part of his face. Blood dripped through his fingers.

"How bad is it?" she asked.

"I . . . I don't know." He took his hand away. The bullet had cut across his chin; a flap of skin hung open and blood gushed. From the location of the wound Suzanne knew it wasn't life-threatening, but it was certainly messy. Mayes leaned towards the rearview to get a look for himself, but when he looked in the mirror he shouted, "They are still coming!" He covered the wound again with his hand.

Another pop from a pistol behind them, then the sound of tearing metal in the trunk of the 535i.

"It's Carmichael!" Mayes said.

Suzanne Brewer knew he meant it was Carmichael's Saudi Arabian proxy force, but she did not correct him. Obviously this was Carmichael's doing. The Gray Man was capable of many things, but she had seen no intelligence claiming he also ran a team of motorcycle hit men.

Another crack of gunfire. This round must have missed the car completely because she heard no impact. She shifted lanes again, then raced forward.

Suzanne didn't want to take her eyes off the road to check her navigation screen so she called to Mayes. "How far to the next turnoff?"

"I . . . I don't know."

"Well *look*, dammit!"

Mayes did so, still holding his bleeding chin. He looked to the navigation map on the console display. "In about a mile we come to a T intersection. Jesus Christ! We'll have to stop! They'll kill us! Even if we make the turn without them overtaking us, we'll be on the 495. There's nowhere to go!"

Suzanne Brewer put the pedal all the way to the floor, but she knew Mayes was right. She could not hold the motorcycles back in this traffic for that long.

She squinted rainwater from her eyes as she weaved between two semis, pushing her speed to ninety miles an hour now, but soon she had to brake again to avoid rear-ending a van.

Another crack of a pistol behind them. The nearest bike was less than twenty-five yards back and closing.

Suzanne knew Jordan Mayes was right. There was no way she could outrun the six assassins on her tail. It was only a matter of seconds before she was either hit by gunfire or miscalculated and crashed her vehicle.

The BMW shot under the Turkey Run Road overpass and began a half-mile-long curve to the left. On the right side was a long gradual drop-off that went down a hill covered in trees and shrubs.

Suzanne looked at the drop-off, then in the rearview again. A plan formulated in her mind quickly, and she knew what she needed to do now. "Get Denny on the phone!"

"*What?*"

"Tell him to call it off."

"Are you insane? He won't answer a call from me!"

"*I'll* talk to him. Get my phone."

He looked around the center console. "Where is it?"

Another crack of gunfire, and the back window shattered high by the roofline. Brewer and Mayes both tucked their heads low.

"In my purse in the backseat."

Mayes reached back, grabbed her purse, and dug through it. "It's not here!"

"Then it fell out back there! You have to find it! It's our only chance!"

Mayes reached back and felt around, but he couldn't locate it. "Forget it!"

"Hurry!" she screamed at him. Another pop from behind shattered her driver-side mirror. On her right an SUV slammed on its brakes as a two-door compact in the next lane veered in front of it, trying to get out of the way of the car chase overtaking it. "We have to do *something*! Get back there and find it!"

Mayes unfastened his seat belt so he could look for the phone. As he turned around to reach between the seats he said, "This is crazy! Calling Denny isn't going to work!"

Suzanne Brewer looked to Mayes, saw him out of his seat and up on his left knee, his upper torso twisted and turned, leaning halfway into the back.

She gripped the steering wheel until her knuckles went white. "Not for you, it won't."

And with that Suzanne Brewer closed her eyes, jacked the wheel hard to the right, and sent her BMW across a lane of screeching traffic and off the road, crashing through a thicket of brush along the shoulder and then hurtling down the hill at nearly seventy miles an hour.

67

The 535i went airborne, careered nose-first down the decline, and then crashed into a copse of saplings, flipping it onto its right side. Brewer's arms and head whipped in all directions, but Jordan Mayes, who was out of his seat, flew completely into the back of the sedan, his body hurtling from one side to the other like a rag doll as the BMW began tumbling. The air bags deployed like cannon fire, restraining Suzanne's movement for a moment, but Mayes's body slammed into the rear windshield, and then his head dropped straight to the left side of the car when it bounced hard once more, snapping his neck on impact.

The BMW finally lost all its momentum, finishing its long crash sequence with its wheels spinning in the air and the roof lying in a relatively flat portion of wet grass, 150 yards down the hill from the George Washington Parkway.

All was still for a moment other than the rain on the metal undercarriage of the sedan. Soon Suzanne Brewer's bloody hand reached out, away from her body, pushing the deflated air bags out of her way so she could orient herself. She hung upside down, her bruised waist and her scraped shoulder and neck held secure by the seat belt.

In another second searing pain crept into her left ankle, and it seemed to amplify more and more with every single beat of her racing heart.

She drooled blood that flowed up into her nose.

Still dazed by the crash, she wiped her face, and then, finally, she opened her eyes.

Jordan Mayes lay in front of her sight line, dead in the dark, facedown in the mud fifteen feet from the BMW. Suzanne took this in without emotion, then her eyes were drawn up the hill. She saw three pinpricks of light above her, back in the direction of the George Washington Parkway. They moved like fireflies, dancing in the blackness, but growing larger, some-times shooting out in wide arcs, then returning to their original shape.

It did not take her long to realize what she was looking at.

Three flashlights, each one carried by a man, no doubt a Saudi Arabian assassin. They closed steadily on her position 150 yards down the hill.

And she understood. They were coming down here to make sure their work was finished.

She did not reach for her seat belt release button. Her leg seemed to be stuck and her ankle was clearly broken—she'd never felt pain like this in her life. But even though she couldn't get away if she tried, her original intention had never been to run away; it had been to make a deal.

With a pathetic sob and a boyish grunt of pain she looked in the other direction, back inside the shattered vehicle. She strained against her seat belt to reach out across the roof of the sedan below her. She opened the armrest storage compartment, pulled out the Faraday cage that held her phone.

It had been by her side all along, and not in the back like she had told Jordan Mayes.

She opened the case and dialed a number with a thumb that trembled almost too much for her to accomplish the simple task. Holding the ringing phone to her ear now, she looked back in the direction of the men negoti-ating the hill and trees, descending the rain-swept hillside to finish her off while she hung upside down like meat in a market.

Her ankle throbbed with sharp, murderous agony, but she forced the pain from her consciousness, because she had to give the performance of her lifetime now, and she could not allow for any distractions.

"Denny Carmichael."

She coughed; the blood on her face splattered the phone. "Listen to me carefully, Denny." Another cough. "Don't make a mistake."

A pause. "And what mistake would I be making, Ms. Brewer?"

"Don't remove someone who's on your side. Someone valuable to you, someone who can help you manage the fallout till the end of this crisis. Mayes is dead. *I* killed him, not your assets. You need to understand that you *need* me. Now, more than ever."

"I don't know what you are talking about. I'm very busy, as a matter of fact."

The jittering orbs of light came closer. They were only seventy-five yards up the hill now; they bathed the broken trees and brush around them with a yellow glow as the men followed the route of the wreck through the foliage.

Brewer spoke more quickly. "Mayes told me everything. *Everything*, Denny. You might think that makes me a liability, but that's not how I operate. I am an asset. Your *best* asset, at a time when I know you could use a friend at HQ. Let me help you solve your problem."

Denny chuckled, the epitome of calm. "Solve my problem? It seems I am in the process of doing just that."

"You couldn't even kill Jordan Mayes without my help! What makes you think you can kill Violator without me?"

Denny did not reply.

The flashlights closed to within fifty yards. It looked like the men carrying them had picked up speed on the treacherous hill. "What is it they say in this town?" Suzanne asked. "It's not the crime, it's the cover-up." Blood dripped from her lips, ran up her face and into her eyes. She listened for a response on the other end of the line, but nothing came. "You *know* what I bring to the table here. You *need* support. You need a witness in-house who saw Gentry kill Mayes. The other cars on the road are going to report multiple attackers. You can't sell your story this time without help."

Still nothing. She wondered if he'd hung up.

"You've come so close, Denny, but you are getting sloppy. Desperate. I can give you the backing you need to see this all the way through."

The flashlights were only twenty-five yards away. She could already make out the silhouettes of the men behind the moving beams.

She thought of something else, one more Hail Mary. If this didn't work, she'd be dead in seconds. Hanging here upside down, a bullet in her brain. "Morvay!"

Denny spoke now. "What's that?"

"Kevin Morvay. He is a senior tech in SIGINT. He has the Dupont video. He's seen it. He showed it to Mayes." She sniffed tears and blood. "You see? I am helping you."

All three flashlights centered on Jordan Mayes's body.

Denny said, "And I appreciate your help. Good-bye."

"I can get it from him! *And* get it off the system. I know how, do you? I can do so much more. I can . . . hello? *Hello?*" It sounded like Denny had either hung up the phone or set it down on a table. Suzanne Brewer started to cry openly. She shook hard against her seat belt, but she couldn't get it off. She thought of screaming, begging, *pleading* into the phone, but she just bit her lip. No, it wouldn't work, and she told herself she wouldn't die like that.

The lights were on her now.

A man knelt down, peered into the vehicle, and the high-lumen light shined right in her face, unbearable, worse than her broken leg.

She shut her eyes and sobbed again. Her bloody nose almost gagged her.

Then, with a shocking suddenness, the light turned away.

She heard the wet slapping of feet on rain-soaked brush, the *clap clap* of boots trudging through mud. Suzanne opened her eyes and looked around. Through the stars in her eyes she saw them now, the dark silhouettes. They stood around the body of Jordan Mayes a brief time, then they began retrograding up the hill, back in the direction of the motorcycles parked along the road.

Denny Carmichael's voice came back on the line. "Are you badly hurt?"

Suzanne wept openly into the phone. "Thank you, Denny. *Thank you.* You won't regret this."

"I don't know what you mean, Suzanne," he said. "You aren't making sense. I think you must have hit your head. I'll send help to the geo coordinates on your cell phone so we can get you to a hospital."

And then he hung up.

Suzanne Brewer vomited upside down, covering the roof of the car below her with blood and bile.

68

After swimming ashore and changing into warm, dry clothes, Court lay in the forest for several minutes, allowing his ears to tune in to his surroundings. He'd seen only one patrol boat on the water, and he'd remained well clear of it, but he had no way of knowing how extensively the Harvey Point guard force patrolled the woods.

Court knew from his time here that this was the absolute best place to come ashore. Most of the activity at the Point was well to the east of this part of the grounds. Over there was an airstrip, along with dozens of buildings: administration and planning offices, barracks, logistics stores, and weapons caches.

This portion of the Point, by contrast, had no great value. The large forest Court moved through now was used primarily by CIA, DIA, and JSOC for escape and evasion training, small-unit tactics training, and jungle and riverine warfare exercises. To the north of the forest were a bombing range, an explosive ordnance testing ground, and two mock cities for close-quarters battle work, along with an Air Branch helicopter center, an automobile and motorcycle training facility, an underground SAD weapons cache, and an array of buildings used as a testing ground—for who and for what exactly, Court had no idea. During his time in SAD Court had had the highest-security clearance, but he wasn't read into any code word ops that did not directly relate to him, so even though no one in America had had access to higher-level secrets than he did when he was in the CIA, there were all sorts of things going on around him that he didn't know about.

Especially at a facility like Harvey Point.

Court's hopes that he would get information at the AAP facility were buoyed as he picked his way through the grounds nearby. Two Humvee patrols passed, giving him the impression there was something this far west of the Point that needed protecting. Both times he hid himself completely behind trees as the patrols neared, fearing the men inside the vehicles would be using infrared scopes to check the woods for trouble.

But when he came upon the AAP compound itself, his heart began to sink. The main compound building was there, even several of the old trailers in the parking lot next to it, but everything was dark and deserted. Weeds grew a foot high from cracks in the lot. To Court it didn't look like anyone had been here in years.

After watching through Zack's night sight from the trees for a few minutes to make certain no one was around, Court rose, then walked through the wide-open gate at the front of the compound. He passed a sign that read Secure Facility, then he crossed the parking lot in front of the entrance to the building everyone in the program referred to as "The Center," and he pushed on the front door.

It was unlocked.

Inside it looked like a typical public high school, but a high school during summer vacation. No light, no movement.

The floors were covered with dust and leaves that had blown in through a broken window somewhere, and there was water damage on the baseboards, as if the area had once flooded. The smell of mold filled the dank air.

Court wandered around for several minutes, checking the different floors and wings, and he found the entire building abandoned, and not a scrap of paper or a sign on the wall to give any hint as to what was once here.

He stood in the medical ward, he walked through the dormitory, he checked every locker in the locker room off the empty swimming pool.

Nothing.

Back outside in the parking lot he walked among the trailers on the north side of the building. These were individual classrooms for AADP recruits; Court had spent part of virtually every day for two years studying with his principal trainer in trailer 14b.

Many of the trailers were gone now, but 14b was still there, the last one on the second row, almost all the way to the perimeter fence around the parking lot. Court walked over to it. Where before the grounds around the lot had been manicured lawn, now it looked like the forest on the other side of the chain-link fence had pushed through. Young pine and oak dotted the ground almost up to the back of the trailer, and the asphalt lot the trailer rested on was buckled and broken, with weeds growing through the cracks.

The windows of 14b were all broken out, as well, and there was evidence of water and storm damage here, just like at The Center. The aluminum door was bent and it hung wide open.

Court looked in, shone his flashlight around. It was all but empty. He went inside and stood there in the middle of the dark space, flipped off his light, and thought about his time here, more than fifteen years earlier.

A small swivel chair was the only piece of furniture that remained—Maurice's chair. Maurice had been his trainer, the one man he worked with 365 days a year for two years. Maurice nearly killed him multiple times, and Court wanted to kill him back more than once, but Court loved the man like a father.

Maurice was dead now, and Court found himself wishing, more than anything in the world, that the old bastard was sitting in that chair so Court could ask him what the hell he should do now.

Exhausted suddenly, and overcome with failure, Court sat down against the wall, leaned his head back, and asked *himself* what the hell he was going to do now.

Just then he felt the vibration of his phone in his pack, letting him know he was getting a call via RedPhone. For a moment he just let it buzz. He had no desire to talk to Catherine King at the moment. As far as he was concerned right now, she was just one more dead end.

Finally, though, he fished out his phone and opened the app that put the call through.

"Yeah?"

"This is Catherine."

"No one else has this number."

"I've been calling. I was worried something happened to you."

I'll just bet, Court thought to himself. He wondered what her excuse would be for not going to Israel. "I'm fine," he said. Three shafts of dull light entered the dark space through the door and two windows, as the moon broke through the cloudy night.

"Where are you now?" she asked.

Court looked around at the old empty trailer. "I'm at a Starbucks on Pennsylvania Avenue."

"Really?"

Court didn't answer. Instead he said, "How 'bout you?"

"I'm at Heathrow. My flight home boards soon. I'm so glad I caught you between flights. I tried you before I left Tel Aviv, but you didn't answer."

Court sat up straighter. "You actually went?"

"I did."

"Did you find . . ."

"The man you shot? Yes. His name is Yanis Alvey. He has fully recovered."

"That's good."

There was a slight pause, then Catherine said, "I need to talk to you about something. Are you somewhere you can listen for a minute?"

Court considered his immediate surroundings. He could probably sit here for days and no one would know. "Yes, I'm secure. What did you find out?"

"I'll tell you. But before I do, I want you to understand something. This was not your fault."

"My *fault*? You're goddamned right this isn't my fault."

She hesitated. Then said, "The man you killed in Trieste was not an al Qaeda assassin."

Court's jaw flexed in anger, but he said nothing. *He'd* been there; she hadn't. *He'd* seen the man kill two Serbian guards, then raise his gun towards the Israeli spy.

"Then who was he?"

"I'll tell you, but you have to understand, you aren't going to like what you hear."

Court closed his eyes. "Who . . . *was* . . . he?"

Catherine hesitated again. Just before Court asked her a third time, she said, "I got this from Alvey, who got it from the head of the Mossad. The Israelis did a multi-year investigation into the affair, piecing it together from primary evidence and interviews with survivors. They are absolutely certain of their findings."

Despair grew in the pit of Court's stomach. Softly, he said, "Tell me who I killed, Catherine."

And she did.

Six Years Earlier

Hawthorn sat quietly in his room in the Italian villa just outside of Trieste, but inside he was raging against Mossad and Manny, furious with himself for believing he would be kept safe.

Manny Aurbach had promised his agent Hawthorn he would protect him, but like other things the old Jew had told him, that had been a lie.

He wondered if he was really mad, or if he was just terrified, diverting his fear into action, as he had been trained to do long ago.

Hawthorn was a spy, and he spied for the Mossad, which was an immediate death sentence to any Arab. Compounding this fact was that he had penetrated al Qaeda in Iraq and now served as a logistics operative for the organization, and he knew it would just take one small piece of evidence to convict him. If *anyone* in his organization thought he was working for the Jews, he would be killed, likely in a most horrible fashion.

He'd not wanted to come to Italy to meet with the al Qaeda operatives from Pakistan, but he'd seen no way out of it. The danger for him was that he had cultivated his legend among the AQ leadership, and they trusted him, but exposing himself to an entire new group of individuals, individuals with contacts and intelligence networks who could check his backstory with their own resources, or poke holes in his legend, meant this trip could put him in front of the wrong person at the wrong time.

And just as he had feared, so had it come to pass. When he and his colleague stepped off the launch this afternoon at the dock they'd been met by a small contingent of AQ men from the Tribal Areas, and a larger group of Serbs. Soon after Hawthorn greeted the men from Pakistan, he knew he was in serious trouble.

In the driveway of the villa everyone climbed out of the vans to begin carrying luggage inside. As Hawthorn started to leave the vehicle, he felt a hand clutch his arm. One of the al Qaeda men from Pakistan sat next to him. He whispered, "I know who you are. If you try to run, I will alert them. They will tear you to pieces and enjoy it."

Hawthorn sat dumbfounded. The other man said, "One of us will not be leaving this city with his life."

"What . . . do you want?"

The man from Pakistan just smiled. "I am not afraid to die. Are you?"

The man pushed past Hawthorn on his way out of the van, leaving the Israeli agent to sit alone in the driveway.

For the rest of the evening Hawthorn had known he would have to act: either run or kill. Doing nothing would be a death sentence. Running seemed impossible, considering the man from Pakistan specifically threatened to alert the others if he tried.

Hawthorn had no idea what the other man's game was, but he knew he needed to act first.

Both Hawthorn and the other spy were carrying weapons. Pistols with silencers. It was standard outfitting for AQ operatives working in the West. The guns were both a means at their disposal to fight their way out of trouble, as well as tools given to them so they could end their own lives before they were taken into custody.

The Israeli asset had not planned on using his weapon for either purpose, but now he felt both comforted to know he had a gun, and terrified to know the man sitting in a room on the other end of the villa had an identical weapon.

As afraid as Hawthorn was now, he did take solace in his belief that he had some time to come up with a plan to get himself out of this mess.

And then the football match began. One of the Serbs had mentioned it earlier in the evening; apparently all work would stop so the twenty or so Balkan men on the property could enjoy the match on the television in the living room; minus those men needed to protect the property, the Serbs promised.

At that moment Hawthorn knew the situation had just changed. Would the other spy come for him, knowing the entire force around them would be distracted for two hours or more?

Shortly before the match began, both Hawthorn and the other spy made excuses to return to their rooms for the evening. They'd also made eye contact at that time, as if to say to each other, "Let's do this."

As soon as the match kicked off and the noise from downstairs rocked the villa, Hawthorn told himself he would not sit here on his bed and wait to be murdered.

If he was going to act, he was going to act now.

He screwed the silencer into the CZ pistol slowly, steeling his body and his mind for what was to come. He was no assassin. Yes, he'd had training in weapons and hand-to-hand action, but that was long ago and he'd not been particularly good at it.

He dressed in the darkest clothing he had, he slipped the weapon into the small of his back, under his shirt, and then he left his room.

It was a unique feature of the villa that all the second-floor bedrooms had windows that looked out on the grounds. For this reason there was no inside access from one room to another, but rather two hallways that cut the second floor into sections, and each hallway led to outdoor walkways that wrapped around the second floor.

The walkways, one to the south and one to the north, each had a pair of guards walking back and forth the length of them. Hawthorn knew the only way to get to the room on the far side of the villa without encountering these sentries was to climb to the tile roof and move carefully all the way to the other end.

He stepped outside his room, climbed onto the roof, and almost fell immediately. But when he had his footing he began moving slowly, up and over on his hands and knees. It was slow going; it took him ten minutes to cover one third of the distance.

He checked his watch and realized his lack of progress, and he began to panic. He knew the match would last at least another hour, but at half time some of the men might return to their rooms to check their e-mails or attend to other things. He hadn't thought about half time till he'd foolishly climbed onto the roof and committed himself, and now his heart pounded with terror. This realization that he did not have as much time as he thought he did made him rush now; he rose higher, and he moved faster.

A weakened tile cracked loudly, broke free, and then began sliding along the roof down towards the northern outdoor walkway.

Hawthorn went flat and prayed.

He heard the two guards below him, and he lifted his head and leaned out a little to see. Two Serbs stood on the walkway. Clearly they had heard the noise, but they only looked around in confusion.

He wanted to give them time to move on, but he didn't think he had the time to spare. It occurred to him that if he killed the men, he could make better time to his target, because he would be able to move along the walkway instead of the roof.

He tried to think of another alternative, but he came up with nothing else.

The realization that he was going to shoot these two guards came slowly, but it did come. He lay flat on the roof, a gun in his hand, trying his best to justify the actions he was about to take. They were Serbian gangsters, working with al Qaeda to equip them with weapons.

Yes, he could do this.

He steeled himself to accept the necessity of his actions.

He rose a little, pointed the pistol at the first man, and waited for the crowd two levels below him to roar again.

A bad call from the referee caused a dozen men to shout at the television.

Hawthorn fired once, striking the first guard in the back of the head. The flash of light from the gunshot shocked the Mossad asset, but he recovered quickly, shifted his aim to the second man, and fired again. The second shot came right before the shouts below died down.

Both Serbs lay dead on the walkway, but Hawthorn worried they could be seen by someone in the back garden, or even on the hillside beyond. He slipped the gun, its barrel scorching hot, into the small of his back, and then he slid down, over the side of the roof, dropping down the rest of the way.

It took all his strength to drag the men and their guns inside. He pulled, then pushed, and even rolled them, one at a time, into a closet in the hallway on the second floor. While he was doing this, the noises from the living room came up an open stairwell. It sounded like the men below were just feet away, and their voices caused Hawthorn to have to fight the urge to run.

He did what he could to push the fear out of his mind. By the time he finished stashing the bodies, the noise had abated, and he relaxed a little.

The Israeli asset moved down the walkway now, towards his target's room. He knew he'd have to move quickly, and after the act, he could not return. No, he would continue on downstairs, and make his way out the front gate, hopeful the guards there would be distracted by the match.

He entered the hallway off the walkway, and he stepped up to his target's door. With his hand on the latch he hesitated, tried to get control of his heart before it hammered its way out of his chest.

Hawthorn opened the door slowly. There, on the bed just five meters away, the Arab spy saw him. Hawthorn checked the man's hands and saw nothing but a silver pen in his right hand, and some papers in his left.

The papers fell to the floor.

Hawthorn braced himself to kill again, and he raised his weapon, hoping like hell this room was far removed enough from the main floor so no one would hear.

He locked his arm to fire, aiming for the man's chest.

No words were spoken.

And then, just ahead and on his left, movement through the open window. A black form. Hawthorn thought it too small to be a person at first, but the form grew as it entered, sailing through the air, and he watched as a man landed silently and adroitly on both feet. A gymnast, but a gymnast in black, his face masked.

A gymnast with a gun. He held a black pistol in his hand, a long suppressor protruding from the end of it.

Hawthorn felt relief wash over him. The Mossad *had* sent a killer, after all. A *real* killer, here to save him. Manny Aurbach had promised to keep Hawthorn safe, and the old man had come through. Manny had cut too close for comfort, certainly, but—

Hawthorn saw the armed man raise his gun—not at the Arab spy by the bed, but at Hawthorn himself.

No!

"Istanna!" Wait!

The Israeli asset never felt the bullet that killed him.

69

Catherine King spoke in soft tones to convey her sympathy to the man on the other end of the phone. "The man you rescued *was* a spy, but he worked for a Middle Eastern intelligence agency. After all this time the Israelis still aren't sure which one. He'd also infiltrated al Qaeda—the core AQ in Pakistan. The Mossad thinks his job was to discover the identity of the Israeli plant in al Qaeda. He'd done this somehow, and then he lured Hawthorn to Italy to murder him. You happened to show up when Hawthorn realized he'd been compromised. It was kill or be killed, so Hawthorn decided to act."

The pain his Court's stomach moved to his back, to his chest. He'd heaved early in Catherine's story, as the details began to fit his reminiscence, but with everything turned upside down.

With Court as the villain.

Now his head hung between his knees. His lips were rimmed with vomit.

Catherine said, "Listen carefully to me. It was an honest mistake you made. You saw what you expected to see. Confirmation bias, they call it. An assassination attempt. You reasonably assumed the assassin was the man you came to stop, and the would-be victim was the man you came to rescue."

Court spoke in a near whisper. "But . . . but I got PID."

"I don't know what that means."

"Positive ID. I saw his picture. I identified him before I moved on the villa."

"I'm sorry, Six. You must have been mistaken. It's confirmed by the head of the Mossad. He told Alvey personally that Hawthorn was shot to death in Trieste six years ago while at a Serbian safe house for a meeting of senior al Qaeda operatives from Iraq and Pakistan."

"No," Court said, but his voice held no conviction.

"Why is it you can't believe?"

"Because I don't make mistakes."

"Everybody makes mistakes."

"Not when you face the consequences I face."

Catherine said, "This was six years ago. You can't blame yourself."

Court shouted into the phone. "Of course I can! The man I rescued hugged me after I got him out of there. He must have known I was American. An infidel assassin. He must have known I'd fucked it all up. He hugged me anyway. He was so relieved that I'd failed so miserably."

Catherine did not know what to say. After a time, though, she just said, "I am sorry, Six. But I have to catch my flight. Please tell me we can talk when I get back home. I won't write about any of this, not until we talk. I promise you."

"Okay." Court's voice was barely audible. "Catch you later."

He hung up the phone and put it back in his pack.

Suddenly every last vestige of energy melted away from him. He had nothing left to give.

He no longer cared.

He could hear Maurice's voice in this little room. Gravelly from chain-smoking and the wear of middle age, yet powerful and commanding.

What would Maurice say now, seeing his student broken and defeated, sitting on the floor?

Court knew. Maurice had said one line to him when Court found himself wallowing in his own misery and unable to complete his objective.

"Suck it up or you'll fuck it up."

Court didn't know if he could suck it up this time. He didn't think he could go on.

He didn't hear the truck pull up, but he should have. He had been trained to remain in condition yellow, always on guard. The very idea he could be sitting in a dark and silent location and not hear a truck pull up a gravel drive to within twenty-five yards of his position was impossible to fathom. And yet it happened.

The trailer brightened with the beams of a vehicle's headlights. He'd been compromised. He had failed again.

He only heard the sound of a car door shutting.

Court decided then and there that he had no more fight in him. He could shoot the men outside the trailer, but why? None of these static security guys who would be converging on him right now were responsible for the murder of the most successful deep-penetration agent ever to infiltrate al Qaeda.

These guys are blameless, Court thought. Unlike him.

He thought about standing, walking out the door, and pointing his gun at the armed guards—suicide by security goon—but he didn't feel like getting up. No. He'd stay right here, here in the little room where it all started so many years ago.

Court decided this would be the perfect place to end the miserable saga that was his life.

He pulled the Glock from his bag, opened his mouth, and jammed the muzzle in, biting it with his teeth. Tears streamed down his face, wet his lips, and carried on down the barrel of his gun.

He had no fear of dying; he never had. His fear had always been failure.

And now he saw his failure in Trieste as the realization of his greatest fear.

He moved his thumb inside the trigger guard and placed it on the trigger. Took a short sharp breath and began to squeeze his hand.

"I sure hope you don't expect me to mop up that mess you're about to make."

The voice came from the doorway. Court spun the pistol around quickly and pointed it there, a reaction to a surprise threat, an instinctive move, nothing more.

Zack Hightower stood in the doorway silhouetted by the headlights. His hands were empty. He grinned. "Make up your mind, bro. You gonna shoot you, or are you gonna shoot me?"

Court quickly wiped wetness from his face with his forearm. He lowered the gun. "What are you doing here?"

"Hanley sent me."

"Who is with you?"

"All by my lonesome. Matt wants a word."

Court shook his head. "No need. I know everything now. I killed the wrong man."

Zack shrugged. "Yeah. I kinda told you that, didn't I?" He moved into the trailer and sat down across from Court, placing his back against the wall. He looked around in the little room. The lights from the truck outside reflected off the walls, though it was still dim.

Court said, "I was *so* sure of my intel, Zack."

Another shrug from the big man with the silvery blond hair. "Fuckin' towelheads. They all look alike to me, too. Hey, Six, you really thinking about eating a bullet? That's not your style."

Court found himself embarrassed. "It wasn't my first choice, but my masterful plan to prove I did nothing wrong went tits-up the moment I found out I did something wrong. I'm not going to be taken alive, and I don't much feel like running anymore. Not sure where that leaves me."

"Looks like it leaves you sitting on your ass in a moldy mobile home with puke on your face and a gun in your mouth."

Court said, "Still telling it like it is, I see."

"You want some advice?"

"What's that?"

"You'll want to angle that pistol up to about sixty-five degrees. Roof of the mouth. You'll hit the brain stem that way. I won't have to watch you flop around like an idiot for more than a second or two."

Court closed his eyes. Despite himself, he chuckled. Gallows humor. "With friends like you, Zack."

"On the other hand," Hightower said, "I came a long ass way. Would it kill you to talk to Hanley on the sat phone for two minutes? If you do that for me, I promise I won't get in the way of your little art project."

"Why?"

"I don't know, amigo. I *do* know my orders are to put you two in touch, and I know Hanley will kick my dick if I don't deliver."

"I thought you were Denny's bitch."

"Hanley's a smart guy. He's a brasshole, everybody at Langley is, but he's one of the better ones. Give him a couple of minutes."

Court sighed and held his hand out.

Zack took an Iridium Extreme sat phone unit from the side pocket of his cargo pants, pulled out a pair of reading glasses from the breast pocket of his shirt, and put them on. He fumbled with his eyeglasses as he dialed the unit.

Court looked at him. "Need some help with that, Dad?"

"Fuck you, kid. Can't see shit up close without these but I can still shoot the right nut off a gnat at fifty paces." Zack said it without looking up from the phone, then his voice rose in both volume and sophistication. "Good evening, Director Hanley. I have Six in pocket. Passing you to him now, sir."

Hightower tossed the phone across the width of the trailer.

Court caught the phone and brought it to his ear.

"How did you know I was here?"

Matt Hanley said, "You were fixated on AAP from the start. I had to dig around to see what the hell it was, but when I found out about the old building at Harvey Point, I sent Hightower to check it out. I've also got a guy shadowing Catherine King at Heathrow. She was in comms with you, which means I know that *you* know about BACK BLAST."

"I do."

"And at this point, I figure I know what you are thinking about doing."

Court said nothing. He still held his Glock in his right hand.

Hanley continued, "Right now it feels like the ground underneath your feet isn't solid anymore. Like everything you thought you were turned out to be a lie."

Court closed his eyes.

Hanley said, "Give me a second, and I might be able to give you something to stand on. Something to believe in."

"Is this a Scientology pitch?"

Hanley ignored the joke. "Court, about two hours ago Jordan Mayes was murdered on the George Washington Parkway."

Court opened his eyes quickly, then leaned his head back against the trailer wall. "I didn't *fucking* do it!"

"Relax, I know you didn't. Carmichael had it done. But he's already pinned it on you. You need to know that."

"Whatever," Court said, defeat obvious in his voice.

"I need your help. I can't do anything within the confines of the Agency, because if this goes public it will burn the Agency to the ground."

"And you think I give a shit?"

"Of course you do. You won't let Denny beat you, and if you eat a damn bullet right now you are handing him a golden ticket to sweep the past week under the rug and move on. I don't care about your motivation. Don't do it because you like yourself. Blame yourself for your mistake in Italy, just like everybody else does. But do it because you hate Denny Carmichael."

"Do *what*?"

"You and Zack, with me running you from distance. I'm talking about getting the band back together for one quick op."

"Going after Denny?"

"Negative. We can't touch Denny, unfortunately." Hanley paused. "He's sequestered away in a safe house somewhere, probably has fifty guys covering him in a blanket of guns. But we sure as hell can go after the foreign goons he's using to fight his war against you. We take them down, we get some people at HQ asking questions about a bunch of dead foreign operators on the streets, and then, sooner or later, Denny's crimes will be exposed to the right people in government. The ones who can force him out without any comebacks on the rest of the Agency."

"Who are the foreign hitters?"

"We don't know for sure, but Denny is tight with the intelligence chiefs of several Middle Eastern countries. Some say too tight. I never thought he would use back channels to run his own foreign hit team on the streets of the USA, but if that's what he's doing here, just think about the other shit he's gotten away with."

"You know where they are?"

"I put Jenner's unit on the tail of the JSOC team looking for you. Had them stand off and keep their eyes open for these foreign assholes. They ID'd them, then tracked them back to a home in Arlington. We count about eight to ten fighting-age males inside."

"And you can't go after them because SAD can't work in the U.S."

Hanley finished the thought. "And I can't just report them to local authorities, because the media would indict the entire CIA for crimes nobody but Denny had any part in."

"Why don't you tell the director of the CIA what you know? He has the juice to shut Denny down."

Hanley replied, "He's a pol, Court. He doesn't give a damn about this Agency. He'll run to the *New York Times* and say he is saving America by shuttering his own organization. He'll destroy U.S. intelligence just so he looks good to the press.

"You and Zack, Court. Face it, you two outsiders are the only chance we have."

Court thought it over for a moment. "I don't know, Matt."

"*What* don't you know? This is your job, Six. We all have to make sacrifices for the good of the country."

Gentry rubbed his eyes. He started to get up, the pain in his ribs still slowing him. He said, "What the hell have I been doing for the past twenty years?"

Hanley softened. "Make all that count for something. Save this Agency. Take away Denny's proxy force."

Court looked across the trailer to his former team leader. Zack couldn't have heard Hanley's side of the conversation, but he was obviously on board with the plan. He just gave Court a sly grin and a slow thumbs-up.

Court ignored Zack and addressed Hanley again. "There are two of us. We'll need some equipment to do this right."

"I gave Zack the authority he needs to gain access to a cache there at the Point. It's got anything you could possibly need."

"I don't have credos to go anywhere on base."

"Taken care of. Plus, I'm sending Travers down in a helo to pick you guys up and bring you back into this area."

"Chris Travers? He's a pilot?"

"Not much of one, but he's learning."

Court didn't feel terribly comforted by this, but he had a feeling he'd just taken on an assignment where dying in a helicopter crash would be the least of his worries.

70

Court and Zack both felt like two kids who had been left alone overnight in a candy store. By the time they turned on all the lights in the massive underground storage facility to see what they had available to them, the two ex–CIA employees felt like they could fight a small insurgency.

The underground warehouse was the size of a supermarket. On shelves, in lockers, and in numbered squares on the floor for reference and restocking, thousands of items sat ready for the taking. Small arms and ammunition, knives, motorcycles, rubber boats, parachute rigs, night vision devices, and communications gear. Climbing equipment and helicopter fast ropes, camouflage uniforms, and snow skis. Explosives, crossbows, medical supplies, GPS units, and even horse saddles.

They selected kit for their job ahead, although there were a lot of questions about just what they would be getting themselves into. Two guys hitting a building with an opposition force of eight to ten was bad enough, but Court and Zack knew precious little about the capabilities of their enemy, and absolutely nothing about the building itself.

They went with general-purpose gear: pistols and carbines, a sniper rifle with a suppressor for Zack, and an ultra quiet small-caliber suppressed handgun for Court. They stocked up on ammo and magazines, body armor, radio headsets, medical equipment, ropes, knives, and other accessories useful for men in their profession.

They also equipped themselves with grenades and explosive breaching charges.

Zack whistled after he and Court looked at everything they had selected to take with them on their op. "What do you say you and me say screw it to Hanley and instead go invade some Caribbean nation? I think we could orchestrate a coup in Dominica, maybe even Grenada. Make our own laws and live like kings."

Court ignored him, because something had caught his eye: a door that read Experimental Locker.

He went inside, flipped on a light, and began looking around. Zack followed him in. They walked between several shelves packed with a large collection of more esoteric equipment. Microdrones, robot cameras, even a heartbeat detector for tactical teams that looked useful to Court until he tried to lift it, then decided he'd rather check back in a few years when the eggheads got it miniaturized into something he wouldn't have to schlep around like a medicine ball.

They read the tags and printed material attached to several other different pieces of equipment. Hightower said, "I don't think you and I are smart enough to figure all this shit out."

But Court knelt down over a black watertight case and pulled a laminated instruction booklet out of an attached plastic pouch.

Hightower walked over to the unit and bent down to see what had Court so engaged. He read the label on the case, then he read it again. Then he shook his head. "*Hell* no."

"Hell *yes*," replied Court.

"Why?"

"Why *not*?"

"You're a hero, dude. But you're not a superhero. That right there is a one-way ride to hell."

"I can make it work."

"You're gonna die."

"Gotta die of something."

"Shit, man, die of something *else*."

Despite continued protests from Zack, Court lifted the twenty-five-pound case and lugged it out with the rest of the gear they would take back with them.

Zack followed him out. "Seriously, Six, what the hell are you thinking about doing? It's eight dudes in a house. We go in, hit it, and quit it."

Court said, "I'm planning ahead. I'm going after Denny."

"Fuck that. Denny's untouchable. Hanley would never sanction it."

"Then it's a good thing I don't work for the CIA. I'd probably get written up or something."

Just after nine thirty a.m., a small blue and white helicopter flew low over the trees at the west end of Harvey Point, and then it slowed to a hover over a grassy field just south of the SAD storage facility. Zack and Court stood next to all their cases and packs of gear and watched the helicopter land.

The aircraft powered down and Chris Travers climbed out of the right seat, then walked directly over to the two men.

There was no greeting. He just said, "I hope you dumbasses don't think you are taking all that shit on board this helo."

Zack said, "We weighed it. Two hundred forty-five pounds of kit. That's a Robinson R44 you're flying there. You can carry this, us, and more."

Travers did not press the issue; even though Hightower was nearly fifteen years Travers's senior, he was still an intimidating character.

The three men loaded the aircraft, then they climbed in themselves. Travers took off into a sunny morning and flew the men to the north.

As they flew, Zack and Court discussed their options. Using Travers's tablet computer with a cell connection, Court pulled up all the imagery on the Arlington safe house he could find. Looking it over, he saw it was a large but nondescript building in a middle-class neighborhood with a fence around the yard. The one interesting feature was that it backed up to an industrial area, with a large parking lot just behind the property.

"It's going to be defended," Court said.

Zack agreed. "We can hit it at night, use NODs."

Court moved the map around the area. Just north of the location was a small park, with trees, two baseball diamonds, tennis courts, and a soccer field. And just beyond that was a large mall.

"Maybe instead of attacking into an enemy position, we can draw them out into the open."

"How so?"

"We bait them with the one thing they are after."

"Where are you going to find seventy-two virgins?"

"I mean me."

Zack understood immediately. He joked, "Just one virgin, then. I like it."

Catherine King had only been back in the States a few minutes when she learned about the death of Andy Shoal. She rushed from Dulles to the crime scene, stood there on the sidewalk just like she'd stood on the sidewalk with Andy many times in the past week, surrounded by cops and flashing lights, searching for answers as to what had just happened.

She didn't know why Andy had been killed by Denny Carmichael, and now she wondered why he had yet to come after her.

No, not for a second did she think the man known to the American press as Jeff Duncan had anything at all to do with this. The media had already convicted him, of course, and their reporting had gone beyond ridiculous, with experts on all the twenty-four-hour news stations opining about every possible motivation and tactic. Video games were being blamed; antigovernment anarchists were implicated; a four-year-old local high-profile missing persons case had been brought up by reporters at a press conference to a bemused FBI spokesperson who didn't have a clue how to respond.

Every American with the common name Jeff Duncan was being sought, not by the police or the feds, because they all rightly assumed that it was a pseudonym, but by local reporters. A man in Illinois with the right name, the right general age, and the right general description had been frustrated by a reporter's demands he account for his whereabouts, and he threw a punch at the man. Now Jeffrey Duncan of Peoria was behind bars and a hundred reporters from around the globe stood outside the jail in the rain, thinking the D.C. assassin might just possibly be this loudmouthed tire store clerk with a right hook that couldn't even drop a spit-shined J-school grad.

And Catherine felt a sense of responsibility for it all. It had been her reporting that started everyone looking in the wrong place, had taken eyes off Carmichael and his Agency.

And she wondered if, once the shock wore off, she would feel responsible for what had happened to Andy, as well.

For the twentieth time since she'd been off her flight from Tel Aviv she tried to call Six. As with all the other times, there was no answer. She wondered if he was still alive, or if all this commotion in the country about him was continuing on long after he was no longer around to take the blame for all these things he did not do.

Catherine headed back to her office, knowing good and well that the second she arrived she would be surrounded by her investigative team and the executive editor, and they would want to know everything about Tel Aviv and how it all related to Andy Shoal's murder. Most would agree that the man who kidnapped her at Union Station three days ago was an assassin, and that Catherine's Stockholm syndrome had just blinded her to this fact.

And she wouldn't argue with them; she didn't have the energy.

The Fashion Centre at Pentagon City was a large multistory mall with a luxury hotel and several restaurants. The average shopper would not realize it, but the mall also had dozens upon dozens of security cameras.

And all of these cameras were part of the network of image feeds that ran through the software at the Violator tactical operations center.

At six p.m., video monitors at the TOC came alive with images and facial recognition hits. While the men and women working in the TOC struggled frantically to pin down the location on a map of the building, they saw shot after shot of Court Gentry's face, totally exposed without a hat or sunglasses. He entered the north entrance of the mall at the ground floor, walked south through the food court, stood in line for a minute to buy a cup of coffee at a kiosk in the center of the large crowded space, and then took his drink to the escalator.

By now the TOC had him fixed and they had live feeds from the Fashion Centre camera network, so they were able to track him in real time. While one analyst contacted the JSOC operatives, who were twenty minutes away in the center of D.C., a second analyst ordered all CIA contract officers in the area into the location.

A third analyst, under orders to do so, contacted the head of the National Clandestine Service. Due to the death of Jordan Mayes, and Suzanne Brewer's hospitalization with a broken leg, Denny Carmichael had taken over operational control of the Violator TOC. Denny had the live video feed patched through to his Alexandria safe house, and he immediately disconnected the call.

Court Gentry took the escalator up to the second floor of the mall, and then he walked directly to a rear entrance of the adjoining Ritz-Carlton Pentagon City. He wove through the back of the hotel until he came to the front lobby, and here he stepped up to the elevator bank.

He took the elevator to the fifth floor, where he walked down the hall to a corner suite and entered with a key card.

All eight operational Saudi assets arrived at the Ritz-Carlton just ten minutes later, which was only possible because the hotel was less than a half mile from their safe house. The men wore suits and ties, they came through the two entrances in groups of four, and they looked calm and casual, like businessmen returning from a day at a conference, as they split into four groups in the lobby.

Two men took the main stairs, two men took an elevator to a floor above Gentry's hotel room, two men entered the Employees Only door and made their way to the service stairs, and two more men waited in the hall.

They all had suppressed Glock 17 pistols and combat knives, and they were all trained killers. At first their earbuds connected them to the director of their service, who had given them the kill order and the room number, but then he had to disconnect for a meeting, so now they just communicated softly to one another.

The team leader, a man named Cha, remained in the lobby with an asset named Jawad. He had the three ascending teams give a final "go check" and then he unleashed them on room 545.

Hani and Kimal moved up the stairs, climbing quickly with their weapons behind their backs. Up on the fourth floor of the stairwell they heard movement, so they raised their weapons, then spun around from the landing just below. There, a hunched-over middle-aged janitor with gray-blond hair mopped the floor, softly rapping along to the Kid Rock song in his headphones. He faced the opposite direction, so the two assets hid their pistols inside their coats and kept going up.

They stepped around the housekeeping cart and passed the hunched-over man without a glance as he continued his rap, and they ignored the words, concentrating on listening for sounds higher up, nearer to their target area.

Until then they both heard the man behind them speak in a loud, low voice. "I *know* you didn't just track across my clean floor."

The assets stood on the stairs above the janitor now. They spun back, looked down, and found themselves facing a large handgun with a larger silencer. Behind the weapon, where the janitor had been, now stood a surprisingly large man holding a mop in one hand and the pistol in the other.

Zack Hightower stood up fully now, adding six inches to his height. He said, "Nighty-night, bitches," and his Heckler & Koch pistol barked twice in the stairwell. He stepped back on the landing and moved his mop out of the way, and two bodies slid down into the space he had just occupied. Both men were on their backs, their eyes open, holes in their foreheads.

He shot both men once more in the head, just to make sure.

Hightower held a small microphone in his left hand, hidden behind the mop handle. He quickly brought it to his mouth as his slipped the pistol back in the housekeeping cart. "Two down. South stairwell clear."

Four Saudi operators closed on room 545 at the end of the hall, their suppressed pistols trained on the door. They all wanted to know where their two partners from the stairs were, but they were operating in radio silence now, so they could only listen in while Cha downstairs called over and over for Kimal and Hani to check in.

One of the assets kept his eye on the stairwell, far behind him, worried something must have gone very wrong, but the other three stayed focused on the mission. They moved all the way to the door, and one man raised his foot to kick it in.

Court lifted his head from the peephole quickly, took several steps back, and raised his pistol. At a distance of ten feet from the door he calmly fired the gun at waist height, raised it slightly and fired again, cycled a few inches to the left and fired, then to the right. Over and over and over.

His Glock 17 carried eighteen rounds and he emptied the entire weapon, dropped the magazine, and expertly reloaded it with a fresh one. He moved back to the door, now riddled with holes, and he stepped to the side. Reaching carefully for the latch he opened it, then he lowered into a squat and leaned around, his pistol leading him.

Three of the men here were dead, their bloody bodies draped haphazardly over one another and their blood draining out on the beautiful hall carpet. A fourth had been shot in the lower back; he writhed in pain and tried to roll around to get his pistol aimed in Court's direction.

Court fired once more into the back of the man's head, sending a spray of blood and gray matter across the hall carpet.

He then hefted his backpack off the floor next to the door and spoke into the microphone in his hand. "Four men up here. They are all down. I'm clear. We're missing two."

The reply from Zack came back quickly. "Not for long, bro. Movement below my poz."

"I'm coming to you."

A soft reply now. "Better hurry up, or you'll miss the festivities."

71

Murquin al-Kazaz sat in a private room in the back of Marcel's restaurant in Washington Circle. In front of him was a seventy-dollar filet mignon, and just beyond that were three members of a visiting Chinese trade delegation, here in D.C. for a meeting with American energy officials.

Kaz had wanted to cancel tonight's meet but these three were potential intelligence sources. China was a nation where Saudi needed a better intelligence presence, and these men were only in town for a day. He decided to go ahead, although he pushed the meeting from the reasonable dining time of eight p.m. to six, which meant the restaurant was mostly empty.

But not totally. He was surrounded by security here, ten men in all, with two more drivers in the lot outside with the vehicles. The three Chinese men had asked about the entourage of obvious security officers, but Kaz had passed it off as his standard operating procedure here in America, where crime was, unfortunately, so much worse than it was in the kingdom of Saudi Arabia or the People's Republic of China, two places where governments knew what to do with their criminals.

That won him some agreement from his potential sources.

During dinner the Saudi's mind bounced back and forth between the past week's hunt here in the area and the conversation with the Chinese businessmen, but just when he'd managed to push most of his worries away about all the compromises in Carmichael's campaign to kill his ex-assassin, Kaz's phone rang with a distinctive ring.

He excused himself, stood up and walked towards the back wall of the restaurant, and held the phone to his ear.

"Yes?"

"We are under attack!"

Kaz walked all the way into the corner of the room now and leaned into the phone. It was Cha, the team leader of the assets, and his voice echoed as if he was in a stairwell.

"What?"

"Kimal and Hani are dead, Mohammed and the others are not reporting. I think they are—"

"Where are you?"

Kaz heard the man scream. "Jawad! Jawad! Cover—"

"Listen to me, Cha. Listen carefully. Do you have anything on you that relates back to the embassy? Anything at all?"

"What? I . . . I don't know. You have to send another team."

"It's up to you, Cha."

"Jawad? Jawad, are you still with me? Jawad is not answering! I have to—"

Kaz heard the soft pop of a suppressed gunshot, then he heard the phone fall to the ground, bouncing several times. The line stayed open, and the Saudi Arabian standing in the restaurant dining room just pressed the phone tighter to his ear.

Sweat covered his brow and trickled down the back of his neck. He looked up to his dinner guests, halfway across the room. They spoke among themselves a little, but they looked back at Kaz as they did so.

A few seconds later Kaz heard a scuffing sound, possibly of the phone being picked up from the floor. Then a soft voice spoke into the device. It was almost nonchalant, but utterly convincing. "I'm coming for you now. I don't know who you have protecting you, but you'd better hope they are a lot better than these guys here." A pause. Then, "These guys were shit."

Kaz said nothing, but he did not hang up.

The man on the other end said, "I know. I know *everything*. Trieste. Denny. Israel . . . You."

Murquin al-Kazaz panicked. He hung up the phone and snapped his fingers, summoning his principal protection agent. With only the quickest and barest of explanations to the men at the table, the Saudi intelligence chief raced for the front door of the restaurant, his detail scrambling to form a diamond pattern around him.

The three Chinese businessmen sat at the table staring at one another, wondering who the *fuck* was going to pick up the check.

Court did not, in fact, know everything. He assumed the operative would have been speaking with his control officer, and his control officer would know what this was all about. For this man to so brazenly run operatives to do the bidding of the CIA told Court this man was deeply invested in the outcome.

The fact that Court had no idea who this man was, or why he was so involved, made his threats difficult to construct, but he'd done his best to act like he knew what the hell was going on.

He could only hope this would encourage the man and his cohorts to scatter like roaches in the light.

At which point, if it all went to plan, Court would stomp on them all.

Denny Carmichael had an eight p.m. meeting with the Violator Working Group here at the Alexandria safe house but for now he just listened in to Dakota's JSOC team as it converged on the Ritz-Carlton Pentagon City. The TOC had lost camera coverage of Gentry after he left the lobby, but by checking the elevator he entered they knew he went to the fifth floor, and by pulling information from the hotel's server they saw the only door to have a card key placed in it at the right time was 545.

Now JSOC moved through the lobby, Denny watched them on the feed, and they disappeared into the elevators and stairwell.

It was his fervent hope these men did not find their target. Or at least didn't find him alive. Denny had sent Kaz's men as soon as he'd received the report of Gentry in the mall, and since this location was only three or four minutes' driving time from the Saudi safe house, he knew his foreign assets would arrive well before the army boys of JSOC.

While he waited he looked at the television monitor next to the Ritz feed. CNN was on and, he had to admit, their story about the death of Jordan Mayes was perfect. An artist rendering of "Jeff Duncan" appeared on the screen as they spoke of a lone motorcycle assassin who raced up next to a vehicle carrying two senior CIA officers and opened fire.

There were witnesses who appeared on camera claiming there was more than one shooter, but the surviving CIA official in the vehicle—CNN went to great lengths to point out she was female, as if that was surprising— verified to authorities and in an off-camera interview with the network that she only saw one attacker.

As usual, CNN was going virtually wall-to-wall with the story, and they were helpful with the "lone gunman" narrative, dismissing the other witnesses by devoting a segment to errors in witness memory, and even having a psychologist on set to explain how the PTSD the witnesses were experiencing from this traumatic event was, no doubt, causing them to misremember.

Denny had to admit it; Suzanne Brewer had come through.

He couldn't have been happier about that, but what he heard from the JSOC radios a few seconds later caused his heart to drop.

"This is Dakota. I have bodies. Wait one." A pause. Then, "Jesus Christ. I've got four dead in the stairwell. None are the target. These are armed men, fighting-age males. All dead. All head-shots."

Another call came over the commo net. "Harley to Dakota. We've got four more up here on the fifth floor. All DOA, multiple gunshots. I do not see Violator among them. Suggest we get the fuck out of here, boss, local PD might already be en route."

"Roger that. Everybody exfil."

Denny sat alone at his desk. He remained still for a moment, until his phone rang, startling him. Looking down, he saw it was Kaz.

"Yes?"

"Gentry killed them. All of them. He's coming for me now. He knows!"

Denny Carmichael breathed heavily into the phone now. Things had spun completely out of control. Kaz was the calmest intelligence official Denny had ever worked with. If he was losing his cool, Denny knew he was in trouble. "Calm down. He doesn't know anything."

"He *knows*! He told me he knew about Trieste."

"You spoke to him?"

"Yes."

"And what does that mean? Trieste. It means nothing. He's flailing, Kaz.

That's all. He's trying to get into your head. To get you to expose yourself. If you stay calm you will be—"

Kaz said, "I can't help with this anymore. My exposure is too great."

Carmichael shouted into the phone, "Listen to me, Kaz, you aren't going anywhere till this is over!"

"Forget it! The local police will take control of the scene. My men are dead. The dead will be identified as Saudi, it will link my nation with the hunt for Court Gentry, and everyone will know. It is only a matter of time before they connect the pieces." He paused. "I have to get out of the country."

"No! We'll come up with a story for the press. I'll talk to them personally. We've manipulated it so far, we will control it."

"*What* story?"

Carmichael said, "Come to me here. We can talk about this. I'll put it on the books as an emergency liaison meeting between our offices. They won't let you bring your detail to the safe house, but I can send an armored motorcade to pick you up and bring you to me."

"I don't know what you think we can accomplish."

"Damage control, Kaz! We stop the bleeding on this op, and then we go back on offense." Carmichael looked at his watch. "I have an emergency meeting with the Working Group at eight, but I'll send the cars to pick you up now and you can wait in my office till I'm finished."

There was a long pause. Then, "Send your very best men."

Court and Zack exfiltrated the Ritz hotel and then began driving south, out of Arlington. The plan was to return to Court's safe house, of sorts, in the woods an hour south of the District. Zack didn't think much of the plan; he wanted to stop for celebratory pizza and beers, but Court insisted they lie low for the rest of the night.

They were most of the way down I-95 and nearing the turnoff to the little airport when Zack got a call from Matt Hanley. He put it on speaker so Court could hear.

Zack gave Hanley an after-action report on the events at the Ritz, and Hanley seemed pleased, but quickly it became clear he had something else he wanted to talk about.

"I just got some interesting news from a guy who used to be in Ground

Branch. Now he is driving in the secure motor pool. I put out feelers with a few outside the division yesterday saying I was trying to find out where Denny was spending his nights, and this guy came through."

"What did he say?" Court asked.

"The U.S. head of Saudi Arabia's Mukhabarat in D.C. was just transported to a CIA safe house in Alexandria."

Court asked, "Why is that significant?"

"The place he went to is a damn citadel. It's called Alexandria Eight. It's been around forever. It's old, but the Agency doesn't have a more fortified installation anywhere in the District. *That's* going to be where Denny is hiding out."

Court understood. "And this Saudi is going to be the guy I talked to on the phone. Who is he?"

"His name is Murquin al-Kazaz. Denny has known him for over a decade."

"Do you know him?" Zack asked.

"No. I never did liaison intelligence shit. I don't trust the House of Saud the way Denny does."

Court said, "We need to identify al-Kazaz's involvement with Operation BACK BLAST."

"Easier said than done. I don't have any access to that."

"It doesn't matter, Matt. We have access to *him*. You just have to get me into Alexandria Eight. I'll get him to talk."

Hanley snorted into the phone. "Did you not hear what I just said? It's Fort Knox, Court."

"If it's a safe house, then you have schematics on it."

"I do. I have blueprints, and the defensive plan from security. *That's* how I know it's impenetrable."

"Prove it. Let me see the prints and plans."

Hanley thought it over a minute. "All right, I'll send them to Zack's phone and you can look. But that's only to prove to you that I'm right. You aren't getting in there, and I'm not going to let you go on a suicide mission."

Court spent nearly a half hour looking over the defenses at the CIA safe house while Zack drove. The facility was impressive, to say the least, but Court was motivated to find a way in.

He found himself significantly less motivated to find a way out.

While Court worked, Zack listened to country music on the radio. He sang along with Dwight Yoakam, then hummed along with Johnny Cash. When some cornball and sugary new country artist came on the radio, however, Zack just sat there and bitched about the state of the music industry till Court told him to shut the hell up so he could think.

An aircraft flying low overhead on its base leg to Stafford Regional Airport, just a mile to the south of where he sat, gave Court an idea. After a few more minutes' work, he called Hanley back.

While Zack and Matt listened quietly, Court laid out his plan in as much detail as he could.

When he was finished, Court said, "So, Matt. What do you think?"

Hanley replied with one word. "Disallowed."

"Why?"

"Because it's suicide, that's why."

"I can do it."

"No one can do it. Plus, you told me how you'd get in, but not how you'd get out."

Court cocked his head. "I *did* tell you how I'd get out."

Hanley said, "I . . . I thought that part was just a joke."

"It might still be. But I'm willing to try it."

"Are you insane?"

"No, sir. But I am in a hurry. If we do this we have to hit right now, while al-Kazaz is there."

Hanley wouldn't budge, so Court said, "Matt. Denny is going to figure out you helped me. The war between you two is going to get worse."

"That doesn't mean I'm going to green-light you on this. Denny is a criminal, and he's an asshole, but I'm not going to kill him."

"Why not? He killed Jordan Mayes."

Hanley replied quickly. "We can't prove it. The one real witness says it was you."

Court said, "I'm not going after Denny. If I get to him, I'll talk to him, but I swear to you I will not hurt him. No promises on this al-Kazaz fucker, though."

"Sorry, Court. The answer is still no."

"Matt. I *need* to do this."

"That's where you are wrong, Six. If you pull this off, it won't change what happened in Trieste."

"That's not what I'm doing."

"Are you sure about that? This sounds like simple revenge."

Court did not reply to this. Instead he hung up the phone.

Zack said, "You should be happy he disallowed that shit. There was no way in hell you were going to survive."

"Get out."

"What? Here? In the middle of the woods? It's another mile to your safe house."

Court drew his pistol and pointed it at his former team leader. "I'm not joking. Out."

"Court, I know what you are going to do. It won't work, it won't change a thing, and you won't survive it."

"I will if you save me."

"How am I supposed to do that?"

"You know how."

"That is crazy, bro."

"You're my only chance. I trust you."

"Then I'm talking to a dead man."

"Get out," Court repeated, and he put the muzzle of the pistol on the top of Zack's knee.

Zack climbed out of the truck, and he started to lean back into the window to talk to Gentry, but Court fired up the engine and pulled back onto the dirt road. He raced off to the south, spraying mud all over his former team leader as he sped away.

72

ngus Lee flew the Bell 206 JetRanger news helicopter for D.C.'s Fox 5. Stafford Regional wasn't his normal airport, but he had just flown down to Richmond for a story and was stopping off here to top off fuel before heading back to the District. There had been a mass murder this afternoon at the Ritz-Carlton Pentagon City, and his station wanted him circling the building for live shots during their full evening special report coverage of the D.C. spy murders.

He'd just finished fueling up on the helipad, and he waved Fox 5 videographer Robert Robles over from inside the hangar. Robles immediately ran over and climbed into the JetRanger, anxious to get to the skies over D.C. so he could get to work.

As the helicopter began spinning up, a black pickup truck appeared on the pad racing towards it. Robles pointed it out to Lee. "Hey, looks like you forgot to pay for your gas."

Lee chuckled, but quickly he got the feeling something was wrong. "That's not an airport vehicle. And he's moving fast."

The Fox photog knew a good shot when he saw one, so he shouldered his camera and began recording. The vehicle stopped just feet from the nose of the helicopter, and the driver's door opened. To the astonishment of both men, a man climbed out with a pistol in his hand, pointed it at the pilot, and walked around to the right side door of the helicopter.

The gunman was head to toe in black and, at first, Robles thought the man was African American. But as the man came closer it was clear his face was covered in greasepaint.

He tapped on the Plexiglas door of the right seat.

"Get us out of here!" Robles shouted to his pilot, but Lee wasn't going to take off with a gun to his head.

He opened the door and put his hands up. Robles did the same.

The man leaned in and spoke to Lee, because with the noise of the engine above them, Robles couldn't hear. "Get out, go to the truck, and get the gear bag from the bed. Bring it back here."

"What are you going to do?"

The man with the greasepaint turned to the side, used the barrel of his pistol to tap the parachute rig strapped on his back. "I just need a quick ride. Your partner there will win himself a Pulitzer for what he's about to film."

Lee kept his hands up, but he said, "What about me?"

"You just keep us out of restricted airspace so we don't get shot down. That should be enough motivation for you."

"Oh . . . Okay."

Court watched the pilot move the forty-pound gear bag from the truck to the spinning helo, then Court climbed in the backseat with it. The pilot got back in and strapped himself into the right seat again.

The videographer was too scared to turn around and look at Court, but Court put on a headset and spoke to him. "Cameraman, throw your phone out the door. Pilot, you, too." Both men did as instructed. Court read off a series of GPS coordinates to the pilot, then said, "Take me there exactly. Get us to an altitude of six thousand feet."

Angus Lee punched the coordinates in his computer. "Yes, sir. What do I tell air traffic control?"

"Tell them you are flying to Baltimore. That will get you close enough to where we're going. After that tell them there was a gun to your head. That will get you out of trouble."

"I'll do what you ask. *Please* don't hold your gun to my head."

"It's a figure of speech, dude. Do what I say and we'll all stay friends. Cool?"

"Yes, sir."

The helo took off and headed north. Court had his own GPS unit on his wrist, and he used it to make sure the pilot complied with his instructions.

While they flew he also consulted a small tablet computer in his hand and looked over the schematics of the building he was about to hit, working over each detail of his operation again and again, trying to think of everything and anything that might come up.

Court's big backpack was next to him on the bench seat, not on his back, because his parachute was using that real estate at present. The pack was bungied to Court's waist, and it would hang from him as he parachuted down. If Court didn't make contact with the enemy during the landing phase of his jump he would pull a knife from his chest rig and cut the pack free right before he touched down. Otherwise he would simply land with a forty-pound weight hanging between his legs, which wouldn't be optimal, but it was nothing Court had not dealt with before, both in training and in operations.

He was well versed in dealing with Murphy's Law.

He put the tablet computer away, then he grabbed another bag from his pack. One by one he pulled out five mobile phones and placed them on the seat next to him. Once he had them lined up, he opened the Uber car service app on each phone and fiddled with the map on each screen for a few seconds. It took longer than he would have liked, but after less than five minutes, he had accomplished what he'd set out to do.

He then opened the door of the helo and leaned out. Looking down, he realized they were flying over Huntley Meadows Park, a large forested green space that would be closed for the evening. Court took all five phones and tossed them over the side of the helo, then closed the door again.

The pilot flew to six thousand feet, checked his GPS, and told Gentry they were two minutes from the target. Court checked one more time to make sure all his kit was secure on his body.

He saw the videographer moving his camera into position. Court turned away, his back to the lens. He spoke into the mic. "No lights."

"I understand," said the videographer.

Court took off his headset, opened the rear door, kicked his legs out over the side, and looked out.

He saw nothing but clouds. His pounding heart skipped a beat.

From the front the pilot shouted now, "Ten seconds!"

Court checked his own GPS and confirmed this, then hefted his backpack in his lap and pushed to the edge of his seat. The cold night pressed against his face as he looked out the side of the helo.

Then, "Three, two, one. Go!"

Court went over the side, dropping his forty-pound bag from his hands as he did so. It pulled at his waist for a moment but as both he and his equipment bundle reached maximum velocity, he knew he wouldn't think about it again.

Not until he pulled the rip cord. He did this at four thousand feet, he felt the canopy catch above him, and instantly the bag yanked hard below him. He checked his chute; it was almost impossible to see in the cloudy night above, but he saw his lines were taut and he realized he had a good, full canopy.

Checking the GPS on his wrist, he began steering to the left, then he looked down, trying to pick out the large clock tower of Alexandria Eight. It took him some time, but on his right he saw the lights of a jet on final approach to nearby Reagan National, and he used this as a reference point. His eyes tracked south from the airport, along the Potomac River, then he looked along the lights of King Street, which led from the river all the way to the massive George Washington Masonic National Memorial, the highest building in the city. From here his eyes tracked to the left, to the west, and within a few seconds he centered on Alexandria Eight.

Once he had the clock tower of the safe house in his sights, he looked at little else, because the tower was his landing zone.

He thought the darkness would improve his chances of parachuting all the way to the tower without being seen by the guard force on the property, but he had wanted to do something to improve his chances even more.

Below him on North Quaker Lane, five pairs of headlights moved slowly to the edge of the property at the front of the safe house grounds. When they rolled under the streetlight closest to the driveway, this revealed them to be five large black SUVs. They stopped one hundred feet in front of the guard shack and just sat there. They weren't threatening anyone or anything, but they were a curious sight indeed.

The five SUVs were from Uber, and Court had ordered one to go to that location with each of his five phones. He'd texted each driver with instructions to wait at the end of the driveway. The drivers inside the vehicles didn't know anything more than that; when they found themselves forming into a motorcade with other drivers, they likely assumed a group would be coming down the driveway from the big property any minute and piling in to go to dinner or to another location.

But Court didn't care what the drivers were thinking. He was only concerned about what the CIA guards on the property were thinking. He knew everyone would see a motorcade of big black SUVs and immediately think "feds" or other government entity. He had planned this so that every eye on the property would look out to the cars at the end of the drive. If he had created some threatening diversion, explosions or fireworks, for example, he knew security here would order the south wing of the property locked down tight, so he kept his diversion mild. Just government-looking vehicles forming in the distance.

Court turned his attention from the five SUVs and focused again on the clock tower. The defensive plan of Alexandria Eight, Court had read in the plans sent by Hanley, had called for either one or two guards on the clock tower landing. Court was hoping for one, but when he got his NODs centered on the tower and then looked just below it at the landing, he saw three men standing there.

Shit.

He reached for the weapon on his right hip. It was a Ruger Mark 2 Amphibian, a stainless steel .22 caliber rim fire pistol with an integral suppressor.

But then he decided to change his tactics on the fly. As he descended closer to the men he took his hand off the pistol, and he let go of one of the brake handles on his parachute rig and quickly pulled his knife. At thirty feet above the landing he cut away his equipment bundle, then quickly grabbed his quick-release harness, pulling it to release the entire rigging from his back.

The backpack crashed on the landing and Court landed right behind it, hitting the surface and dropping low, just inches behind the first sentry, who swung around at the noise right behind him. Court came up under the man's M4 rifle, ripping the weapon away with one hand and pulling against the guard's rifle sling. This yanked the man forward, with his chin leading the way.

Court rocked the man with an uppercut palm strike to his chin.

The first guard crumpled to the ground unconscious before the other two men even knew what was going on.

Both remaining security officers spun into action now—one reached for the radio on his shoulder while his hand went down to draw his pistol, and the second brought his rifle up towards the movement less than ten feet away on the landing. Court drew his suppressed Ruger .22 and shot the first man in the forearm, knocking his support hand off the rifle and causing the weapon to drop free, where it hung by its sling.

Quickly there was a second snap of Court's integrally suppressed pistol and a small flash of light. The radio handset in the second guard's left hand shattered. As he drew his pistol with his right hand Court fired another round from the nearly silent pistol. The small round slammed into the barrel of the pistol in the man's right hand, knocking it away. It bounced off into the darkness on the landing.

The officer in front reached again for his rifle hanging from his chest, but Court closed the distance, slapped the gun to the side, and pressed the long suppressor of his Amphibian into the man's forehead. In an aggressive whisper he said, "A lot of dumb assholes have died for Denny Carmichael. That ends tonight. You don't want to be the last one to die, do you?"

Though Court's gun was pressed to one man's head, his eyes were on the second man, ensuring he wouldn't try to run for the door to the stairwell. When the man turned to do just that Court took his steel pistol and struck the right temple of the man under his control, dropping him unconscious to the ground. Then Court turned and aimed at the fleeing guard.

Court fired twice, striking the man once in each thigh. The security officer dropped flat on his face, unable to operate his wounded legs.

The dark figure who had appeared from the sky now advanced along the narrow landing, overtaking the young guard as he kept crawling for the door.

Court reached into a pouch on the wounded man's own load bearing vest, and he retrieved two tourniquets. While the man squirmed Court applied one high to each of the two thighs, stopping the bleeding instantly, but also completely disabling the appendages, as they went numb in seconds. He spoke softly to the terrified man below him.

"I doubt I hit anything vital, so you probably don't need the tourniquets, but I don't know how long it's going to take for you to wake up and call for help."

"Wake up?"

Court smashed the Ruger pistol into the side of the man's head, and the security officer slumped back on the landing.

Court stood, heaved his pack, and headed for the stairwell.

When he drew up his attack on Alexandria Eight, Court knew the weakest link of his entire infiltration would be the period—maybe no more than fifteen seconds—between exiting the tower stairwell and entering Denny Carmichael's private suite. Court would have to move down a winding open staircase from the third floor to the second floor, completely exposed to everyone and anyone in the main hall of the building. For all Court knew there could be two dozen armed men standing around on the ground floor or on the second-floor landing, and they would all have a straight line of fire on him until he made it off the landing and through the entry to the hall of the south wing. And perhaps even more importantly than the fact that he'd be exposed to the guns, it would only take one person triggering a warning for the security office of the building to flip a switch, at which point the steel doors would close and the pneumatic locks would engage, sealing the south wing off from the rest of the property.

He couldn't stay invisible and he couldn't crawl down the stairs, because he would still be in view. No. He just had to run for it and hope no one saw him, at least until he was close enough to the hallway door to get through before it was shut and locked from the inside.

And Court had to do all this with forty pounds of gear on his back.

He moved out of the tower stairwell and onto the winding staircase around the main hall. The light was good here, which wasn't good news for Court, but he was happy to find no CIA security officers on the stairs or on the higher floors.

He began moving down the stairs. Below him at least a half dozen armed guards stood at ground level, congregated at the main entrance to the building. They all appeared to still be looking outside at the five SUVs way down the driveway.

This ruse worked for a while, but finally Court saw one of the men turn away from the front door, idly look up, and see a man head to toe in black, his face darkened with greasepaint, and a massive black backpack on his back.

As much as he hated it, Court was impressed with the speed at which the man reacted.

"Contact!" The guard below raised his weapon, and Court picked up the pace, rushing towards the hallway doors half a floor down and twenty yards away.

With the first echoing cracks of rifle fire in the huge room, Court knew the security officer positioned behind a desk just inside the south wing would be reaching for the button that would close that part of the building off from the rest of the property. This would slam the door shut, drop steel over the windows, and lock steel doors to the attic above. Court would have zero access to Carmichael and al-Kazaz once the door—now fifteen yards away—slammed shut.

Masonry on the open stairway exploded just in front of Court but he ran into the dust and bits of debris. He didn't bother with fighting back; even firing a couple of rounds in hopes it would force his adversaries to take cover would cost him more time than he could afford to lose.

He just kept running down the stairs, taking them three at a time. The backpack strap bit into the ragged wound on the right side of his rib cage.

All the M4s in the entryway were firing now; the noise was insane in the three-story-high room, and Court felt the jolt of a round slamming into his backpack behind him. It pushed him against the wall but his momentum kept him moving onward, and his balance was good enough to keep him from stumbling and falling down the stairs.

A light above the south wing door began flashing when Court was just ten yards away. He saw the double doors closing quickly in front of him. A squawking alarm that kept time with the flashes rang out but it was drowned out by another half dozen rounds. Court felt the overpressure and heard the zing of a bullet passing a foot from his face, but he ignored the desire to duck and instead he dove forward, arms outstretched, and he landed on his chest on the marble floor, and then tumbled right past the closing steel doors.

As soon as he was through he tucked his feet to his body and the doors slammed shut right behind him.

But his problems had just begun. There were two men at the far end of the south wing hall, one hundred feet away and looking in his direction. The security desk was just on his right by the double doors, so he rolled out of his backpack, then rushed behind the desk. Here a lone security officer drew his pistol to fire at the man in the black greasepaint but Court slid under the man's aim and took him out at the legs.

The security officer fell on top of Court, but as he dropped down, Court fired a straight right jab up. The crack of bone on bone echoed in the hall, and the guard was unconscious before he landed face-first on the floor next to his attacker.

Court leapt to his feet, then started running to a room just off the hall. While he did this he heard shouts from the approaching security officers. Court opened fire as he ran, aiming low. One man took a pair of .22 caliber rounds in the shins, the other a single bullet through the top of his boot and into his foot.

Both men tumbled down in pain.

Court scooped his pack off the floor by a strap as he ran, then he dragged it along next to him. He made it into the room across the hall as pounding gunfire chased him, and crashed into an armed CIA security officer rushing out. Both men fell to the ground, and with the impact both men fired their weapons. The sound of Court's .22 was drowned out by the report of the other man's HK MP7 Personal Defense Weapon discharging a round, but both bullets struck a bookcase filled with dusty old books.

Court's ground-fighting skills were superior to those of the other man, so he managed to get on top of him quickly, delivering a punch to the man's jaw, and then lifting his head up and knocking it back into the hardwood floor. The security officer went limp under him.

Court dove off the man and back towards the open door behind him, slammed it shut, and then crawled to his knees and bolted it.

He stood up, then doubled over in pain, holding the right side of his rib cage as he did so. The gunshot wound bled a little, but mostly it just hurt. He fought the incredible desire to just slide back down to the floor and lie in the fetal position. Instead he used the locked door to steady himself, then he turned around slowly to survey the room behind him.

There, much to his surprise, fifteen men and women sat silently around a massive conference table. They all stared up at him, eyes wide. A blond in her thirties put her hand over her mouth. An African American male in his forties stood slowly and balled his fists, but he did not approach. Others raised their hands in surrender, and the rest did not move a muscle.

Court lifted the guard's MP7 and trained it on the group, then he reached down into a pouch of the big pack on the floor. He dug around inside for a moment, then he pulled out a device no larger than a deck of cards. He held it up to the men and women at the table.

"Wireless detonator." He motioned with his head to the backpack. "C4 antipersonnel charge with an anti-tamper switch and a motion detector. Enough demo to level this wing. Anybody moves, we all go on a moon shot together. Any questions?"

An attractive redhead began to cry.

Court said, "Sit tight a second, I'll be right back." He moved past the table and entered a narrow hallway off the conference room. He knew from the blueprints and the security plan Hanley had sent him that this hall had a narrow staircase to the attic off to the left. At the top of this was a steel-reinforced door to the attic. Beyond the staircase sat Denny's office and private quarters.

As Court passed the stairs to the attic he raised his weapon out in front of him, and as he neared the door to Denny's office, it opened in his direction.

73

DeRenzi had made it to Carmichael and his Middle Eastern guest within seconds of the alarm sounding, with the plan to barricade them in place. He locked the door to the conference room—the Violator Working Group members were guarded by a security officer named Suarez—then he bolted the other door from the office to the main hall. After a few seconds he heard gunfire right outside in the hall, which likely meant the attacker had made it past the doors into the south wing before they closed. DeRenzi rushed now to the conference room entrance. He listened at the door a moment, then opened it, intending on calling out to Suarez, to order him to fall back to DeRenzi's position to help cover Carmichael. Two men could protect the two entrances better than one, DeRenzi reasoned. This would leave the Violator Working Group on their own, but DeRenzi knew the Gray Man was in the building, and he also knew Denny Carmichael was the target.

The employees of the Violator Working Group weren't his problem.

Slowly the veteran CIA shooter opened the door to the conference room hall, got his gun up, and saw a man head to toe in black, just a foot away.

DeRenzi fired his M4 but the Gray Man used his MP7 to strike the weapon just as it fired, sending a burst of 5.56 rounds into the wall of the hallway by the bathroom door. The Gray Man took hold of the handguard of the weapon, then raised his MP7. At point-blank range he fired directly into the steel chest plate of DeRenzi's body armor, knocking the CIA security officer back on his heels. A second shot from Gentry's gun, then a third, a fourth, a fifth, and a sixth sent DeRenzi stumbling backwards the length of the office. Court ripped the M4 from the security officer's hand as he fell back.

DeRenzi lay on his back on the parquet floor. He wore a pistol on his hip, but just as he thought about going for it, Court said, "You try it and the next six rounds won't go in the middle of your chest plate. I'll put them in your face."

DeRenzi raised his hands in surrender.

Court had him remove his drop leg holster and slide the entire unit across the floor, then he ordered him onto his stomach with his legs crossed and his hands behind his head. Once DeRenzi complied, Court turned to Carmichael, who stood in front of a shuttered window.

With him was Murquin al-Kazaz.

Court showed no emotion as he approached both men. He planned on checking them for weapons quickly, but as soon as he reached for the Saudi, he realized there was no way this man would have been allowed in the building with a firearm or a blade. He turned to Denny. "You wearing a gun, Denny?"

Carmichael shook his head. "I put it on the desk, son. I'm not pointing a gun at the world-famous Gray Man."

There was sarcasm in the comment, but at least Carmichael was telling the truth. Court saw a semiautomatic lying on the desk fifteen feet away. He searched Denny anyway, and he found nothing on his person save for a mobile phone, and a curious item on his left wrist. Just larger than a watch, it had a small glass screen and a function button. Court touched the button, and the screen lit up. He realized the device was a master security panic button. By scrolling left or right on the screen, he could then give the wrist computer different commands. He could alert his security force of an emergency, close and lock his living quarters, or close and lock down the entire south wing. He also had the option of opening and closing any door in the wing, and even overriding commands from the south wing security desk.

Court was pleased to see that the big double doors were still closed and locked, then he pressed the icon that would keep them that way until he signaled that he wanted them open. He put the device on his own wrist, then led the three men back down the hall and into the conference room without a word. He had Denny and al-Kazaz both take a seat at the table, then he pushed DeRenzi against the wall at the back of the room, flipped them on their stomachs, and tied them expertly with pieces of Kevlar rope.

The conference room was a full house now.

A middle-aged man at the table said, "There was no motion detector on that bomb, was there?"

Court said, "Are you kidding? That would be dangerous." He checked the locks on the conference room doors and decided they were solid. Confident he had a semi-secure perimeter, he finally took a breath, then looked around the room at the crowd. "Who are all you people?"

No one answered.

He turned to the youngest, most junior-looking person in the room, a scrawny kid with Coke-bottle glasses who sat at the far end of the table by the wall monitors, a laptop computer and a few peripherals on the table in front of him. The man was terrified, clearly, and to Court he looked like he couldn't have been twenty-five years old. Pointing the HK rifle at him, Court said, "Who are you?"

A meek cough. "William, sir."

"And what's your function here, William?"

"I'm in charge of the video-conferencing suite. That's all I know, sir."

"Who are you conferencing with?"

The young man glanced over to Carmichael. Court said, "Denny can fire you tomorrow. I can shoot you now. Pay attention to *me*."

"I am connecting the Violator Working Group here with the Violator tactical operations center at Langley."

Court nodded. "The Violator Working Group?" He looked around at the men and women at the table. "All these years I pictured the faces of the people who were after me. Not the shooters on the ground, but the suits pulling the strings. And here you are."

After a slow pan of the room, he looked back to the young man. "William, are we connected with the TOC right now?"

"Yes, sir."

"These assholes at the table needed the TOC to locate me, but I'm here, so they don't really need it anymore. I want you to pull the plug on everything. Shut it all down for me."

William slowly moved his hands up to the laptop and began shutting down the connection.

Court turned back to the group. "Toss your phones in the middle of the table." Everyone did so. "Guns, knives, Tasers, pepper spray?" No one moved. "*Anything?*"

Nothing but shakes of the head.

"None of you have any way of protecting yourselves from me? I was just some name on a sanction list, some vague personality that needed to die. I wasn't a real person, so you didn't see me as a threat to you. Now here I am, and you don't have a clue what to do about it."

Denny Carmichael said, "Court, this is—"

"Shut the fuck up!" Court screamed, his outburst of rage in stark contrast to the calm demeanor he'd used to address William seconds before. He raised his PDW and stormed around the table, aiming the weapon's laser pointer on Denny's forehead the entire time.

More women sobbed now, and some of the men trembled with terror.

No one in the Alexandria Police Department was aware that the twelfth largest building in their city was, in truth, a Cold War–era CIA secure facility that was now being used as a safe house by America's senior operations officer, so when the first call came through about a hostage situation at the property on North Quaker Lane, they did what they would do for any other similar event; they dispatched squad cars, tactical units, supervisors, and detectives.

The Agency employees at the facility had been ordered to keep a low profile, which meant they couldn't very well tell the cops that rolled onto the grounds to get off their lawn. They did confirm there were government employees inside, which caused the local police to inform the FBI, but as far as the Alexandria cops were concerned, this was their town, so this was their scene.

Within minutes a massive cordon was set up around the building, helicopters were flying overhead, and police filled the main hall. Above them, on the second-floor landing, two dozen armed men screamed down at the cops, refusing to come down or turn over their guns, claiming that they were responsible for what went on here, and they would take care of it.

The police were disinclined to just pack up and call it a night, however, so a tense standoff developed.

The FBI arrived ten minutes later, in the form of six Special Agents. They called in their vaunted Hostage Rescue Team, but it would take HRT a half hour to deploy from Quantico. In the meantime the FBI men pushed their way through the cops, made it to the bottom of the stairs, pulled their credentials, and began walking up into the cordon of armed plainclothes-men on the landing. Nobody shot anybody, which was something, but the shouting and the yelling only got worse with the arrival of the FBI.

Suzanne Brewer had been sleeping—the dark hospital room along with the painkillers they gave her every six hours made it hard to stay awake—but her eyes opened when she heard the door squeak. A shaft of light raced across the room to her. Her guards outside were ordered to keep everyone out but hospital personnel, and her nurse had told her she would not be disturbed for the rest of the night. As she turned her head to look, for one brief, heart-stopping moment she thought of Violator, but this vision drifted away instantly and, in a second moment—this one lasting twice as long because to her the threat was twice as real—she thought of Carmichael.

Could he have changed his mind about their arrangement? Could this be one of the Saudi hitters roaming the District?

But the man in the doorway was not the Gray Man, and he was no one doing the bidding of Denny Carmichael. On the contrary, Matthew Hanley stood big and broad, a thin smile on his face and a large bouquet of flowers in his hand.

For some reason Suzanne could not put her finger on, the sight of Hanley with flowers felt to her more menacing than seeing a Saudi assassin at her door.

"Hi, Suzanne, how are you feeling?"

She pressed a button on the railing of her bed, turning on a light on the wall behind her. She pushed a second button, and this raised her up into a sitting position.

"Matt, so nice to see you." This had yet to be determined in Suzanne's mind, but she said it anyway. "Flowers personally delivered by a division director? I must say I'm surprised you took the time to come all the way over here."

Hanley said, "They tell me you are going to be fine. A broken leg, a concussion, lots of cuts and bruises, but it could have been worse."

"Yes," she said. "Much worse." After a moment she added, "Poor, poor Jordan."

Hanley said nothing.

Suzanne could not stand the silence of the moment. "Sorry, Matt, I don't want to look a gift horse in the mouth, but is there some reason you are here, other than the flowers?"

"You don't know what's happened, do you?"

Suzanne Brewer shook her head slowly. "I know nothing. I've been lying here in the dark since mid-afternoon."

Hanley sat down in the chair next to her bed. "At this moment Denny Carmichael is being held hostage by Court Gentry in a safe house in Alexandria."

She closed her eyes. Her mind raced. "Oh my God. What are we doing to get Denny out of there?"

"Everything we can, I'm sure, but Gentry holds all the cards at the moment."

Suzanne's head began to spin. She tried to sit up. "I'm going to Langley. I can manage this better from the TOC."

Hanley shook his head. "You are going to stay right here." He picked a dead petal off of one of the chrysanthemums. Dropped it on the floor. "Suzanne, you are a winner. You can still come out of this ahead, but the walls are closing all around you, and there is not much time."

"I . . . I don't understand."

"You've chosen sides. That's all right, we all need an allegiance. But your side is losing. Even if Denny walks out of that safe house with his life, he won't hold the power he held when he walked in. His operations have been compromised. His connection to Gentry and the origins of the shoot on sight will be scrutinized.

"I'm not telling you anything you don't know, I'm sure. You are a lot more politically astute than I am, so you know when you are standing on a sinking ship."

The metaphors were piling one on top of the other, but she certainly understood the message.

She fought for the right words. "I'm not sure I understand you, Matt. I'm sorry. My involvement in this matter is limited to the work I did in the Working Group, and my presence at the scene of one of Violator's assassinations. I am not aligned with Director Carmichael any more than anyone else in the Clandestine Service."

Hanley stood. "Well, if that's the case, then you can turn on CNN right now and watch the action in Alexandria with only a passing curiosity. With no stake in the outcome. If there is something else, some other string that tethers you to Carmichael, then you should consider cutting it before he goes down. Denny's descent won't be pretty, and he will take a great number of people with him. That is unfortunate for them, but it will create a power vacuum that the Agency will need to fill."

Hanley continued, "The NCS is going to need good people in its ranks when this is over. Winners."

He headed for the door, but Suzanne called out to him.

"Matt, I'd say you are a lot more politically aware than you make yourself out to be."

Hanley turned. "Me? No, I'm just an old straight-legged army guy who's learned how to roll with the punches." He smiled a little. "That's all. Hope you feel better." He left the room, leaving Suzanne Brewer alone with a terror that began welling up inside her.

Within twenty seconds, she reached for the telephone.

74

Things inside the conference room had gotten testy. A few of the male CIA officials were preparing to make a move, and DeRenzi had tried to climb back to his feet. Court held up the detonator, and this quelled some of the enthusiasm from the agitators, but he knew he needed to thin this herd immediately.

He announced to the crowd that everyone would be leaving other than al-Kazaz and Carmichael. DeRenzi protested, Court threatened to shoot him, and then DeRenzi shut up.

Court then ordered everyone to stand and head to the door.

A square-jawed CIA NSA liaison officer sat straight in his chair. "I am not leaving Director Carmichael!"

Court just sighed. "Yeah, you are, asshole."

"Fuck you! I'm staying." The man showed no fear. He looked Court in the eye. "You'll have to shoot me."

Court turned to Carmichael. "Denny, you can either order this man to hit the bricks, which will make you look noble and benevolent, or I can shoot him in the head. He'll be dead, and you'll look just like the jackass you are. Your call."

"Dale, it's okay."

"No, sir."

"I order you to leave with the rest of the Working Group."

"Sir, I—"

"Christ. *Fucking* go, Hamilton!"

Hamilton complied, but the entire time he walked around the table and towards the exit he gave Court a look of pure hatred. Court returned the evil eye, but said nothing.

When all seventeen men and women were lined up at the door, Court taped Carmichael and al-Kazaz's hands behind their backs and ordered them to stay seated at the table.

He then opened the door into the hallway and everyone filed forward, directly across to the heavy steel doors that led into the main hall. The three security officers out here Court had dealt with earlier were still out of the fight; two men were tending to their wounds and the third, the man from behind the security desk, was just coming out of his stupor. Court removed the weapons from the men and put them in the group with the others.

Court stepped to the side of the door and lifted his weapon, training it on the crowd. "Everybody hold your hands high. When those doors open you will have five seconds to get out, then I'm closing them again. If you see anybody trying to come in, you need to just run over them and keep going, because I will open up with automatic fire if I'm engaged."

He heard spoken prayers and loud sobbing. "Here we go."

He pushed the icon on his wrist controller to open the pneumatic doors, and they swung inward quickly. Outside on the second-floor mezzanine the dozen or more security officers in sight stood or knelt or lay prone, their guns trained on the movement. Several FBI agents just yards from the doors were caught in the open. They drew pistols and crouched low, ready to respond to an ambush by the attacker inside. Men down on the ground floor rushed to swing their weapons to bear on the threat.

All the men with guns held fire when they saw the large group of men and women, everyone with their hands up, moving through the doorway.

Court pressed the icon on his wrist controller to shut the doors just as fast as they opened, and he locked them down with another command.

He stepped back into the conference room and locked these doors, as well, then he stood in front of al-Kazaz and Carmichael. "It's just us now, gents." Court hefted his big pack and left the room, heading up to the attic.

Five minutes later he returned to find the phone in the center of the conference table ringing. Court looked at his watch, then stepped over and pushed the button to put the call on the speaker box.

"Must be a jurisdictional fight out there. It took you guys forever."

"Who am I speaking with, please?"

Court didn't answer.

"Is this Jeff Duncan?"

Court shrugged. "Sure, why not?"

"Mr. Duncan, this is Allen Reynolds with the FBI. I need to make sure everyone in there is safe."

"Buddy, there's nobody in here that's safe, and if you and your friends come in here you'll be the least safe of all."

"Is Director Carmichael with you?"

"Yes, he is. He is unhurt."

"I'd really like to check in with him, if that's okay."

Denny sat silently at the table, his hands behind his back and sweat on his brow.

Court said, "Denny, meet Allen. Allen, this is Denny."

"This is Carmichael. There is one gunman." He looked at Court with malevolence. "Just one."

The FBI negotiator said, "I also understand there is a Saudi diplomat present, is that correct?"

Now Court said, "Al-Kazaz, meet the guys."

Murquin al-Kazaz spoke in a loud and authoritative voice. "Contact Jabar Almlhan at my embassy immediately. Inform him of the situation. Then, notify—"

Court pressed the MP7 to the Saudi man's temple, and he stopped talking.

Court said, "See, he's fine. A little bossy, but that's not my fault.

"Let me tell you what's what, Allen. Right now your HRT guys are looking at the blueprints of this building, and they are figuring that the attic above the south wing is the best avenue into my location. The roof isn't steel like the windows and doors, and it's not reinforced with iron like the walls and the floor. It's a reasonable assumption to make, but it's up to you to let your guys know they are wrong. I've rigged a rather large explosive to a motion detector, and it will detonate if anyone tries to enter the attic. I really don't want to blow up a bunch of poor FBI working stiffs, but now that I've warned you guys what will happen if you try to come through the attic, my conscience is clear on that matter, so you guys decide what you want to do."

"I understand, Jeff."

"That's all for now. I'm going to talk to Denny a bit, and then I'll be back with you."

He heard the negotiator say "Jeff?" right before he pushed the button to disconnect the call, but Court hung up anyway.

He sat down at the table in front of the two men and positioned the MP7 on the table in front of him, the barrel pointed at Carmichael's chest, six feet away. He said, "So much trouble to get a meeting with you."

Al-Kazaz said, "I have nothing to do with any of this. I have diplomatic immunity."

Court smiled again. "I'm not so diplomatic, so you aren't immune from me. In fact, if you don't tell me what I want to know, I can guarantee you I will be your proximate cause of death."

Kaz clenched his neck muscles, but he did not speak.

"Now," said Court, "I am going to sit here and pick your brains till I know what Saudi Arabian intelligence had to do with Operation BACK BLAST. You were clearly involved, because you were willing to risk your operation here in the States to silence me."

Al-Kazaz shrugged his shoulders, an awkward gesture with his hands behind his back. He said, "I offered my agents in the hunt for you simply as a courtesy to Director Carmichael. We have a good relationship, and I wanted it to continue."

"Bullshit," Court said. "Denny was worried that if local PD got to me first they might accidentally take me alive. He wanted foreign hitters that would do his job for him. But for you to send a kill team into the streets here, he had some major leverage over you. What was it?"

"Our nations are simply partners against terrorism." His eyes narrowed. "Denny told me you were a terrorist."

Carmichael said, "Court, I initiated the shoot-on-sight order because you killed your team. Yes, I sent your team to pick you up for what happened in BACK BLAST. But you overreacted, you started shooting, they shot back, and then there were four dead SAD Ground Branch officers lying in the dirt."

The gunfight had happened in Gentry's Virginia Beach apartment; there was no dirt; but he did not correct Carmichael on this trifling point.

Court did, however, disagree with the larger premise. "That's a lie, Denny, and I've shot men for lying to me. My team was ordered to term me."

To Court's surprise, Denny did not push back on this. He just said, "You know BACK BLAST was your doing. I had every right to term you after what happened in Trieste."

"I know I shot Hawthorn, I must have screwed up the ID of the target, but that's not a reason to terminate me." He looked back and forth between the two men. Suddenly his tough act softened. "Just tell me what I'm missing here."

Denny said, "Why would I tell you a goddamned thing? You are going to kill us anyway."

Court shook his head. "Wrong. I promised Hanley I wouldn't kill you." Court shrugged. "I'd love to back out on that promise, but I won't." He then turned to al-Kazaz. "I might shoot this fuck just because I don't like him, though." He leaned closer to the Saudi. "You better impress the hell out of me in the next couple of minutes."

Carmichael said, "Courtland, you made a very serious mistake that hurt U.S. national interests gravely. You expected to see the assassin targeting Hawthorn. Instead you saw Hawthorn making his own move, *against* an AQ assassin. You didn't bother to get proper PID." Carmichael stared at the gun while he spoke. "You fucked up. You killed the best agent the West had in al Qaeda, crippled us in the War on Terror for years. Hell, a decade, perhaps. And to make matters even worse, you rescued an al Qaeda operator."

The phone rang again. Court sighed, then he snatched it up. "Allen, I said I'd call you."

"I want to help you, Jeff. Can I get you something to eat or drink? I just need to—"

Court interrupted. "Listen very carefully. This is bigger than you know. Sometime in the next few minutes a van is going to arrive and a bunch of men are going to pile out of it. Somebody with an ID that will confuse the hell out of you is going to walk up, and then a phone will ring, and someone far above your head will tell you to stand down and leave the premises. FBI and HRT will be sent packing with your tails between your legs."

Allen Reynolds said, "Jeff, that's what *we* did to the Alexandria police. Trust me, son, *nobody* does that to the FBI. You are stuck with me for the duration, so we should just open up a healthy dialogue here. I need to know what you need."

"I need for you to wait for the other guys to get here. They'll take over the scene. They'll probably be assholes about it, they don't hire these guys for their manners, but you won't be able to stop them."

The FBI man revealed a little swagger in his voice. "Who do you think is going to come for you?"

"The men that come will have orders to kill me, not to arrest me. They can't let you guys try and hit this room, because you might take me alive."

There was a pause.

Court said, "Allen? You there?"

"Uh . . . Jeff, I'm going to have to put you on hold for just one—"

Court gave a tired smile to Denny and al-Kazaz. He spoke into the speakerphone. "They're here, aren't they?"

"Uh . . . I'll be right back."

Court snorted out a chuckle. "No, you won't. You're done." He hung up the phone.

On the second-floor landing outside the steel doors, many of the men of the FBI HRT team took their eyes out of their gun sights and looked to the stairs below them. Heading up the staircase was a large group of armed men wearing civilian attire covered in body armor and ammunition. Their rifles were newer than the FBI shooters' own equipment, and the night vision equipment they wore on their helmets was a generation better, something the HRT boys had only seen in classified briefings about new technology.

One of the HRT snipers muttered, "Who the hell are these guys?"

FBI negotiator Allen Reynolds pocketed his phone and stepped in front of the approaching men. "Excuse me." They kept walking. "Hey! FBI! What the hell do you think you are doing?"

A man in his early forties stepped up to Reynolds and stopped while his cohorts continued on. He wore a beard and held an assault rifle and a helmet adorned with state-of-the-art communications gear, cameras, and other gadgetry Reynolds could not identify. "Good evening, Special Agent Reynolds. Your phone will ring in five seconds. It will be the deputy director of the FBI. But don't worry, it's good news. You get the rest of the night off."

The bearded man patted Reynolds on the shoulder and passed him by.

"Who the fuck do you think you are?" The phone trilled in his hand. He looked down at it a moment, then answered. "Special Agent Reynolds."

Dakota had already moved on. He and Harley walked up to the doors. Two other JSOC operators had begun looking for places to attach the breaching charges on them.

A minute later Reynolds stepped back up to Dakota. The JSOC commander was setting up a laptop and establishing communications with the CIA TOC.

The FBI negotiator stood next to him, waiting to be noticed. When he realized he was being purposefully ignored he said, "Okay, it's your scene."

Dakota didn't look up. "Yep."

"You guys must be—"

Dakota interrupted him. "Nope. That's not us."

"Right. Hey, look. No hard feelings. I was in myself. Seventy-fifth Ranger Regiment. Did five years."

Dakota turned dials on his interteam radio. "Is that right? Well, now you're a cop, so go find yourself a donut shop and get off of my scene."

The JSOC commander walked away, heading back over to the doors to check on the placement of the blast charges.

Special Agent Reynolds stood on the landing fuming for a moment, then he headed down the stairs towards his car.

75

The three men sat at the conference table, staring at one another in silence. Kaz shook perspiration out of his eyes, struggled against his bindings.

Carmichael sat motionless, looking even more drawn than usual.

Court looked tired himself, but his focus remained sharp.

To Carmichael, he asked, "Do you know the identity of the man I rescued?"

"Yes."

"What happened to him?"

Denny shrugged. "I took care of him."

"Meaning?"

"I put a warhead on his forehead."

"You drone-killed him?"

"That's right. Peshawar. 2011. Once I knew his involvement in this, I took him out." Carmichael went on, "You see why I had to term you, don't you? If the Israelis knew my man killed Hawthorn, there would be hell to pay with them. And if AQ got wind of it they would use it to their advantage. A propaganda coup that would destroy the CIA."

Court muttered, "So I had to die." The strain and adrenaline of the last thirty minutes had drawn most all of his energy reserves.

Denny said, "Of course you did. Think about it, Gentry. Put yourself in my shoes. Why would I even care? Do you think I sit at home at night and ponder the fate of one damn trigger-puller? The work I have done in my career has created nations. It's dissolved governments. A Ground Branch shooter thinks he got a raw deal? I'm sorry, but so *fucking* what?"

Court looked off into space.

So fucking what?

Softly, he said, "I can call Catherine King right now and fill in the pieces, tell her everything she doesn't already know from the Mossad."

Carmichael shook his head. "That's not going to happen, and we both know why. That information would be damaging to the Agency, and the Agency protects the interests of the USA. You know how political winds blow, son. You can't just damage a single element of the CIA by revealing this. If you try to destroy me for vengeance, you will destroy the entire core of U.S. intelligence."

And Carmichael was right about that, Court knew. He wasn't going to the media with this. Anything damning that Carmichael did would simply be used against the entire philosophy of human intelligence collections and operations. CIA scandals, as a rule, became political and ideological footballs, and the CIA never came out on the right side.

Court would not burn down the village to save it.

Denny looked coldly at Court. "Haven't you done enough damage to the cause you devoted your life to protect?"

The speakerphone rang again. Court knew this would be the new team, and they wouldn't be calling to offer pizza and soda. He found himself surprised they called at all.

Court checked his watch and he hit the button. "Who is this?"

A new voice said, "I have someone here who would like to speak with you, Violator."

Court cocked his head. "Who is it?"

A woman's voice came on the line. "Hello? This is Catherine King."

Shit, Court thought; this was turning into a fucking circus. "I don't really have time for an interview right now, Catherine. We'll have to reschedule."

King said, "Six, I have information you need. I have to come in and tell you."

"Come in *here*? That would be a really bad idea."

King then turned her attention to Denny Carmichael. "Director Carmichael. Please listen. I have told the men out here that I think I can stop this from turning into a bloodbath. It's not necessary for anyone to die. *Please* let me come in."

"Ms. King, it might not surprise you to know certain classified information is being discussed in here. Since you don't have a Top Secret security clearance, I can't allow you to come in."

"Does Murquin al-Kazaz have a Top Secret U.S. security clearance?"

Denny did not reply.

Catherine said, "You *need* me in there, Denny. I can make this better."

Carmichael said, "It's not really up to me. I'm not the one holding the submachine gun."

Court just smiled. Carmichael was warning the JSOC boys about the defensive setup.

Catherine said, "Six. I know you want to protect the Agency, even after everything that has happened to you. You have my word there will be large amounts of the information I know that will never make it to print if you let me in that room to talk."

"What information?"

"Do we have a deal?"

Court sighed. "You do know this is life-or-death in here, don't you?"

"I do. It is my intention to save lives."

"Mine, or his?" Carmichael asked.

"I don't want *anyone* in there to die today, Mr. Carmichael."

Court didn't know what to do. He wanted to hear any intel he could get on this, but he fully expected JSOC to breach at some point, and then it wouldn't be safe for King to be here in the line of fire.

She pressed. "Open the door, Six. You need to hear what I have to say."

"If this is some kind of a trap, Denny dies first."

"It's no trap."

Court opened the door to the hallway, then he crossed to the security office by the pneumatic doors. He positioned himself out of the line of fire, but he used the reflection from a hall mirror to keep his eyes on the doorway.

He tapped a button on the security controller on his wrist, then he readied his weapon. The pneumatic doors opened. Catherine King entered the hall with her hands raised. She wore warm-ups and tennis shoes. It looked to Court like she'd been called out of a yoga class to come here. Her hands were empty.

Court reclosed the pneumatic doors, then he approached her in the hallway. He turned her to the wall and frisked her quickly, finding nothing on her.

Turning her around, he led her back into the conference room. "Anything for a story, right?"

King forced a little smile. She looked nervous, but steadfast. She sat at the table with the others, and Court sat back down himself.

"So," Court said, turning to King, "you have brought some news? Some way to resolve this crisis?"

She nodded. "I hope the way I can resolve this crisis is by keeping those men outside from coming in here shooting. Maybe with me here, they will be afraid of the bad press it would cause if anything went wrong."

Court shook his head. "They don't care. Maybe you bought me ten minutes while they talk about how to account for you, but no more."

"Look, Six, I know what you are planning on doing. I've been following all your actions for the last eight days. You are here to go out in a blaze of glory. You plan on punishing Carmichael for all he did to you, but you are also planning on punishing yourself for what you did to Hawthorn."

Court did not reply.

"But I know the truth. I have a new source, deep in the CIA. She has filled in some important pieces in the puzzle. Things the Israelis didn't know. What I told you the other day wasn't the whole truth."

With faint hope in his voice he said, "I didn't kill Hawthorn?"

"You did kill him, I'm afraid. Neither you nor I can ever take that back."

"Then nothing else really matters, does it?"

"Not true. You shot Hawthorn, the Israeli penetration agent, *not* because you made a mistake. You shot him because Denny Carmichael ordered you to."

"What?"

Carmichael instantly shook his head. Al-Kazaz remained silent.

"Denny gave you the image of the man you rescued. Denny wasn't trying to save Hawthorn. He didn't even know about Hawthorn. He had no idea an Israeli asset was in that villa.

"He was trying to save the other man. And you did just what he asked you to do. You rescued the man you were ordered to."

Carmichael protested, but Court just lifted his weapon off the table and pointed it at him till he shut up. Looking at Catherine he asked, "How do you know this?"

"Denny assassinated Jordan Mayes yesterday. He framed you for it, but someone in the car with Mayes at the time he was killed confirmed it was not you. Before he died, Mayes told this source of mine that Denny had revealed the truth of Operation BACK BLAST. It was an attempt to rescue the other Arab, because *he* was the spy for the United States. Carmichael didn't know Hawthorn was an Israeli asset. He thought he was just an AQ hit man out to kill *his* agent."

Court leaned back heavily in his chair, his MP7 lowered into his lap, though it remained pointed in the general direction of the two hostages.

"Who was Denny's agent?"

Catherine King looked to Murquin al-Kazaz. "He's sitting right here, Six."

Court turned to the man slowly. Looked at his face. He tried to add a beard, and to take off six years. He wasn't sure.

Al-Kazaz yelled now. "This is an outrageous lie! I know nothing of this!" He turned to Carmichael. "Denny, tell them this is not true. Don't join their lie to save yourself. You *need* me!"

Court lifted the HK assault weapon off the table and pointed it at al-Kazaz's head. "Well, I sure as shit don't need you."

Kaz shut his eyes.

Catherine King screamed, "No, Six! Don't do it!"

Court held the gun there, the laser sight painted on the man's forehead. Finally he lowered it. With his eyes still on Kaz, he said, "Denny, your only chance at surviving the next fifteen minutes hinges on you coming clean on all this. Right *fucking* now."

Catherine King did what she could to defuse the situation. "Denny, anything you say will be considered off the record. You have my word."

Denny Carmichael spoke in a defeated voice now. "You have to understand the opportunity that I had. It was one of the most successful intelligence operations of the past half century, and it was all me. No one knew I had a highly placed man in al Qaeda, *and* a highly placed man in Saudi intelligence."

He paused for a moment, then turned to Kaz. "It was the same man.

"It's true. Kaz had been feeding me al Qaeda intel for two years, but he knew he was burned. AQ discovered he was a Saudi intelligence officer. He'd been tipped off that the trip to Italy was cover to get him out of Pakistan so he could be assassinated without causing a rift between al Qaeda and their Saudi benefactors. He asked me to save him. I needed to keep Kaz secure, but I couldn't pull him out by going through normal channels, because the relationship was not approved. I sent you, Six, gave you an old image of Kaz he'd taken in Tel Aviv, and told you he was an Israeli asset."

Carmichael continued, "I swear to Christ, Court, I had no idea the *assassin* was an Israeli asset. Kaz didn't know, either.

"I made a quick decision, the only rational decision I could have made. I *had* to save him." Carmichael leaned forward, straining against his bindings. "And lo and behold, it worked."

Court was still looking at Kaz, but he spoke to Carmichael. "The only problem was the man I killed was the best penetration agent any service had in the enemy's command structure. Higher than Kaz. He was core AQ."

Carmichael lowered his head. "A few days after BACK BLAST I got a call from Manny Aurbach at Mossad. He said he had a man go dark in Trieste. He told me he was undercover as AQ. Manny asked me if we'd heard any chatter. Immediately I suspected, but I asked for a picture. I sent it to Kaz and he confirmed it was the man you shot. I had to cover it up from the Israelis, not to protect you"—Carmichael shrugged when he said it—"but to protect Kaz. By this time he was back in Saudi Arabia, but if I told Manny the truth, that it was an honest mistake, he would know I'd been trading intel with the Saudis at an unapproved level, and he would have gone to others here in the U.S. to have me derailed.

"So I lied to Manny. That should have been that."

"But?" Catherine asked.

Denny continued, "But a full year later a Serbian who was at the villa in Trieste gave the Mossad a picture of you standing over Hawthorn's body."

Court cocked his head. "How the hell did he happen to get a picture of that?"

"It was a covert camera set up in Kaz's room. It's a picture of you standing in front of a window, silenced pistol. Hawthorn is in the doorway falling to the floor after you shot him. God knows why the Serbian gangsters set the camera up, or why they sent it to the Mossad, but they did. At that point Manny knew his man had been assassinated, and he knew the only force that could pull it off was the Americans." He paused. "I couldn't deny. I told them you must have gone rogue, done the job for money. I had to terminate you so the Israelis couldn't talk to you. If they did, they could just show you a picture of Hawthorn and you would know that wasn't the man you were sent to rescue. If you told the Israelis then they would know BACK BLAST was a lie."

Court looked down at the floor for a minute, saying nothing.

Finally Catherine called out to him. "Six, are you okay?"

Softly he said, "The Serbians did not have a camera in that room."

"They must have. How else did they get the image?"

"They didn't." Court turned to al-Kazaz. "You took the picture. I remember."

"I don't know what you are talking about."

"The pen. The pen in your hand. I remember it now. All your other items in that room, papers, luggage, your computer. Everything else could stay, but you had to put that pen in your pocket. I thought it was strange at the time, but I had too much going on to worry about it."

"What does a stupid pen have to do with any of this?"

Denny Carmichael's face reddened with fury. "I gave you that pen. It contained a pinhole camera. You son of a bitch!"

Catherine connected the dots. "Al-Kazaz gave the image to the Israelis." She looked at the Saudi in the chair across from her. "Which means you knew Hawthorn was a Mossad agent the entire time. The whole damn thing was a setup."

Carmichael roared, "Goddammit, Kaz! No!"

Court said, "Denny, you were wrong before. Kaz wasn't your man in al Qaeda. He wasn't your man in Saudi intelligence. You were *his* man in the CIA. He ran you. He still does."

Denny's hands were bound behind the chair, but he looked like he might try to kill the man tied next to him with only his gnashing teeth.

Kaz surprised everyone in the room with a slight smile. He turned to Denny, on his left. "I ran you for years when I worked inside AQ. Giving you enough information to solidify me as a source, to make me look good, and passing disinformation when it suited Saudi interests. I fed you intelligence that I knew would go straight to your friend Manny Aurbach at Mossad. You believed it all because I'd proven myself. And Manny believed it all because it came from you, and he never knew I existed."

Denny said, "I'm going to kill you."

Kaz laughed now. "No, you won't." He pointed his forehead at Gentry.

"This man will do the honors. You and I will die tonight, but I can die in peace, because although my scheme was discovered at the end, my efforts succeeded for many years. I can be proud of my service to my kingdom." He laughed again, more cruelly this time. "You, Denny, will die knowing you failed your country."

Denny Carmichael turned to Catherine King. "I did not know. You *have* to believe me. Whatever happens to me, you can't report that I did anything to hurt the CIA."

King said, "You were next in line to become director. If you had succeeded in killing Six, as you tried so hard to do, then al-Kazaz would have been able to manipulate the director of the CIA."

It was a statement, and Denny had no reply to it.

Kaz was about to speak again, but the lights in the conference room went off suddenly, shrouding the scene in darkness.

76

Five seconds after cutting power to the south wing of Alexandria Eight, Dakota spoke into his helmet-mounted headset. "Breach!"

The explosive ordnance expert on the team depressed the detonator, and a breaching charge on the wall just to the left of the steel double doors blew. A large water bladder covering the outside of the charge tamped the explosion, both keeping the men outside the wall safe from the backblast, as well as pushing the majority of the explosive power into the fortified wall.

Within seconds of the explosion the first two JSOC operators had their weapons through the oval-shaped hole in the wall. While they covered ahead, two more operators climbed through, took a knee in the hallway, and searched for targets in prearranged geometries of fire. The hallway was pitch-black, but both of these operators, as well as all the other men on the team, wore GPNVG-18s, state-of-the art night vision goggles that rendered the darkness before them in varying hues of green in a wide, ninety-seven-degree panoramic view.

Assaulters five and six were through the breach an instant later, and they moved down to the far end of the hallway to the small door that led straight to Denny's office. They set a small breaching charge on the lock of the door, planning to enter and then take the other exit out of the office. They would then move up the small hall past the attic stairs and into the conference room.

Seven and eight moved straight between the cordon of armed men covering all angles, and these two ran to the wall just left of the conference room doors. One man carried a large shield-looking device in his hand, and he shoved it against the wall, affixing it with pre-placed adhesive. This large breaching charge was also backstopped with a water barrier, but it was designed to minimize the inward blast, so that hostages inside would not be injured.

Nine and ten, Dakota and Harley, moved into the hallway last. They each set two more small charges wide of the first two, both at shoulder height. These would blow small holes in the wall, creating gun ports so operators could cover the assaulters moving into the main breach.

While one operator connected the det cord to all three charges on the wall, the other men moved wide of the area, lined up in two stacks, one on each side, and prepared to execute the dynamic entry.

When the lights went out, Catherine King could not understand why Court Gentry sat calmly in his chair for several seconds, apparently sending a text message. And when the explosion in the hallway rocked the room and Catherine King screamed in shock, Denny Carmichael could not understand why Gentry cut him free from his bindings. It was too dark in the room to see any faces, but Denny wondered if Gentry was afraid of the attack to come and had some plan that involved Denny being ambulatory.

But Gentry just moved over to al-Kazaz and cut him free, as well.

Denny's first inclination was to dive for Kaz's throat. He wanted to kill the man who had ruined everything, the man who had hurt Denny's nation and destroyed his reputation, the man who had tricked him and deprived him of everything in the past decade he had counted as a success. Nothing else mattered to Denny now, not even his own life.

But he didn't go for Kaz's neck, because when the JSOC men entered, as they would in mere seconds, Denny knew he'd only survive if he remained perfectly still.

Getting shot by army commandos would end his attack on Kaz long before he could strangle the life out of the younger man.

Catherine grabbed Gentry by the arm while he was still cutting the rope binding Kaz's wrists. She implored him, her voice cracking with panic. "They will kill you as soon as they get through the door. They will not take you alive. You have to trade Carmichael for your freedom. It's your only chance!"

"No. Once I entered here, I knew I would not be walking out."

"You don't have to do this! You know everything now. You can get out of here and—"

Court took her by the wrist and pulled her around the table, away from the two men. He walked to the wall next to the doors to the hallway, then he moved all the way to the end of the long table, close to the narrow hallway towards the attic stairs and Denny's office. He could see Denny and Kaz just barely in the dark; they remained in their seats next to each other, facing the doorway to the hall.

They looked to him, straining to see him in the darkness.

Court checked his watch, then he unhooked his HK MP7 from the sling around his neck, and he placed it at the end of the long conference table.

He kept his hand on the weapon for a short time, while he tried to think of something to say. No words would come to him now. Catherine pulled at his arm, trying to get him to lie on the ground, but he pulled back, still staring at the two men in the low light.

"I promised Hanley I wouldn't kill you, Denny. So I'm going to give Kaz a gun so he can do it for me."

Court Gentry surprised everyone in the room by sliding the loaded weapon across the long, shiny conference room table, in the direction of the two men. As the HK spun towards them Court rushed down the hall to the attic stairs, pulling Catherine along behind him.

Denny Carmichael and Murquin al-Kazaz both launched to their feet, reaching for the gun skittering by on the table. They both knew the assault team would breach within moments, but they both also knew they were in danger as long as the other had access to a loaded weapon.

Kaz grabbed it by its short barrel, near the muzzle, but Denny managed to take hold of the grip of the weapon. While Kaz screamed in fear, Denny ripped the gun off the table and twisted towards Kaz, who still held on to it for dear life.

Carmichael jammed his finger onto the trigger, yanked it back, and fired a long fully automatic burst of 4.6-millimeter hollow point rounds into Kaz's stomach at a range of one foot.

The weapon lurched in Carmichael's hand, so he took hold of the forward grip to steady it.

The loud roar of the gun drowned out the tamped explosions on the wall fifteen feet away, and Denny's eyes were locked on Kaz, whose expression of pure shock and agony shone bright as day in the fat red flames of the gunfire.

Denny emptied most of the magazine into the flailing body of al-Kazaz, then he spun to his left, aware suddenly of the noise, light, and motion there.

He turned wildly with the gun in his hand still firing, and then Denny Carmichael rocked back on his heels, slammed into the bookshelf behind him. The HK flew from his hand and then he dipped forward, dropped onto his knees, and fell down flat on his face behind the conference table, coming to rest across the legs of al-Kazaz.

He'd been shot twice in rapid succession, straight through his necktie and into his heart.

Dakota raced through the ragged breach and into the conference room. One of his assaulters in the gun port had just shot a hostage, he'd seen it through his NODs as he entered, but his main objective all along was to kill Violator, and that had not changed.

He lined up in front of his men, cleared the room, and moved right, towards the hallway there. With three operators on his heels, he led the way.

At the foot of the attic stairs he met up with the two men who had breached the door to Denny's office. They'd reported no joy on the target, so they knew he was in the attic.

All six operators began moving up the steps.

Court shouted to Catherine King, twenty-five feet away in the attic. "Lie flat on the ground, facedown, hands out to your sides. Cross your legs at the ankles. No matter what happens, you don't move till they move you. You do all that and you'll be safe."

Two decades of yoga had not instilled in Catherine the sense of calm necessary to endure all that was happening around her. She thought her heart would burst, but she complied with Court's instructions, lying on the dusty old wooden floor near the stairwell. Looking across the darkened attic, she could barely see him, kneeling in front of a large backpack.

She called out to him. "Let me talk to them! Maybe I can—"

"No! Do not move from where you are!"

"Six, lie here with me! They will kill you if you don't—"

"Just stay there, Catherine," he ordered.

She looked at him again. Cocked her head. "What are you doing? What . . . what is *that*?"

Harley set the breaching charge on the door to the attic, unwound the det cord, and backed down a few feet. He called, "Fire in the hole!" and the explosion blew dust and splinters on the men all around.

Dakota took the second position as the assaulters rushed up and past Harley and through the blown door. As soon as they were in the dark room the first operator in the stack shouted, "Don't move! Don't move!"

Dakota stepped to the side and saw the woman from the *Washington Post* lying on the floor, in a compliant stance. Her head was down, her arms were out, and her legs were crossed behind her. Someone had given her a lesson in how to not get shot by a tactical team.

While the first assaulter kept his gun trained on her, a massive explosion to Dakota's left knocked him off balance, all the way down to his kneepads.

The room filled with smoke, and when he spun around and looked in the direction of the noise he couldn't see a thing, even through his panoramic night vision goggles.

All the men in the stack were in the attic now, covering the main part of the room with their rifles, desperate to find a target through the thick smoke.

Another noise came from the smoke. It wasn't an explosion; more like the sound of an electric engine.

Dakota didn't want his men running into a trap. "Hold positions! Hold till you can see your way forward!"

The smoke cleared a little, but the NODs weren't cutting through it. Dakota called, "White light!" into his mic, then he flipped up his goggles and actuated the flashlight on the bottom of his rifle. Quickly the other operators followed suit.

The smoke was still thick, but they could see him now. Twenty-five feet away their target stood still in the middle of the room, his arms wrapped tightly around his body, his legs together.

His eyes on the six men in front of him.

Above him Dakota could see stars—there was a jagged eight-foot-long hole in the roof above Violator's head.

Dakota shouted, "Contact front!" and he pressed his trigger.

And then, just like that, their target was gone. He fired straight up, into the air and through the hole in the roof.

The six JSOC operators stood there, guns trained on empty space. Dakota had gotten one round off, but he didn't think he'd hit anything.

The team leader was the first to run forward. He looked up at the hole in the ceiling now, and he saw nothing but the nighttime sky.

Harley stepped up next to him. "There is no *way* that just happened."

77

ourt soared through the broken roof, his eyes closed and his appendages tight against his body lest he rake them across the jagged edges
marking the border of the breach created by the charge he'd affixed to
the ceiling soon after his arrival here at Alexandria Eight. Once he felt the
cool of the night air on his skin he opened his eyes, and he watched the
large CIA safe house fall away below him as he rose, shooting upwards as
fast as he would if he were flying in a plane.

He still wasn't feeling great about his chances—his heart pounded and
his stomach cinched tight with terror—but he'd made it out of the range of
the JSOC boys, so he knew there was nothing else he could do to affect his
chances now.

Court told himself he should just sit back and enjoy the ride.

Instead, however, he fought a wave of nausea as the motion and the
nerves played havoc on his insides.

t the Special Activities Division cache in Harvey Point, North Carolina,
Court had run across a new piece of equipment that immediately
reminded him of something very old.

The Fulton recovery system, more commonly known as the Skyhook,
was something of a legendary device in special operations. Invented in the
1950s, the Skyhook was a personnel ground-to-air retrieval system consisting of a large balloon attached to a rope, which connected to a body harness. When the device worked as advertised, the balloon rose to several
hundred feet, and an aircraft equipped with a capture device grabbed the
rope under the balloon and then heaved the person in the harness up into

the sky. Once alongside the aircraft an operator in the cabin could then use a device to reel in and recover the "victim."

It sounded great in theory, a little too Buck Rogers, perhaps, but for a spy behind the lines with no other options, it was much better than nothing.

But Court had heard of no more than five or six times where a Skyhook recovery had been successfully executed in the field.

The item Court noticed in the experimental locker at the Point was a modernized and miniaturized version of the Skyhook. Named the Buzzhook, instead of a huge balloon and helium tanks, this ground-to-air retrieval device employed a 16-by-16-inch quadcopter that could climb vertically at fifty miles an hour carrying a payload of fifteen pounds.

Behind the quadcopter, three hundred yards of four-millimeter bonded Kevlar rope spun out quickly from a large, spring-loaded spool in Court's backpack. The rope was black in color and it had been invisible in the dark attic, so thin that even with rail lights from the JSOC assaulters' firearms they could not see it, especially with the smoke from the breaching charge in the air.

As soon as he'd blown the roof, Court pressed a preset button on the drone and it fired straight up through the hole created by the breaching charge. The Buzzhook pulled its cordage to a height of nine hundred feet in just seconds. Here it stopped suddenly and began hovering, staying perfectly in place with its onboard GPS receiver and its gyroscope.

An infrared light blinked on the drone, and a second infrared light, attached to the cord a hundred feet below the Buzzhook, blinked as well.

Within moments of the drone launching out of the roof of Alexandria Eight, a de Havilland Twin Otter with a painted-over tail number flew to the exact same GPS coordinates, but at an altitude of only 400 feet. The hundreds of people on the ground—the media, first responders, local cops, FBI, and interested CIA officials—all stood and stared. Police helicopters had seen the craft coming in from miles away, but it had claimed to be on its base leg for nearby Washington National Airport, and it only deviated from its flight path forty seconds earlier, so there was no time to begin tracking it before it arrived.

Timing had been everything, of course, and here Court had had to make a few educated guesses. He'd told Zack to plan on arriving directly above Alexandria Eight at twelve thirty a.m., but to plan to have an excuse ready for air traffic control that could speed them up by five minutes, or slow them down by the same amount.

That gave Court a ten-minute window.

The Twin Otter captured the Kevlar cord and pulled Gentry into the sky at twelve thirty-three, yanking him almost straight up by entering a steep climb.

Court looked down at an altimeter on his watch and saw he had ascended four hundred feet. He looked up and behind him, and finally he saw the aircraft, flying black now, all its lights extinguished. He kept his body tucked as tightly as possible, felt the incredible wind and cold and even the thick mist as he was pulled along through a small cloud, and he told himself that this was not nearly as bad as he thought it was going to be. As long as the tiny cord that served as his lifeline held, then he would be fine.

But as he was looking at the dark aircraft above him, he saw something that made his heart stop. The Twin Otter suddenly banked to the left . . . *hard* to the left.

Court knew physics well enough to understand what would come next, so he closed his eyes and held on to the harness inside his clothes by wrapping his arms even tighter across his chest.

Two seconds later he felt his harness wrenched hard in the direction of the plane above, then he whipped around at over one hundred miles an hour. He screamed a volley of curse words and he kept his eyes closed, but when he felt the pull direction change again, and he sensed he was now flying forward and not backwards, he gave in and opened them.

The Fox 5 helicopter he had flown in forty-five minutes earlier was now right in front of him, no more than one hundred yards away, its rotor blades churning the air.

The harness pulled harder now, Court seemed to climb faster, and he passed fifty feet above the whipping blades of the Bell 206.

Court vomited into the night.

Thirty seconds later and only a minute and ten seconds after leaving the attic of the CIA safe house, Court found himself hanging right next to the open cabin door of the aircraft. The pilot had made no more evasive maneuvers; Court knew the massive starboard-side propeller of the Dash 6 was only fifteen feet behind him, so he prayed no more aerobatics were forthcoming. He looked into the dark cabin and saw Zack Hightower wearing a flight suit, a large earmuff headset, and goggles. His blond hair whipped in the wind as he reached out with a hooked device in his hand. With this he grabbed onto Court's harness and pulled him towards the cabin doorway.

Court's feeling of weightlessness went away in an instant when Zack grabbed the harness with his hand, then pitched backwards, heaving himself and Court to the floor of the cabin. While both men lay there in a heap, Zack spoke into the mic of his headset. "Punch it, Travers!"

Court looked up and forward into the open cockpit. Chris Travers sat alone in the left seat, a baseball cap turned around backwards and big earmuff headphones on his own ears. Immediately he reached up to the throttle above him and shoved it all the way towards the windscreen. The pitch of the engine outside the open left side door rose markedly. Court climbed up to his knees and off of Zack, but Zack remained on his back. For some reason Court saw him sniffing his gloved hand.

"Did you puke? That's nasty, bro."

Court helped him shut the cabin door.

The Twin Otter wasn't the fastest aircraft in the CIA's inventory, but this one was one of the few that Matt Hanley could plausibly deny as belonging to him. It had been stripped of all markings in preparation of reregistering it and using it on special operations in Central and South America, and since the new registry had not been completed, the aircraft remained in a perfect state of limbo to be employed in the Gentry rescue operation.

It was also a dependable aircraft, and although its top speed was barely two hundred miles an hour, that was fast enough for the plan devised by Court and Zack, and then tweaked by the pilot.

Just two hours earlier when Hanley called Travers asking for some quick help, the young Ground Branch operator ran some numbers and looked at some maps, then he rushed frantically to attach the tubular polymer capture "horns" to the port wing of his aircraft and get the bird in the air.

While he did all this Zack worked on acquiring the gear the three men would need for the next stage of this operation. Namely, food, water, camping gear, and three parachutes. All this he had stowed in the cabin and strapped down, and while Travers set the autopilot just five minutes after picking up Gentry, the other two men began quickly donning their chutes. Travers had already turned off his radio because he got tired of listening to air traffic control yell at him, but he assumed Air Force F-16s from Langley Air Force Base had been scrambled and were en route to intercept the illegal flight. He knew a Dash 6 didn't have much of a chance against a World War I–era fighter plane, much less an F-16, so he wanted to be long gone from this poor bird before they got in range.

Three minutes later, after a quick handshake from Travers and a forced hug from Zack Hightower that made Court's gunshot wound to his ribs hurt like hell, Court opened the cabin door and leapt out. The other two men did the same, each far enough apart to where, in the darkness, there was no chance they'd find one another on the ground.

By design, all three men landed in different parts of the foothills of the Blue Ridge Mountains.

After he buried his chute and put on his backpack, Court checked his GPS and found himself only five miles west of the town of Sperryville, Virginia. His first inclination was to walk those five miles, arrive by daylight, and then stop at the first Waffle House he could find.

But he fought that urge with a wistful smile, and instead he turned east, heading away from civilization and deeper towards the dark mountains.

Zack Hightower splashed down in a dank oxbow lake alongside the South Fork of the Shenandoah River. He cussed and bitched as he climbed out of the murky water, slicked slime off his clothes, and slung his pack over his back. Checking his GPS and looking over this terrain, he decided he'd make camp right here, just so he could get out of his clothes and get some sleep. First thing in the morning, he told himself, he'd walk east to Luray, Virginia, and he'd hop a bus back to D.C. He had no idea if he would have a job at CIA, but tomorrow was a workday, and he wanted to be ready for work, just in case his new master called.

Chris Travers sat alone in the back of the aircraft for a few minutes, then he jumped out himself. He misjudged the wind around his landing zone and ended up stuck in a tree in the mountains on the Virginia/West Virginia border. He wasn't hurt, but it took him till well past sunup to untangle himself, climb up his lines to the canopy, and get out of the pine tree.

By noon, however, he walked into the town of Brady, West Virginia, sat down in a diner, and ordered a turkey sandwich and a Diet Coke. While he ate at the counter he watched TV coverage of the event the evening before in Alexandria, culminating with an airborne rescue and an attempted escape.

Travers hid his smile behind his sandwich when the reporter then said the aircraft had crashed into a desolate field high in the Allegheny Mountains, and all on board were presumed dead.

He left the diner minutes later and headed off in search of a bar. His first operation as a CIA black ops pilot had gone off perfectly, and he wanted to toast himself with a shot, or three, of Jameson.

78

Catherine King stepped off the elevator on the seventh floor of the CIA's Old Headquarters Building. Her assigned control officer escorted her into a conference room—the same room she'd visited a week earlier to interview Denny Carmichael—then offered her a cup of coffee. When she declined, the young woman disappeared, and soon the door opened again.

Catherine had never met Matthew Hanley, the Acting Director of the National Clandestine Service, and she knew very little about him. All she knew of his CV was that he'd been a Green Beret, an SAD officer, and then had worked as station chief in Haiti. He'd been back here running SAD until yesterday, when he was tapped to take over NCS for the late Denny Carmichael.

She assumed Hanley knew the man she called Six, but she had no idea if Hanley still had any association with him, or even if Hanley had been involved in the manhunt for the ex–SAD operator.

But that didn't really matter, because Catherine knew this morning's meeting would not be about Six. It would be about Catherine. Or, more specifically, it would be about what Catherine planned on publishing. There was no other earthly reason why first thing in the morning on his first day in his new position, the new top spook in the United States would want to speak with an investigative reporter for the *Washington Post*.

When Hanley stepped through the door she found herself surprised. Where Denny had been lean and stately, Director Hanley looked like an old linebacker. She could tell from his eyes and his nose that he liked to drink, and she could tell by his frame that he liked to eat, but his ruddy complexion made her think he could handle both without ill effects.

He shook her hand gently and sat down. Smiling while he talked, he seemed night and day different from his predecessor.

There was significant chitchat at first—Hanley seemed to enjoy talking—but when he got down to business she realized he had a definite objective.

"Ms. King, I want to offer you a great opportunity."

"An opportunity to do what, exactly?"

"An opportunity to help your country."

She rolled her eyes. "By not talking about what happened at the safe house, you mean?"

"You can talk about it. I hope you will. But I hope you are . . . fair. Deliberate about what you say."

"Have you read anything I've written?"

"Every week."

"Then you know I am both fair and deliberate."

Hanley seemed to consider a moment. Like he was playing chess and thinking over his next move. "I'm ready to make a deal. A really nice deal."

"And I'm listening, Director Hanley."

And then, for the next several minutes, Acting Director Matthew Hanley offered Catherine King unprecedented access to the inner workings of the CIA. Exclusives, tips, personal tours, and visits to places she could not have dreamed of getting into. Introductions to players, background intelligence on world figures, and data that she had never thought she would obtain from anyone in government, least of all from the top spy in U.S. intelligence.

Hanley finished his spiel by saying, "Denny Carmichael was not an evil man. I didn't like him, never did. But that was because his methods were too top-down. He thought he was a puppet master and a king, and that's not what this place needs at all. Everything bad that has happened, everything classified you've learned about in the past week . . . it was all Denny Carmichael. When he died . . . I'd like to hope that could all die with him." He spoke in a pleading voice now. "Don't destroy this Agency by reporting the crimes of a man who no longer needs to be stopped. Instead, watch this Agency closer than anyone in the Fourth Estate has ever watched us. Make sure I don't become Denny. You can have a real positive impact on this organization, on this nation." Hanley winked. "And you can probably write some damn fine stories in the process."

Catherine kept her poker face, but she had already decided to be extremely sparing in her reporting. She knew the power of the media to destroy, and she knew that despite all the nuance in the world, a thorough piece on the front page of the *Washington Post* about rogue bands of assassins killing their way across the nation's capital under orders from the number two man at the CIA would cause politicians to gut the Agency down to nothing.

She wouldn't do that.

That the new guy running NCS just offered her unparalleled access almost caused her to jump out of her chair.

Instead, she forced him into specifics, hammered out dates for meetings and general ground rules for sharing information, and then she kept her poker face as long as she could. Finally she reached out a hand. "I look forward to following your tenure here very closely, Director Hanley."

Hanley shook her hand, and she could see on his face that he recognized he'd just paid dollars to someone ready to accept dimes.

"I bet you do, Ms. King."

Arthur Mayberry opened the wooden door to his home, but he left the storm door locked. Through the Plexiglas and bars he saw a white male in his thirties standing in the morning sunshine. He wore a suit and tie, and a serious expression.

The media had moved from his sidewalk a week or so after Jeff Duncan nearly blew up all of Columbia Heights, but these damn cops just kept coming.

Bernice appeared at Mayberry's side just as he said, "I've told you boys everything I know."

"I'm not here to ask questions."

"Then what can I do for you?"

The young man held out an envelope. "You can take this, and not ask *me* any questions. To be honest, I don't care for them any more than you."

Mayberry looked at the envelope. "Well, what is it?"

"*That's* a question, Mr. Mayberry. Please pay attention."

Mayberry unlocked the door, took the envelope. He opened it. It was a fat stack of one-hundred-dollar bills.

"Lord have mercy," he said softly.

The young man smiled a little. "Someone wishes to apologize for any inconvenience you might have endured in the past week or two. He asks that you accept this as repayment for the damages."

Bernice looked at the money. She whispered, "Drugs."

The man in the suit took no offense. "Not at all, ma'am. This is something else. Are you familiar with the FBI's Witness Protection Program?"

Bernice said, "I . . . I believe I saw it on *Law and Order*."

"Yes . . . well . . . things aren't always how they appear."

Arthur gasped. "You mean to tell me Jeff Duncan was in the Witness Protection Program?"

The young man raised an eyebrow and, with it, he gave a little smile.

Arthur Mayberry said, "No questions?"

"Exactly right, sir. Have a nice day."

The man returned to his car, the car rolled off, and Mayberry locked the door. Only when this was complete did he pull the cash out of the envelope.

"How much is it?" Bernice asked.

Arthur Mayberry took a moment to thumb through it, making sure all the bills were hundreds. They were. He said, "It's enough to where we won't ever have to rent out the basement to another crazy man."

The Mayberrys looked at each other and shared a smile.

EPILOGUE

Court Gentry wore a full beard and mustache, and his dark brown hair was pulled back in a tight ponytail. This, along with the leather jacket, faded jeans, and work boots, gave him the look of a man who fit in well here. There were tens of thousands of miners, farmers, and other industrial workers in southern Pennsylvania, and most all of them dressed like this—more or less, anyway—so he did not look out of place at all.

Not even here, at Somerset Regional Airport—not that his look mattered much, because all the commercial flights had flown for the day, he was far from the terminal in a private hangar, and there was no one else around.

Just Court and a sleek white executive jet, its turbines spinning slowly.

Court sat alone in the hangar's tiny executive lounge, his small backpack at his feet and a bottle of water in his hand. The TV high on the wall was set to CNN. Court had watched several stories about the crazy happenings a couple hundred miles to the southeast of here in D.C., but he'd learned nothing new.

A second aircraft landed in the dark distance, then it taxied over and parked in the hangar, next to the plane right outside the window of the executive lounge. Court waited quietly for a few minutes, then watched a single man deplane and walk down the air stairs and up the steps into the lounge.

Matt Hanley wore a wide Cheshire cat grin, but to his credit, he didn't try to hug his former employee. The two men just shook hands. Matt sat down in the chair in front of Court, then he produced a flask from inside his coat, along with two shot glasses.

"You bring those all the way from Langley?"

Hanley shook his head. "Stole them off the plane. Actually, it's an Air Branch aircraft, so as long as I give them back or expense them, I can do whatever I want with them."

He poured two shots of neat scotch and passed one to Court, and they drank them together.

Hanley said, "You've been up in the mountains two weeks?"

"Yeah."

"Shit. How much did that suck?"

"It beat D.C."

Hanley chuckled, but moved on. "Been digging into NCS files. Old code word programs and ops. I'll be unraveling this shit for months, years maybe, but the short version is this: Carmichael was in some sort of a dysfunctional three-way relationship between Saudi Arabia and Israel. He fed both sides intel pulled from the other, kept both in the dark about where he was getting information."

"What could possibly go wrong?" Court quipped. He took Hanley's flask and poured himself another drink.

Hanley continued, "Al-Kazaz figured out Denny's game early on. This meant the Saudis had a disinformation conduit into the Mossad. Kaz gave up some legit operations to solidify Denny's trust, and he gave up even more to make Denny look good to the Mossad. It was like setting up an IV, and putting good drugs through it.

"But after a while, Kaz started pushing poison through the line.

"Then came Operation BACK BLAST. Kaz knew about the Israeli infiltration agent in al Qaeda, but he couldn't remove him, because it would tip CIA and Mossad off to the fact that they had a breach. So he concocted the perfect scheme. He organized the meeting between the cells in Italy, and he got Hawthorn to attend. He convinced Denny someone was going to kill him at the meeting, and that he had nowhere to turn. Denny sends his best assassin to rescue him. Kaz survives, the Mossad agent dies, and no one knows Saudi intel is the puppet master of the entire debacle.

"But it got even better for Kaz a year later, when he decided to create a rift between CIA and Mossad by leaking proof the CIA killed Hawthorn. Just imagine how much fun that must have been for al-Kazaz. Aurbach learns CIA schwacked his best man, Carmichael is put on the spot. Carmichael is pissed at al-Kazaz, but he is convinced the Saudis made an honest mistake with the bad intel; he doesn't suspect he's been tricked."

"Why not?"

"Simple. Kaz gave up AQ assets left and right to backstop his story.

Carmichael knew he'd been getting gold from Kaz. And he knew that gold had helped him climb his way up in the Agency. He couldn't let himself think for a second he'd been played because it would mean everything he'd put forward as a strength was now a weakness."

"Kaz bought Carmichael's trust and allegiance."

"That's right," Hanley said. "When Aurbach dug for answers, Carmichael had to give you up. He knew he couldn't let you talk to Mossad because you were the only one who knew you killed the man in the photograph you were given. If you were silenced, then the entire incident could be chalked up to a CIA assassin gone rogue, taking money to smoke the wrong guy, not a massive intelligence failure involving an illegal program."

"But I didn't play along."

"No, you didn't. Carmichael ordered your own team to terminate you. If you had died that night, the truth would have died with you, but you got away, went on the run and off grid. Carmichael then spent five frantic years trying to remove the compromise that could ruin him."

Hanley downed another scotch, then said, "If you ever knew what this was all about, you could have walked right into an Israeli Embassy and explained it to Mossad. But you were kept in the dark as to why you had to die. You never knew BACK BLAST went bad, you never knew you killed Hawthorn, you never knew you were the one loose thread in an illegal operation that, if unraveled, could bring the entire U.S. intelligence community to its knees."

"Now I know," Court said. He looked out the window at the two planes. "Where does that leave me?"

Hanley said, "I want you back."

"Back in the Agency?"

"Not exactly." He paused. "Back running from the Agency."

Court looked back at Hanley. "What the hell does that mean?"

"For the five years of the shoot on sight, you were out there, doing CIA dirty work, with no comebacks to us. You were the epitome of plausible deniability. All the other intel services knew we were after you, so whatever you did, we were in the clear."

Court understood, but he said nothing.

"I want to harness that, Court. I want to run you, make you operational, keep you on target with our intelligence, close-hold stuff you can't get any-where else. I want you out there, going after bad actors we don't have sanc-tion to go after any other way. You could be our best direct-action weapon ever."

"What's in this for me?"

"What do you want?"

Court thought it over. The question stumped him for a moment. "All I wanted was to come home."

Hanley patted him on the shoulder. "You have a home. You just can't stay here. It wouldn't be safe. You have to keep moving, to remain in the shadows. We were never the only people out there looking for you."

Court said, "If I stayed in the States, the government could protect me."

Hanley did not disagree. Instead he just said, "You are an operator. You will always be an operator. Work for me. I'll help you do what needs doing."

Court thought a moment. "Two years."

"What about two years?"

"Two years and I'm out. Done. Back home and under your protection."

Hanley rocked his head from side to side while he mulled this over. Soon he said, "Done."

Court said, "I approve all contracts. I get to take jobs from others if I want."

Hanley nodded. "Of course. You are a subcontractor. Self-employed." Hanley smiled. "I just aim to be your biggest and best client." He stuck a hand out, and Court shook it.

Hanley said, "Glad that's settled. Court, I want you to know that you always have a direct line to me. Always."

Court understood what was coming next. "But since you're D/NCS now, running all Agency ops, you will bring in a handler to deal with me directly."

"That's right. But don't worry, I'm giving you one of the best officers in the Agency. Trust me on this, you're in excellent hands."

"Sure," Court said, not convinced.

Hanley pulled out his iPad, touched a few keys on the screen, and then handed the device over to Court. He took it, somewhat confused, then suddenly he realized he was on a video chat. He saw an empty chair.

He looked up to Hanley. "*Really*, Matt?"

"A shitty way for a meet and greet with your new handler, I'll admit. But she had to man the fort while I snuck around out here in the boonies."

"*She?*" Court asked.

As he said this, a woman appeared on screen and sat in the chair. She looked to be in her late thirties, not unattractive, with brown hair pulled back, fashionable frames, and perfect makeup. She beamed into the camera with a wide smile. "Good evening, Mr. Gentry. My name is Suzanne Brewer. I am so looking forward to working with you."

Court looked up to Hanley for guidance, then, when none came, back down at the screen. "Uh . . . yeah. Me, too."

"Matt let me know just a little about your career here, and I will get up to speed quickly. I just want you to know all the unpleasantness of the past is behind us. I am going to treat you with the respect and deference you deserve."

Court nodded, feeling awkward about the exchange, but satisfied Hanley hadn't pawned him off to some young case officer just out of the Farm.

"Cool," he said awkwardly. The three of them talked a minute more, then Hanley disconnected the video chat and slipped the iPad back in his briefcase.

Standing up, D/NCS said, "I can't begin to thank you for all you've done for the Agency. We didn't deserve you. We still don't, but with me and Suzanne on your team, I think you will know you are back in the fold. The family."

Together the two men walked back out to the hangar. In front of the two aircraft, they shook hands again.

"What about Zack?" Court asked.

Hanley said, "I have a role for Zack. He's not you, but he's not half bad."

"What will he—"

Hanley put up a hand. "Sorry, Court. Can't tell you. It's classified."

"Cute." Court let it go with a little smile. "You're going back to Langley?"

"Yeah. Meeting tomorrow with the director. He's got his head so deep in the sand he probably won't hear a word I say, which is good, because I'm going to bullshit the hell out of him."

"What about me? Where am I going?"

Hanley patted Court on the shoulder. "Something's cooking in Hong Kong. Need you there, stat."

"I have approval on all my contracts. Did you forget that deal you made with me ten whole minutes ago?"

Hanley chuckled. "You'll get the intel on the flight over. If you say no, then you just got a free flight around the world." Hanley winked. "But you won't say no."

"Why not?"

"Let's just say it involves an old friend."

"I have friends?"

"Not if you don't get your ass to Hong Kong, you don't. Don't dick around with this one, Court. No time to waste." And with that Matt Hanley turned around, headed up the stairs into his Gulfstream, and disappeared.

Court stood there a moment, then he looked up to the other aircraft. *His* aircraft. With the faintest of shrugs, he turned for the stairs and began climbing.